RIDES A STRANGER

2 GREAT BOOKS IN 1

A BULLET FOR BILLY

THE JOURNEY OF JIM GLASS

RIDES A STRANGER

2 GREAT BOOKS IN 1

A BULLET FOR BILLY

BILL BROOKS

wm
WILLIAM MORROW
An Imprint of HarperCollins*Publishers*

RIDES A STRANGER. Copyright © 2007 by Bill Brooks.

A BULLET FOR BILLY. Copyright © 2007 by Bill Brooks. All rights reserved. Printed in the United States of America. No part of this book may be used or reproduced in any manner whatsoever without written permission except in the case of brief quotations embodied in critical articles and reviews. For information, address HarperCollins Publishers, 195 Broadway, New York, NY 10007.

First William Morrow mass market printing: March 2019

Print Edition ISBN: 978-0-06-289082-5

Cover design by David Cook

William Morrow and HarperCollins are registered trademarks of HarperCollins Publishers in the United States of America and other countries.

19 20 21 22 23 QGM 10 9 8 7 6 5 4 3 2 1

CONTENTS

RIDES A
STRANGER

2 GREAT BOOKS IN 1

A BULLET FOR
BILLY

RIDES A STRANGER

For Carmen and Laura,
God's Own Children

✂ PROLOGUE ✂

The Hondo Daily Reporter
Eyewitness Account of Slaying

My name's Kip Mulligan and I own a saloon in Hondo County just outside Mordecai, New Mexico Territory. I have owned the place for three years and never seen such violence all at once. About noon, three men came into my establishment and took seats at a table and ordered drink and food. They were secretive in their manner and spoke in low voices. I took them at first to be cow-boys, for they were dressed like drovers and wore long dusters and spurs with small rowels.

I brought them whiskey and stew and they took to it like they had not eaten in quite some time. I tried to make small talk but they were reticent to be engaged in conversation. One of them had his hair in a long braid that fell halfway down his back. That was the only outstanding feature among them.

I noticed that their horses were all lathered when I stepped outside to empty a spittoon. They looked like they had been used pretty hard.

My assistant, Miss Emily Rose Sherbrooke, entered the room shortly after the trio arrived and took up residence with me behind the bar. Some words were exchanged between she and the men not fit for print. I tried to intervene on her behalf after they insulted her, making reference to what they perceived her profession to be. Miss Sherbrooke has worked for me for several years and is an entertainer and nothing more, let the record show.

It was at this point that I became concerned for our safety, for all three of the men acted gruff and in a threatening manner and I could see by then they were well-armed with revolvers. I asked Miss Sherbrooke to take her leave so as to calm the situation. She refused, calling one of them a son of a—! after he again insulted her looks. This is when he parted his duster back and showed us he was wearing a badge—the sort I'd seen whilst living in Texas and quite common down in that country, the sort the Rangers wear.

I offered them a free bottle of spirits in order to improve the situation and they readily accepted, and I thought that pretty much the end of the matter even though Miss Sherbrooke was still distressed over the insults they'd cast her way.

Things had settled down considerably by the time another stranger entered and approached the bar behind which I and Miss Sherbrooke were yet standing and ordered a glass of beer. He took notice of the painting I have hanging above the bar—a rendering of a nude entitled *Eros in Recline*, which I purchased a year earlier at an auction in Santa Fe in order to provide my customers some respite from the isolation of the territory, which only adds to a man's great loneliness. The painting is quite revealing and free to view for any paying customer.

Nonetheless, the stranger seemed like everyone else who comes in for a drink—nothing at all unusual about him. He was middle-aged, maybe, tall, dusty from the trail like the other three. When he first came in I thought maybe he was part of that bunch because he was wearing a duster of similar fashion.

He kept glancing up at that painting before letting his gaze fall to the mirror behind the bar, and I did not understand what he was doing until he done it.

Cool as a cucumber, he reached inside his coat, I thought to pay for the beer, but when he withdrew his hand, it was full of a nickel-plated Russian model Smith & Wesson .44–40, I do believe. I feature myself as something of a gun fancier and have studied the various models of revolvers, and the Russian model is a mean piece of iron, that when you've emptied its firepower on your opponents you can use to bludgeon them with if needed. I've seen it done.

Miss Sherbrooke and I were warned off sounding the alarm by the stranger's hard gaze—not that I would have alerted them anyway considering their earlier behavior toward Miss Sherbrooke.

And as smooth as silk the stranger swung 'round and pointed his piece at the trio and warned them to lay their own pistols on the table they were sitting at. I never saw a man hold a gun so steady, and you'd have to be a complete fool to not think he meant business.

But I guess those three *were* fools. The one with the braid swore a curse and made his play but by the time he'd cleared leather, the stranger shot him dead center. Dust spanked up off his shirt and he flopped back out of his chair like a carp yanked out of the river.

The sound of that Russian model going off in such close quarters left my ears ringing. Miss Sherbrooke screamed just as the remaining pair went for their guns, coming up quick out of their chairs as they did. I don't know what those boys were thinking—whether they had a death wish or whether maybe just because they were peace officers they knew all about looking into the face of danger and terrible odds and were not fazed by what they just witnessed happen to their friend. I know those Texas Rangers are tough hombres.

The stranger killed them both so quick it sounded like he only fired a single shot. *Bang bang.*

I never seen anything like it in my life, and I've resided in such places as Dodge City and Tombstone and Del Rio, Texas too.

Then before I could even think to breathe he wheeled about and aimed his weapon at me— the muzzle of that big Russian model breathing smoke an inch from my face, and he said, "Whatever you're thinking about doing, don't."

And I said, "No, sir, I ain't thinking about doing nothing and I ain't going to either." And then he looked at Miss Sherbrooke and said, "Miss, please stop that god— screaming." It shut her mouth right up like a door that had been slammed shut.

We watched as he walked over to the dead men and removed their badges and put them in his pocket. Then just turned and went out and got on his horse and rode off toward the north. That's how it happened. I don't know how I'm ever going to get those bloodstains out of the floorboards. If any of your readers want to come by and see where those three Texas Rangers got dusted, they can see the exact spot. That's all I've got to say about what I seen.

No, I never seen the man before in my life, nor did I see those three Rangers. It seemed odd to me that they had come to Hondo County from across the border in Texas, and I remember when I first saw their badges that I asked them how it worked, them enforcing the law in New Mexico, and what the one said—the one with the braid of hair—was, "We ain't surveyors." *"Surveyors!"* I said, taking it to mean they didn't care nothing about where borders began and ended. I don't know what else it could have meant. I reckon now they're sorry they *weren't* surveyors. My place is open for business all the time.

1

After I turned the badges into Captain Rogers in Eagle Pass, he thanked me for what I'd done and said, "Jim, I wish you could have brought those murdering bastards in alive so I could have hanged them myself."

I told him I wished I could have too but they didn't give me much of a chance to negotiate.

"It's one thing to kill one of my men," he said, "another to kill three and steal their badges and guns. To me, it's robbing the dead, which only makes the crime worse, and even though I am sworn to uphold the law, had I been you I don't think I would have negotiated with them either."

Captain Rogers was a short, blue-eyed man who'd spent most of his adult life fighting for the right things. He'd pulled me out a jail cell where I was doing thirty days for drunk and disorderly and bought me a decent meal and said he was sorry to have seen me go downhill like I had done. I said I was sorry too. Then he told me about the killings and said, "You want to be a Ranger again?" I'd most likely have turned him down but I knew all three of those boys—Frank May, Billy Higgens, and Josiah Barkley. Two had wives and children, and I knew them too. And when the Captain told me how they'd been ambushed and then executed by being shot in the back of the head, I could see myself finding the men who did it. And I could see myself doing what I did to their killers—which is exactly what happened that day in Hondo County where I found them.

Then I told the Captain I was quitting for good, I didn't want to wash my hands in any more blood. He asked what I'd do, and I said I thought I'd go work at something peaceful like on a ranch some-where, and we shook hands and that was the end of my Rangering days and the start of all the rest of my days.

And now I was on the drift again like I had been since I quit.

I'd bet a dollar that the crow watching me from atop the wobbling sign wondered what such a raggedy looking fellow like me was doing riding a twenty dollar horse with a forty dollar saddle into a town that looked like little more than some old lumber somebody had spilled off the back of their wagon and had been hammered up into badly constructed buildings on a prairie so lonesome even the wind never stopped to take a rest.

And I'll bet another dollar I wouldn't have an answer.

The sign read:

COFFIN FLATS POP. 756
NO DISCHARGING OF FIREARMS
BY ORDER OF CITY MARSHAL
WELCOME

Summer was dying and winter hadn't woke up yet. Some called it "Indian summer." All I know was it was a sweet time of year—not too hot, nor cold—and I'd come a long ways from the last place I'd been and was thirsty and tired. I was also down to my last few dollars from the last job I quit, when the ramrod told me to go dig Mr. Watts some postholes, which was the last straw for me, considering what all had preceded it.

I told the ramrod I didn't dig postholes, and he said that I'd better go collect my pay then because he was only paying for a posthole digger that day and not some fancy duded-up cowboy who thought himself too high and mighty to do work except from the back of a horse. I said that was about the size of it. But where he got the idea I was high and mighty escaped me even though I wasn't about to disabuse him of his notions. Hell, I figured I'd already gone the extra mile by mending fence wire, something no man worth his salt should ever do.

So I went on up to the big house where Mr. Watts lived and knocked on the door, and his wife answered and looked surprised to see me. I told her I was quitting. She asked why and I told her my hand didn't fit a posthole digger was why and she rolled her eyes.

"Lord, Jim, it seems like such a little thing to be quitting over."

"It may well be, Fannie, but that's the way it is."

But we both knew it wasn't *just* about me digging postholes or not digging them. It went a lot beyond all that.

Now I guess a stranger listening in might wonder why a saddlesore drover like myself would be talking so familiarly with the ranch owner's wife on such a pretty day as it was, standing there on that big wide wraparound porch so freshly painted you could still smell the mineral spirits. And I'd have a hard time explaining it except to say that Fannie Watts and me had gotten on familiar terms ever since about the second week I'd come to work on the place.

Some things just happen you don't have any control over—like the feeling that comes over you about certain women and horses and other potentially dangerous creatures. That's the way it was with us—we didn't have any control over it.

The way it happened was, I was out riding fence, looking for busted wire I could fix so all Mr. Watts's cattle didn't run clear to Colorado or some such, when this black buggy topped a grassy rise and come on down the fence line.

She pulled up and stopped where I was banding wire back together and set there watching me. I was at first pretending like I hadn't noticed because I knew who she was and what the ramrod had warned me of the first day I hired on.

He'd said, "Jim Glass, don't make the mistake some other of these old waddies have made and gotten run off for."

"What mistake would that be?" I had told him as I threw my bedroll onto an empty bunk in a place you could tell was lived in by nothing but men because there were chaps hanging on pegs and run-down boots 'neath the cots, several decks of dog-eared playing cards, and lariats and everything smelling of sweat and tobacco smoke.

"Flirting with the boss's wife," he'd said with a

face like a preacher that just learned there wasn't any Jesus.

"That been a longstanding problem?" I asked, looking around at my new home—for how long, exactly, I didn't know, but knew it wasn't someplace I'd likely retire in.

"No, no problem," he'd said, "long as you keep your eyes to yourself and your manners proper. She's younger than the old man and cute as a button and sometimes these old boys just fall all over themselves whenever she comes around. Some don't rightly know where to draw the line 'cause they was raised without manners."

"Maybe it's her that's the problem then," I said. "Maybe she oughtn't to come around men who don't see a decent woman but maybe thrice a year whenever they hit a town where there might be some decent women to be seen."

"You hold your tongue or you can just saddle that broomtail and keep riding," he'd told me. He was a stumpy little fellow hard as weathered blackjack tree who'd left any personality God had given him back home somewhere.

So anyway, I tried to keep everything to myself whenever I saw her—Fannie—and not talk about it with any of the other hands, about what a pert young gal she was, with hair like spun gold, to be somewhat poetical about it, and eyes as crisp blue as a Kansas sky on a real good day. She looked more like the boss's daughter than his wife whenever you saw them together.

Jack Watts was tall and slightly bent forward like a nail that had been struck slightly wrong. And you'd never see him without his standing under a big white Stetson that looked like he'd just taken it off the merchant's shelf. He had flowing white moustaches, and most of what hair he had on his head was all white as well and shagged over his collar. He wore black waistcoats and white shirts. Flint, the ramrod, said old Jack Watts started out as a drover back in '68 and eventually gathered his own little herd made up of mostly mavericks and maybe more than a few brand-altered cattle and started buying up other surrounding ranches, owned by many who had abandoned life on the high lonesome for the goldfields of California.

"Everything that old boy touches turns to gold," Flint said. "Like that fella, Midas."

"Including the wife?"

"Yeah, her too, I reckon."

So there she was, sitting in that little black buggy with the wind blowing down the grass and letting it back up only to knock it down again, and even a man laced with sweat and sore hands could look upon that sea of green and see it was a damn pretty sight, when the wind waved through it. Mrs. Watts—Fannie—sat there in that buggy looking at me with those eyes looked like the kind painted on the face of a bisque doll, and she was even prettier than the land.

She said "Hidey," and I said "Hidey" back and let go of the wire and the wrecking bar and took off my old Stetson and wiped my sleeve across my sweated face while I watched her reach down somewhere under the seat and come up with a mason jar sweating about as much as I was and hold it forth.

"Would you like some cold tea?" she said, and

it didn't take me very long at all to answer that I would. And each of us stood there holding onto it a moment, looking into each other's eyes, and you could just feel whatever it was dancing between us like the heat waves you see wobbling off a road in the summer.

Then she asked did I want something to eat, was I hungry?

Of course I was, even if I wasn't, and she reached down into a basket where she'd brought the jar of tea from and I could see other jars in there as well and handed me a sandwich wrapped in butcher paper.

"Hope you like roast beef and onions," she said, handing it to me.

"Love 'em," I said.

Then we stood there looking at each other a good bit longer before she said she had to ride on and deliver some of the other men their lunch, and I said, "Yes'm," because there wasn't any words for what I was feeling and thinking that I could have said other than yes'm.

I watched her drive off and my heart wasn't in any more work that day, or the next, when she didn't return. Instead it was Flint come riding up and pitched me down a jar of tea and a sandwich without those same loving looks.

"I was sort of hoping it would be the boss's wife bringing me lunch," I said. "It sort of breaks up the meanness of this type work."

He looked at me so hard with those dark empty eyes of his it was like looking down the barrels of a shotgun.

"I ain't gon' warn you twice," he said, and drove

off in that rickety buckboard like some sort of king riding in a one man parade.

Next two days it was the same thing, Flint bringing me and the rest of us lunch, and I'd bet another dollar the other boys were just as disappointed as I was and did believe those sandwiches and that tea didn't taste as good as when the boss's wife brought them.

Then come that Friday there she came, up over the rise in that little black buggy pulled by the bay, and I quick sniffed my shirt to see how bad it was I stunk and it was pretty bad considering the weather had been awful hot for days and days, so bad even the wind laid down and didn't blow half the time. You could look off in the distance every now and then and see a windmill that wasn't turning, and the sky was empty of birds flying, and stream water was warm as fever.

I knocked dust out of my hat by slapping it against my leg and set it back on my head and tried to seem casual about it as she pulled up and stopped. This time I didn't try and pretend I hadn't noticed her coming and instead stood there with my hands stuffed down into my hind pockets like I was at some pie dance waiting to be asked to join in a quadrille.

"Hidey, Jim," she said, only this time she said it using my first name.

"Hidey, ma'am," I said back, still unsure what little game we were engaged in.

I wasn't completely bereft of the ways of women. In fact I'd known my share of them. But most of them were what you'd call "improper" types—Cyprians, Brides of the Multitudes, Fallen Angels—

that sort. Goodhearted girls as long as you had a dollar or two to buy them a drink or afford their services. Sad women, lots of them were, looking for a man richer than a cowboy to take them out of the life and set them up proper. Some made it too, and some drank mercury. But it had been a quite a little time since I'd been in the company of a woman like Fannie Watts, and I guess I was acting like it too.

We stood there staring, not saying much, and it felt a little like ants crawling in my shirt from the trickling sweat and the anticipation so much so I could hardly stand it.

"Been a while," I said.

"Oh, I had to go to visit my mother," she said. "But I'm back now."

"I reckon you got to get on and take the others their lunch," I said, testing the waters because I'd just as soon she was gone as to stand there and have to be around her knowing she was as illegal as that whiskey they sold down in the Indian Nations.

"No," she said, reaching into her little basket and taking out a sandwich and a jar of tea. "I saved you until last today, Jim. Would you give me a hand down? I'd like to stretch my legs."

Well, it just all got better from there on. As we were later lying in the grass together looking up at big white clouds drifting overhead that had no rain in them, I was thinking about the warning Flint had laid on me the first day. But the truth was, I knew that it didn't matter because nothing good ever lasted very long anyway and you learned to take the good where you found it and expect the worst to come along right behind it.

Fact, I told myself Flint and the rest could come and shoot me and string me up and shoot me again, and it would have been worth it the way I was feeling just then. I believe a man can die happy if he tries hard enough, and I sure gave it my all. I think the look on Fannie's face could attest to how much of my all I gave it.

And so we met like that two or three times a week until I had pretty much fallen down in the well of love over her and was planning how many banks I'd need to rob to give Fannie the sort of life she was accustomed to if she ran off with me when the cold hard truth came down like a bad rain.

Truth had a name: Junior Bosch. He was another hand working on Watts's spread. Junior was a good ten years younger than me, and admittedly of a pleasant disposition. On top of which he had dark curly hair and teeth that shone like ivory that caused even some of the old punchers to look upon him with a certain envy.

It seemed I wasn't the only one getting those special delivery lunches from Fannie—that she often alternated days between Junior and me as to which of us got our lunch delivered last. And once all the dirty laundry got washed, I learned there were some days when Junior and me both got our lunches delivered back to back. And that little trip she said she took to her mother's turned out to be a trip to meet up with yet another fellow in Council Bluffs. Most disturbing to me was having to think I was mixing in where Junior might have earlier been.

The real kicker was, I think Flint knew the whole while what sort of woman she was and was laugh-

ing out the side of his ugly mouth at those who'd
been fool enough to fall for Fannie's charm. He
fired Junior when it came to light because Junior
had a loose mouth on him when he got to drinking
and ran the whole tale down in front of me and the
others one night. I didn't get fired because to that
point nobody knew about me and Fannie. 'Course,
Flint told everybody to keep it under his hat what
Junior had spilled, that he didn't want Mr. Watts
hearing such things or he'd fire every one of us. But
I knew then and there I was gone.

So I made a big show of quitting the next day after I learned about the two of them doing the grass
dance together—an image that set with me about
like a rancid steak washed down by snakehead
whiskey. Flint had come up to me first thing in the
morning and told me to go dig some postholes up
on the west forty. That's when I told him what I
thought about such work—and it was by God the
truth even if it wasn't the real reason I quit.

But my pride wouldn't let me come right out and
tell Fannie face-to-face what I was thinking, the
reason I was quitting. And hers wouldn't let her
ask any deeper than the reason I gave her; I think
in a way she was glad I was going.

And so there I stood and there she stood and
you could tell it was all broke and never going to
get fixed between us and the only difference was I
think I cared a whole lot more than she did. Out
of work cowboys were as plentiful as ticks on a
wet dog, and beautiful young women were about
as rare as a butcher with all his fingers, so you can
see which the odds favored.

So she went and got my thirty dollars a month's pay and handed it to me.

"I'm sorry things didn't work out, Jim," she said, and I could hear the old man inside somewhere coughing and it dawned on me just then he must have known of her dalliances, past and present. How could he have not? And knowing he must have known left me feeling pretty lowdown to think that she done what she done with his knowing it and I'd become equally as guilty. Still, when I looked into those sweet eyes I couldn't get mad at her.

"You even feel a little bit bad about all this?" I said.

She glanced up at me and said, "Well, it all works out somehow, doesn't it, Jim."

"Goddamn if it don't," was the last words I said to that woman, my heart broken, my mind messed up like it sometimes got when I drank the better stuff.

So I rode on away from there just following the sun because it was as good a direction to go as any, and then here I come to this sign all about no discharging of firearms and population of 756, thinking it wasn't too big of a town where a man would feel crowded, but not so small either that there wouldn't be any job opportunities. I needed some grub and to find work of some sort, or me and my horse would end up just another of life's tragic victims—our bones bleaching on the plains like a lot of others who'd gone in search of something they weren't ever going to find—men, women, and children. Here and there along the roads you could often see little wood markers with names burned into them half knocked over by the wind and rain and I didn't feature joining them as part of that grim landscape.

I never thought my stopping in such a place called Coffin Flats, with such low expectations, would lead to what it did. But then, after my last go-round, I told myself, Jim, don't even try and guess what is writ in the book of life under your name.

I just rode on in and tied off in front of the first drinking establishment I found. Place called Bison Bill's Emporium.

If the beer was cold and wet and not over a dime a glass, it was my sort of place.

2

I rested a foot on the rail and waited for Bison Bill or whoever it was tending bar this mid-morning. A one-armed man with handlebar moustaches said, "Beer or whiskey?"

A chalkboard listed the prices. Beer was a nickel, whiskey two bits, pickled eggs a dime.

"Beer," I said, "and two of those pickled eggs."

It was early yet to be drinking, but then, I never owned a watch. There was just me and the one-armed bartender and a man sitting by himself in the corner at a table reading a newspaper—holding it up to the window light because it was dim inside the place.

He lowered his paper when I ordered my beer, looked over the top of the pages at me then went back to reading.

I put two bits on the bar and the one-armed man picked it up and put it in a big brass cash register after he punched a button and the drawer clanged open. I wondered how much money a big register like that could hold; just weighing my options for a future career as desperado in case nothing better came along. I sure didn't want to go mending any more fences, even if the ranch owner's wife was pretty and liberal with her body.

"What time you put out the regular eats?" I said, plopping one of the eggs into my trap before washing it down with a swallow of beer.

"Not till the lunch crowd," he said.

I ate the other egg and sipped more beer and it was cold and that's all that mattered, cold and wet, something to cut the trail dust.

"You in town looking for work?" he said.

I heard the newspaper rattle behind me.

"Could be. You know of any?"

"Not much."

I waited for him to come up with a name maybe. Some towns are just friendlier than others.

"Where you hail from, you don't mind my asking?"

"Bar Double Z," I said. "Nebraska."

"I fell drunk off a horse once in Nebraska," he said.

"I imagine you'd not be the first to do so," I said.

It was aimless talk not leading to anything I could see.

"Noon you say, about the lunch?"

"Yes, that's right."

I glanced at the jar of pickled eggs again.

"You do your own pickling?" I said.

The barkeep smiled.

"I seen you," he said, "I was wondering if maybe you'd come in for the big fight tonight." He was wiping out the inside of a drink glass, then holding it up to the poor light and wiping it some more.

"What fight's that?" I said.

"Gentleman Harry Ford is in town taking on

all comers. Champeen prizefighter from back East somewhere. Middleweight they say."

"Middleweight, huh?"

He pointed to a poster tacked up on the wall just inside the door.

"Cost you five dollars to get in, but if you can knock the champ out, his manager will give you fifty dollars."

"Ten to one," I said, scratching up under my hat. I needed a bath and a shave and some clean clothes. "Not too bad of odds."

"No sir. If I had both arms, I'd fight him myself."

"You say all a fellow has to do it knock him out?"

That's when the fellow reading the newspaper lowered it and said, "You'd be wise to save your money and your face."

I glanced over at him.

He looked like a banker with his derby cocked to one side and frock coat and checked vest. All he was missing was a horse collar and a necktie. He folded his newspaper and set it beside his coffee cup. I could see the window light glance off a pinky ring.

"What makes you think I'd lose?" I said.

He lifted his cup and took a drink, his eyes watching me the whole time like I was a dog he was thinking of buying.

"I know you cow punchers all think you can fight, especially when you're all liquored up. You believe you can whip Jesus himself, but trust me, this old boy will use you like a redheaded step-child. I saw him fight an exhibition in Dodge last year."

Well, shit, it sure didn't help my confidence none

having a stranger tell me he could tell just by the looks of me what I could and could not do in a fistfight.

"Where do I sign up for this Gentleman Harry Ford?" I said to the barkeep, and he smiled like he'd just grown a new arm.

"The fight's to be held down at Bucky's Corral. Starts at seven o'clock sharp. Bring your money."

"Goddamn right," I said, and looked back over my shoulder at the man. He simply picked up his newspaper and tucked it under his arm and walked out into the mid-morning light that seemed to just swallow him whole.

"Who is that fellow?" I said.

"City marshal Chalk Bronson," he said.

"Awfully sure of himself."

"Yes, awfully."

I hung around till lunch and bought another beer and dug into the meats and bread and cakes and went off and found myself a table—the same one the lawman had been reading his newspaper at—and sat there eating and sipping my beer like I owned the place. I counted out my money. I was down to seventeen dollars and two bits. Add to that the fifty I planned on winning and I'd be aces once again. Figured maybe I'd sell my horse and saddle and buy a train ticket to California and put both my feet in the ocean just to say I did and then look around for some real opportunity. I heard there was a lot of it out there. These old prairies hadn't shown me anything but the ass end of cows and fence lines and a sea of grass. I didn't even want to think of what it was before I took up punching— the faces of the men I'd killed.

The buffalo was all shot out and the farmers were taking over and it was getting so peaceful, most of it, it was goddamn pitiful. Everybody knew if you wanted to make something of yourself you had to either go east or west.

I sat around till the lunch crowd thinned out again then offered to help the one-armed barkeep put away the leftovers. He paid me by giving me a free beer. I thanked him and he poured himself one while four old boys with long beards played dominoes at a table and told each other jokes and laughed and shuffled their ivory.

"So you think you might know somewhere I could land a little work?" I said.

"You like whores?"

"I never held anything against them but me," I said.

"Pink Huston is looking for a bouncer at his cat-house."

"Shit, wasn't exactly what I had in mind as a career move."

"Career move?" He laughed like hell and swiped the beer foam from his moustaches.

"You know what something like that pays, bouncing at his hog farm?"

He shrugged. "You'd have to ask Pink but I imagine, knowing him, he'd want you to take some of your wages out in trade with his gals."

"Where do I find him?"

"You see them railroad tracks just south of here when you rode in?"

"Yeah, I seen them."

"That's where he is. Marshal keeps all the for-sale pussy across those tracks—the dead line, he calls it. Crib whores, Chinese whores, all of 'em. Chalk's got the biggest hog farm within a hundred miles of here. You can't miss it—look for the one with the mansard roof."

I thanked him and went out and mounted my horse and rode down toward the railroad tracks. I could see a line of shacks and one structure with a mansard roof that looked like it belonged north of the tracks, not south. It loomed above the others. The horse was skittish about crossing over the tracks. I patted his neck in a gentle way and said, "Hell, old son, we been south of tracks like these before."

I rode down the one and only street and noticed a lot of the whores had hung out their laundry by draping their underthings and bedsheets over railings, and some were washing clothes in big galvanized tubs set out front of the cathouses. Several of the ladies were sitting lounging around on porches and balconies—the places that had balconies—in their bloomers, and smoking cigarettes and chatting like schoolgirls.

Most of them whooped and called out to me when I passed by. I made it a point to pass by slowly.

"Hey cowboy, come on in!"

"Hidey Lonesome."

"I could sure use a good man like you, honey."

"Hey you tall drink of water, come and see Alice!"

Some stuck their rumps out and slapped them just to show me the product. I let it cross my mind briefly that whoremaster might not be a bad profession.

I smiled and touched my hat brim and tried not to think of all that temptation as I rode down to the end place with the mansard roof. There were girls lounging around on the porch there too, four or five of them, and one had a black cat sitting on her lap she was petting. When I dismounted and tied off my horse at the hitch post and stepped up onto the porch she lifted her sloe eyes to me and said, "You like my pussy, honey?" The cat purred contentedly, its eyes closed.

"It's a real fine-looking pussy, ma'am," I said, and the other girls laughed and so did the one holding the cat.

"I'm here to see Pink Huston," I said.

"Pink's inside. But he can't do you half as much good as these girls can."

I leaned over and scratched the cat's head and its ears twitched and I said, "Probably not," and went inside.

It was like something out of the Arabian nights—lots of red damask and heavy wine-colored drapes, settees with carved wood feet, and even a crystal chandelier. A man in spats was sitting at a small burl-wood desk counting money.

"You Pink Huston?"

"Who'd be needing to know?" He had an English accent.

"Barkeep over at the Bison Club said you might need a bouncer."

"You any good with your dukes, mate?"

"I'll find out just how good tonight," I said. "I'm going down to Bucky's Corral and sign up to fight Gentleman Harry Ford."

The man stopped counting. "You ever see that bloke fight—Gentleman Harry?"

"No."

"He's a first-class pugilist," he said. "D'ya even know what a pugilist is, lad?"

"I'm from Nebraska, not China," I said.

His laugh sounded like someone strangling a chicken, and he went back to counting.

"What about the job?" I said.

"We'll see how ya do tonight, then I'll decide whether you're the bloke for me."

"Fine," I said. "How much for the one out front with the cat?"

"Lorri? She's not fer sale, laddie. She's me personal snatch."

"We'll talk later then," I said. "After I knock out the Gentleman."

"Yar," he said. "After you coldcock him, eh."

I went out and got on my horse and Lorri stroked her pussy while giving me that look you'd expect a woman with her talents would give and I touched my brim and said, "Destiny is a funny thing, ain't it, ma'am?"

"What do you mean?" she said.

"I think you and I have a date with destiny— that it's something that was bound to happen since before either of us was born."

"Careful, cowboy, Pink is a jealous man, especially when it comes to smooth talkers."

"Yeah, me too," I said, and reined the horse around and headed back across the tracks.

I killed the rest of that afternoon by taking a long soak at a small bathhouse run by a Celestial while waiting to get my clothes cleaned at his laundry in back. Then I got a shave before heading back to the saloon, and nursed a beer or two until the evening hour of seven o'clock, when I walked down to Bucky's Corral. A sizable crowd had gathered.

I stepped up to the corral, which was set up as a boxing ring, and saw the touted Gentleman Harry Ford standing on the other side wearing tight britches with a red sash around his waist. He was bare-chested, no doubt to show off his muscular frame. He had short-cropped black hair and black handlebar moustaches and looked cool as a block of ice as his gaze swept the crowd, no doubt seeing future broken noses, split lips, and busted teeth. A short bald man stood next to him, rubbing Harry's upper arms and shoulders and talking to him, the fighter tilting his head to hear better what the man was telling him, rolling his broad shoulders. Another man stood in the middle of the corral with a megaphone, telling everyone that Gentleman Harry was ready for the first challenger and anyone who had not yet signed up should see him.

"Come on, now, who will be the first to challenge the champeen?" the fellow with the megaphone asked, and a well-built man climbed over the top of the corral and jumped down into the dust and said, "Me."

Somebody standing next to me said the challenger was the town blacksmith—Andy Toe.

"Old Andy will hit him like a mule kicked him," the fellow said. I sure as hell hoped old Andy wouldn't knock the Gentleman out before I got my chance to win the fifty dollars.

"I'll take five on the champeen," I said, and the fellow said, "You're on."

The two fighters were called to the center of the ring while the megaphone fellow gave them instructions about no hitting below the belt, no gouging of eyes or biting off ears. Then he nodded at the bald man who rang a dinner bell, and the blacksmith rushed out to meet the champ and threw a haymaker that the Gentleman ducked easy and as he came up, slammed a right hand to the side of the smith's head that collapsed him like he'd been shot. The megaphone man who had now turned referee counted the smith out, and some other men came and dragged him out of the ring by his arms. I took my five dollars from the kid next to me. He didn't look quite so sure now.

"Who's next?" the referee said.

The kid raised his hand, then got into the corral. He was tall and wiry as a terrier, with little blond hairs on his upper lip.

"Yer mudder know yer fighting?" the referee said jokingly. The boy nodded, and you could see he was nervous the way he shifted his weight from foot to foot like he was dancing on a dime, trying to make it give change.

The man with the dinner bell struck it with a hammer and the boy began to dance around the Gentleman, who more or less stalked the kid, waiting for him to throw a punch. The crowd began to boo the poor exhibition, and the Gentleman stopped and stood there waiting for the kid to do something, to come close enough. Finally the kid got up nerve enough to throw a long looping right hand that hit the Gentleman on the side of his face. They both seemed surprised.

It went like that for a few minutes or so—the kid dancing, throwing slaps against the placid face of the Gentleman, the Gentleman standing there taking it, letting the kid get more and more confidence up until at last he moved in close enough and the Gentleman snapped a straight right hand that landed flush in the center of the kid's puss, snapping his head back like he'd been assassinated. The blow knocked him straight back and dumped him into the trampled dirt and horseshit. The kid sat with his legs splayed out in front of him and spit teeth and waved his feeble hand in resignation. The crowd laughed and booed at the same time.

"Next!" came the call, and a succession of local oafs took their turn with the Gentleman, who knocked each one out, or hit them so hard they quit.

Finally I figured it was as good a time as any and climbed over the top rail and dropped down and paid my money to the referee as he gave me the same instructions about not biting or gouging or hitting in the nutsack. I took off my clean shirt and hung it on the top rail and waited for the dinner bell to ring.

I noticed Pink Huston and Lorri, the cat woman, in the crowd; I wanted to ask if she'd brought her pussy along but this was no time for joking around. I looked down just then and saw some bloody teeth lying in the dirt.

The bell rang and I came in fast and low and popped Gentlemen Harry Ford with a couple of hard left hooks to his short ribs and moved out just as he dropped his own left hand down, grazing my ear and causing it to feel like it had been stung by a wasp.

"Ah, we've got a true lad, now don't we?" he said, grinning so some of his gold teeth showed.

I feinted with a right and threw another hard little hook into his ribs sameplace and saw how that affected him. Some of the smile went off his face. Everybody wants to knock you out in a fistfight, so they try and hit you in the head. But the body is a bigger target and can't move out of the way easy as the head does. A lot like when you have to shoot a man—you aim for the biggest target.

The Gentleman was quick of foot and moved well and came in and hit me with a couple of shocking blows that mostly glanced off my arms, which helped to soften their power, and several off my shoulders as I turned to give more of an angle. I knew I couldn't go long with him; he was a pro and would figure me out, and my teeth would end up with those of the others.

He moved in, his hand already cocked, and I sidestepped just as he threw a fist that whistled past my face. I bent and hooked two more hard lefts into his ribs, same place as before, and I thought I heard something crack. He threw a wild overhand that clipped the back of my head and bounced off my shoulder blade. I staggered like I was hurt and he moved in fast, ready to make the kill, and I brought a right uppercut from down near the border that caught him just under his chin. I put my full weight behind it and it was like hitting rock and I heard him give a hard grunt as his teeth clashed. The blow had caught him completely un-awares and stopped him in his tracks, which was all I needed as I smashed a sharp left cross to the bridge of his nose, smashing it like a strawberry hit with a hammer.

He staggered back and I moved in fast, hitting him with as many rights and lefts as I could swing, driving him back and back and back until he was up against the railings and I could feel that hand-some face giving way, bones and flesh softening— like hitting a grapefruit—with every blow. Then his eyes rolled up in his head and I stepped back and watched him collapse to his knees before fall-ing facedown in the dirt.

The referee took his time about counting the Gentleman out but the crowd got on him and fi-nally he did and then reached in his pocket and gave me the fifty dollars. I went and put it in my shirt before realizing I had a cut over my left eye that dripped blood, which I temporarily stopped by pressing the heel of my hand to it.

Pink Huston came up then and said, "I lost a hundred dollars on you. Come around later and we'll talk about your job duties."

Lorri slipped me a silk hankie when Pink turned his back to walk away. She gave me a wink. "Mr. Destiny," she said.

City Marshal Chalk Bronson found me as I was holding Lorri's hankie to my face and feeling flush with the new money and the scent of her whorish perfume. Something about a good fight makes a man want to drink and have sex.

"Hell of a fight," he said.

"You lose money on me too?"

"No," he said. "I bet on you."

"Why?"

"I get hunches about people," he said, and then, "Come on, I'll buy you a drink at the Bison. I've got something I want to discuss with you."

3

He'd been a worried man looking for an answer he did not think existed. Then he saw the stranger and took note of him and as soon as the stranger started to speak, saying how he was looking for work, and Chalk began to have hope, that this man might be the answer.

So he took careful study of him there in the Bison, saw the way he carried himself, the way he seemed to take note of everything in the place, unafraid to state his case. And the lawman noticed something else too—the bulk that was under the linen duster riding the stranger's right hip.

And when Bill mentioned about the fight, the stranger didn't hesitate. A man like that, who doesn't hesitate, was just the sort of man Chalk figured he needed. Lately he had felt very alone. Saddled with a problem he couldn't tell anyone about, even his Nora. A secret about a woman you once loved was not something you talked to your wife about. And this particular secret was full of danger for everyone.

So he went on about his business after observing the stranger and suggesting directly that the stranger would be smart to save his money and not

put himself in the ring with a professional prizefighter, because more than anything he wanted to
see how the stranger would react to such negative
comments. It hadn't even fazed him. And so Chalk
Bronson thought there was one more test before
he made his pitch to the stranger—to watch him
actually fight.

That little traveling show had come into town
the night before and set up a tent just outside the
town's limits, and he had gone out and looked them
over. The fighter, himself, this Gentleman Harry
Ford, sat eating an apple as calmly as a horse while
his manager scurried about directing the local men
he'd hired to put up the tent, his face red as the
apple his fighter was eating.

Chalk warned them both not to *skin* the locals
and that he expected everything to be on the up
and up. Sure, sure, the little man said. "My boy's a
pro. We don't need to skin nobody."

Chalk told them both he'd be at the fight keeping
an eye on things, and the little man did not object,
but seemed rather pleased that the local law itself
would be in attendance and said, "I don't suppose
you'd be putting up the dukes with the Gentleman
here?"

"No," said Chalk. "I only fight when it is necessary and not for the sport of it," and went home
with his mind still troubled about what had happened earlier in the day when the two punchers had
ridden out from Johnny Waco's with the letter of
demand that said he had till Friday to make it happen. The letter fully stated what the consequences
for him and the town were if he failed to deliver.
They were dusty, horse-smelling punchers, the sort

he was more used to arresting and throwing in jail for drunk and disorderly than from taking any sort of orders from. But they were fully aware of their own immunity, being the hires of Johnny Waco.

So he went down the night of the fight to watch the stranger, to see if his backbone and fists matched the rest of his confident manner, and placed a ten dollar side bet on him, believing himself a better judge of the human character than most. Then he stood and watched as the Gentleman quickly dispatched his first half-dozen opponents, if they could even be called that, with professional ease and blows that struck the unschooled like hammers.

Then the stranger got into the ring and it was a different story, and Chalk felt vindicated and blessed all at the same time when he saw the stranger was no stranger to using his fists and nerve, and he went home that evening feeling the slightest ray of hope in an otherwise dark world.

Chalk convinced himself that the stranger had arrived when he did for a reason. What else could explain it? Chalk Bronson was not a God-fearing man in the normal sense, but he didn't disbelieve in good fortune either. He believed it was more than just dumb luck that had thus far kept him from getting assassinated in a profession where assassination was not uncommon.

And so he had approached the stranger after the fight and offered to buy him a celebratory drink and then lay out his proposal.

The stranger listened as Chalk told him the deal.

The stranger listened with interest.

"A job's a job," he said to the stranger.

"No it isn't—not always."

"You need money, I'm offering you a good bit of money. More than you can make prizefighting or doing anything else this little burg has to offer."

For Chalk Bronson knew one thing that was common to most men—money, and that everyone had a price. All you had to do was learn what their price was.

The stranger didn't seem to be any different in that way.

4

The barkeep chipped me off a chunk of ice from a block he kept out back to keep his beer barrels cold and put it in a cloth and I held it against my face.

"You knocked that sucker out like you owned him," he said.

"Trick is to keep moving and keep throwing punches," I said. "Some days you get lucky."

Marshal Bronson stood sipping his coffee and listening.

"You said you had something you wanted to discuss with me," I said.

"You found work yet?"

"Yes, I think so. Pink Huston offered me a bouncer job at his hog farm."

"Let's set over there," he said, pointing with his chin to an empty table.

We carried our drinks over and set down and he took off his derby and set it on the empty seat between us and I could see he was losing his hair though still a young man, younger than me, I guessed, by a few years.

"Here's the thing," he said. "I need me a man to do me a special service."

"What sort of service?"

His eyes glanced up toward the bar and then around the room—the place was nearly full that hour, men still talking about the prizefight, working girls, horses, their wives, the weather.

"What I'm going to tell you, you need to keep to yourself. Can I trust you on that regard?"

"Sure," I said.

He reached in his waistcoat pocket, took out a folded piece of paper and unfolded it and said, "You learn to read somewhere along the line, did you?"

It wasn't an insult the way I saw it, just a legitimate question. Lots of fellows dropped out of school before they learned to read, and some never went.

"This arrived yesterday in the noon mail," he said.

I read what was written:

You have one week to return my Antonia or I will come with plenty enough men and burn your town and kill anyone who tries to stop me.
                                        J.W.

"Who is she?" I asked. "Who's he?"

"*He* is Johnny Waco—biggest damn rancher in this part of the state. *She* is his wife and currently an employee of Pink Huston—your future employer."

"Why doesn't he just come and get her, he wants her back?"

"Long story," he said. "Just that it is my town

and I'm responsible for seeing it doesn't get burned down. It's what I get paid to do."

"Where do I fit into all this?"

"I want to hire you to help me deliver her to him."

"Me? Shit, what'd I do to piss you off?"

"That your idea of humor?"

"No, seriously, why me?"

"Like I told you, I get hunches about people. My hunch is you'd be a good man to have on my side."

"Good and dead, I reckon, if the threat in that letter holds any water and you can't get Waco's wife back to him."

"How's five hundred dollars sound?"

"I miss something about this place?" I said. "I never met a lawman yet who made over thirty a month."

"Special case," he said. "I can get the money."

"What makes you think I'm any sort of man for this?"

He looked at the butt of the Merwin Hulbert riding my hip.

"The way you wear that hogleg," he said. "Like a man that can use it."

"Could be I just want folks to think that."

"Well, do you know how to use it?"

"Yeah," I said. "I do. Don't mean I will, though."

He eased back in his chair.

"You're half as good with a gun as you are your fists then you're worth the money."

I weighed my options. I could turn him down and go bounce drunks and peckerwoods at the hog farm and probably get plenty of free quim for my troubles as well as a steady paycheck, or I could make a lot of money fast and probably get killed before I could spend it. Or I could get on my horse and ride the hell out of there and forget I ever heard of Coffin Flats. Thing with the bouncer job was, if this Waco *did* come riding in with a bunch of men and burned the town to the ground, my bouncer job would get burned with it, especially if Waco's wife was working for Pink. So that was no good. Leaving was probably the smartest thing to do— after all, I had over sixty dollars in my pocket. But five hundred sounded like a lot more than sixty if I remembered the mathematics right I'd learned in a West Texas schoolhouse when I wasn't daydreaming about girls, horses, and fighting Indians.

"Who else you got to help you on this?" I said. "I mean if things don't work out getting Waco's wife back to him?"

"Got two deputies I don't know if I can count on."

"Maybe you should fire them then and get you someone you can count on."

"I don't want to sit around here bullshittng, Mr. Glass. You're either in or out. We can't pull this off, this whole town is going to burn and maybe a few good folks will die."

"Including you."

"I'm not afraid to die," he said. "I've been close to it a dozen times already. But I got this sick wife . . ."

"I get the five hundred either way it turns out— long as I'm around to collect it?"

"Either way long as you don't cut and run."

"So if we can get the woman and deliver her to Waco, we're aces."

"That's the size of it."

"Where's this old boy's place?"

"A full day's ride from here."

"Why the hell doesn't he just come and get her is the question bothering me. The one you says got a long story behind it. I don't mind putting my neck on the line long as I know what I'm putting it there for."

Chalk sipped his coffee and stared into the cup.

"Because he wants *me* to do it."

"You want to level with me or just sit here pulling my dally rope?"

"It's complicated," he said.

"I already figured as much. How *is* it complicated?"

"Antonia and I were engaged to be married once—a long time ago, before she met Waco. But I went off to fight in that goddamn war because I thought it was my duty and I got hurt and lost in my head and didn't come back when I could have. I was gone two years longer than the war lasted. And when I *did* come back, she was with Waco. She thought I was killed—lots of men were and their families never knew it. Waco had money and could provide her a life I couldn't even think about even if I had come back—"

Somebody shouted from across the room and Chalk looked up suddenly, saw it wasn't anything but some drunk being a drunk.

"Sounds like maybe you didn't lose all that much in losing her."

He looked at me hard then.

"You don't know anything about her," he said.

"You're right, I don't. So Waco took up with her, but how the hell did it go from that to where she's at now—moonlighting at Pink Huston's hog farm?"

"Time I come back here, I was a drunk myself, run-down and wasted. She was married to Waco. I met Nora and she pulled me out of the bottle and I hired on as a deputy, stayed sober, and when the marshal quit, I was offered the job. Thing is, I'd run into Antonia now and then when she'd come to town. We'd talk—privately. She wanted me back. I told her I couldn't, even though I was still weak when it came to her. I messed up this once with her and later she told me she was pregnant with my child. I said I was sorry, I'd do what I could but I wasn't leaving Nora. She tried to kill herself but all she managed to do was kill the child with the poison she drank. Afterward she got hooked on the laudanum Doc gave her to keep her sedated—found out she liked the world better when she wasn't sober. When she couldn't get laudanum, she got into opium and booze. Christ! I have to explain all this to you?"

"I can pretty much guess the rest. Pink kept her in dope in exchange for her working for him."

"Yeah, that's pretty much it."

"I still don't get why Waco just doesn't come and shoot Pink and take her back."

"He blames me, thinks I run a game on her to get her to leave him. She must have told him about the child. Believes if I hadn't come back, none of this would have happened. He's probably right, none of it would have happened. He wants to embarrass me, make me pay for my sins—show her what sort of no account I am."

"Why not just tell him to go to hell?"

"'Cause I never mentioned any of this to Nora, for one thing. Now she's sick, and if I lose her, I've got nothing to live for. And for another, I've swore to protect these folks and this town. I guess as much as I messed up, I owe somebody something."

I studied on it and what I saw was a worried man— but worried more about others than himself—and I knew all about that, having been down that road myself a time or three.

"It sounds like a lot more than wanting to embarrass you," I said. "It sounds like pure revenge."

"Yeah," he said. "It does, but so what?"

"No matter what, you lose."

"Probably so."

"You could always take your wife and just ride away and not look back."

"That wouldn't end nothing. He'd come and burn this town and then he'd come after me. He just wants me to grovel awhile before he puts his boot on the back of my neck. Maybe I give him back what he wants he'll let things go. Then Nora and I can leave and find someplace to ourselves."

"Tell you what," I said. "I'm supposed to go see Pink about that job. Let me go see what I can find out with regards to Antonia. Then I'll find you and see we can't work something out."

"You want the job or no?"

"Yeah. Maybe."

"I should go over there with you."

"And do what?"

His gaze dropped to his coffee cup; a small black mirror that reflected a troubled face.

"Where can I find you when I come back?"

"I'll be right here."

I stood and went out into the cool night. You could feel the seasonal change, and the sky looked like it had holes poked in it with silver pins. I rode down to the railroad tracks—the dead line—and could see the lights on in some of the bagnios and crib joints. Behind those doors and walls and windows, there was some serious action going on and everybody was playing the hand they'd been dealt.

I tied off in front to Pink's place and knocked on the door and it was answered by the woman, Lorri. She was wearing a green silk dress and holding that same cat.

"You come back to play with my pussy?" she said, smiling, stroking the fur between the cat's ears. The way she said it made me want to.

"I've always been a cat lover," I said.

She smiled and held the door wide for me to come in, and there were several women of various ages and sizes lounging on the furniture. Pink was there at his little desk, dressed in a silk smoking jacket and smoking a cheroot like some Arab sheik watching over his harem.

"Ah, the pugilist," he said. "Y've come for the job then, laddie?"

"Tonight," I said, "I've come simply for the pleasure."

"Certainly, take yer pick—anyone but me and Lorri, that is." The two of them exchanged looks.

"Somebody told me that a gal named Antonia was a good choice," I said.

"Ah, right you are. Step forward, my angel, the man has requested your services."

A thin strawberry blonde lifted herself unsteadily from one of the horsehair divans and wobbled forward. She was pretty, with a thin emaciated face and dark shadows under both eyes and hollow cheeks, and I'd bet a dollar she used to be a lot more attractive.

"Tell you what," Pink said. "It's on the house tonight, in spite of what you cost me already. Just to show you I'm a generous bloke."

She took me by the hand and we went up a carpeted stair to a room that was narrow with striped wallpaper. The flame from a small lamp by the bedside danced inside the glass chimney.

"What's your pleasure, cowboy?" she said without the least bit of enthusiasm, and began to undress from the robe she was wearing. The robe fell away and what was left was a too thin woman with sallow flesh covering her ribs and bony hips. I picked up the robe and wrapped her in it.

"Hey . . ."

"I just want to talk to you," I said.

She sat wearily on the side of the bed. "You got anything to drink?"

"No."

"I could use a cigarette."

"I don't smoke," I said.

"Jesus, what are you, a damn priest?"

She rested her face in her palms.

"I came to see you on behalf of Chalk Bronson," I said.

She looked up, her eyes red, tired, half closed.

"What's *he* want?"

"He needs to take you back to Johnny Waco."

"Yeah, like hell."

"Look, you've got the man between a rock and a hard place, miss."

Her mouth twisted with displeasure.

"Cowboy, what I do is fuck, I don't talk, and I don't care if he's between a rock and a mountain." She started to rise but I put a hand on her shoulder and pushed her back down again.

"Waco is going to burn the town down if the marshal doesn't bring you to him," I said.

She looked at me like I wasn't there.

"Well, it's going to be a tough place to make a living then," she said. "Because no way in hell am I going back to Johnny Waco."

"Can I ask you something?"

She shrugged. "Why not."

"You happy with this situation?"

She looked at the flame dancing in the glass chimney of the lamp, the light catching in her eyes.

"It beats living with Johnny Waco."

"I can make it better."

"How?"

So I told her the plan—the one I'd just made up there on the spot. The one that was mostly desperate and probably would get me killed and maybe her too. But what the hell were the choices? Okay, so I knew I could still ride away and not look back. But it isn't always that simple. Maybe if I'd never known what would happen, it could have been easier, but now I knew and I'd have to live with it—whatever I did or didn't do for a very long time. And if I could pull something off that maybe saved some lives, maybe a lot of lives, then maybe it was worth a try.

When I finished telling her, she said, "You call that a plan?"

5

She had been waiting forever it seemed.

First there was the wait for him to come home again from the war. And when he didn't, there was the wait of mourning. The wait of mourning was followed by wait for light to come into her life again after all the long lonely dark nights.

Then came the wait for new love, if there was such a thing.

It had not come exactly as she had hoped. But then what great love could repeat itself?

Johnny Waco wooed her. He was wealthy and in some ways larger than life. But he was a great mystery to her as well. He had a reputation as a hard man without forgiveness toward his enemies, and later he would prove to be a man who kept his secrets secret, a man of interminable silence. But in the beginning of his courtship, he showed her none of that. He arrived in carriages pulled by pretty horses and took her for long rides and showed her the width and breadth of his holdings.

He arranged picnics beneath large cottonwoods that guarded clear running creeks and rivers. He could be wildly generous and often was. He once bought her a hat on a whim—a hat she knew she'd never wear—that he'd ordered from a catalogue simply because he thought she would like it. It had ostrich feathers.

He let her know from the outset his intentions to marry her. He professed his love and his desire for her. Even if he wasn't Chalk Bronson, it was still flattering in a way.

There was no one else that came even close to being marriageable. Just old men, punchers, gamblers, the occasional drummer selling tinware or elixirs from the back of a medicine show wagon.

She'd told him no at first, said she wasn't ready for marriage. Her heart still longed for the man who'd gone away and never came home again. Dead, lost, disfigured, out of his mind? She couldn't be sure. No word had come. He had been simply swallowed by a distant war she only read about in the newspaper. Time left her without answers.

Johnny Waco was a force in his own right. Tall and good-looking with smoke-dark eyes, a man who did not hesitate to brag that he always got what he was after.

He seemed just decent enough, and after a time her resistance broke down; it was easier to marry him then to keep finding reasons not to. They were wed in the church by the priest even though Johnny made no claim to any particular religious belief. He would do what was right by her. And afterward there was a huge wedding feast prepared by his hired help, Maria Montero, his housekeeper, and her husband, Pedro, along with some of the hired hands who carried out long tables into the yard for guests to sit at, decorated with white crepe.

They took the train to San Francisco for a honeymoon.

The ocean startled her. The ships in the harbor seemed to be waiting to take her to exotic places. Weeks after their return to the desert she could still hear the creak of ropes, see the lighthouse light floating on the black water at night. The hotels in San Francisco had electric lights.

Their lovemaking was for her the hardest part. She still remembered the hands of Chalk Bronson, the scent of his skin, the landscape of his body. Everything with Johnny Waco was different, hurried, and in the end unpleasant. She told herself she would give it time, that she could not expect him to be her late lover. Men are as different as horses are different, as the days are different, the seasons.

But time did not ease her unease around him. And by the time of their return home again, she felt as if he found pleasure in her for only one reason.

His personal bar is where she developed her taste for liquor—a glass in the early afternoon relaxed her. Another at supper made the long hours leading to bedtime seem less dull. Later she would learn to calm her mind after he had fallen asleep by going to the cabinet and pouring herself a glass of brandy. It made her feel less stained.

After two years of this new but unhappy life she heard news that nearly stopped her heart: Chalk Bronson had suddenly appeared in town. It was exactly as though a dead man had risen from the grave—the shock of it.

She fought the urge to go and seek him out. Her husband warned her against such indiscretions.

"If he thinks he's come back for you," he said, "he's badly mistaken."

She vowed that she no longer could love a man who would abandon her for so long. How could she? Posing such a question to Johnny Waco seemed to calm him.

But then she went. And she found him staggering drunk down the street. She hardly recognized him. His face was haggard, his cheeks hollow and grizzled with graying beard. He'd lost a great deal of weight. He wore moustaches long and unkempt.

He seemed just as surprised to see her.

They were formal at first, like strangers being introduced. Her heart ached to touch him and make him new again. He ended up weeping into his rough beard.

"I'm sorry," he said over and over.

Whatever they had once had was broken and they both knew it.

She rushed home and locked herself in her room and wept. She'd never felt such anguish. And that afternoon she got fully and maddeningly drunk for the first time, and her husband found her huddled in the corner of the room raving in her anguish.

"You saw him, didn't you? Against my wishes, you saw him!"

She didn't bother to try and explain.

He warned her again to stay away.

"Will you beat me if I do not?" she said.

"No, but I will beat him in ways you will not like."

The next time she went to town she planned carefully, waiting until he had gone away on a cattle buying trip.

She learned where Chalk Bronson was staying, which room at the hotel, and went up the back stairs and knocked on his door, and he opened it, standing there wearing just his trousers, his hair tousled, his eyes red and anguished.

He let her in and they talked.

Their talking eased them beyond many of the old barriers that had been built up in his absence. He confessed he still loved her. She asked him why he hadn't come home after the war.

"I can't explain it," he said. "It changed me. I felt like I'd lost myself. I needed to find who I had once been and went in search of it. I couldn't bring myself home to you the way I was. You wouldn't have cared for what I'd become."

His truth became her own. She ordered the copper tub brought up the room and filled with hot water and soap and towels.

"I want to wash you," she said to the man who should have been her husband. She did not know if he legally still was, but in her heart he still was.

He stripped, and she could see how pale his skin was, how thin he'd become, the ridge of bone in the center of his back as he bent to get into the tub. She took the bar of the soap into her hands and delicately began to wash him, his back and shoulders and neck. He closed his eyes. She washed his hair and rinsed it and he sat there with his eyes closed. For her it was like washing away their sins, past and present.

"I heard you married Johnny Waco," he said, his eyes still closed.

She told him why she had. He asked if she was happy.

"Do you think I would be here if I was?"

He reached up across his chest and laid his hand on her damp wrist and held it there on his shoulder.

"There is someone I've met," he said.

"I don't want to know who it is."

He told her the woman's name was Nora Hancock. She worked in the dry goods store. "She's a widow," he said.

She knew who the woman was, had seen her often when she'd shopped at the mercantile. A rather plain woman of quiet disposition. She tried not to compare herself with this Nora, this widow.

"It doesn't matter," she said.

"It does."

Then for the first time in three years they kissed, and it was like the very first time they kissed, as though nothing had been forgotten or left out. Certain things do not change.

Later they lay on the bed together. The room quiet except for a man coughing next door.

She knew then she'd been changed, that he had put new life into her. She did not say this; it was a secret she would keep for a little while longer until she was sure. She kissed his rough hands.

"Are you sorry?" she asked.

"I think I've dishonored us both."

"No, you haven't. I came because I wanted to see you. I wanted to erase the past, to start again. I hated you after I saw you the other day. I've hated you for three years. I told myself I could never not hate you. But it isn't true, Chalk. No matter what you might do to me, I can't hate you."

He didn't know how to tell her he'd changed, that his love for her had changed.

"I'm not the same man," is what he said, hoping she'd read into it the truth of who he was now.

Someone knocked on the door. They lay together silently. The knock came again, followed by a woman's voice asking if he was in there. He looked at her but did not answer. Then they heard footsteps fading.

"That was her," he said. "That was Nora."

"You could have answered it," she said.

"No, I couldn't have."

"You're ashamed of me?"

"No. I just wouldn't want to shame her."

She wasn't sure of where she stood with him now. It would take time, she told herself, to make things back to where they once were. She would ask for a divorce. She knew what she wanted. But something warned her not to be too hasty. Something in his voice, his not answering the knock at the door, warned her against rushing to a decision.

And then weeks later when she broke the news she was pregnant and saw the look in his eyes, the near sadness, she understood that he would not marry her.

It was like someone slamming shut a door suddenly in the middle of the night, a sound that both startles and has finality.

"You have to understand," he said. "I've given my love to Nora. She has been good and kind to me, she has saved me from maybe killing myself. I couldn't let her down by leaving her . . ."

"Yes," she said magnanimously, even though her chest felt crushed. "Of course you couldn't."

"I'll do what's necessary, of course," he said. "As far as the baby is concerned."

"No. There is no need to trouble yourself with it," she said, and left and went back to the ranch of her husband and found his liquor and drank it until she couldn't stand.

Every day after was like that, and Johnny Waco would find her in bed late in the afternoons. He thought she had a sickness until he discovered the hidden empty bottles. He assigned Maria to watch after her, to keep her away from the liquor. But by then she'd become quite clever in getting it and hiding it.

A fall caused her to begin bleeding.

Dr. Flax declared she had a miscarriage.

"Your husband should be here with you," he said.

"No, he doesn't know," she said. "And I'd ask that you not tell him."

"Of course, of course."

She went and packed a few things and left the following day. If she was to be what she thought herself as, a whorish person, there was only one man in town who could make her such. Pink Huston.

They worked out an agreement over a pipe of opium. He called it "chasing the dragon."

He said, "You have lovely breasts, Antonia."

She closed her eyes as his hands sought her out.

"This is the first test," she remembered him saying.

After that it no longer mattered.

6

I told her to think about it, that I planned on taking a room at the hotel and if she was agreeable to come see me in the morning. She looked at me like I was asking for a line of credit.

"Just think about it before you say no," I said.

"What about the other thing?"

"You mean what I paid for? I didn't pay for it, you were a gift."

I saw the look in her eyes, that of being used to the lowest level, and knew I'd driven in a wedge to pry her loose from this place, the pimp out in the other room.

"Come see me in the morning, unless you like being treated like this."

As I walked out and past the parlor, Pink Huston called, "Well, laddie, how was it?"

"Worth every penny," I said. He laughed at the joke.

"What about that job offer?"

"I'll let you know tomorrow." Lorri was there with him, draped over him like a wounded angel. She and Pink both had dreamy looks. I'd seen that look in other eyes. There was an opium pipe there on the stand next to them and the room smelled sweet. I went out and rode back over the tracks under a night pinpricked with stars.

I found Chalk still there at the Bison.

"Well?" he said.

"I might have a plan."

"You want to let me in on it?"

"I won't know for sure until tomorrow morning if it's actually a plan that might work."

He ran his fingers through the threads of his hair.

"And if your plan doesn't work out?"

"I've got a backup plan."

"I'd never have taken you for a planner."

"Looks can be deceiving."

"That's not what I meant."

"How sure are you about raising that five hundred?" I said.

"Then you're accepting my offer?"

"Maybe."

"I can probably have it tomorrow. I need to talk to the city council."

"Then I'll see you tomorrow."

"Where?"

"I'll find you."

He stood and put on his derby and patted the crown, then strode out, leaving the doors swinging behind him. Nobody seemed to notice his departure. In fact everyone seemed to be enjoying themselves. It seemed like just any other night in a bar with men drinking in it and I thought about the way people are before a bad storm they don't know is coming, the kind of storm that brings a cyclone down on them and tears the shit out of everything in its path, killing people and animals, the guilty and innocent alike. They are always oblivious until it's too late. I understood and respected Chalk Bronson for not panicking the townsfolk with his lament.

I went and found a hotel room at a place with the word Hotel painted on its face. Simple, the way I prefer it. Not the Coffin Flats Hotel, or anything pretentious, just *Hotel*.

An old man under an eyeshade sitting behind the desk reading a book peered over his spectacles when I came in.

"Need a room," I said.

"Front or back?"

"Back," I said.

"Got none in the back. Give you one in the front."

"Okay, front then."

He pushed the register at me. "Sign your name, please."

"What are you reading?" I said, curious.

"*Don Quixote*," he said.

I'd heard of it.

"Crazy old bastard puts a piss pot on his head and thinks he's a knight," he cackled. "Damnedest story I ever read."

"Sounds interesting. How much for the room?"

"How long you staying?"

"I'm not sure."

"Two dollars a day or ten for a full week. Cheaper by the week, you break it down."

"Let's just do a day at a time."

"Let me know by noon if you're staying another day or if you're not."

I put the money on the counter and he handed me a skeleton key.

"You got a boy who can take my horse over to the livery and get him fed and watered down?"

"He'll be along soon. He's over cross the tracks getting his wick wet. Boy's plum pussy crazy. Ever time he gets a dollar he spends it on one of those crib whores. I tried to warn him he's going to get the pox and go blind someday. You think a randy boy will listen to an old man like me?"

I put another dollar on the desk.

"Tell him to tell the liveryman I'll settle up with him when I come to pick up my horse."

He looked at the name I'd written on the register.

"Mr. Glass." He looked at me. Grinned till his mouth looked like a row of shoe peg corn. "Shit, I know who you are," he said.

"I don't see how, I've never been here before."

"I seen you once in a gunfight in El Paso," he said.

"It's news to me. I never been in El Paso either."

"Yessir, Mr. Hardin," he said. "Far as I'm concerned, you're just Mr. Jim Glass, like it says here."

"Hardin?"

"No sir, I didn't mean nothing by it. Last thing I'd want to do is get on your bad side," the clerk said.

The only Hardin I knew was one called John Wesley—real bad son of a bitch if even half of what I heard about him was true.

"That who you think I am, John Wesley Hardin?"

He raised his hands in supplication.

"No sir, you are whoever you say you are." His

raised hands trembled like a pair of leaves in a stiff wind.

"Well, you just keep to your business and we'll get along just fine," I said.

"Yessir."

"Where's my room?"

"Up them stairs, turn left, second door on your left."

When I got up there I set there on the bed and pulled off my boots and then my pants and shirt after setting my Henry rifle in the corner and hanging my gun rig on the bedpost above my pillow, then stretched out and it felt damn good.

John Wesley Hardin. Hmmm. I wondered if the mistake would be any advantage to me or if it would simply inspire somebody to come up and stick a gun in my ear and pull the trigger.

I thought about my plan. I never stole a woman before. Never even tried. Closed my eyes and went to sleep. The one thing I got from reading the Bible, which I did a time or two when I was younger and scared and feeling especially sinful, was that worrying didn't change a hair on your head. I sleep like a dead man.

Knocking at the door awakened me. Morning light fell into the room through a dirty window. I pulled on my pants and opened it. It was the woman, Antonia.

"Come in," I said.

She was dressed in trousers and a coat and had her hair twisted into a braid. She looked wasted, like a puncher home from a three day drunk, but you could still see her former beauty lurking somewhere behind the weary eyes, the hollow cheeks, the grim mouth.

"How do I know I can trust you?" she said after I closed the door. "How do I know you won't just hand me over to him and leave?"

"You ran away once, you can do it again if that's the case."

"Like I said, that's your plan?"

"No, I told you what my plan was."

"He'll kill me," she said.

"If that's his intent, he'll do it anyway if he comes for you. I think all he wants to do is rub Bronson's face in it and drag his name through the mud, show him who's the boss dog."

"He wants to humiliate me just as much."

"You want to do this or not?"

"I could use a drink."

"No, that's the last thing you need."

She looked at me. "The hell you know what I need?"

"You're right, I don't."

"The way I see this is I'm the sacrificial lamb to save this town of do-gooders. Let me tell you something, mister. They're not all good. Half the big shots here have paid me and the other whores Saturday night visits while their wives wait for them at home and then go stand in church Sunday morning like saints. They're no better than those dirty punchers. Why should I care if they get burned out?"

"Maybe not them, but their wives and kids," I said.

I could see how that affected her—the mention of kids.

"Chalk tell you about me and him?"

"He did."

"About our child?"

"Yeah, that too."

For the first time I saw a moment of softness in her eyes.

"You know, there's another way out of this," she said.

"If it's a better plan than mine, I'm all ears."

"I could just kill myself."

"Shit, I never thought of that."

"Don't be a wise ass."

"I'm not. But I figure if you did that, it would just piss this Waco off and he'd probably blame it on Chalk like he has everything else, maybe more, and what do you think he'd do then?"

"I guess it wouldn't matter—at least to me it wouldn't if I was dead."

"Give my way a shot and if that don't work I'll loan you my gun."

"You're a hard son of a bitch," she said.

"Yeah, so I've been told."

"We'll see how hard when it comes to Johnny Waco."

"Wait here, I've got to go see Chalk about the money."

"Two hundred and fifty, isn't that what you said?"

"Half of five, yes."

"Not a hell of a lot for a fresh start somewhere."

"What were you thinking?"

"Maybe you could get him to squeeze these paper collar saints for more—a thousand or two."

"That's an idea."

Something akin to a smile played at the corner of her mouth.

"We're no different, you and me," she said.

"How so?"

"We're both whores—that's our nature."

"Because we do things for money?"

"Isn't that what being a whore is—selling yourself for money?"

"I guess I never thought of it that way or I'd have charged more along the way."

"Yeah, like anyone would have paid."

"Now who's being a wise ass?"

"Go on before I change my mind."

"See you in a while."

"Yeah," she said, and sat on the bed looking glum.

As I was going past the desk I saw a young fellow with carrot red hair sitting in a chair with his eyes half closed.

"Hey," I said. His eyes went up like sprung window shades.

"Are you the one who took care of my horse last night?"

"Yessir, if you're him."

"Who?"

"Mr. Hardin . . . er, I mean Mr. Glass."

"I am. I just wanted to make sure you took care of my animal."

He nodded, looked scared.

"Don't wet yourself, son."

"You got anything else you want me to do for you, sir?"

"Yeah," I said, and put two dollars on the desk. "Go and get a breakfast and take it to the woman up in my room."

He had front teeth like a rabbit when he grinned.

"She's one of those high-priced ones, ain't she?" he said. "I seen her once or twice coming out of Pink Huston's hog farm."

"She's a guest of mine," I said, "treat her with respect."

"Yes sir."

I walked over to the jail and saw Chalk through the window sitting there at his desk with a cup of coffee looking like he hadn't slept. I opened the door and went in.

"I'll need a thousand instead of five hundred to make your troubles go away," I said.

"Yeah, and I need to be twenty-one again and have all my hair back but that's not going to happen either."

"How do you know—about the thousand, not the hair, I mean—unless you ask?"

"I know these old boys are businessmen, not fools," he said.

"Exactly."

"Why the extra?"

"Need half for her."

"Antonia?"

"Yeah."

"I don't get it."

So I told him the plan.

"You call that a plan?" he said.

"Funny, but that's the same thing she said."

"Take her back and then steal her?"

"Yeah, simple, but sometimes simple is better."

"It's a fucking joke."

"Maybe. But what's he want? He wants you to bring her to him so he can make you look bad, like he owns you. But what do you care if you can save this town yourself? You have to ask yourself is it worth it—to look bad in front of her and to drag your reputation through the mud. He's checking your pride, Marshal. Figures once he's ruined your reputation you'll quit and leave. Pride's killed as many men as guns."

I could see the lines deepen in his face.

"Then I what, quit, after he's made me look like a fool?"

"Better quit and looking for another job than the alternative."

"I'm not so sure."

"Nothing else, you've got a wife you say you love, just like these councilmen have got wives they say they love. You lay it out for them—how Waco will come and burn their town down and scatter them like sheep and a thousand will look cheap."

He stood and put on his derby.

"What the hell," he said. "I guess it don't cost nothing to ask," and went out.

I waited till he came back pretty sure none of this was going to come out right. He was right about me, I never was much of a planner. I just did whatever needed doing at the time it needed it. I remember something my old man told me a long time ago: "Don't ever do something just for the money."

Less than an hour and Chalk Bronson was back in the office. He took an envelope from his inside pocket and tossed it on the desk. It looked fat—like a thousand dollars fat.

"Your move," he said.

"I'll go get your ex."

"Leave off with that shit, okay?"

"Okay."

I picked up the envelope and went back up to the hotel. She was sitting there on the bed the same as she had been when I left—the plate of food untouched.

"You should have eaten something," I said.

"What are you, my father?"

"No, but if I was, I'd make you eat something."

I threw the envelope on the bed.

"Count out half and put on your coat."

She looked at it listlessly.

"I need a drink or something." Her hands were trembling as she counted out half the money, folded it and put it in her coat pocket then put the coat on.

"I'll stop at the Bison and pick you up a bottle."

"Thank you," she said, and I felt she really meant it.

"This will work out," I said.

"I don't even care anymore," she said.

I felt like I was leading a lamb to slaughter, looking at her, the sad way she seemed. She reminded me of everything wrong there was about life and little there was right about it.

Don't ever do anything just for the money, Jim.

7

We walked over to the jail and went in and Chalk was there standing at the window and he looked at her with eyes that were full of some deep sorrow only the two of them knew about.

"Antonia," he said.

She started to speak then didn't.

He looked at me.

"I want to know something," he said.

"Go ahead, we're all friends here, right?"

"I got word you might be John Wesley Hardin."

I had to force myself not to smile. "The kid at the hotel, right? Or the old man."

"Raford," he said. "The old man."

"What if I was, how would that make any difference about what we're doing here?"

He chewed his lower lip. I could see he was armed with a bulldog revolver in a short holster.

"The council knew I just handed over a thousand dollars of their money to John Wesley Hardin, I'd be fired."

"Might be a stroke of good luck for you then, considering."

"I'm not fucking around here, are you or aren't you?"

"No," I said. "Jim Glass, like I told you."

"Shit," he said, and put on his hat and coat. "I rented a buggy, Antonia. I got it pulled around back."

"I thought I'd tag along," I said.

"Suit yourself," he said.

I fell in behind them on the westbound road. Wind blew in our faces, sharp and cold. You could tell it was going to be an unpleasant day, and I had to tug my hat down tight to keep it from blowing off my head and turned up my coat collar. I figured the two of them had some things in private they would probably want to talk over—or maybe not, so I maintained a good distance behind them. At one point, about two hours into the ride, he stopped the buggy and I heard the two of them arguing and saw the bottle I'd bought her go flying. I spurred ahead and said, "There a problem?"

"The fuck you buy her whiskey for?"

"Because she asked for it and looked like she could use it."

She looked at me with half-lidded eyes.

"What the hell do you know about anything?" he said.

"She's entitled," I said, "considering she's putting herself on the line for you, wouldn't you say?"

He lowered his gaze then dismounted the wagon and walked out on the prairie until he found the bottle. He wiped the dead dry grass from it and walked back carrying it in one hand and held it out to her, and she took it and cradled it against her as he climbed back up into the wagon and snapped the reins. We rode on the rest of the day like that and I felt like I was part of something that was not only unkind but downright cruel, and I had to keep thinking about sacrifice. Only it wasn't my sacrifice but hers, and it was easy for you to think about it if it wasn't you doing the sacrificing but someone else. And it didn't make me feel any better by a long shot.

We stopped before the darkness behind us caught us and swallowed us whole.

I said, "I thought it was just a day's ride?"

Chalk said, "It is if you're riding a good horse and not a buggy and hauling a sick woman."

There was a stream that ran crooked as a dog's hind leg through the dying grass, and I gathered pieces of kindling and started a fire while he set up a small pup tent he'd taken from the back of the buggy along with a sack of foodstuff and a coffeepot. She sat there on the ground sipping from the bottle, staring off into the long nothingness and empty places.

Time everything was ready, he scraped her some beans and salted pork onto a plate and held it out to her. She refused it.

"Eat something, please," he said.

"You eat it," she said. "I don't want it."

I got myself a plate and sat back against my saddle and the night folded over us till there was just our shadows playing in and out of the firelight, the flames licking at the night.

"I don't feel good about this," he said to her, the fire between them. "Just so you know."

"Why should you care, Chalk? Why should you care?"

He looked beat in every way a man can look beat.

I ate fast then set the plate aside and laid back and pulled my blanket up around me with my head propped on my saddle and pulled my hat down over my eyes like I was sleeping. I didn't want to be part of their intimacy even if it was conflicted.

"You think we could just not argue?" he said. "Just this once?"

"Yes, Chalk. Our arguing days will be forever over come tomorrow when you hand me over to Johnny."

I thought of all the ways a woman can hurt a man and the ways a man can hurt a woman, and it wasn't like they were trying to hurt each other, they just didn't know how not to anymore.

I waited until everything fell silent for a time before I let myself go to sleep to a low wind moaning over the grass like sorrow itself.

We rose with the daylight and took turns going off into the bushes and had some fresh-made coffee and some bacon and cold biscuit sandwiches—at least he and I did; she still refused to eat anything, and I saw the bottle was empty on the ground next to her blanket. A soft rain began to fall by the time we broke camp and I thought it was just an unpleasant morning. My half of the money wasn't much comfort.

We rode till about mid-morning and then turned off the main road up a wagon trace and followed it for maybe half an hour more till we topped a rise and there in the distance was a windmill turning in the wind and beyond it some buildings.

"That's his place?" I said.

"We've been on his place since last evening," Chalk said. I could see shorthorn cattle scattered all over the grasslands and riders working in among them cutting some out for branding, which was being done down closer to the buildings. Work sort of stopped as we approached; the hired help stood watching us ride up to the main house.

I could see Chalk's features were set hard as stone as we neared, and the woman next to him with her eyes downcast. Three men stood on the porch of the long house.

"Which one's him?" I said.

"The middle one," Chalk said, and my eyes shifted to him.

He was tall and wore his pants stuffed down inside mule ear boots and wore a short coat and a pancake hat. He had a long red scarf tied around his neck and looked like something out of a dime novel. The other two flanking him were heeled with revolvers riding high on their hips and one had a quirt in his left hand and they both stood slouched slightly in that loose way men with bad attitudes will stand.

Chalk halted the buggy a few feet from the porch and nobody said anything, but Johnny Waco was looking at me, trying to assess my reason for being among them, and I didn't flinch because you just didn't do that with the sort of man who knew how powerful he was. The other two took notice of me as well. I had made it a point to unbutton my coat before we got there so they could see I was heeled too and had slid the Henry from its scabbard and rested it across the pommel of my saddle. Best way to keep trouble from happening is to be prepared for it. Let a man know what stuff you're made of so there's no guesswork to it. If it comes anyway, there was no stopping it but with a bullet.

Johnny's eyes finally shifted to the woman.

"Get down from there," he said, "and come here to me."

She started to get down but Chalk laid a hand on her forearm and stopped her.

"I want assurances this is the end of it," he said to Johnny.

Waco cocked his head like a dog that had just heard something it didn't know what it was.

"You get down too, Chalk."

They both got down. I kept an eye on the two who were heeled. Any trouble breaking out would come from them first. Waco didn't look like he was armed, but then you didn't know what he might be wearing under his coat.

"Come up here on the porch," Waco said to the woman. She looked at Chalk then went and climbed up onto the porch and stood there while Waco looked her over like a horse he was considering.

"Go inside," he said. I thought maybe she'd look back at Chalk one more time, but she didn't, just went inside like a beat dog.

"Then it's over," Chalk said.

"No, not quite," Waco said.

"What else?"

Waco's gaze again shifted to me.

"You don't want none of this action, mister."

I noticed some more men had gathered 'round, all of them armed.

"You don't interfere here, or you'll not even have a chance to regret it," he said.

Chalk looked back at me.

"Stay out of this, Glass, no matter what happens."

"You sure?"

"I am."

I slid the Henry back into its scabbard.

Waco nodded his head and three men stepped forward and two of them took Chalk by the arms and the third man took the lawman's bulldog revolver and tossed it in the dirt. I felt something go tight in my guts.

"You know I can't just send you back without folks knowing there is a price to pay for everything when it comes to dealing with me," Waco said. Then he looked at me again and said, "You pay attention here, in case you ever get it in your mind to cross me, mister." I didn't have to look 'round me, behind me, to know that several of the others had drawn their guns and had them aimed at me.

He nodded again and the man who'd taken Chalk's pistol from him slammed a fist into Chalk's ribs, doubling him over, then crashed another blow to his chin, knocking him to his knees even as he was being held up by the two men holding him by the arms.

It was a hard thing to watch, the way they beat him till his face was a bloody mess and he no longer groaned when the cowboy hit him. The one doing the hitting was a big strapping fellow with long arms that lashed out like whips, and every time he struck Chalk you could hear it, his knuckles smacking meat and bone.

Finally the two holding him turned him loose and he sank to his knees in the dirt, his blood splotching the ground with drops the size of half dollars. He lay there without moving. Waco nodded toward a man standing by a fire they heated their branding irons in and the fellow pulled one of the irons from the coals and brought it with him as the one who'd done the battering bent and ripped Chalk's shirt, exposing his back muscles and shoulder blades.

"Do it," Waco said to the brander.

Chalk jerked even though he was out cold when the brand burned into his flesh. The sound and smell was something I knew I'd never forget.

"Now break his hands," Waco said. The slugger went to a shed and came back with a hammer and smashed Chalk's hands with it. I flinched but didn't look away. I owed him at least that much—not to look away.

"Now get him the hell off my land," Waco said, giving me one last hard look. "And don't you or him ever come back here."

I dismounted and lifted Chalk and spilled him into the buggy, then tied my horse on back and climbed into the seat and took the reins and snapped them. It was all I could do to keep my hand off my gun.

I drove steady the rest of that day and through the night, stopping only when I needed to give the horses a blow. I washed canteen water over Chalk's face and checked his heartbeat. He'd come to then and would go under again. I did the best

I could to keep him comfortable, but there wasn't much could be done. We finally reached the out- skirts of Coffin Flats about the same time as dawn did. The streets were fairly well deserted, the town still asleep.

Chalk was by then shivering and muttering in his delirium, his face swollen terribly, blood crusted in the corners of his eyes and ears and nostrils. I kept seeing in my mind the way they beat him, smelled the burning of his flesh when they branded him. He held his broken hands out away from him like shattered birds.

Johnny Waco wanted to make sure that he was never out of Chalk Bronson's thoughts. I knew looking at the lawman, Johnny Waco was never going to be out of my thoughts either.

I pulled in at the hotel and went inside and found the kid there half asleep behind the desk.

"Where's there a doctor?"

He looked at me through lidded dull eyes.

"Doctor!" I said.

"Doc Flax has a place up the street above the druggist," he said. Then he realized I didn't know anything about the town and pointed. "That way."

I quickly drove there and pounded on the door at the top of the stairs but nobody answered. Went back again to the hotel. The kid was picking his nose and staring at his finger.

"Where's the marshal live?"

"Up that way," he said, pointing the opposite direction of the doctor's. "Little yeller house end of the street and over one—to your right."

So that's where I went.

I pounded on the door till a woman answered.

She was wearing a checked robe and her face was puffy with sleep.

"You Mrs. Bronson?"

"Yes," she said.

"Help me get your husband out of the buggy."

Together we got him in the house and onto a bed. She was distressed, asking me over and over again what had happened. I told her we needed to get a doctor and did she know where he lived and she said yes and I told her to direct me and she did. I went and found the medico and he hurried back with me his shirttail hanging out, and when he saw Chalk he said, "Good God!"

I stood out in the living room while they attended to him, and realized I'd not slept in the last twenty-four hours and the world seemed otherwise a shitty place to be. I went and stood out front and watched the soft falling rain that had started and quit and started again ever since the day before— rain like sorrow, like God's own tears—and wished I had a drink and a place to lay down. I paced then, thinking I ought to do something but not knowing what, if anything would make a difference.

Finally they came out, the doctor and the woman— Chalk's wife.

"He'll live," the doctor said. "But it will be some time before he's back to anything close to normal. His hands are all busted and I . . . well, I did the best I could for him." He looked at the wife.

Chalk's wife's eyes were red and teary. They saw I had blood on my clothes.

"Ma'am, if it wouldn't be any trouble, I could use a cup of coffee and a place to wash up."

They wanted to know what happened and I told

them—the part about the beating but not why, or delivering Antonia; that was a little more complicated, considering. I could see the strain on Chalk's wife as it was and figured why make it worse.

"Thank you for bringing him home," she said in a very soft voice. She was dark-haired and broad-faced with gray eyes—what you might call plain, but she had a sense of goodness about her, that deep-down kind of goodness you don't sense many people have. I thought about how different she was from Antonia, how they must have compared in Chalk's mind—the two of them, different as night and day on the surface, but maybe the same in ways a stranger like myself couldn't see.

Chalk's wife showed me where I could wash up and then poured me a cup of Arbuckle and I drank the coffee and said I was sorry I had to bring her husband home in that condition and I was sorry there was nothing I could do to prevent it. She wanted to know why anyone would do what they did to him and I said I didn't know because the truth wasn't in play just then. She wept, and I stood and said I needed to go but that I would stop back by and look in on her and Chalk. The doctor walked out with me and when we were outside he said, "What the hell is the story here?"

"It has to do with a woman," I said.

"Antonia," he said.

"Yeah."

"Goddamn it."

He looked back toward the house.

"I warned Chalk to stay away from her."

"It's not exactly like it sounds."

"I knew them from before," he said. "They were

good together once, then it all went to shit and now look what's happened. Somebody ought to go out and shoot that Johnny Waco in his goddamn face. Chalk's a good man, maybe too good for his *own* good."

He tucked his shirt in and said, "Whatever your interests are here, you'd be wise to get on your nag and ride away."

"Shit, I'm already gone," I said.

He looked at me and I knew those eyes had seen a lot of bloody things but I don't know if they'd ever seen a man branded and his hands broken with a hammer.

He walked away shaking his head.

I just hoped Antonia remembered the plan and stuck to it.

8

I needed rest bad and I went to my hotel, and the old man, Raford, was behind the desk again still reading that same book about Don Quixote and grinning as he followed his finger underneath the sentences. He looked up when he saw me enter and stopped grinning.

"You tell Chalk Bronson I was John Wesley Hardin?" I said.

He shook his head.

"I've been known to kill men for less than lying."

The color drained out of his face.

I held my gaze on him then said, "Don't be running my business out on the streets, you hear me?"

He nodded.

I went up to my room and undressed and lay down on the bed and for once I didn't sleep like a dead man—only a half-dead man.

I woke and there was still a little light in the room coming through the window and I rose and got dressed and armed myself and carried my Henry downstairs. The old man was still there only he avoided my gaze. I went out and slipped the rifle into the scabbard of my horse and walked

him down to the livery and told the man to feed
and rub him down and I'd be back later for him.

I walked to the town's only restaurant and went
in and it was full of diners and I had to stand by the
door to wait for an empty table. Then the waitress
came over and said, "The lady over in the corner
wondered if you'd care to join her?" I looked and
it was the prostitute, Lorri, Pink Huston's woman.
She was looking twice as beautiful as the last time
I saw her—and sober and without the cat.

I worked my way past tables and said, "Nice of
you to offer."

She smiled up at me. "Well, a man has to eat,
right?"

"Right."

I took off my hat and set it on the floor next to
my chair opposite her.

"Where's your . . . what should I call him, Pink?"

"Whatever you like. The steaks here are wonderful," she said.

So that's what I ordered, a steak and a glass of
beer. Lorri was eating a small round steak, cutting it into delicate pieces. Her eyes were large and
wet looking. She looked like she was dressed for
the opera, with a black beret decorated with small
white beads, a white blouse with lace tatting and
black bone buttons and ruffled cuffs. I couldn't see
without being obvious exactly what sort of skirt
or shoes she was wearing, but her fingers were be-
jeweled with a variety of rings, mostly silver with
rubies and other precious stones. She looked like
something you'd want to keep.

"So, how are you and Antonia getting along?"
she said as I waited for my meal.

I shrugged, said, "Antonia?"

She sipped from her wineglass and tilted her head far enough back to make it seem she was looking down her nose at me.

"I know she went to meet you the other morning after you'd come to the hog farm," she said.

"What else do you know?"

She smiled coyly and cut herself another little piece of steak and chewed it in a way I've never seen a woman eat anything before.

"I know she hasn't come back to the hog farm and Pink's more than a little pissed he's lost one of his best girls."

"I thought you were his best girl?"

She stopped chewing.

"I'm my own woman," she said. "I'm with Pink because I choose to be with him, not the other way around."

"Seems like an odd pairing, you don't mind the observation," I said. "You and Pink."

"Call it convenient," she said.

"You can tell him Antonia probably isn't coming back," I said.

"And can I also tell him why that would be?"

"She's gone back to her husband Johnny Waco."

I watched her mull that one over as she took another sip of her wine.

"I guess I'm a little relieved," she said after she set her glass back down again. The waitress brought my steak and I dug in right away, my belly crawling with anticipation. She waited until I took a break.

"What?" I said, from the way she was looking at me.

"I thought maybe Antonia and you had taken up together. I never thought she'd ever go back to Johnny Waco."

"Me?"

She smiled.

"And if she had taken up with me, so what?"

"I'd be disappointed."

"Why is that?"

"I sort of thought about taking up with you myself," she said.

It was my turn to smile. "Yeah, I bet a dollar you did."

Her hand reached across the table and rested atop mine, the one I held the knife with.

"You'd lose if you did bet a dollar," she said.

"It's a tempting offer," I said. "But my dance card is sort of full right now, Lorri."

She removed her hand slowly.

"You don't find me attractive?"

"Quite the opposite."

"Then why not act it and ask me to leave with you right now and go back to your hotel room?"

"I'd like that," I said. "But I don't need trouble with Pink, and I've got something I have to do tonight."

"Funny," she said. "I never figured you for a man who would be afraid of Pink. Maybe I misjudged you, Mister . . . I guess I don't even know your name."

"Jim Glass," I said. "That's my name, and you can think whatever you want about me. It doesn't matter—not really."

I finished eating my steak and she watched me and it was damn tempting to just say to hell with it and take her back to my hotel room. But I kept seeing Chalk's battered face, those smashed and broken hands, the wounded look on Antonia's face when she was being ordered around by Johnny. I kept smelling the stink of flesh burnt by a branding iron.

I reached in my pocket and my fingers felt the fat envelope—half a thousand dollars. Riding money, or riding around money? It was something I needed to decide. But then again, I'd already decided.

I called for the bill—both bills—Lorri's and mine, and paid for both our meals and left a nice tip because I was either feeling magnanimous or suicidal.

"Jim . . ." she said.

"Maybe another time," I said.

"I won't count on it," she said.

I stood and adjusted my hat and looked at her one last time. She really was beautiful and I really was a goddamn fool.

I went out and it was still raining softly and the night sky had that red to it—that faded red that feels ominous. The rain pattered off my brim as I walked back down to the livery and had the man saddle my horse. I said, "I'd like to buy a spare horse from you and a saddle."

"I got one I could let go for forty dollars, saddle included."

He showed it to me, a smallish mare that seemed sound after I ran my hands over her. "Lace her up," I said.

I undid my bedroll and took out my slicker and put it on then tied things back together and mounted my horse and took the reins of the spare after paying the man.

"Piss poor night to go riding," he said.

"Don't remind me."

I rode over to Chalk's place and tied both horses off out front then stepped up under the overhang and shook off my hat before knocking on the door and waiting for Chalk's wife to answer.

She stepped aside to allow me entry.

"How's he doing?" I said.

"He's awake, but I just gave him a spoonful of laudanum."

"Maybe I should just go and see him later," I said.

"No, he said earlier if you came 'round he wanted to talk to you."

"Okay."

She opened the bedroom door for me and then closed it. He was on his back on the bed, his hands bandaged, and when she closed the door he turned his head and looked at me, the lamp's light glittering in his half-swollen eyes.

I pulled up a chair next to the bed. His voice was raspy when he asked me where things stood.

"I'm on my way back there now," I said.

"You saw what he did to me," he said. "He'll do worse to you if he catches you."

"Unless she changes her mind, I should be okay."

"Where will you go—the two of you?"

I shrugged. "Someplace far away from here. Better you don't know."

"I don't—" He coughed and you could see it hurt him to do that. "I don't know why you're doing this," he said.

"The money," I said. "Why else?"

"You could just let it go . . . long as she stays with him, he won't do anything to this town . . ."

"Yeah, I could, couldn't I?"

His eyes shifted behind the swollen lids. They went from my eyes to his ruined hands then back again.

"I made her a promise," I said. "I took your money so I guess I made you a promise too."

"You see what it cost me . . ."

"Yeah. I'm sorry I didn't do anything."

He shook his head. "He'd have killed you."

"Some things can be worse than dying."

"No," he said. "They can't . . ."

The door opened again and his wife said, "Chalk, are you needing anything, honey?"

He shook his head.

I stood away from the bed.

"I was just leaving, ma'am."

She seemed relieved. She walked to the front door with me.

"There's more going on here than you're telling me," she said.

"No ma'am."

"I'm not so young and naive I don't know when a man is lying to me, Mr. Glass."

"No ma'am, I didn't reckon you were."

"Please don't come back around here anymore."

"Yes ma'am."

She closed the door, and it was just me and the two horses and the rain outside and a long road back to a dangerous place.

I saddled up and took the reins of the spare and

headed back to Johnny Waco's spread. I had the little map Antonia had drawn for me there in the hotel room when she agreed to my plan—the map to where she would meet me. I had to get there by tomorrow night—to the grove of trees she'd drawn on the paper, by a stream a mile from the main house.

"It's the only place I can hide for a short time," she'd said. "I'll wait until Johnny's asleep and sneak out—let's say midnight—and wait for you there. But if you're not there by one in the morning, I'll have to go back or he'll send his drovers for me. Bring a horse. A good fast horse."

Words wrote on paper but like words branded on skin, far as I was concerned. I figured to ride steady till daylight and beyond, stop and rest till it got dark then make my way in the night to the grove and be there waiting for her. After that I thought we'd figure out together where to go— Texas, maybe.

The rain let up and pretty soon the moon broke between clouds that looked like black silver in the night sky and helped light the road ahead of us like it was something meant to be.

I could have spent the hours thinking of all the things that could go wrong, but what was the point? Either things would go right or they wouldn't. Either I'd live to someday tell the story or I wouldn't. The way I looked at most of life was that in a hundred years nobody would care what you did or didn't do. The only thing that mattered was what you knew for yourself you did or didn't do.

This felt like the right thing to do.

It was a little like what the late Mr. Lincoln said about religion: "When I do right I feel right, and when I do bad I feel bad, and that is my religion."

I guess it was my religion too.

⇥ 9 ⇤

When the stranger offered her salvation, she took it. For enslaved she was and enslaved she knew she would forever be. But she'd rather be enslaved to her vices than to a man like Johnny Waco. She would rather be dead than to be enslaved to Johnny Waco. So she'd taken the man's offer, that he would come for her and that he would take her to a place called refuge. All she had to do was say she wanted it. And so she'd said it, hopeless as it might seem.

She craved the dragon more than she craved life. But the dragon would not come as long as she was in the clutches of Johnny Waco. He would have Maria tie her to her bed, as he had done before. And she would wretch up her insides and her head would hurt until she was nearly blind from the pain. Maria would force cold soup down her and call her privately a *puta* in disdain and stare at her with eyes as cold and calculating as a snake.

She suspected Maria of being Johnny's *puta*, of wanting to replace her as his wife. She cared not for Pedro, her dark, slump-shouldered and meek husband. She treated him cruelly and ignored his efforts and criticized him in front of Johnny.

She'd heard Maria whispering one time—the two of them, Johnny and she—and noticed the way Maria's demeanor softened whenever Johnny was near. She was openly flirtatious, even when Pedro was there; especially when Pedro was there. She flaunted her heavy breasts in low-cut blouses, the weight and shape of them like large loose fruit.

She was surprised that Maria did not slap her face when she was ill from the sobering effects.

So she tried to escape down the dark tunnel of her dope-filled dreams, escape reality for a different reality. She knew that if she did not try and leave, she would end up dying in the household of Johnny Waco. He would kill her slowly and indirectly.

In fact he had said to her not long after her secret bloody visit to Dr. Flax, "Was it mine, the child you lost?"

Dr. Flax had betrayed her no differently than she had been betrayed by any other man.

"No," she said. "It wasn't yours."

"Then I'm glad you lost it."

At that moment she knew she could not feel any more hate for anyone than what she felt for Johnny.

"I'm glad I lost it too," she said.

He slapped her hard across the face. It was nothing compared to the pain she'd already felt.

"Hit me again."

He hit her again, with his open hand. The sound of it was like someone letting a screen door slam shut.

The taste of her own blood gave her a private satisfaction. Would that he crucify her and make the act complete. Would that he shoot her, she could not have wanted more from him.

Instead he called Maria and told her, "Take care of my wife!"

"Sí, señor, Johnny."

That bit of familiarity that had become so common, shared between them. She saw the looks the two of them exchanged and was sure of her suspicions.

Now she'd gone back to him again, at the request of the stranger.

She was already making plans.

If he failed her, well, what surprise was there in that? She had her own plan. She did not trust completely even the stranger, but there was one man she felt she could trust, and she had summoned him earlier that day of her planned escape.

"Pedro," she said. He was standing in the shade of the house, smoking a cigarette. Maria was somewhere in the kitchen preparing supper at the opposite end of the long house.

He looked up at her, his eyes sorrowful from what she guessed was long years of marital misery. His rough straw hat was broken in places.

"Sí, señora."

"I want to ask you a favor."

She took the money and put it in his hand.

"I want you to do me a favor you cannot speak of to Maria or Señor Waco . . ."

He looked at the money. It was a lot of money.

"It is not necessary," he said, handing it back, but she refused to take it. "The money isn't only for the favor," she said. And when he continued to look baleful, she said, "It's for everything you've done until this moment. Do you understand?"

He nodded. "Yes, I understand," he said.

She wanted him to get her a gun from Johnny's cabinet and bring it to her unseen.

He demurred at first.

"Will you do it?"

"Yes. But I don't want your money . . ."

"No. You keep it. You don't have to say anything to Maria about the money either." His gaze revealed nothing, whether or not he'd do it, whether he'd tell Maria, whether he'd tell Señor Johnny, his boss. Pedro was inscrutable.

"Something small," she said. "And loaded."

10

I made steady time, and after what seemed forever dawn broke over the prairies bright and clean as a new penny. I knew from what Chalk had told me before that I was well onto Johnny Waco's spread and I'd need to keep an eye peeled for any of his hands. Here and there windmills clattered and shifted around in the uncertain morning wind pumping up groundwater that spilled from lead pipes into water tanks. I took advantage of them to water the horses and wash my face and neck, and to try and awaken my weary senses.

I climbed one of the wood towers to get my bearings, and way off in the distance I could see the tin roofs of the buildings gleaming. I swung my gaze wide of them, following the directions on Antonia's hand-drawn map until I spotted the grove of trees—like the bristles on a paintbrush now that the leaves had shed off them. Then I climbed down and looked for a likely spot to hole up till nightfall.

There's something consoling about the sound of the blades of a windmill clacking in the wind.

I rode off in the general direction of the grove,

taking my time, looking for a lay-up. I finally spotted an old line shack with the windows all busted
out and the door missing and chose it.

Tired as I was I knew I had to be on my guard
for any of Waco's men. I led the horses inside with
apologies to them then settled down for the long
day to unwind.

Wind blew through the open spaces—the windows and door and holes in the rotted roof—and
I spent some time reading the old catalogue pages
whichever old boys who had lived there before had
tacked up over the years. I wondered where those
old punchers were today, what they'd seen and how
many of them died as broke as the day they were
born and how many had married and how many
of them came to bad ends or ended up preachers or
store clerks or outlaws or lawmen.

Thing with old buildings is they got a history
same as any man—the history of all who lived in
them—the weddings and funerals that took place
in them, the love and hate that hid between their
walls, and that was something that always interested me, the history of buildings.

The horses snorted their restlessness and I
talked to them, some in Spanish, the little bit I'd
learned down in Texas, calling them sweetheart
and just making up things to talk to them about.
And before I knew it my thoughts turned to Fannie and our time spent there on that prairie grass
together where the fenceline ran true as God's finger, the wire glazed by the sun, and I couldn't help
but smile even in light of the heartbreak she caused
me, because no matter how bad those things turn

out—and they always turn out bad—your mind just naturally remembers the good parts. And in spite of nothing what we shared being true, I still considered myself a lucky man to have been part of it. Anytime a beautiful woman gives herself to you, consider yourself lucky.

Clouds passed before the sun, creating great shadows over the grass—dark shapes moving like something alive—and it made for a pretty sight.

Then I heard the whicker of horses and all that pleasant mood changed in a heartbeat.

Two riders topped a slight rise and sat surveying the lay of things. One looped his leg 'round his saddle horn and fumbled in his coat pocket till he came out with makings and rolled himself a shuck. They were both wearing bat-wing chaps and I could see they had rifles in their scabbards. They sat there for a time, the wind carrying smoke from the one's cigarette. One of their horses whickered and then one of mine answered. The riders both turned and looked toward the line shack.

A piece of bad luck on my part if they decided to ride down and take a look.

They did.

I drew my revolver because I sure as shit didn't want to have to shoot those old boys with my rifle, which I easily could have. I didn't want to shoot them at all, but if I did shoot them it would be because they wouldn't leave me any choice, and it would have to be close-in work.

They rode down the slope cautious, looking for where the sound of the horse had come from. It was that little racer I'd bought off the liveryman.

They got close then circled the shack, never suspecting a horse would be inside with another horse and a man holding a pistol.

"Where you think it come from?" one of them said.

"Hell if I can make it out, down from around here somewhere."

"I don't see no horse, do you?"

"I don't see no horse neither."

"I heard it said they's ghost horses in this country."

"I ain't never heard nothing like that. What the hell's a ghost horse anyways?"

"I guess it's just some old horse or something, I don't know. It was a Indian told me."

"Indian?"

"Pawnee Indian."

"Listen."

"What is it?"

They stopped circling the shack.

I stepped out behind them with the Merwin Hulbert cocked and aimed.

"You boys step down from those horses."

They looked 'round slow.

"Don't make me shoot you all."

One was young, the other quite a bit older.

The older one said, "Why you want to shoot us?"

"Because you all might ride back and get some others and come back here and shoot me."

The younger one said, "Shit, that don't hardly make no sense."

"Yeah, it does," the older one said. "That's the fellow was with Chalk Bronson the other day."

"This isn't a debate," I said. "Get off those mounts. And do it cautious; I've not had my coffee yet and my hands are a little shaky, and I've got the pull on this trigger set light anyway so it wouldn't take much—might even just go off by itself."

They stepped down holding their reins.

"What you all doing back here?" the older one said. He had iron gray moustaches—an old boot who wasn't ever going to do anything but run cows and ride fence and work for men like Waco. "You got some sort of death wish?" he asked.

"Take that rope, junior, and tie your partner up," I said to the younger one.

He looked sheepish.

"I'll shoot you in the knees," I said. "Do it."

He unhooked his rope and wrapped it around the old man, and I said, "Truss him up good, like a mossy horn steer."

He said, "I'm sorry, Bob."

And the old man said, "Don't you worry none about it, I know it ain't nothing personal you got against me, Torrence."

When he got old Bob trussed up, I said, "Sit down on the ground." And when he stood defiant, I went and shoved him down and told the kid to lay facedown next to Bob, and he did and I took Bob's rope and trussed the kid up good.

"Now what?" Bob said.

"Now nothing," I said.

"Well ain't this the shits."

"I reckon maybe it is."

I hauled them one by one inside the shack and set them up against the wall and said, "Once I get my business done here, I'll let some of your pals know where you are if you ain't worked yourself loose from those ropes."

"They's wolves all over this country," the younger one said. "And snakes."

"Too cold for snakes and I'll bet there's not been a wolf seen in these parts for ten years," I said. "I don't guess you have to worry about nothing but me."

"We all just gone sit here till what?" the old man said. "I got to take a piss. Piss all the time here lately—ever' hour or so. Then when I try it takes me a while to get started and a while to stop. Goddamn but it ain't like my life ain't miserable enough, now I got to run into you."

"I sure as hell am sorry about your problems, Bob. You give me your word you won't try anything stupid and I'll untie you."

"You got my word. I spent all my stupid letting you catch me once."

I untied him and walked outside with him and watched as he went and stood off with his back to me and fumbled at his front and stood there with his back arched trying to relieve himself.

I could hear him groaning. I felt bad in a way, because I knew we all get there someday—old like that with our plumbing messed up and our dignity gone but there wasn't nothing any of us could do about it—and I hoped when it came my time somebody would show me a little respect.

We probably stood there ten minutes before Bob finished up his business and I walked him back inside. I trussed him up again and he set down on his own accord next to his companion.

"How many men has Waco got working for him?" I said.

"All told? Maybe fifty," he said.

"They all stay close to the main house?" I said.

The old man raised his tied hands and knuckled back his hat. He had a grizzle of growth on a face looked like scrub growing out of dry land cut by rain and wind.

"Nah, they're scattered all over this here land."

"You aim to kill us, mister?" the younger one said.

"No, he ain't aiming to kill us, Torrence," Bob said. "He was aiming to do that, he'd already of done it."

They both looked at me.

"He's right," I said. "Bob is."

They sat there with their legs crossed at their boots. We all waited for nightfall.

It come dark and I led the horses outside after telling the two they best just keep quiet and let me go and do what I come here for, and Bob said, "What'd you come here for?"

"I come for the girl," I said. "And if you two follow me, help the others to follow me, and I get the chance, I'll shoot you both, just so you know."

Bob shook his head, said, "I'm a puncher not some man killer. Torrence ain't either."

Torrence shook his head too.

"Well, then, you all take care. I fixed those ropes so you all should work free of them shortly enough."

Outside, I spanked their horses with my hat, slapping them hard two or three quick times till they run off, knowing they wouldn't run off all that far but far enough to take those boys a while to catch up to them. Then I mounted up and rode off toward the grove.

It took me about an hour to make my way to the trees, and I could see them against the night sky standing stiff and dark and went up toward them figuring if she was there she'd recognize me.

She did, and stepped out.

I handed her the reins to the racer and she mounted up. She had a satchel and said it was spare clothes, and I said we ought to get moving and rode away toward the south, away from the main ranch buildings.

"How will we make our way?" she said, and I pointed up toward the sky.

"Stars," I said. "We'll navigate like sailors do."

"That what you were once, a sailor?" she said.

"No, but it don't mean I can't read stars."

We kept moving till sunup then stopped, rested the horses and let them graze a bit.

"I figure we can make the border to Texas in two, three days," I said.

She was dressed in man's clothing, rough coat, britches, low-heeled boots, and a felt hat with her hair tucked up under it. I watched her throat when she drank from the canteen. It was a nice delicate throat.

I stood watching the direction we'd come from to see if we were being pursued. It was flat where we were now and you could see a pretty good distance. We'd left the main road earlier and cut overland but the grass, tall and dry as it was, left a clear trail for even a half-assed tracker.

I didn't see anything. Not yet, at least.

"How you holding up?" I said.

"I could use something for my head," she said.

"Maybe this would be a good time to consider getting off the booze and dope," I said.

"Yes, thank you for your advice," she said sarcastically.

"Just meant a clear head might be of some advantage when you're being chased by a man like Johnny Waco."

She looked too at the direction we'd just come from.

Except for the whisper of the wind over the brittle grass there didn't seem to be anything alive except her and I.

I shrugged and said, "Maybe he's not going to come after you . . ."

She laughed a short hard laugh.

"He'll be coming," she said.

"Maybe not. Maybe he figures you keep running away, what's the point. Maybe he'll just find himself another woman—one who will stay home."

She tightened the cinch on her saddle like a woman who knew a lot about such things, then mounted.

"He's coming," she said and patted the satchel.

"What's in there besides some of your underthings?"

She smiled. "Enough of his money to last me a very long time."

"The five hundred wasn't enough for you?"

"It's not a matter of how much," she said, "but whose."

"So you robbed him?"

"Blind as a bat."

I looked back again and saw the column of dust from the road about the point we left it and cut across country.

"Yeah, he's coming," I said.

And we rode like hell.

11

We stayed ahead of them as though we were out-racing our own shadows, and at one point Antonia came alongside me and shouted, "Follow me!" and I did without hesitation. I saw the town rise out of the grass and heard a train whistle blowing.

We were practically off our horses before we fully had them stopped, the train just pulling away from the station. I helped lift her aboard one of the cars then ran to catch up and finally got aboard just as the train picked up speed. You could smell the steam off its engine, the hot cinder along the track.

We found seats in one of the cars and sat across from each other and in a little while the train conductor came down the aisle asking for tickets. When he reached us I said we didn't have any tickets and could we buy some from him.

"Where you headed?" he said.

"Where does this train go?"

"All the way to Refugio."

"We'll take two tickets to Refugio, then," I said. "How much?"

He was a short thick-set man in his middle years

wearing a black cap and coat and his shoes were polished. A silver watch chain with a fob hung from his waistcoat buttonhole to the pocket.

"It's not policy to purchase tickets onboard," he said. "I'll have to put you off at the next stop and you'll have to pay the ticket master there."

"Look," I said, taking the envelope from my pocket with the city council money in it. I peeled off fifty dollars and held it out to him. "Do you think that will cover it—the fare?"

"Mister, that's way too much."

"You got a private car for rent on this line?"

He nodded.

"Would that cover the trip and a private car and your troubles?"

"Yes sir, it would."

"Then if you wouldn't mind."

He led us back up the aisle and into another car and through that one into a third that had private rooms on one side. He opened the door to one of them and let us in and told us that the dining car was one car back and lunch would be served—he pulled out his watch, the one hooked to the silver chain, and looked at it—in half an hour. I thanked him and closed the door.

Antonia had taken off her hat and set it on the velvet-covered seat beside her. Her hair tumbled down to her shoulders, a nice dark brown thicket. She unbuttoned her coat and I could see the free weight of her breasts inside the peasant shirt, the V of it held loosely together with a thick string. She didn't have those sleepy doped eyes now. They were alert and alive with excitement or whatever it was she was feeling after the chase. I sat down opposite her and took my own hat off and ran my fingers through hair that needed a cut and had shagged over the back of my collar. I felt the stubble on my jaw as well and realized I probably smelled like horse sweat but knew this wasn't any time for worrying about formalities. She smelled like a cake of soap, what I smelled of her.

She still held the valise on her lap, gripping the handle with both hands.

"Did you take it because you wanted to make sure he'd come after you?" I said, thinking it was a damn dumb thing of her to do if she really wanted to be free of the guy.

"He owes me this much and more," she said. "But it's not that."

"Then what is it?"

"I just wanted to take something from him I knew he cared about—like he took from me."

I looked out the window, the prairie slipping past in a hurry, the telegraph poles like tall straight lines, the train's own squat shadow just down below. I could feel the vibration up through the soles of my boots.

"Once we hit Refugio you feel safe enough to strike out on your own?"

"Yes."

"Then that's what we'll do."

"What about you?" she said. "Where will you go?"

"Better neither of us knows where the other is headed."

"Why? I mean we pulled it off."

"I doubt a man like Waco will quit that easy. And if either of us is caught we can't say about the fate of the other if we don't know."

"You'd tell if he caught you?"

"I might. You might too. I saw what he did to Chalk Bronson for some perceived slight."

Her light demeanor changed just then.

"What do you mean?" she said.

"You were there."

"No, I went inside, remember."

"You weren't curious?"

"No. I mean I didn't want to know, I suppose."

"He broke his hands," I said. "He branded him and broke his hands after he had him beaten by a couple of his cowboys."

She turned her face away and I could see she was fighting back tears.

"You still love him?"

"Who, Johnny? I never loved Johnny."

"No, I mean Chalk."

She wiped at her wet eyes with the heel of her hand.

"No."

"I think he does you, a little, as much as loving two women at the same time allows him to."

She looked at me then again, fiercely, intently.

"Once it's gone, it's gone," she said. "Love is."

"I wouldn't know," I said. "I only come close to it one time, and not all that close."

"It hurts to the same degree it feels good."

Then we seemed to run out of words and after a little while she lay down across her seat using the satchel as a pillow and I said I was going to walk out on one of the platforms and have a smoke. She closed her eyes. I didn't smoke, but used it as an excuse to go and have a drink in the dining car alone. The last thing I needed was for her to get drunk.

I found an empty table and a black porter came over wearing a white shirt and black trousers and said, "Suh, we don't serve nothin' to eat for 'nother half an hour."

"Can I get a whiskey?"

"Yas suh."

He went off and returned in a few moments with a whiskey and I paid him for it and sat there looking out the window and taking my time with it. In spite of everything, it seemed like high adventure to me—having a runaway wife of a real bad guy and a satchel full of his stolen money. And to think I could be clerking in some general store somewhere, selling notions to fat ladies in big hats. I asked the porter to bring me another whiskey when he came to get the glass and asked him when we were scheduled to pull into Refugio and he said around ten o'clock that evening.

I figured when we got there, I'd send a telegram to Chalk letting him know the plan had been successful, if nothing else to give him the satisfaction that Waco no longer had possession of Antonia. Small comfort, I'm sure, but comfort nonetheless I guessed.

I finished the second drink—not as good as the first, because the first of anything is always better than what comes after it—and walked back to the car. She was sitting in the corner of the couch, her feet and bare legs tucked up underneath her, her trousers and boots lying on the floor. She held a silver flask in her right hand and I could see whatever she was drinking was already starting to take its effect, for her face was flushed and her eyes dreamy.

"What the hell is that?" I said.

"Absinthe," she said, holding it to me. "Have some."

"No. I know all about it."

She smiled warmly.

The valise was open next to her and I could see lots of loose money in it—so much so it didn't even seem real.

"Tell me about the women you never loved but almost did," she said.

The sky outside was gray again and little drops of rain streaked the car window even as the world seemed to be moving one way and we another. The two whiskeys I'd had were just enough to make me reconsider her—the wan and almost vulnerable creature, half naked, all that money, daring me to play the game.

I sat down across from her.

"Is that what you really want to do, talk about the women I almost loved but never did?"

"Or something like it," she said.

She leaned over and placed the hand holding the flask in my lap and let it rest there.

"Are you sure you won't have some?" What I saw in her gaze was the promise of all things.

Everything about it was wrong. But then temptation always has a wrongness to it. We ended up falling asleep pressed together but that was all, the rhythm of the train stealing our resistance to sleep—stealing it like money.

We awoke to the rapping of our door, the conductor calling, "Refugio ten minutes!"

I fumbled around in the dark for my boots, found a match and struck it to the small lantern above the couch. I tried not to stare at her while she dressed. The feelings I had were the same feelings I had when I found out Fannie had been keeping time with me and Junior Bosch at the same time. Only instead of Junior doing it to me, it felt like it was something I was doing to Chalk Bronson, coveting his woman, the woman he entrusted me to save, even though by all accounts she wasn't his woman at all. She was legally Johnny Waco's woman and I didn't know *how* I felt about that part.

"What will you do when we get off the train?" I said.

"I thought we weren't going to tell each other."

"That was about where we'd go once we hit Refugio."

"I don't know what I'll do," she said. "Possibly see my father again."

"He a good man, your father?"

"Yes."

"Mother?"

"Dead," she said. "Long time."

"Brothers or sisters?"

She shook her head.

"Five minutes to go in our coexistence," she said, "and we're having a real conversation. That usually comes before what we did."

"I apologize."

"For what?"

"It felt like I wanted to take advantage of you, Antonia."

"Maybe you should have."

I offered her my best leer. "Another time and place, different circumstances, who knows."

"Yes," she said. "Who knows . . ."

We felt the train slowing and then at one point it lurched ahead after we'd thought it stopped and it threw us together and we held each other not knowing if the damn train had finally stopped or not or if we should unhand each other or what.

Finally we did.

"Good luck," she said as we stepped off the train into a cloud of steam, the night dark around us except for the lights of the town up ahead.

"You too," I said.

What we didn't know was there was only one hotel in town and we both ended up taking rooms there—but not together.

"You hungry?" I said as we climbed the stairs.

"Yes, you?"

"Starved."

"I guess taking a meal together wouldn't commit us to anything."

"Don't see how it would."

"You buying?" she said after we'd set our things in our rooms and locked the doors and gone down to the dining room and been given seats.

"You are," I said. "I paid for the train tickets, remember."

She smiled and we ordered steaks and I could still see that dreamy doped look in her eyes and wished it wasn't there, but it was what it was and there was nothing I could do about it except maybe privately grieve that a woman with such potential wanted to waste herself.

We ate slowly and I asked her to tell me more about herself.

She shrugged. "What is there to tell, really?"

"How did you end up with Johnny Waco, for instance? He seems the complete opposite of Chalk Bronson."

"Long story, but the short of it is, I thought Chalk had been killed in the war. I waited a long time without hearing anything from him and finally gave up hope that I ever would. The selection of men wasn't much as you can imagine in a place like Coffin Flats. Johnny had a big-time reputation of being a powerful man and at first he was charming as hell. You probably don't know it, but most of the real bastards can be charming as hell when they want to be." The look she gave me didn't fail to register.

"Yeah, some gunfighters are like that too."

She smiled again and sipped the last of the wine in her glass and waited for me to refill it for her and I did, reluctantly.

"You're pretty charming yourself when you want to be," she said.

"You think so?"

"You see, that right there, that boyish innocence you sometimes put on."

"Well, it's worked in the past a time or two, I won't deny it."

"Me, I like to deal straight off the top of the deck, Mr. Glass."

"You sure know how to take the starch out of a man."

Her laugh was short, sharp, as she lifted her wineglass.

"To scoundrels and women like me," she said.

And when I didn't toast, she smiled and drank half the glass.

She went on to tell me about her father, an attorney for the railroad at one time who'd made a lot of money through wise investments and was now semiretired. She said his name was Dalton Stone and that he lived in Denver where he took on cases he mostly couldn't win but ones he believed innocent men had been convicted of crimes they didn't commit or where there was a real sense of injustice. I thought it interesting.

"How did you meet Chalk?" I said.

She smiled warmly, the candlelight infusing her eyes.

"Him," she said. "He was part of a medicine show that came to Denver when I was nineteen. Doc Rainey's Patent Medicine Wagon. Chalk was driver and helper to Doc Rainey. They even had an Indian princess who claimed she'd been healed from crippling diseases . . ." She shook her head, remembering. "Chalk was dressed in a bright blue bib shirt with white buttons and a pair of woolly chaps." She clapped her hands happily. "God, he had a hat on big enough to block out the sun. But he was so handsome I couldn't take my eyes off him. And after the show my father took me to meet Doc Rainey—who also performed magic tricks. Chalk was there by Doc's wagon lounging around spinning a rope."

She sighed and took another sip of her wine.

"He was young and handsome and shy as a colt and that's what attracted me to him. I went back to the show the next day alone and made it a point that we meet."

"A case of love at first sight?" I said.

"Yes, exactly. We'd decided to elope, have a

preacher marry us and go off to Niagara Falls for our honeymoon. I knew my father wouldn't be happy, even though he'd come to like Chalk quite well . . ."

"It must have hurt when he went off to the war and didn't come back."

"Like you can't even imagine. I met Johnny and thought I could be happy again, but all I was was miserable and eventually I started doing this stuff." She held up the wine. "Then a friend introduced me to cocaine pills—washing them down with whiskey. It took some of the heartache away— quite a bit of it. I discovered the pleasures of opium after . . ."

"Hooking up with Pink," I said.

The pleasantness of her face changed to something other.

"I didn't mean to pry," I said.

"Yes, you did."

"Not to dredge up hurtful things."

"I want to write Chalk a letter. One last letter to let him know I'm sorry for all that's happened to us. Do you think that would be all right?"

"Don't see what it could hurt."

"I wish I could go back and change everything to the way it was," she said.

"We all do—sooner or later."

We finished dinner and went up the stairs together and I walked her to her door and she paused for a moment as though wanting to say something, but then put the key in the lock and said only, "Good night."

I walked down to my room and did the same thing.

I kept telling myself I shouldn't be thinking what I was thinking.

The last thing on my mind was Johnny Waco and his bunch.

It should have been the first thing.

⇥ 12 ⇤

Morning light had filled the room and I was sitting on the side of the bed rubbing the sleep out of my eyes when the door caved in. Three men, two of them with shotguns aimed at me, suddenly made it crowded. The shorter one with the sugarloaf hat, holding only a short black revolver, said, "If you reach for that hogleg there won't be enough left of you to put in a cigar box." My Merwin Hulbert resting in my holster that hung from the bed frame above my pillow looked a mile away.

Then he turned over the lapel of his coat to show me the badge.

"Sheriff Joe Bike," he said. "You're under arrest."

"For what?"

He looked at me as if I'd just asked if his mama was still a virgin.

"How about wife stealing? We take that shit 'round here fairly serious, mister."

I could hear voices out in the hall, one of them Antonia's: "Turn me loose you dirty bastard!"

I started to rise off the bed.

"I'd move real fucking slow I was you," the lawman said. "These boys are the nervous types, seeing how they're new on the job."

I looked from the one to the other. They did indeed look nervous.

"Got her, boss," a fourth man said from out in the hallway, and Sheriff Bike turned his head to have a look then turned his attention back to me.

"Well, at least you got good taste," he said. "Take her on down to the jail, Tobe." Then to me, "Get dressed."

Twenty minutes later I was sitting in the man's jail, such as it was. I could hear Antonia cursing our captors in another room.

"Let me go, you son of a bitches."

"Holding you till they come get you, woman. You might as well shut that foul mouth of yours."

She continued to curse them and they continued to try and settle her down. This went on for nearly an hour.

Finally Sheriff Bike came back to where I was—a small eight-by-eight-foot (I measured by stepping it off) cell with naught but an iron cot.

"Real she-cat Johnny got himself," he said.

"You know Johnny Waco?" I said.

He looked at me with cornflower blue eyes you'd expect to see on a woman.

"He's my cousin," he said.

"How'd you track us down?"

"Telegraph, son. You heard of the telegraph, ain't you?"

"Yes, but how'd he know we were coming here?"

"Easy enough. That flyer you all took out of Coffin Flats—there's only one town between here and there worth even getting off at. Guess which one? You're in it."

"You know anything at all about your cousin?"

"Know he's rich and is generous to those who lend him a hand."

"He'll kill her if you send her back."

He looked toward the door and the room beyond it, where I'd heard Antonia's voice.

"True love," he said. "Never does run smooth, they say. It ain't my place to get into a man's marital affairs. It ain't yours neither."

"I was just trying to do her a favor. Trying to save her life. Seems to me that should be the job of the law, not the other way around."

"Real philosopher, ain't you?"

He turned and went out again, slamming the door closed behind him, shifting the bolt.

I waited all day for nothing to happen. Every so often I could hear Antonia laying into whoever it was and the one male voice said, "Now ma'am, there ain't no use to talk to me like this. I'm a Christian. There ain't no use to you abusing me so . . ."

Time dragged mercilessly.

Finally, sometime very late in the day, I heard new voices. Male voices. A shuffling of boots on wood, a door clanging open, Antonia's voice, then a slap then nothing. More doors closing again then silence.

An hour or so more and the door to where my cell was opened and dull light fell in and Sheriff Bike came in with two of his men.

"Well, she's on her way back home to her worried husband, exactly where a woman ought to be," he said. "Lucky thing for you is, Johnny don't want to press charges."

I waited for him to open the door and let me go, but knew it wasn't going to be that simple.

He nodded and one of the deputies stepped forward and then Bike opened the door and said, "He's just goin' put these handcuffs on you. Don't give him no shit, now, hear."

"Why handcuffs if you're letting me go?" I said.

"Because we're gonna ride you out a little ways then turn you loose, make sure you don't come back here no more. You look like the dangerous type. It's a precaution."

"You don't have to worry about that," I said. "I've got no reason to come back here."

"No, you sure as hell ain't," he said. "We just gone make sure is all."

I had a bad feeling—maybe the worst one I'd ever had.

"You try and fight this," he said, "I'm gonna shoot you in the head and say you tried to escape."

I let the kid deputy put the handcuffs on me.

"Now walk out the back there," Bike said.

They escorted me out the back door, where four saddle horses stood waiting. I was ordered to wait until two of them mounted their horses, and then Bike told me to do the same and then he mounted his too. Then one rode over to me and said, "Turn your head." And when I did he tied a kerchief over my eyes.

The air was chill and the wind tunneled down the alley where we were. The two riders in front led out. One of them had taken the reins and my horse followed. I could hear Bike behind me saying, "Let's take him to the meeting place, boys."

That bad feeling I had only got worse.

I tried to time in my mind how far we'd ridden or in which direction, but it was impossible. We rode for what seemed a goodly amount of time. I settled into the rhythm of life itself, figuring if they were going to kill me, there wasn't much I could do about it, and it sure seemed like that was exactly what they aimed to do take me somewhere out into the backcountry and kill me.

We rode along to the creaking of saddle leather, the jingle of bits, the clop of hooves against the hardpan.

Seemed at some point we rode down a slight incline and back up again after going through some water. Not long afterward Bike said, "Hold up here."

One rode up and took off my blindfold and I could see we were standing under a big spreading cottonwood, its leaves all but shed, its branches low. I figured it was a hanging tree.

"Get him down from there," Bike said, and they came and took me off my horse, my wrists still cuffed.

"This where you let me go, right?" I said, half mocking because I knew they'd not ridden me this far just to let me go.

"Something like that," Bike said and nodded at the two with him, who took hold of my arms. Bike made a show of it, pulling a pair of leather gloves he had hooked on his belt and putting them on.

"Hold him steady, boys," he said, then slammed his fist into my belly and almost as soon as it doubled me slammed another into my jaw and my world tipped over.

"You understand I'm doing this for your own good," he said. I tried to shake the ringing out of my ears. "So's you'll know there is always a penalty for doing wrong."

He hit me again and I think he broke a rib because it hurt like a son of a bitch, like something sharp going into my lung, and then hit me in the face again, his blow catching me just above my right brow so that blood leaked into my eye. The guy knew what he was doing, snapping off the punch so it'd cut.

I almost went black from it and his voice seemed far away.

"Go bust a nice limb," I heard him say to one of them. They turned me loose and I dropped to my knees trying to wipe the blood out of my eye while trying to breathe. Bike stood there rubbing his hands together, looking at them like they were something he just discovered.

I heard a limb breaking, a splintering crack like a pistol shot.

"Stand him up and take off the cuffs," Bike said. They were like faithful dogs, those two. Once they had me uncuffed, they stretched my arms out to my sides and tied my wrists to the heavy thick limb they'd broken from the tree.

"Why hell," Bike said when they finished. "You look like Jesus—paying for your sins. Thou shall not covet thy neighbor's wife, ain't that right?"

I figured now was when they'd shoot me.

"You're free to go," Bike said, and I lifted my head as much as I could with the limb yoked to me and pressing into the back of my neck.

They mounted their horses and sat there looking

down at me, the land falling to night all around, the stinging of my face, the blood from the cut above my eye drying to a crust.

"Don't come back to my town," Bike said. "Don't ever let me see you again."

Then they turned and rode off and I watched them go before sinking to my knees. Every time I took a deep breath it felt like a knife going into my lungs. I worked my wrists but they'd been lashed to the limb with rawhide strips. I knew one thing: I couldn't allow myself to fall on my face or back or I'd never be able to rise again. Those old boys knew a thing or two about putting a man in a bad way. I forced myself up finally and realized that with night coming on fast I'd be a fool to try and make my way in the dark.

I went over to the tree and placed my back against it and eased myself into a sitting position. With the support of the tree holding me up, I could at least sleep if I needed to, wait out the night, hope for better things in the morning. Where I was I couldn't say. I didn't see a road anywhere, no sort of trail.

With the night came a steady rain that soaked me through to the skin, and after a while I couldn't tell if what was flowing down my face was blood, rain, or tears.

And that money I'd done this for, well, they'd taken that too, back when they arrested me and put me in the jail. I was broke and yoked and abandoned, and with my luck running the way it was, I'd probably be dead in a few days.

Unless.

It was a big *unless*.

⇥ 13 ⇤

The metaphor, he told himself, was a boat adrift, its mooring rope cut, the water wide, turbulent, always astir. He was the rudderless boat guided by the unpredictable winds after her death. The winds were mighty, carrying him along with no real sense of purpose. The winds were nothing more than God's angry breath.

His name was Tom Twist. And somewhere in the distant past were the mountains and a grave on a plateau with her in it. It was as though God had come to visit and then simply stood suddenly and said good-bye and took her with Him.

He thought in metaphors these days. His heart had been assassinated. He had lived a good life for so long that now he felt the need to see the darker side. He bought a pair of fancy pistols off a man who said they once belonged to the famous but long dead Wild Bill, complete with matching holsters. Their weight felt right on his hips, balanced, deadly. He felt dangerous at last, a man to be feared.

He thought he could find solace in the sort of women men fought over and spent their last dollar on. The whorehouses of Cripple Creek and Silver City and all up and down the goldfields offered him plenty of opportunity.

In every whore he searched for a little bit of his dead wife, the woman he had loved so hard and true. They disappointed, left him wanting, ashamed, sick. One girl came close; a small darkhaired twenty-year-old from Iowa. She said her name was Alice Blue and that she'd been raised on a farm and could still smell pig stink. He did not know how much of what she said was true. Every girl had a story of sorrow, every one had a certain sadness.

"My daddy would probably kill himself to know what I was doing now. Him and Mama were good Christian people."

The winter had set in. The gulches and hills were socked with wet fog, ice, snow. A dreary time to be a boat adrift. The mud came up to his knees.

Alice Blue had the laugh of a schoolgirl. She was young, naive, childish, and goodhearted— somewhere between a woman and a child, with budding breasts and thick legs. He could imagine her married someday with several children and having grown too fat.

He never told her who he was, what he'd been. He never told her about his dead wife, the life he'd lived. She never asked. She laughed and showed him her stockings, this well-fed Iowa farm girl. He liked that in her; it made her more wholesome than the others with their pocked faces and bad teeth and wasted bodies. But who could blame them for what they'd turned into? The men in those camps were the roughest there were. Hard as the rock they picked to get to the gold. They pried with dirty fingers the gold and the flesh with equal gusto, desire flaming in their brains. They also had rotted teeth and rotted breath from the rotted liquor and lack of personal hygiene. When they rose from the whores' beds, the sheets were filthy.

"Miners are terrible hard on a girl," she said.

She confessed to him many things about her life. She was as open as a book. And for a short while he was enchanted by her, thinking perhaps like God, love works in mysterious ways. And for a moment he allowed himself to believe that he *could* love her.

Then one day he awoke to discover her gone, and with her, his money. He suspected the man she called "cousin" was her pimp. He thought the price of his stolen poke fair wages for the sin. He did not try and find her, but let the wind fill him again, a boat without rudder or sail, the weight of wind mapping his path.

It didn't matter where he had been or where he was about to go, for he was in search of himself and nothing else. The self lost needed to be found again.

He came eventually into New Mexico and saw the dark mesas long and flat and black against the evening sky—reaching forth like gigantic fingers of an outstretched hand. The sky at evening went from a soft pink to a deep rose before becoming like unpolished silver.

He came across the mouth of a cave one evening just after dusk, and from it flew thousands of bats and he sat and watched in amazement.

He had heard stories about New Mexico, about

shape shifters and men who could turn themselves into animals, about the haunted grounds of the Hopi and the sacred grounds of the Navajo.

He knew a young priest who had gone and lived there and come back completely changed and married a woman and had children with her, believing, he said, that God did not want man to suffer alone, but to have himself children and a woman to love. The priest said, with tears in his eyes, that God *was* love and to deny love was to deny God.

Tom Twist heard the echoes of his horse's hooves within the canyon walls and upon loose rock.

The stars seemed closer than ever as he waited for sleep.

He was sure he had come to the right place. He was sure that whatever force was guiding him had led him to this place for a particular reason.

And then one day he saw what looked like a crucified man staggering alone, his arms spread outward, tied to a tree limb, and with the failing light it seemed to Tom that he was having a dream—for how could it be, the thing he was seeing?

And for a moment he held his breath thinking he was having a vision.

But then he saw the man fall and not get up.

He knew then there was a reason it was he who had come across this man and not someone else. But what that reason was, he could not yet say.

He rode forth.

⇥ 14 ⇤

That son of a bitch Joe Bike was right about one thing—after two days I was beginning to feel death chasing me. I was cold and miserable and half out of my head. When I found water to drink, I'd have to kneel and balance myself, leaning forward so I didn't fall flat on my face and end up helpless as a turtle on its back. The rain hammered me on and off through that first night and into the next and the day after that. The wind lashed across my face, at times making the rain feel like thorns, and my eye had swollen shut from the blow Bike struck me so that I had to turn my head to look at what was on my right. Making everything worse, more intense, was my broken rib, just trying to breathe. Every step was painful, but kneeling and rising again was excruciating. And every step I took stabbed more anger in me toward the men who did this to me, and especially the one who ordered it done: Johnny Waco.

At one point near the end of the second day I nearly lost my balance and fell flat and had to retch because my stomach was turning over with probably bad water I'd drank out of a dirty puddle. That night I found a stump of a tree to sit against and the dreams came bad and repeated themselves over and over and I kept waking every few minutes, shivering, my teeth chattering, the pain so great I wanted to scream and did.

The third day broke clean, or maybe it was the fourth, I'd lost track of time, and the sun offered some of its early winter warmth. But by then I might have even been walking in circles. At one point I looked up and saw buzzards wheeling in the sky and wondered if they had found something already dead, or were just waiting.

I knew no matter what, I had to keep moving. Every time I stopped and rested it was harder to get up again. At one point I spotted a cairn of rocks someone had stacked up and figured I'd give it one shot—to throw myself backward on those rocks and try and crack the limb I was lashed to.

I knew the chances of success were not great, that if I broke anything it would probably be one of my arms in trying. But I was desperate and a desperate man will do desperate things when he feels his luck is about run out.

I tried to think of the best way to do it and couldn't come up with a very good plan. So I just stood with my back to the rocks and then flung myself backward as hard as I could.

The pain nearly caused me to pass out.

I lay there trying to get my breath, the plan a complete failure, my hands scraped and cut, my back bruised and aching. I cursed. I wept. I bargained with God. Nothing seemed to help.

It took every last bit of my strength and three tries but I finally managed to lift myself up again.

I staggered on. Toward what, I didn't know. I just knew I had to keep moving.

I recall falling, lying there with the sun in my eyes thinking it would blind me if I stared at it. I turned my face away and insects soon found me. I didn't care. I had no strength or will to care anymore and closed my eyes and let them feast. I just hoped it would be over soon even though I knew it would probably go on a lot longer.

After a time of the bugs crawling on me, pausing, biting, I knew I'd go mad. I managed to shake my head from side to side when it became too much. I cursed their existence. It would stop for a while then start again. Relentless. They seemed to especially like the blood—the cuts on my hands and the one over my eye.

I struggled to get up but couldn't. I'd die just as I was. Someone would eventually find me, or what was left of me, and wonder how it came to pass a man would be like this and stories would arise and be passed from one person to another—told in saloons and quiet rooms—about the man who was found crucified to a limb.

I lay waiting for death.

Death had a peaceful voice.

I felt something working at my hands, perhaps a wolf or coyote gnawing them off. But then whatever it was did the same to the other hand and I managed finally to open my one good eye and saw the shadow of a man kneeling between me and the low sun.

"Easy, mister. Go easy."

He was dressed in black: black hat, black coat.

The sunlight gleamed off his knife blade as he folded it and slipped it into his pocket.

"Who did this to you?"

I could not speak, my throat as dry as sand. I tried lifting my arms away from the limb but my shoulders seemed locked. I curled my fingers.

He raised my head and put a canteen to my mouth.

"Drink slow," he said.

It was like drinking salvation.

He trickled more water into my mouth until it had the quality and effect of oiling a machine. My tongue was swollen.

He tried to help me sit up but my scream made him ease me back down again. Then blackness came over me like a blanket.

I awoke knowing time had passed and stared into a fire lashing flames against the darkness. He sat across from it.

"Thirsty?" he said.

I nodded and again he brought me water to drink.

"How about now, you think you can sit up now?"

"I'll try." The words seemed to break in two when I said them.

He helped me sit up and I nearly fainted but managed to stay upright.

"Hungry?"

"Yes."

"Chew on this," he said and handed me some jerky.

He had a sharp bony face with close-set eyes and white hair nearly to his shoulders; he didn't seem old enough to have white hair.

"Am I dead?" I said.

"Do you think you are?"

"I don't know."

"The thing is, none of us do. We have it in our heads that we're this or that, but are we really, or is everything an illusion?"

It made no sense to me what he was saying. Maybe I was dead, or hallucinating. I closed my eyes and chewed and the jerky seemed real enough and so did the night wind and the surrounding darkness and the flames in the fire licking at the night.

I slept.

I had dreams.

I dreamt I died, that a faceless man had killed me. I awoke.

It was morning and the man in the black hat and clothes and white hair sat across from me, the fire between us.

"How are you feeling?" he said.

"Like I was just taken out of a grave."

"Born again?"

"Maybe."

His eyes were very pale, almost like colorless glass. I noticed as he reached for the coffeepot resting in the fire that he had smooth hands, the sort of hands a working man would not have, the sort of hands that a professional gunfighter or gambler would have.

"Here," he said, pouring me a cup and handing it across.

I shrugged out of my blankets and took it. It was good coffee for trail coffee.

"Who are you?" I said after taking a drink.

"Just a man in search of himself," he said, then

half smiled. "And I found you, which isn't like finding me at all."

"I guess not."

"How did you get yoked?" he said. "It was an unusual sight—like a crucified man fallen from the cross."

"Maybe that's who I am, Jesus, or somebody like that. Don't it talk in the Bible about Him coming back?"

He grunted, said, "Maybe. This is strange country. I've seen lots of unusual things since I've been here, but so far you're the strangest."

"I've heard it said the land is full of spirits—that they live up on the mesas, lots of them, and that there are some who men believe can change shapes, go from men to becoming animals and vice versa."

"I've heard that too," he said. "You believe it?"

"I believe I'm not Jesus or anything close to it."

He shook his head.

"I believe that too. You want some bacon?" He took the lid off an iron skillet and the smell of fried bacon made my belly crawl. He had a Dutch oven setting on a rack over the fire and took the lid off it too and there were half a dozen small brown biscuits baked together in it and he took one out and split it apart and forked on some of the bacon and handed it to me.

We ate without saying much because I was so damn glad to have anything to eat I couldn't think to talk.

"How'd you come to be here?" I said after I ate two more of the biscuit sandwiches and swallowed down my first cup of coffee and refilled it.

"How'd you?" he said.

"Fair enough question." I told him, and he listened.

"They sound like a pretty tough bunch," he said.

"Tough enough."

I asked him if he knew where the town of Refugio was. He shook his head.

"No, I'm new to this part of the country," he said. "I came from north of here, the goldfields most recently."

"You a miner?"

"No," he said. "The farthest thing from it."

"I'm from Nebraska, myself," I said. "I sort of wish now I'd stayed there."

"I bet you do."

"I think I've got a busted rib."

He nodded knowingly.

"I think I will find what I'm looking for here," he said, gazing at the mesas and the landscape of sage.

"Well, what you might find is trouble," I said.

"Maybe, but I think there's a reason I came here and I'm soon to find out."

"How will you know?" I said.

"I am not sure, but I believe I will know when I find it."

Sun broke over the mesas and the air was crisp and way off in the distance I could see snowcapped mountains.

"You come across a town nearby lately?" I said. "Someplace I could maybe find a horse, a pistol? Those old boys robbed me of everything I owned including some of my dignity and I aim to go and get it back, but I'll need a horse and a gun to do it."

He sat there squatting on his heels looking for all the world like a man in no hurry to be anywhere soon. He turned his head slightly.

"I came across a small village a few miles back. It was just some Mexican people mostly, a church, a cantina, some casitas. I'm not even sure of what its name was or if it even had a name."

"Which way was it and how far do you reckon?"

He shrugged. "Three or four miles, perhaps."

"Well, I might as well get started then. I'm not sure how to thank you for what you've done."

"No thanks necessary. I'm sure you would have done the same thing for me."

I'd like to think I would have but the way my life had been going, I'm not sure how much good I had in me.

I stood slowly and it hurt still and I was sore from head to toe and my shoulders ached like hell and I wouldn't have paid a nickel for me even if I had a nickel left, which I didn't. I was broke and afoot and a man in my condition couldn't get much worse off.

I started to walk in the direction he had indicated.

Then he said, "I can ride you back there," and stood himself and tossed the remains of the coffee into the fire's ashes, causing them to steam and hiss, and wiped his fry pan out with sand and put away his Dutch oven and all the rest into a large canvas sack, telling me I'd have to carry it if we were going to ride double.

He had a fine black horse—a Morgan, I'd judge— that seemed too proud to even be a horse. It stood our weight and its owner clucked his tongue and we started off at an easy walk.

We made the village in an hour and he was right about it—there wasn't much there except what he'd said was there. All the buildings were adobe and some of the casitas had strings of red chilies hanging by the front doors and brown-skinned kids played in the only street and women stood at a community well with clay pots.

"This is it," he said and stopped in front of the cantina. I slid off the horse and handed him his sack and he dismounted and lashed it behind the saddle horn.

A woman sweeping the street in front of a small casita eyed us suspiciously.

"We're probably the only white men here," he said.

"You know I didn't even get your name," I said.

"Tom Twist," he said.

"Jim Glass," I said.

"You think it matters?" he said. "The names they give us?"

"I guess it's how we know when to pay attention," I said.

He seemed to consider it.

"I guess," he said.

He was stranger than the New Mexican wind.

"I guess as long as I'm here I'll see about restocking some of my supplies," he said. Then he paused and looked at me. "You have any money?"

"No. Like I said, they took that too."

"No money, no horse," he said. "You're in quite a fix, aren't you?"

"I don't know when I've been worse off."

"Here," he said, taking a twenty dollar gold piece from his pocket and extending it toward me.

"I'd like to be able to decline your kindness," I said. "But under the circumstances I can't."

"Take it," he said, and I did.

"Well, I wish you luck, Jim Glass—on your journey, wherever that might lead you."

"Same here, Tom." We shook hands and I watched him go up the street to a small trading post with a number of dark-skinned men sitting out front wrapped in colorful blankets.

I went inside the cantina. You want to know anything about a town, bartenders are the best people to ask.

The man behind the bar was singing to himself. That hour there weren't any drinkers. Singing and rubbing glasses with a hand towel.

"Señor," he said. He was short and fat with hair combed down over his forehead and large ears.

I was torn about buying a drink knowing every dime I had of the twenty dollar gold piece was critical to my survival.

"You speak English?" I said.

"Sí. *Poquito*—a little, yes."

"Anyone in town sell horses?"

"*Cabellos?* Sí. Caesar Hernandez—he have horses sometimes."

I asked directions and he told me this Hernandez had a corral at the edge of town and I thanked him and went out.

I found Hernandez squatting on the sun side of his corral, his eyes closed. He was old, his skin leathery, threads of black hair growing from his upper lip and chin. He was mumbling to himself and running a string of rosary beads through his crooked fingers.

I coughed and he opened his eyes and looked at me like an old turtle.

"I'd like to buy a horse," I said.

"I maybe have one to sell," he said.

"How much?"

He shrugged and sized me up. The wind shuffled his black hair. "You have gold or silver?"

"Gold."

That seemed to suit him and he stood up, using his hands on his knees, and shifted his serape over his shoulders and pointed to a gray inside the corral that didn't look too bad.

"That one," he said.

"How much?" I said again.

"For heem, I take forty dollars gold."

"I've got twenty," I said, showing him the double eagle.

He shook his head solemnly as though I'd just insulted his sister and was contemplating what he was going to do about it.

"Twenty, señor . . . *ayiee*. It is not enough for heem."

"What have you got for twenty?" I said.

He shook his head again. "Nothing," he said. "Maybe you could buy a big dog, eh?" He seemed to take pleasure in his own joke. I didn't think much of it.

"Let me ask you something," I said. "You know of a place called Refugio?"

"Sí." He pointed a crooked finger toward a set of brown hills covered in juniper. "It's that way. Beyond those hills."

"How far?"

He shrugged. "Pretty far," he said.

Goddamn if it didn't look like he was right.

I remembered just then the reason I was standing here trying to negotiate a horse I couldn't afford: Antonia. What had happened to her? Where was she now? It was something I didn't want to think too hard about. Thinking about it just made matters worse. But I'd made her a promise and I intended to keep it.

I headed back up toward town. Somehow I had to raise more cash.

Tom Twist was just coming out of the trading post, his sack weighted down and slung over his shoulder.

"You look as lost as I feel," he said.

"Tried to buy a horse, but twenty dollars doesn't buy you much in this town."

"Wish I could help you out more, my friend, but I'm pretty well empty-pocketed myself now."

"No," I said. "You've done way more than enough."

"What were you going to do if you got yourself a horse?" he said.

"Get a gun and then probably go kill some men."

He shook his head. "Bad karma," he said.

"What?"

"It's something I learned in India. Bad actions this life make your next life more difficult."

"This is the only life I intend to live in," I said. "And I intend to get even with a few people while I can. If there's another life after this one, I'll worry about it when I get there."

His smile was close to pitying.

"Well, maybe you're not wanting a horse bad

enough," he said. "And maybe the reason you don't have a horse is because it is not meant for you to seek revenge. Maybe that's not why you're here."

"You talking God, or what?" I said.

"God could be a part of it. I think it's a lot more complicated than that."

He was by any account the oddest duck I'd ever come across.

"Well, I'll tell you what," I said. "If I have to make a horse out of sticks and mud and a gun out of straw, I'm going to make sure the score gets evened."

He retied his sack to the horn of his saddle then slipped a foot into the stirrup and swung himself onboard.

"I wish you well in your journey," he said and touched heels to his mount and rode to the end of the street, where a small adobe church with white-washed walls stood. I watched as he dismounted and, taking off his hat, went inside. It gave me pause—thinking about stealing his horse did. But I couldn't do it, after what he'd done for me.

I went into the trading post. It was cool inside with a low ceiling of plaster and ocotillo sticks. Cool and dim and I went to the counter and asked the Mexican behind it if he had any guns for sale.

"*Pistolas,* or rifles?"

"*Pistolas,*" I said.

"*Sí.*"

He took out a tray with four revolvers on it. Two of them had pitted barrels and another had loose works. The last one was a Colt Thunderer— something the size a woman might carry. It had hardwood grips.

"This used to belong to Billy the Keed," he said. "I bought it from heem."

"How much you want for it?"

"Fifteen, señor."

"Five."

He shrugged and shook his head. "Twelve."

"Ten and you throw in a box of shells."

"Okay, but only half a box."

I loaded the chambers before I left and put the rest of the shells in one pocket and the last of the money in my other. I walked back down the street to the corral. The caballero looked at me like I was a lost child that had found my way home.

"You come back for the horse, eh?"

"Tell you what," I said. "I'll bet you this gun for that horse."

He looked at the gun. "It's just a gun," he said.

"It used to belong to Billy the Kid."

"So what?"

I took out the ten dollars I had left.

"How about the gun and the money?"

He shrugged. "It's not much, not enough."

I showed him my boots—new ones I'd purchased that spring in Ogallala—and the spurs to go with them. The boots had roses stitched into the shafts.

"I'll throw in my boots and spurs," I said.

"What's the bet?" He was by now nothing if not curious.

"You have a peso?"

Again he shrugged.

"You toss it in the air and if I can hit it on one try, you sell me the horse for ten dollars, and if I miss you can keep the gun, my money, my boots and spurs."

He reached in his pocket and took out a peso. The damn thing looked smaller than I'd imagined it would.

"One try," he said. "Not two."

"That's right, one shot."

He knew it was a sucker's bet and I could see in his greedy little dark eyes he was already feeling his feet inside my boots whether they fit him or not, and my ten dollars in his pocket and the pistol and all the rest.

He stepped away from the building so that we stood in sunlight.

I held the pistol in my right hand down alongside my leg.

"Go ahead," I said.

He flipped the peso high in the air and I let it land in the dirt then took aim and shot it.

"Hey," he cried. "You don't shoot it in the air."

"I never said in the air, I said I could hit it with one shot. And that's what I did."

His face bunched into brown anger.

"The hell, you're still getting ten for a horse not worth twenty," I said. I bent and took off my spurs and handed them to him. "Just to show you my heart's in the right place." It seemed to ease his pain at being suckered.

He called me a fucking gringo in Spanish as he led the horse out and handed me the halter rope.

"*Gracias,*" I said.

Then he called me an asshole.

⇥ 15 ⇤

A gun, a horse. What more did a man need to get by in this cruel old world? I asked myself. I probably looked pretty damn silly to the locals, riding a horse bareback with a pistol stuck down the waistband of my britches. I headed for those brown hills way off in the distance. I rode until nearly dark. The wind blew cold and I was damn near to shivering and hungry as a wolf. Ahead lay a deep purple veil of nightfall and something else. The wink of a campfire.

I rode toward it.

"Hello the camp," I called.

"Come on in, friend."

The voice sounded familiar.

It was Tom Twist there in the light, his Dutch oven steaming.

"You following me?" I said jokingly.

"Maybe I am," he said.

"Hell of a technique you have—following a man by staying ahead of him."

He offered me a plate of food.

"See you found yourself a horse after all."

"I guess I wanted it bad enough, or God wanted me to have it," I said a little sarcastically.

"Maybe so," he said with some degree of confidence.

We squatted on our heels within the heat of the fire and ate.

"You figure out where it is you're going yet?" I said after eating the stew he'd ladled onto a plate for me. It had potatoes and carrots and onions and some sort of meat chunks.

He shrugged. "Not yet, not exactly."

"Well, I'm told the way you're headed—I'm headed—will take us both right to Refugio."

"Where you were when those lawmen got hold of you," he said.

"Yes."

"And it's them you're going to kill?"

"Kill, or use pretty hard," I said. "They've got my horse, saddle, rifle, pistol, money, and some of my blood. I figure they owe me and I aim to collect."

"Might not be worth it," he said. "Results could be the same as they were last time, maybe even worse."

"They've got something else they took too," I said.

He looked at me, the light jumping on his face.

"A woman."

"Oh," he said. "Well a woman certainly does add to the drama."

So I told him the whole story, about Antonia and Johnny Waco and all the rest and that what I was trying to do was something good for somebody and it had ended up costing me.

"We never do good simply for good's sake," he said. "You want some coffee?"

I nodded and he filled two cups and handed me one.

"How so?" I said.

"We mostly do good so we feel better about ourselves," he said. "Yes, we might help another person, but we don't do it for that reason alone. We do it because it makes us feel good. So it's not entirely unselfish."

"Does it matter?"

"Probably not."

"I'm guessing you were in the God business at one time or the other."

He simply smiled and said, "We're all in the God business."

Somewhere in the darkness I heard a dove coo. A moon like a china plate lifted into the night sky. Wind whispered to the fire and the fire whispered back.

"I saw you go into that church today."

"A man needs respite and replenishing sometimes," he said.

"From anything in particular?" I said.

"Most often it is from ourselves," he said. "But today was for the something else."

"You on the dodge, Tom? I mean it doesn't matter one way or the other if you are. What you did for me. That's what matters."

"No," he said slowly, sipping his coffee, his brim down low over his eyes. "I'm not running from anyone except maybe myself."

"Running or searching?" I said.

"Sometimes it's the same thing."

"Sometimes it is, yes."

A star shot across the sky so quick you couldn't be sure it had.

"That a wedding band?" I said.

He looked at his hands, the ring on his finger.

"Yes."

"A woman just adds to the drama," I said.

He smiled. "That it does," he said.

"You want, we can ride as far as Refugio together," I suggested.

"Maybe," he said.

I lay down by the fire, a coat and hat not much for a bed, but it was what I had. When I closed my eyes, the last thing I saw was Tom Twist squatting there holding his coffee cup between his hands, blowing on it then sipping and staring into the flames, and I wondered what all he was made of and how a man like him had drifted so far from whatever or wherever he had been.

I slept like I always did, like the dead.

"How will you do it?" he said the next morning after we'd eaten a light breakfast and cleaned the camp and mounted the horses.

"Do what?"

"Take on those lawmen by yourself?"

"I don't have all the details worked out yet," I said. "I sort of plan things as they come to me."

"Shouldn't that be important, the planning?"

"It should. I never did brag I was any sort of genius. I go along to get along, as they say. But then sometimes these things happen to you you didn't plan and you have to make it up as you go along."

"I don't think violence is the answer, Jim."

"Maybe you should tell them who committed

it on me that," I said. "Wouldn't be no violence in their future if they hadn't done some in their past. I can't just let it go. And besides, there's the woman I owe."

"You can't be responsible for their behavior, only your own."

"We're square on that," I said.

We rode along.

"Turn the other cheek, is that it?" I said after thinking about it for a while.

"It takes a man of some character to turn the other cheek," he said.

"Which I don't pretend to have—character."

"Will you feel better about it later, after you've wrought violence upon them?"

"Some, I reckon. Better than I'd feel if I just let them get away with it."

We reached this side of the brown hills late that day with clouds folding in on themselves in a low sky and the threat of rain or maybe even snow, as cold and damp as the wind was.

"We should make camp early," he said.

My whole backside was sore from riding bareback. I didn't fight him on the idea.

We made a fire and he set up his cook pot and boiled water from a clear running little stream and spilled in some beans to boil and sliced off a couple of good chunks of salted pork. We didn't talk much.

We ate and his silence was complete, as though he was preoccupied with something.

About the time I was set to lay down by the fire again he spoke.

"My wife . . ." he began. I sat there listening.

"She was murdered." Wind rose and fell around us like some great beast breathing and sighing.

"It happened almost a year ago," he said, and bent and poured himself more coffee. "The men who killed her were never captured as far as I know. They're still out there somewhere . . ." His gaze looked toward a darkness as vast as an ocean.

"It's got to be hard knowing that," I said.

"It is," he said. "Annalee was a decent and kind woman. It was her kindness, I think, that cost her her life. The way it looked, what I could ascertain was, she'd let the men into the house, probably thinking to do them a kindness. There were four plates on the table, the food half eaten, muddy boot tracks under it. They probably came by and asked for a meal and she never thought anything but to feed them. She was that way—a Quaker. Peaceful woman without an ounce of hate toward anybody."

I tried imagining her, wondered if she was anything like Antonia, who I guessed was probably a good woman at one time, as all women were probably good at one time.

He reached inside his pocket and took out a silver frame and stared at it.

"That her, your wife?" I said.

He nodded and held it out and I took it and tilted it toward the light and saw the photograph of a sweet-faced woman with light hair and eyes that seemed to stare into vast nothingness; an innocent stare, it was.

"She was twenty-three," he said as I handed the picture back to him.

"Young," I said.

"She was pregnant, that was the very worst of it. I lost them both, Annalee and our child."

"I'd think you'd want to kill the men who did this," I said.

"I do," he said. "That's the problem."

"How so?"

"It goes against everything I ever believed in, everything I ever spoke out against."

"I was right then, you are in the God business."

"Was," he said. "I haven't been for a long time now. And I doubt even if I wanted to be, that I've fallen too far from the vine to be redeemed."

"Redeemed," I said. "I like that word."

He went on to tell me how he had been a preacher and had come to live among the Quakers and met his wife and fell in love with her on first sight.

"I'd been all my young life a hell-raiser till I found the Lord," he confided. "I was saved, born again, and found my own true love all within a couple of years. I was given a taste of the promised land—in her I found everything, including my true self. Then these men came along and destroyed it all and I went back to being what I was before. And now I don't know what I am . . ."

He sighed and drained what was in his cup and set it aside.

"I am lost," he said.

I felt niggardly for having been so complaining about my own circumstances now that I'd heard his.

"I'm sorry," I said. It was all I knew to say.

"So am I, Jim. So am I."

That night I had dreams of Antonia, only she had the face of the preacher's wife, those innocent eyes staring at me, and I heard the thunder of hooves and saw a rider bearing down on me. Death riding a horse. I heard a woman's scream and awoke sitting up, my pistol in my hand ready to shoot the ghosts that plagued me. But no one was there and my heart hammered inside my chest, the broken rib a painful reminder of the recent past and why I was out here now.

I lay down again and stared up at the stain of stars. All man's bloody history had been witnessed by those same stars, and all that was yet to be done would be witnessed by them as well.

The next day we rose and rode on to Refugio without talking because it didn't feel like there was anything worth saying that hadn't already been said. Nothing we needed to share about what haunted us.

We were just two men riding to an uncertain fate, pursued by bad memories, chasing uncertain things.

16

The town was as I remembered it: just a town like any other, without any sign of the violent men that it harbored.

"Well," I said to Tom, "I guess this is where I bid you farewell—in keeping with the drama of it all, of course."

His smile was slight. "I've been thinking," he said.

"About what?"

"You, those men you intend to kill or use real bad."

"Yeah, I know, pretty poor odds, and I shouldn't do to them what they did to me because it will only make me just like them, and all that."

"That's true enough. But I can't let you face them alone."

"Meaning?"

He reached back into his saddlebags and came out with a double rig and strapped it around his waist. Two-gun men were rare in the West, mostly a creation of dime novels.

"Those for real?" I said.

They had ivory handles with carvings of eagles and were nickel-plated—like something you'd see in a Wild West show.

"'Thirty-six Navies," he said. "I bought them from a man named Utter in Colorado who said they belonged to Wild Bill, that he was trying to raise money for a headstone for Bill. They're real enough."

When he saw the uncertain look on my face he took one out—the left one—and handed it to me. I inspected it and it was the fanciest damn gun I'd ever seen anywhere. *J.B. Hickok* was engraved on the back strap.

"I bought them thinking I'd find the men who did what they did to her and kill them. But later I realized that she wouldn't have wanted that. She would rather have sacrificed her own life than that of another human being."

"But you didn't get rid of them. Why?"

He shrugged. "I guess you're lucky I didn't," is all he said.

"And you aim to do what, exactly?"

"Help you."

"You wouldn't take revenge on your wife's killers but you'd help me?"

"I wasn't able to find them, for one thing," he said. "I tried. I guess it wasn't part of my destiny to do so. I realized that if I kept trying, it would have gone against Annalee's wishes, and against whatever my fate is meant to be. It would have been futile, so I quit trying. But you're right here and you could use some help and I'm right here and I'm able to help and maybe that's what I'm supposed to do. Least, that's what it feels like I'm supposed to do."

The town looked peaceful. It was just past noon.

"We never do good just for good's sake," I said. "Isn't that what you told me the other night?"

"No, we never do," he said.

"You ever fire those things, ever shoot at a man or had one shoot at you?"

He shook his head.

"Well, I've been in a couple of gunfights," I said. "It's something that will take your breath away if you live to tell about it."

He sat looking toward the town, down the wide main drag. Then he turned his head and looked at me.

"I think that our entire lives are laid out for us from the moment we take our first breath until the moment we take our last," he said. "If it's meant you do this thing and it's meant that I try and help you, then nothing we say or do is going to change what the outcome of this day will be. Now if you just want to sit here and keep talking about it, that's fine with me."

"I never did meet nobody like you," I said.

He simply turned his gaze toward the town again.

We rode down the center of the street and I spotted the jail to my left and I said, "That's it there," and we reined in and got down and I pulled the pistol out and held it in my right hand down alongside my leg and Tom pulled both his and followed me in. We went in fast.

The kid who'd cuffed me was reading a Bible—a small black one—and he looked up and I said, "You so much as even think about going for your gun I'm going to send you quick to heaven and you'll learn firsthand what it is like and you won't have to read about it no more. You understand?"

He nodded and looked at Tom, who had both those shiny pistols aimed at him, and even I was surprised at how steady Tom held them.

"Where's your boss and the other deputy?" I said.

"Eating their lunch," he said.

"I want to know what you did with the woman."

"Sheriff Bike put her on the flyer back to Coffin Flats with a guard."

"Now that was a mistake," I said and stepped forward and cracked the butt of my Thunderer down across his hat, caving it in and knocking him half out of his chair. He let out a painful whoop and looked like he was about to cry.

"Get on back to that cell," I said.

He did as I ordered and marched back and I found a ring of keys hanging on a peg and locked him inside, and Tom came back there and handed him his Bible through the bars.

"You might want to study on it careful, what it says in there about doing unto others, son," he said.

"I ought to give you as much chance as you gave me and shoot you where you stand for leaving me to die out there," I said.

He rubbed the knot I'd put on his head and looked at his caved-in hat.

"I just do what I'm ordered," he said.

"You ought to learn better," Tom said. "Suppose you'd been ordered to fry children, or something?"

The kid deputy blinked. "Huh?"

"What do you want to do now?" Tom said to me.

"Why don't we just wait for them to come back from lunch?"

He shrugged. "It's your show," he said.

We went out into the other room where the kid had been at the desk and stood by the window looking out onto the street.

"Fry children," I said. "That's quite an image."

"Maybe it will be one that will stick with him for a while next time he's given an indecent order."

"I reckon maybe it will."

We stood around maybe thirty minutes or so.

"That's him, Joe Bike," I said, seeing the lawman and his deputy coming down the walk on the other side of the street. Bike was picking at his teeth with a thumbnail, his deputy was walking with his head down, his hands stuffed in his pockets. They stopped briefly to talk to another man, then came angling across the street to the jail. We were waiting for them, just inside the door, our pistols out.

"Come on in and close the door," I said.

Joe Bike didn't seem all that surprised to see me but his deputy did.

"How—" the deputy started to say.

"Ease your hardware out and lay it on the desk," I said.

"Or what?" Joe Bike said. "You forget I'm a goddamn sheriff?"

"Soon to be ex, or the *late*, take your pick if you don't do what I told you," I said. He looked at Tom Twist, at those pretty guns Tom was aiming at him and his deputy.

"Horace!" he called.

The one in the back said, "Yessir, I'm back here."

"I did you a favor is what I did," Joe Bike said. "I could have just as easily killed you and dropped you in a shallow grave and nobody would have known the difference."

"Yeah, you could have, but you didn't. Your mistake. Now take those guns and put them on that desk."

They eased them out and set them there.

"Where's my horse, saddle, and rifle?" I said. "And where's the money you stole off me?"

"Sold your horse and saddle and guns at auction to cover expenses," the lawman said. "And you're a liar about the money. I ain't no thief."

"Yes you are," I said and hit him square in the face—one short hard punch I'd imagined throwing for days—that knocked him back against the wall and cut his cheekbone open like I'd sliced it with a razor.

Tom stood steady with his pistols.

Joe Bike swiped at the blood running down his face, saw it on his knuckles when he looked.

"You leave a man afoot like you did me is the same thing as murdering him," I said. "I'm a man who believes in squaring things." Some of his blood dripped down onto the toe of his boot and the floorboards.

"Put that expense money and my stole money on the desk."

He snorted. "Yeah, like I've got it," he said.

"You better have it."

I thumbed back the hammer on the Colt.

He began to fumble at his pockets until he found his wallet and brought that out and took what was in there out and dropped it next to the guns. I gave a quick count. Forty dollars. I put it in my pocket.

"Now you," I said to the deputy. He took out his money and looked at it then set it down on the desk. Thirty dollars.

"My month's pay," he said.

I had no sympathy for him and took his money too.

"Now what you stole off me."

Joe Bike hesitated again and I raked him across the face with the barrel of the gun and opened another cut wider than the first one and this time he dropped to his knees, stunned.

"I can keep this up if that's what you're wondering," I said.

"You'll never make it out of this town alive," he said, wiping at his lacerated face.

"Then neither will you."

"Why don't we just kill them all right now and get it over with," Tom said. I wasn't believing what I was hearing coming from his mouth.

The two lawmen swallowed down whatever brave they still had in them.

"Okay!" Bike said. "I'll give you your money . . ."

He stood up shakily and opened the bottom left hand drawer of his desk and took out the familiar paper envelope. "It's mostly all there," he said.

"Put it on the desk and step away," I ordered.

"I still think we should just finish it here and now," Tom said. I glanced at him and saw he was looking at the lawmen like they weren't even there.

"Hold up goddamn it!" Bike protested. "You got what you came for."

I put the money into my pocket along with the rest.

"Walk on back to the cell," I said. I unlocked the door and they went in like trained puppies and I locked it on them again.

"You all know who this man is?" I said.

They looked at Tom and you could see they were trying to put his face with a name.

"John Wesley Hardin," I said. "You all are just goddamn lucky I don't let him go ahead and unload on you because there's hardly anything he likes better than killing traitorous bastards such as yourself, is there, John?"

"I've killed forty-one men," he said. "Might as well make it forty-four."

It was starting to wear on their nerves, being faced down by such a notorious bad man as John Wesley Hardin. First I was him, now Tom was him. The son of a bitch seemed to get around, even though the last I'd heard he was still in the state prison down in Texas.

"Let them live, this time, John," I said.

"I sure don't want to."

"No, it's okay. But tell you what, they make any move to come after us, we'll kill them in ways they haven't even thought of yet."

We went outside and Tom said, "Who's John Wesley Hardin?"

"A very bad man," I said.

"Oh."

"What would you have done if things had gone wrong in there? I mean you were talking tough as hell."

"Just trying to get them to cooperate with you," he said. "I don't know what I would have done if things had gone wrong. I guess we're both lucky they didn't."

"I guess."

"What now?"

"You want to see this through all the way to the end?"

"You mean getting the woman back?"

"It probably won't go near this easy," I said. "I

saw what Johnny Waco and his bunch did to a city marshal and it was pretty ugly."

"You mean uglier than what you did to that sheriff?"

"By a whole lot."

"Why don't I just tag along for a time and see how it goes."

"It's your choice."

He shook his head.

"Like I said, I don't believe we have any choices, Jim." Then he seemed to consider something for a moment and said, "John Wesley Hardin. You think he'd take it as an insult that folks would mistake me for him?"

"Probably shoot you in the eyes."

He smiled then, that same thoughtful smile like someone had told him a clean joke.

"Okay," he said. "Let's go."

He was already starting up the street toward the train depot and I was already thinking I wouldn't have to ride bareback anymore like some damn bummer. But a train ride back to Coffin Flats wasn't the smart move and I stopped Tom and told him we'd have to make the trip on horseback.

He wondered why.

"Telegraph," I said. "You've heard about it, right?"

It was the first time I saw a look of impatience from him.

"Those birds we got caged will get out before we get halfway to Coffin Flats and that sheriff will wire ahead and Johnny Waco will have his boys waiting for us and probably kill us before we get both feet on the platform."

"Well then you better buy yourself a saddle and we'll resupply our food stocks."

"Let's make it quick before they all start hollering."

We found a dry goods store and I bought what we needed including a saddle and a good rifle and were out of town in under half an hour. And like it understood the situation and sided with the jailed lawmen, the weather turned meager and it began to rain.

I looked at Tom and he said, "There's a reason for everything, Jim."

Hell, what'd I know?

17

We followed the railroad tracks. It seemed simplest. The country wasn't familiar to me and it wasn't to Tom either. We shot a jackrabbit the first night and cooked it over a fire down inside a small canyon to avoid any watchful eyes that might be roaming about. I figured by now Joe Bike and his deputies had broke jail and Johnny Waco already had gotten word I was coming.

"How's that rabbit?" I said.

Tom was chewing on it tenderly because of the heat.

"Just like a Philadelphia steak," he said.

"You've been everywhere?"

"Been around to lots of places, that is a fact."

"Asia and Philadelphia," I said. "Don't know that I ever met a man who's even been to either one of them."

"Travel seasons a man," he said.

"Your late wife, did she use to travel with you?"

"No. I did most of it way before I met her."

"You in the war?"

He nodded almost sadly.

"I was," he said. "A chaplain's assistant, in case you hadn't guessed."

"What side?"

"Union. What about you?"

"The other—the one that lost."

"It was a terrible war no matter," he said.

"It was."

"I think of the dead—especially the ones who died on the losing side of a battle—how they just got dumped into mass graves, their names unknown, their causes lost, their families never knowing what became of those lost men. Was always better if you died on the winning side . . ."

His voice trailed off, a sound fading into the distance. The rain had stopped long before and now the air was as cool as it was black and the stars were out and you could see the crescent of a moon riding a ridge of jagged mountains.

"The best friends I ever had were lost in that war," I said.

He nodded understandingly.

"We lost so much, all of us."

"At least you didn't have to kill anybody," I said. "Be grateful for that."

"Does it haunt you much, the men you killed?"

"Some. Not all the time, not every night, but now and then. Sometimes I look at a field of wildflowers and it reminds me, or sometimes, like now, sitting in the dark I'll think I hear voices out there. But not all the time, not as much as I once did."

"I prayed over a lot of those young men in their last hour," he said. "The newly wounded always cried out for their mothers, the really bad ones cried out for God. I don't know that either could or did assuage them their misery."

We ate the pieces of rabbit, cutting it up and sharing it and licking the grease off our fingers and washing it down with fresh boiled Arbuckle and there was something about it—sharing a meal like that with a man like Tom Twist, two of us different as night and day it seemed to me.

"How old were you?" I said.

"Twenty," he said. It surprised me because he didn't look that old now except for the pure white hair. "What about you?"

"Nineteen," I said. "Hasty to get there before it was over. Went the winter of 'sixty-three, afraid I'd miss it all. Then once I got through the winter of nearly freezing to death and setting around most of it, and marching in the spring mud and got into my first foray, I couldn't wait for it to *be* over."

"I watched a lot of it with the generals," he said. "I'd go onto the field of battle afterward and do what I could to bring spiritual comfort. What they really needed were good surgeons and miracles, not my words, most of them."

"Was that when you started to doubt?" I said.

"No, I believed all the more because of what I saw. When I'd see the look that came into some of their eyes there at the very end, that look of peace just before they gave out, I knew it had to be something they saw, some sort of light, some of them said. Some spoke as though they were holding a conversation, but there wasn't anyone there but me. I remember one boy . . ." He shook his head sadly. "He was talking to somebody named James, saying, 'James, I'll be right there. Just wait there for me, James.' I looked 'round thinking somebody was there by the tent but there wasn't a soul. The boy nodded like whoever he was talking to was telling him something and he said, 'Okay, I'll do her then I'll come over there.' Then he closed his eyes and died. It happened more than once like that."

Somewhere off in the distance we heard a gunshot—too far to be concerned about, too close to ignore completely.

"I heard similar stories," I said.

"It was after that I lost my faith," he said. "After my wife."

I knew what he meant.

He took the little silver frame out again and looked at his dead wife's face for a long time then put it back in his pocket.

"I guess if you believe in those things," I said, "then you have to believe she's in a good place."

"It's what I'd like to believe and half the time I do. It's the other half the time it eats at me, my doubt does."

We lay down by the little fire knowing it would die before morning because we'd found the camp spot late and by the time we shot the rabbit and gathered some dried ocotillo wood it had grown very dark in the canyon. We didn't have enough fuel to sustain it but it didn't matter.

"Listen," I said. He lay still and I wasn't sure he hadn't already fallen off to sleep. "Any time you want to pull stakes it's all right with me. Nobody expects you to risk more than what you have already . . ."

He didn't say anything. I shut up. Speechifying in the dark wasn't my strong suit. I watched as the sliver of moon slipped beyond the ridge and the night sky looked like it was shotgunned through with stars.

I could smell the sweat and old hair oil of my hat as it lay low over my face. It seemed like I was so far away from everything and everything was far away from me. I saw a field of skulls when I closed my eyes and heard the moans of men long dead in the silence of my own thoughts. I saw the shattered woods ripped apart by cannon shot, smelled the burning flesh left after the woods caught fire, the flames ravishing those wounded who could not lift themselves to escape it. I saw a young officer speaking with a courier, his handsome face suddenly without its lower jaw, the white of his upper teeth pulsating in a bloody maw, his tongue lolling freely before he slumped off his horse into a heap.

I saw men standing in a ragged line in front of a camp whore's tent, their loneliness and lust tugging at them even though they knew the price they'd pay was two dollars and a visit to the physician's tent afterward.

I saw myself riding away on a dreary afternoon, my hunger for war sated.

Morning came without event. I went one direction to gather fuel for the fire so we could eat a hot breakfast, Tom went another. The sun lit his end of the canyon and I heard a shout. He came back holding his forearm.

"Snake," he said. "Big one. I should have looked where I was reaching."

He rolled up his sleeve and there on the muscled

flesh two drops of blood he swiped away revealed two small prick marks.

"We need to bleed it," I said.

"Go ahead." He sat down, his face a little flushed. "Stupid me."

He handed me his Barlow knife and I opened a blade. No way to clean it but wipe it on my shirt, I took his arm and cut an X over each of the fang marks and squeezed what I could, his blood thick and reluctant.

I took off my kerchief and tied it off tight just above his elbow.

"You think you got most of it?"

I didn't know. "How big you figure it was?"

"Big," he said.

"If it gets to your heart it could be bad," I said.

"All the ways I've thought about dying, this was never one of them."

"I'll saddle our horses and we'll see if we can't find somebody to help."

He nodded and stayed sitting.

I saddled the horses and gathered our gear and we were on the move in quick time. It was wild country and we'd not yet passed a single dwelling nor saw a single trace down which a ranch might stand. We rode along at a good pace knowing that he had less than a fifty-fifty chance if we didn't find someone who could help.

An hour passed, then two. We had to rest the horses and I checked his arm and it was already swollen to twice its normal size and his fingers were fat as sausages and I said, "Does it hurt much?"

"Like you can't believe," he said, putting a brave face on it.

We rode on and still nothing but brown hills and dry riverbeds and red canyons, prickly pear and blue sky.

I saw he was having trouble staying in the saddle, swaying from side to side, his face no longer so brave; the pain etched deeply in it now, his eyes closed against it.

I rode alongside him.

"My heart's beating like a drum," he said. His face was damp with sweat.

Finally around noon we spotted a house that sat south of the tracks a half mile and made for it.

It was made of mud and stone. There were chickens in the yard and a pen of sheep. Two dogs came out barking, both of them black with white cow dogs, their bellies low to the ground. A man was grinding an ax blade on a stone wheel and looked up when the dogs began barking. He stopped turning the wheel and stood up holding the ax. A woman who was bent at the waist in a field of pumpkins also stood and looked in our direction.

The man reached for a rifle he had leaning against the grinding wheel.

I raised an open hand as we rode up, holding the reins of Tom's and my horse in the other. Tom was barely hanging on, lying low over his saddle horn.

"My friend's been bitten by a big rattler," I called soon as I stopped our horses. "He needs help."

The man looked at us suspiciously then set his ax down but held onto his rifle.

"Maize," he called, and the woman stepped out of the pumpkins and walked to where we were.

I dismounted and helped Tom out of the saddle.

The man looked at his arm, said, "Jesus!" Then, "Bring him inside."

The woman held the door for us and the man pointed toward a cot in the corner of the front room. Besides the cot, there was a kitchen stove with three burner plates, a table, two chairs, cupboards, and a dry sink.

Tom groaned when I eased him down.

"When'd he get bit?" the man said, looking closer at Tom's arm.

"This morning."

The man stood and went to the cupboard and got a long thin-bladed knife and a bottle of liquor and came and pulled a chair up close to the bed.

"I'm going to cut your arm, mister," he said to Tom. Then to me, "You two help hold him."

The woman moved to the head of the bed and placed her hands on Tom's shoulders and bore down and I held his other arm as the man drew two long slits with his knife down the length of Tom's forearm. The blood rushed out and the man pulled the cork on the bottle with his teeth and spilled the whiskey into the cuts. Tom jerked like he'd been shot.

"Get me some bandages, Maize," the man said. She left and then returned with several strips of muslin.

The man reached in his shirt pocket and took out a twist of tobacco and bit off a good chunk and chewed and took a sip of the liquor and kept chewing with the liquor in his mouth till he had a good wad then compressed it to the bite marks and wrapped a strip of muslin to hold it into place, his fingers bloody from the work.

Then he said to Tom, "Drink some of this," and held the bottle to his mouth and Tom swallowed some of it down.

"That's about all I know how to do for him," the man said. "Hoping the tobaccy will draw the poison out." Tom's eyes fluttered. "Maize, wench up some cold water and soak cloths and put them on his arm clear up to the shoulder. The cold will slow down his blood." The woman left the house and came back in several minutes with a bucket of water and set about bathing Tom's arm and shoulder.

The man motioned me outside.

"I din't want to say it in there where he could hear me, but your friend's going to die, mister."

"No he's not," I said.

He shrugged.

"Bad break," he said. "Hard country. You want a taste of this?" He handed me the bottle. I took a pull and handed it back.

"How far from here to Coffin Flats?" I said.

He shrugged. "Another two days you keep at it steady. That where you're from?"

"It's where I'm going."

He wore a thin coat. Dark-skinned. Could have had some Mexican or Indian in him; the woman too.

"I thought when I first saw you two coming you were Clancy's men."

"Who's Clancy?"

"A one-eyed son of a bitch," he said.

The sheep in the pen bleated plaintively, the dogs paced restlessly.

"You want you can go on alone," he said. "Maize and me will see to your friend, bury him when he's passed."

"He's not going to need burying," I said.

He took another pull off the bottle and offered it back to me but I declined and he punched the cork back into the neck with the heel of his hand and set it next to him where he squatted on his heels looking at his sheep.

"I need to get them sheep up to Clancy's Crossing and load them on the train and send them to market," he said.

"The same one-eyed son of a bitch, Clancy?" I said.

"Yeah, he's got the market on things round here. All but me and Maize. Wants to buy me out. I won't sell. Hell, where would I go? Where would she?"

"Your wife and you?"

He shook his head.

"Sister," he said. "This place is all we got. My old man fought the Apaches for it and his old man fought them too and was killed by them. Thank God they're all over in San Carlos and we don't have to fight them no more."

The woman came out of the house and the man stood and I stood with him. It was the first I really paid any real attention to her. She was of an age most would consider spinster—plain but not bad looking.

"He's asleep," she said, shaking her head. "I can't tell if he's any better or not."

"I got to get them sheep to Clancy's Crossing," the man said again.

"I can help you get them there," I said.

"No, you stay on with your friend. I can get them there just fine."

"It's no problem," I said.

"No, I got the dogs."

He looked at the woman.

In a short while we watched him head off with his band of sheep, his two dogs working to keep them bunched and moving. He carried the rifle over his shoulder.

"You hungry?" she said.

"I could eat."

She fixed a pot of mutton stew with wild onions in it and we sat across from each other, her eyes lowered most of the time, which gave me a chance to observe her closer. She had a broad face with wide-set eyes. Her dark hair was parted in the middle and roped into braids that hung down to her breasts. Her nose was straight and her lips looked like they'd been finely carved, just right to fit the rest of her face. She had thick hands. She ate with a delicacy as if she were eating in the finest restaurant in a city. I'd seen women with large hats eating that same delicate way. When I finished she asked if I wanted another helping.

"Thanks but no," I said.

"Big man like you should eat more," she said in an almost motherly way.

I didn't know what to say.

She cleaned up the dirty dishes and gathered everything on a sideboard at the sink. "I can dry those plates if you like," I said when she came back from outside with a pail of water she filled a pan with.

"It's not necessary," she said.

"Are you and your brother always so independent you won't accept no kind of help?"

She smiled. "Okay," she said. "The towel is right over there."

We stood washing and drying and I liked how that felt. She stood about as tall as my shoulder.

I checked on Tom when we finished the dishes and he was still asleep, but moaning some, and I couldn't be sure but his arm didn't look any worse than it did before and maybe some better. She made us coffee and we went outside to drink it and the sun glazed brightly beyond the distant mountains that looked so faded as to be clouds on the horizon.

"You like living way out here?" I said.

"No, not really," she said. "But here is where we are."

I tried to guess why a woman would live so far out from anybody, not have herself a man, houseful of kids running around.

"Always just been you and your brother?" I said.

"How do you mean?"

"Have you ever been married?"

"No," she said, shaking her head. "It would have had to have been some lonesome cowpoke, or some no account drummer—way out here; that's about all you ever see this far from town. Why marry something you know you're not going to stick to?"

"You mind I ask about the trouble between your brother and Clancy?"

She shrugged.

"It's pretty simple," she said. "He wants to buy Spence and me out, resents we haven't sold to him. Our place sets right in the middle of the rest of his holdings. He has to run his cattle around the long way. And besides, he hates sheep and those who keep them."

"Why not sell, since you don't care for it all that much?"

"I don't, but Spence does."

"You never got the urge to strike out on your own?"

"Just about every day. But I couldn't leave Spence here to fend for himself."

The wind played with the dust by the empty pen.

"What about you?" she said. "You got a woman kept off somewhere?"

"No. If I had, I'd be with her."

She sipped her coffee, looking at me over the rim of her cup, something in her eyes telling me something, conveying something unspoken but something a man should know when he sees it in a woman's eyes.

"He won't be back till tomorrow afternoon," she said. "He'll get his sheep to the loading station then get a good drunk on, probably buy himself a woman and stay the night. Buy supplies in the morning and come home."

She looked off toward the direction he had gone with the sheep and dogs.

"What about you, you ever go into town for fun?"

"No kind of fun in Clancy's Corners for a girl like me to have," she said. "Unless it's she enjoys wrassling with dirty shirt cowpokes who'd treat her like the morning flyer—all wanting to stand in line and get on board. I never had any urges to be the morning flyer."

"Anything that you do for fun?"

"You asking me to show you?"

"Maybe I am."

She turned and looked at the door of the house.

"I'm not loose," she said. "But I *am* damn lonely."

"I know the feeling," I said. "Seems a little foolish we both are when we wouldn't have to be."

"Let me think on it some."

"Sure," I said.

I spent the rest of the afternoon taking care of the horses, lounging about, uncertain as to where things were headed, concerned about how Tom was making it, whether or not he'd live or I'd end up leaving him in this place. It felt like I knew him a lot longer than I had. I didn't want to think about his dying before I got to know him better.

She and I ate a supper of the same stew. She did not speak but simply looked at me, judging, weighing the possibilities in her mind. I was doing the same and we both knew it every time we looked at each other. We washed and dried the dishes after she got Tom to eat a little bit.

"There's a water hole not far from here," she said. The sun was low over the mountains so all you could see was its light thrown up against the evening sky.

"You ever bathe naked with a woman?" she said.

"A time or two," I said.

"I've had in my mind some time now how I'd like to bathe naked with a man in the moonlight," she said.

We took some towels and a bar of soap and stepped out into the evening air, which was cool now but not intolerable. The sky with the sunlight drained out of it had turned a dark blue metal. I followed her down to the waterhole beyond sight of the house. It was a large flat pan of red rock where a stream ran in from higher up and drained away from the lower end, leaving a natural pool in the middle the water had worn into a bathtub over a thousand years or more. A full moon had risen and seemed so close we could just reach out and rub our hands over its surface. I watched her undress, dropping her clothes casually until she stood fully naked. Then she unbraided her hair and shook it free and half turning to me said, "You just going to stand there and watch?" Then she walked into the water up to her waist.

I stripped out of my duds and walked in to where she stood and I was surprised that it felt warmer than the air. She said it was from the sun heating it all day.

"You sure are white," she said, laughing as she led me into the deepest part of the pool.

I felt like being led.

"You've done this before."

"All the time," she said. "Only alone."

We naturally came together, her head inclined, and I kissed her wet mouth. She urged her body even closer to mine when I did, floated up against me, and everything after that just took its natural course. The weight of her was hardly anything at all, buoyed by the water as I held her, suspended, floating in my arms it seemed. She laughed and kissed my face and lips and neck. I did my best to please her.

"Like that," she whispered. "Just like that . . ."

Later we used the soap to wash each other and it felt like we were children playing and the moon reflected itself in the pool all around us. Then we rinsed and climbed out onto the still warm rock and dried ourselves with the towels and dressed then walked back to the house.

Tom was sitting up at the table, his swollen arm resting atop it, a cup of coffee near his good hand.

"I wondered where you had gone," he said, then looked at Maize, her hair still wet, and said, "Oh . . ."

"How are you feeling?" I said.

"Like I want you to cut my arm off."

"Least you're not dead," I said. "I'd think you would be by now if you were going to be."

"There's worse things than death," he said. "I know that now."

"You think you'll be up to riding tomorrow?"

He shook his head. "I don't know. I'm still feeling dizzy and sick."

Then he asked if I could help him lay down again. I did. And the house had gone quiet. And when Maize snuffed the lamp there by her bed, we lay in the darkness of moonlight.

"I'd like to try that again," she said. "What we did in the water. Only slower this time."

"I was hoping you'd say that," I said.

We could hear the silence of time shifting, and later I could hear her heart beating as steady as a good watch and it brought me peace.

18

From the diary of Maize Walker . . .

July 17, 1881.

Dirt, desert, wind, sky. Days all the same, except sometimes it rains in the summer months when the heat is at its zenith. Spence and me sometimes sit out in it just for relief as we did today. Spence believed it was as hot as it's ever been.

April 3, 1882.

I watched a spider build its web. A construction so fine it seems unimaginable.

May 11, 1882.

Spence gone to town with sheep, am here alone. Sing all day so I can hear the sound of a human voice. In town he will take part of the sheep money and buy himself liquor, a woman. He never talks about it except sometimes in his sleep. Last time he cried out the name

*"Ismeralda" and I could hear him banging
around in his room.*

October 22, 1882.

*Bleeding nine days now, unusual. No doctor
near to consult. One at Consideration
River—90 miles. No pain, but feeling weak.*

November 1, 1882.

*Have harvested the pumpkins. More than we
need. Spence says he'll take a load to Clancy's
Corners and try and sell them. The biggest took
the two of us to lift in the cart. Spence wanted
to know what I was feeding them. Sometimes
he makes me laugh.*

She likes best writing at first light as Spence
goes about his business, as the two dogs follow after him, as the world is still sleeping. On a shelf,
the image of a man in a silver frame with a long
tangled beard, his eyes staring into the lens like a
man about to be executed. Hayes Walker, grandfather, who died grimly (found with several arrows
in his body) seems to keep a watchful eye on her. In
death, his face was more relaxed than in the pho-
tographer's studio in Santa Fe.

December 29, 1882.

*Would you believe it snowed? Went out in it,
let the flakes fall upon my face, like cold kisses,
so lightly they tickled.*

December 31, 1882.

*Last day of the year and have a cold & fever.
Up all night sick. Spence agrees to go get doctor
in Consideration River if I need him. Decide to
wait another day.*

January 7, 1883.

*Saw a badger today near swimming rock
drinking. Its eyes fierce. I told Spence & he
went in search of it and tonight we'll have
badger stew instead of mutton. I'm not so sure
it will taste as good, but a change nonetheless.*

Occasionally a rider or drummer would come
by—men on their way to somewhere else—and
they would give her knowing looks as if to say:
"I know lonely when I see it in a woman and I'm
available if you're in need of a man."

Once it was a young rider whom she feared was
on the dodge from trouble, his black shirt spanked
with dust.

April 19, 1883.

*A young man who calls himself Tate Harrison
arrived at noon today, his horse all lathered.
A blue-eyed boy of no small beauty with dark
ringlets of hair cascading from under his hat
to his shoulders. Hospitality assured he'd be
invited to stay for dinner. I was tempted to
invite him to my bed as I had done on one or
two other occasions—the patient-medicine*

*drummer the summer before, and Henry
Stob, that time he came with a load of Hay
and Spence was gone hunting. But something
warned me about young Mr. Tate—that he was
dangerous in the extreme. Not that he would
do harm to me anywhere except the possible
ruination of my heart. He was quiet and had
the sweet soft mouth any girl would be jealous
of. Now past midnight and I am still awake
thinking about him, my skin crawling with the
memory of his eyes looking at me across the
table at supper. He rode away right after.*

August 22, 1883.

*Henry Stob asked if I wanted to marry him.
Wife dead not three months and already he is
looking for a new one. Claims he can't stand
living alone and can't cook nor clean house
very good. Of course I told him no. He seemed
so forlorn, wanted me to take him to my bed
again. No, again. He wanted to know why not
when I had once already. How does a woman
explain to a man that what she does she doesn't
always do for love alone? Told him instead I
hoped for a younger man who could give me
children. He did not seem to understand, swore
a vow his seed was still good. Went away dour.*

When the heat became too intense to work for
long periods, she would go to the swimming rock
and there remove her clothes and slip into the pool
of water, letting it slide over her skin like cool silk.
She would soak until her bones grew cool and

think of a life unlived. She would like to have children before she grew too old. But where to find a proper man? And closed her eyes in wistfulness.

Some days she did not write in her diary.

Some nights she did not dream.

Some hours she did not think of the children she did not have.

September 30, 1885.

Two riders rode up to the house today, one of them with a hurt arm—bitten by a snake. Arm and hand swollen something terrible. Spence did what he could by cutting and applying tobacco poultice but feels certain the fellow will not live.

The other one is quite handsome and about the right age. Am considering asking him to go for a swim with me if opportunity presents itself. He seems likable.

⇥ 19 ⇤

Day broke. The woman slept beside me. Our lust less now that it had been spent, ardor cold as ashes. I rose from the bed without waking her and went in to check on Tom. He lay on his side with his face to the wall. It hit me then that he might be dead. But when I touched him he rolled over.

"How you feeling?" I said.

He looked at me standing with a blanket wrapped around me.

"How you?" he said.

"Fair to middling."

"I guess I'm about the same. Arm feels some better, not as tight." I couldn't see much difference when I looked.

He said, "Help me sit up." He held his ravished arm tenderly as I helped him.

"Jesus," he said. "I'm so dizzy I can't see straight."

"Just take it easy."

"Don't worry, I'm not planning on wrestling you."

"You want coffee?"

He nodded.

I shuffled over and found the tin of Arbuckle and then went out and pumped a pot of water and shuffled back in again. The morning was cool and bright and I didn't see any sign of Spence having returned.

I started a fire in the stove and set the coffee to boiling.

"You think maybe you should put some clothes on before her husband gets home?" Tom said. He looked pale, like someone had scrubbed all the color out of him.

"They're brother and sister," I said.

"Well, that's a positive note," he said. "Still, do you think he might be a little upset, the two of you having just met?"

"Point taken," I said, and shuffled back into her room and began to dress as quietly as I could.

My back was to the bed when she said, "You leaving, Jim?"

I was pulling on a boot, trying to balance myself.

"Just thought I'd get dressed. Get some coffee going and check on Tom."

She sat up, her long hair covering the dark buttons of her bare breasts, and I noticed again how well formed she really was—not one of those thin, fine-boned women like Antonia or Fannie, but of sturdier stock, like a woman who was built for hard and practical work all her life. I hadn't been looking for that in her the night before, her beauty was of its own kind and not of the classical variety.

"Nothing to hold you," she said, "if you *did* want to leave. Certainly not me." It felt awkward talking to a naked woman and me half dressed.

"Never thought of you as the sort of woman to try and hold a man if he didn't want to stay," I said.

"Something struck me as odd, Jim."

"What's that?"

"You never called me by my name—not once."

"Maize," I said.

"That's better," she said with a smile. "It would be nice if you kissed me good morning. Not required, but nice."

"I'm sorry, Maize. I guess I'm acting like a damn dote." I bent and kissed her.

"Thank you," she said, and rose from the bed without trying to hide anything and began to dress and I had a hard time taking my eyes off her because she was so natural about herself and it wasn't every day you saw that in a woman either.

We went out together and Tom was still sitting there holding his arm and looking miserable.

"Which way is your privy?" he said.

"Out back and beyond the hill," she said.

"You need help getting to it?" I said.

"Let me give it a go on my own. I'm not back in an hour, bring a shovel and bury me."

He rose unsteady and walked out barefoot.

"I like him," she said.

"I do too."

"You brothers?"

"No. Just friends."

"I didn't think you were kin. You don't look anything alike. He looks like butter and you look like hard rock."

"If that's meant to be a compliment, thank you," I said. She smiled at that.

We ate breakfast of warm biscuits, honey, slabs of fried ham, hash, hot coffee. Jim didn't eat much

but he ate some. Said he was still feeling tenuous—
tenuous!—from the poison.

"I knew a woman once who killed three of her
husbands by poisoning them," he said. "Now I
know what they must have felt like."

Maize looked amused.

"You think you're up to riding today?" I said.

He shook his head. "I think it would be better if I waited another day." Then he turned and
looked at Maize and said, "If it wouldn't be too
much trouble for you, miss?"

She looked at me with an unsettled smile.

"No, no trouble at all."

Tom said he'd like to sit out in the sun, that he
felt cold in his blood. We took a chair out and
placed it where the sun was best and he sat in it
and closed his eyes and lifted his face and said,
"That feels a lot better."

Maize went inside and I stayed with Tom.

"I'm sorry I'm dragging you down," he said. "I
know you want to get to Coffin Flats and save that
woman."

"Another day isn't going to matter," I said.

"You don't have to wait for me," he said.

"I know I don't."

He closed his eyes again. Parts of his arm were
black and red like overripe fruit, like a plum split
open. He hadn't died, but he could still lose his
arm. I didn't know what was worse for a man, to
die or lose a part of himself. I hoped I'd never have
to face that choice.

I thought I'd give it another day or two and then
if he still wasn't up to going with me I'd go on alone.

I didn't want to abandon him after he'd thrown his lot in with me, but I didn't want to abandon Antonia either. I couldn't even imagine what she might be going through at the hands of Johnny Waco, especially after she'd run off from him a second time. I hoped he wouldn't be son of a bitch enough to break her hands like he had Chalk Bronson's.

There were plenty of worse things I imagined a man like him could think to do to punish her.

I passed the morning currying the horses and splitting large pieces of cottonwood Maize said her brother had sawn and dragged up to the house and left there to cure. Working the ax felt good to my muscles but reminded me too of the broken rib that hadn't healed all the way and still pinched when I didn't swing just right.

The air was pleasant and a man could work up a hell of an appetite in no time at all. Maize worked in her pumpkin patch and I walked out and did some hoeing with her.

"Did you know that Geronimo raised pumpkins?" she said.

"Interesting."

"The Apaches owned all this at one time, Lipans, Chiracahuas."

"Your brother told me all about his old man and Grandpa fighting them for it."

"They killed Grandpa over it. Father found his body in a canyon shot so full of arrows he looked like a porcupine. That's his photograph inside the house."

She wiped her face with the hem of her apron.

"The funny thing is, we got some Indian in us

too, Spence and me, and all us Walkers, going way back. Cherokee, I think."

"I was wondering," I said.

She leaned on her hoe handle.

"Look at all of it," she said. "All this land. You'd think there's enough for everybody to live on, but it doesn't seem there ever is. Seems like folks are always fighting over it, wanting to fence off their portion and keep others off. Even Spence, when it comes down to it. He doesn't want Clancy to cross it with his cattle and Clancy doesn't want us on it with our sheep. And nobody wanted the Indians on it . . ."

I glanced to where Tom was sitting, his head down now, no doubt dozing, his arm lying in his lap like a useless thing.

"I guess it's just something in folks," I said. "To fight over what they believe is theirs—whether it's land or a woman or whatever."

"You ever fight over a woman?" she said.

"No."

"Land?"

"Never owned any."

"I thought not. You don't seem the type to fight over a woman, but let a woman fight over you."

I smiled at that.

"I don't know of any women who's ever fought over me, or if they have I sure never knew about it."

She laughed and I did too.

"And you *sure* don't look the kind who would own something he'd plant his feet in."

"Just never came across anything I thought was worth owning," I said.

We worked till noon and took a break for lunch and then she said, "Spence should have been back by now." There wasn't any real alarm in her voice, but there was a dark thread running through it.

"Maybe he got a bigger drunk on than usual," I said.

"Maybe."

We ate dinner outdoors, our plates resting on our laps, the sun angled straight overhead. Afterward Tom said he was tired and would like to lie down and he went inside the house.

"Want to take a walk with me, Jim?"

We walked down to the waterhole. In the sunlight the water looked green around the edges, darker in the center where it was deepest. We sat on the warm rock and kissed and leaned back and held each other.

"I could get used to this," she said.

I didn't say anything.

"My time's running out, Jim."

"For what?"

"Children."

Again I didn't say anything.

She sat staring into the water and I didn't know what to make about her comment but I had an idea where she might be headed.

"That what you want, children?"

"It's been something on my mind. But without a proper man . . ."

"I wouldn't be him, Maize."

"Oh, of course you wouldn't, Jim."

"I don't even know who I am," I said. "Don't know how I'd be able to let someone else know me enough to trust me with such responsibility.

Kids need someone they can count on. I've never worked steady in my life or stayed too long in one place. It isn't something I plan, just something that has worked out that way."

She smiled.

"It was just a thought that come to me is all," she said. "I didn't mean to imply nothing by it. I'm sorry."

"No need to apologize."

A soft wind wrinkled the water. The few clouds that floated overhead were mirrored in the green surface.

"You want to go for a swim?" I said.

"No, I guess not."

Whatever had been there between us, that feeling two people have when they're new to each other, when there is a mutual hunger, wasn't there any longer. Whatever it was had passed and we both knew it wouldn't come back again, that no words or actions could make it like it was for that brief time.

"Want to just sit here then?" I said.

She nodded.

You could see dusk coming half an hour before it arrived, like purple dust. Maize kept going outside the house and looking toward the north.

"He should have been home before now," she said the last time she came in again, this time with worry in her voice. "He's never been gone this long." Darkness had dropped down all around us.

"Maybe because he knows there are men here he might have seen it as a chance to take a little extra time away," I suggested.

"No," she said. "It's not Spence's way. He's a homebody. Whatever fun he wanted to have, he's had it by now. Something's wrong."

"You want me to go and try and find him?"

She looked at me with eyes that begged the question but she remained silent.

"I'll go," I said.

"I don't want to put you out."

"You've done plenty enough for us."

Tom was sitting there at the table, some of the color back into his face, his swollen arm resting next to his cup, his fingers still fat.

"It's no use going tonight," she said. "If something's happened to him along the way you won't find him in the dark. If he's not home by morning . . ."

"I can leave now."

"No. Maybe he'll come tonight. If not you can go in the morning. If something's happened and he's fallen along the way, you'll be able to spot him."

"You sure you don't want me to go right now?"

She nodded.

We all went to bed early, only this time I slept on the floor by the stove and Maize didn't say anything about it when I suggested it.

But sometime during the night she came and lay next to me and took my arm and put it around her and I pretended that I didn't hear her crying softly.

20

I was already up and saddling my horse when Maize came out of the house carrying a cup of coffee she handed to me. Bunches of gray clouds had gathered off to the north and it looked like they had rain in them, and a cold wind blew loose sand and rolled tumbleweeds across the open places.

I took the coffee from her and sipped it and our eyes met and held for a moment.

"Don't worry," I said. "I'll find him and bring him home."

"I know you will."

She put her hands over mine as I held the cup, an embrace of friendship more than love, it seemed to me. Comforting.

"About yesterday and what happened the night before . . ."

"It was what it was," I said. "I don't regret it and I hope you don't either."

"No," she said. "I don't regret it either, Jim."

I asked her for directions to Clancy's Corners—the direction Spence would have gone, and she gave them to me.

"It's just a place with a whorehouse, a saloon,

small trading post, and a loading pen for the train when it stops," she said. "If he's there you'll be able to find him."

I nodded and drank the rest of the coffee and tightened the cinch and slid my rifle into the scabbard then forked the saddle.

"Tom's better," I said. "He was awake when I checked on him."

"I'll see to him," she said. "And thank you."

"No thanks necessary, Maize. If we aren't anything else, we are at least friends. You and Spence."

She touched my knee and I handed her back the cup then rode off toward the north.

It was about five miles, she said, from their place to Clancy's Corners. I looked for his body along the way, one of his dogs perhaps, anything that might indicate he never made it there, or made it back. I didn't see anything until I saw a few buildings below as I topped a slight rise of loose rock and sand. There were the railroad tracks, a water tower, a large wood pen, and two buildings that looked like hastily thrown together shacks. The place had the look of impermanence, like in a few years it wouldn't be there anymore; that it would all be blown away and forgotten and nobody would remember it ever having been there.

I rode down cautious, not knowing what to expect.

There were several saddle horses tied up out front of one of the buildings. No sign or nothing to indicate what it was. Just some scoured gray boards nailed together under a rusted tin roof. The stock pens were empty, the tracks quiet, their worn steel rails dull in the cloudy light.

I tied off and went in.

Several men, the number matching the number of horses out front, stood at a rough plank board propped on two wood barrels on one side of the room. The opposite side looked like a dry goods—the trading post, I assumed, Maize had spoken of. A man in a plug hat stood behind the plank bar pouring liquor from a bottle into one of the glasses in front of the men. They all looked up when I came in. None of them looked friendly.

I said, "I'm here looking for Spence Walker."

Their eyes fell on me like I'd come to collect taxes.

Nobody said anything. So I repeated myself, something I hated to do.

The man behind the bar in the plug hat had sideburns like tangled wire that came down to his chin. He wore a black eye patch over his right eye.

"Spence Walker, you say?"

I walked up to the bar.

"I'm a friend of his," I said. "You must be Clancy."

He looked at me close with the only eye he had like he was trying to see through water, his eyebrows bunched. He had an odor like something old and sour with a hint of cheap perfume mixed in. His striped shirt was soiled with dark stains all down the front like spilled coffee or tobacco juice.

"That's right," he said. "I'm Clancy and I own everything your eye falls on 'round here and Spence Walker is no friend of mine."

You could feel men tighten their shoulders, shift in their boots. It was like some sort of threat but it wasn't, quite.

"So I heard," I said. "His sister's worried about

him. Sent me to look for him. That's what I'm doing, looking for him."

One side of his mouth curled into a cur-dog smile showing a broken eye tooth, and he poured whiskey in a glass and pushed it forward with the tips of stubbed fingers missing the first joints.

"Have a drink, stranger. On the house this one, but you buy the next."

"I don't drink before breakfast," I said. I could see he wasn't used to being turned down. "But I'll make an exception this time." I tossed the drink back and it was something like you might imagine if you were to drink coal oil.

"Better give me a beer to chase that nasty sumbitch down," I said.

He seemed to enjoy my discomfort and said to one of the men at the bar, "Farge, piss in that empty glass so this man can have himself a warm beer." Then looked at me and added: "Farge here is our beer manufacturer."

Farge was obviously the oaf who took a big glass mug off the bar top and undid himself and took a hearty piss into it then handed to me. I took it and held it aloft, as though to judge its quantity and quality, then swung it in a swift downward arc, smashing it against the side of the oaf's head so hard it rained piss and broken glass all over that dull smiling face. At the same time I was swinging the mug I pulled the pistol from my belt before the oaf fully hit the floor and jabbed the muzzle against Clancy's eye patch before he could finish hooting.

"Now you stupid bastard, tell me where Spence

Walker is or there's going to be a new owner of everything my eye falls upon."

The others in the place shuffled back like I just announced I had the plague.

Clancy jerked his head back so hard his hat fell off but I grabbed him by the front of his shirt so he couldn't go anywhere and cocked the hammer back. The oaf lay out cold on the floor, no doubt dreaming of some past glory he never had, his pecker shrunk back in his trousers like the neck of a turtle.

"He come yesterday and loaded them damn stinking sheep on the train," Clancy said, his eye bulging. "Kellogg paid him then he went and bought him a gal at the Cajun's is all I know."

"Where's the Cajun's?"

"Cross the way there by the water tower."

"I'm leaving now," I said. "Don't try and fool with me or I'll ruin your day. And if I find out different about Spence, that you're lying to me, I'll be back."

I backed out of the place knowing they probably would not *fool* with me. You judge a man by his actions not his talk, and I'd shown them I wasn't about a lot of talk.

The only other building that looked habitable was a small adobe standing in the shadow of the water tower. I was still trying to work that terrible taste out of my mouth from the oily liquor.

I wrapped on a heavy wood door and waited until it opened and a skinny woman who looked like she'd just gotten out of bed stood there in a dingy nightgown.

"We don't do no business before noon," she said. "Come back then."

She started to close the door but I wouldn't let her.

"I'm looking for Spence Walker," I said.

"And I'm looking for a rich husband, honey, and if you find one let me know."

"If Spence is inside, send him out, I want to talk to him."

I heard a masculine voice with a thick accent ask, "Who dat at dey door?"

She turned her head and said, "Some damn cowboy is here looking for Spence."

"Tell him he can go fuck himself."

"He said to go fuck yourself, mister." She seemed to find her relay amusing until I shoved her aside and went in. A consumptive looking man sitting in a chair with a blanket around his shoulders smoking a pipe seemed lost in a cloud of blue smoke. I didn't give him a chance to set the pipe aside but instead slapped it from his skeletal hands.

"I come for Spence and I'm not leaving here without him," I said.

The woman started cursing me, asking what right I had to bust in and lay down threats, and I told her to shut the hell up, and she did when she saw I was serious.

The man looked at me dully as though I were some apparition he couldn't quite believe in, possibly a dead relative or the like.

"Spence?" he said. "Who dey fuck is Spence?"

"Oh, honey, you know Spence," the woman said. "That stinking sheepherder comes around here to plink Carmella."

"Sheep," he cackled. "Carmella? Where dey sheep?" And he looked 'round like a kid at Christmas trying to see where the presents were hid.

The place smelled of sex and worse.

"Come and gone, Spence is," the woman said. "Was here yesterday, bought himself two pokes off Carmella and left."

It didn't sound right, what she was telling me, what everyone in the Crossing had told me so far.

I saw a door and went and threw it open and there was a naked brown woman sleeping facedown on a narrow cot.

"Carmella," the other woman said. "You satisfied? He ain't here."

I went outside again. The wind was blowing hard, throwing sand up against the buildings, rattling the pen rails. The spout on the water tank swung back and forth. The clouds had lowered themselves threateningly. I looked about. Nothing but a spot in the road. Then I saw something small limping way off on the far side of the tracks. A black and white dog. I went to get my horse. Clancy and the others were standing out front of the storefront, some holding drinks, curious to see what I'd do, as though they had all bought tickets to some theater spectacle.

I mounted without acknowledging their presence and rode across the railroad tracks out a couple hundred yards to where I'd seen the limping dog.

I found the dog licking the hand and face of Spence Walker, who looked like someone had tossed him from a moving train. His face and hands were bloody, his clothes torn, one of his dogs lay dead a few feet away. I washed the shepherd's face with canteen water and he opened his eyes and looked at me.

"Spence, it's me, Jim Glass."

"Oh," he said.

I checked to see if he'd been shot anywhere. He hadn't.

"What happened to you?" I said.

He shook his head. "I ain't sure."

"Can you stand?"

"No, Jim, I think something's wrong with my foot."

I looked down and saw his one foot was turned wrong.

"I'll be back," I said, and rested his head down gently again and forked the saddle and rode back toward the Crossing, pulling the rifle from the scabbard as I went.

I don't know what made me say it other than I was pissed off they'd do this to a man then just let him lay there. I knew what it was like to be such a man. When I reined in short of the storefront I said, "I am the Redeemer, the swift sword, the slayer of evil! And you sons a bitches better get that man a horse and whatever money you stole from him and go and bring him here to me, or I'll start killing you where you stand!"

It was like a sudden hard wind knocked them all back on their heels as my horse danced around, my rifle held in my hand. And when they did not move fast enough to suit me, I shot out the only plateglass window in that snakehead whiskey joint and it crashed raining glass.

"Do it, boys!" Clancy himself said. "Jeez Christ, mister, what the fuck is wrong with you?"

I aimed the rifle at him and said, "You're about to find out if you don't do what I tell you."

Several of them took a wagon out and came back with Spence in the back with his dog. Spence looked confused. One of the men untied a saddle horse standing out front and handed me up the reins and those in the wagon lifted Spence onto the horse's back then lifted him up his lame dog and I looked at Clancy and said, "Where the hell's his money for the sheep he sold?"

"He spent it on whores. Go ask the Cajun."

"I will burn this trash heap to the ground and scatter you like the wind."

Clancy reached in his jacket pocket and came out with an uncertain amount of money and handed it to Spence, who took it without question and pocketed it. He'd lost his hat somewhere. It wasn't important. He could buy another one.

"I'll be staying out there awhile, my friend and I, in case you're thinking to seek your own redemption," I said to Clancy. "My friend's name is John Wesley Hardin and mine is Jim Glass and I've murdered almost as many men as he has. We got this running bet going—who can kill more men. So far he's ahead, but I aim to catch up fast. Keep your men at home or you'll be burying them like winter potatoes." It was about the longest speech I ever gave anyone. They took it like kids to medicine.

I spanked the rump of Spence's horse with the barrel of my rifle and waited till he was well started south again, then I followed and didn't bother to look back. I wanted them to think I was invincible, and by God I think they must have thought that because no one tried to follow us.

Tom was sitting in the yard when we rode up, and Maize was hanging fresh washed clothes on a line of wire, shirts, pants, a dress, her underthings.

She cried out when she saw Spence's rough condition. He grinned through the cuts on his face. He had a missing tooth. She helped him out of the saddle.

"I think my ankle's busted," he said.

She noticed the dog limping too when I set it down on the ground.

"Where's Tater?" she said.

Spence shook his head.

"Dead," he said. "That's all I know."

"They killed your dog?"

"I don't know what they did, Maize. I was drunk or doped or something. All I know is I woke up on the ground, my ankle broke, Tater dead next to me, Bo limping around. Then I seen this rider with the sun behind him so I couldn't see who it was. But I knew from the way he rode in here the other day who it was and thank God for him."

"You damn fool," she said.

"I know it," he said.

She helped him limp to the house and I sauntered over to where Tom was sitting.

"How's that arm?" I asked.

"I can almost bend my fingers," he said. "Sounds like you raised a little hell out there."

I looked back the direction I'd come.

"Don't be surprised we get company tonight," I said.

"You think we will?"

"If not tonight then I think they'll leave it alone.

I told them I had John Wesley Hardin out here with me. It might make them think twice."

"You think it will?"

"No."

"I couldn't swat a fly with this hand," he said.

"You're a two-gun man. If they come, kill 'em with your other hand, you need to."

His grin wasn't quite a happy one.

"Trouble is thy name, Jim," he said.

"That's very damn poetic."

"I stay around you much longer, I'll be cussing and acting like a killer."

"You know what I told 'em?"

"What?"

"That I was the Redeemer, the swift sword that would cut them down."

"Maybe that's what you are and you just don't know it. Maybe God has sent you on a mission to redeem the lives of others."

"Ha, now you *are* talking foolish. I don't know why I said it. Just mad as hell is all it was."

You could hear the deep rumble of thunder off to the north where the clouds were bunched. It would come rain soon, and maybe a whole lot more. I couldn't help but believe that a man with one eye and half his fingers missing was not going to be cowed by somebody like me. With men like him, respect and fear was everything. Maybe he'd see what I'd done as a good excuse to wipe out Spence and Maize, and maybe old Jim Glass and John Wesley Hardin too.

— 21 —

From the diary of Maize Walker . . .

October 1, 1885.

Whether I am in love or not with Jim Glass is yet to be known. My heart says one thing, my mind another. He is the closest to any man I've ever known to rousing in me long slumbering feelings. With him, I'd have children and they'd be beautiful and bright. But practically speaking, he is a man I suspect who disdains any thought of settlement. He told me as much.

We swam like fishes. We made love in the water and later in my bed and now it is too soon over. His eyes look to the distance. He is as eager to go wherever it is he is bound as a racehorse is anxious to start the race.

October 2, 1885.

Spence gone to town and not back yet. Unusual. Woke this morning with Jim's side of the bed yet warm. Watched him dress. His

*flesh pale except for his face, neck, hands, and
wrists. Struck me as strange how, till I asked
him, he never spoke my name. Then when he
did, it sounded wonderful coming from his
mouth. I do my best not to let him know how
great an effect he has over me. I think he knows
anyway.*

*He volunteered to go look for Spence
and bring him home. Am worried about my
brother. I am relieved Jim is going. I trust he
will return with Spence in tow.*

*Spent the day in and out of the garden,
Jim helped me with the weeding. We hoe in
the pumpkin patch together. I tell him about
Grandpa, the Indians. It feels natural enough—
like two souls long together.*

*Jim says if Spence is not back by nightfall he
will go look for him in the morning.*

*Outside I hear the sound of ax against
wood. It sounds like my heart being split
apart.*

*Jim chooses to sleep on the kitchen floor.
Already my bed feels empty without him.*

She sits propped up in bed, the shadows and
wavering lamp's light dancing over the page as
she writes. How, she wonders, did she allow herself to hope when long ago she'd given up all such
hope? *Is it worse to hope than not?* Her breasts feel
heavy, swollen from the wanting of his touch. She
is restless without knowing why—a vague feeling
that has plagued her all day.

It is time to stop writing.

She lays down her pen and stoppers the small bottle of ink and closes the diary and sets it under her pillow then turns down the wick until darkness fills the room. She closes her eyes then opens them again, staring into the blackness, then rises and goes out to where he lies near the kitchen stove on a pallet and lies down beside him, her back to his front and reaches around and takes his arm and drapes it over her. And at last she is at peace.

October 3, 1885.

Jim came home with Spence looking like he'd been dragged through the chaparral, all cut & bloody with his ankle hurt. One dog dead, one also hurt. Spence claims he can't remember how he got in such a condition. I wanted to say, "You lay down with whores and drink their whiskey, there is no telling the outcome." But instead did the best I could to repair him.

Jim expresses concern there may come trouble from Clancy and his boys after nightfall. Says we should all be ready. A world full of land and we have to fight over a small patch of it.

I ache to run off with Jim.

22

Dusk brought with it the anticipated rain. Tom sat at the table with his hand resting on a pillow Maize had gotten him. Spence with his foot propped on a chair, the toes purple. The dog lay in the corner, its head between its paws, eyebrows twitching whenever one of them moved or said anything. Maize fretted about getting us all supper, saying that we should eat and moving back and forth between stove and table. I stood at the window until it got too dark to see beyond the curtain of falling rain.

"I'm going to go outside for a while," I said.

I took my hat and rifle and went out and stood under the bit of overhang there at the front door—a small sheet of corrugated tin nailed to the top of two poles just there in front of the door. The rain hammered the tin like small stones. Lightning shook through the bruised sky. The darkness and rain obliterated everything between the flashes of lightning. "Maybe they wouldn't come in this weather," Tom had said earlier, just as it started to rain.

I could see the destruction they'd leave behind.

Four of us dead, the place burnt to a pile of smoldering gray ash that the wind would eventually carry away. In short enough time there would be nothing left to mark our having existed.

Maize came out in a little while.

"You hungry, Jim? Come on in and eat."

"I better keep watch," I said.

She looked into the uneasy darkness. The rain was gathering in puddles near our feet and it looked and sounded at times like the water was boiling up from the ground.

"You think Clancy and his men will come in this?"

"I don't guess the rain will stop them if they're looking for a fight. It wouldn't me."

I saw the look on her face when I said that, the interior light of the house falling softly on her cheeks.

"I can shoot a gun, Jim. I'm a better shot than Spence."

"That's good to know," I said. "You might just have to practice your skill."

She stood close to me and I could smell her washed hair.

"Maybe it's just as well they come," she said. "Maybe we can end the conflict between us one way or the other. It would be better in a way than just waiting all the time for them to come. I am surprised that Clancy didn't kill Spence."

"He wanted to put the last bit of fear in him," I said. "Sometimes there are worse things you can do to a man than killing him."

"Well, if they come tonight he might be sorry he let Spence live."

"You prepared for that? Is he?" I said. "To take lives?"

"It has to end sooner or later."

"I think I'm going over and wait under that tool shed," I said. "It might be better if we can catch them in a cross fire if they come."

"Tell me what to do," she said.

"Get a rifle and put out the lights and stand here in the doorway. Give Spence a gun and set him by the window. Tom will know what to do, even if he has to shoot with his off hand. You hear or see anything coming, strike a match just inside the door so I can see it but they can't. I'll do the same."

"Jim . . ."

I ducked out through the rain before she could say whatever it was she was thinking and made it across to the toolshed and stood in the door frame. The house was close enough I could see its shape even through the curtain of rain. Time would tell. The rain hammered down with fury at times, letting up, then coming hard again. The night sky vibrated with lightning, rumbled with thunder. The sound of the rain was a steady hiss like you'd imagine a roomful of demons would make.

An hour passed, then two.

Suddenly they were there, at the edge of the property. One minute it was just the rain and darkness, then a flash of light from the storm lit them: several men sitting horses near the house. I struck a match and snapped it out. I hoped Maize saw it.

Between the lightning, you couldn't see much of anything. I aimed the rifle at where I'd seen them. Then waited. As soon as the next flash came I fired, jacked lever and fired again. They cut loose soon as

I fired my first round, and so did the others inside the house. I could hear glass breaking. I could see the flashes of their guns and I unloaded into them and when the rifle went empty I pulled my pistol and emptied it too. Then almost as suddenly as it had begun, it stopped, the sound of gunfire dying in the rain. It couldn't have lasted more than a minute, two at the most—the whole fight.

The storm marched off in the distance and with it the lightning. The rest was silence. I waited. All night we waited in silence. Then the rain quit just before dawn, leaving the first morning light to shimmer on the wet dark land.

There were three dead men near the house. Two of them were facedown, their arms spread out and above their heads. The third man lay on his side facing away. I crossed to the house and went inside.

Tom and Spence were there. A trail of blood led from the doorway to the cot they'd laid Maize on. Spence looked defeated.

"They shot her, Jim," Tom said, shaking his head.

Her eyes were partially opened and I bent and touched her cool face and closed her lids. It was like touching two small smooth stones. The bullet had struck her through the breast, leaving a drying flower of blood on her clothes.

Something heavier than anyone could describe was in the room with us. She looked like she'd simply gone to sleep. I took a blanket and pulled it over her. She looked cold and lonely and I wanted to lie beside her and hold her but it was way too late.

"Maybe you could say something," I said to Tom.

He said, "Yes . . . if Spence would like me to." He looked at Spence, who sat there with his head hanging down, his longish brown hair fallen over his face.

"She wasn't a churchgoer," he mumbled. "Neither of us were. No time for God and godly things in this godless land. But I'd be grateful if you said something if you know how."

So Tom spoke softly as though he were confiding in a friend: "Lord, take this woman's spirit into your bosom and let her there reside for all days eternal. In your kingdom she will be an angel, for she is now free of all her earthly bonds, all obligations, all regrets and pain and suffering. Amen."

Spence rubbed his eyes with the heel of his hands and looked up through his lank hair and said, "Those were nice words, Tom. I know she'd have liked them."

I rose and went outside because I didn't want to have to look at Maize in death one more minute. One of her earthly bonds had been me, and I was still tied to her in a way that any man is tied to any woman he's shared intimacy with. And that is not something so easily forgotten.

I took in a deep breath and let it out again. And then walked over to the dead lying in the quickly drying mud, the sun risen now over the mountains, its heat gaining strength.

One by one I turned them over and recognized the first two as being men I'd seen at Clancy's. The third one, the one lying on his side, was Clancy himself. I knew before I turned him over, by the stubbed fingers on the hand that lay twisted back behind him. His mouth was agape as though the bullet had caught him by surprise. I hoped to hell it was Maize's bullet that got him.

Tom helped Spence hobble out and they stood there looking at the dead men.

"Clancy," I said, standing over the body.

"Help me over there," Spence said and leaned on Tom, and when they got to the body of Clancy, Spence spat on him and said, "You son of a bitch."

Tom and me just looked at each other. I understood Spence's grief and anger, and maybe Tom did too.

"I'll dig the graves," I said. "Is there any place special you want me to bury Maize?"

"She liked that swim hole down yonder . . ." He pointed with his chin but I already knew where it was. "Somewhere down there would be nice."

I went down with a shovel and found a spot above where the swim rock was, where you could look down onto the water, and dug a good deep grave then went and got her body and carried it down and buried her as gently as I knew how. I patted the last shovelful of dirt down with my bare hands and smoothed it out and then sat down next to her, my shirt soaked with sweat.

"You'll get to look at your swimming place every day," I said. "And, I'll remember it and you long as I live."

The wind whispered to me and I wanted to believe it was her whispering farewell even if it wasn't.

"You gave me everything, including your life, and I'm sorry Maize Walker. I'm sorry as hell."

I went up and loaded the dead men one by one onto the backs of the three horses—mine and Tom's and Spence's—and walked them all three a good distance out of sight of the house and dug one large grave. It took me a while but I finally got one dug. Maybe not deep enough to keep the coyotes and critters from catching the scent and digging them up eventually, but probably a better grave than the one they would have dug for us if the situation had been reversed.

I dragged them and dropped them in and it was onerous work and I cursed them for their stupidity at having made it so I had to do this. When I finished, I went back to the house and tied off the horses and then went down to the swim hole. I stripped naked and plunged into the cool water and looked up through it at the sunlight filtering through its greenness. I felt as though I could simply stay down under it the rest of my life and did not surface until my lungs were burning for lack of air.

I tried washing away the stink of death but it did not want to wash away completely. Tom was sitting on the warm rock when I surfaced.

"I feel terrible about what's happened," he said after I climbed out and dried myself and began to dress.

"So do I, but there's not a hell of a lot we can do about it. Everybody who is responsible for this is already dead."

"Bad karma," he said, shaking his head. He sat with his legs drawn up, his forearms resting on his knees.

"So you mentioned once before."

Dressed now, I sat down next to him and we stared at the water and not at Maize's fresh dug grave.

"Were you in love with her?" he said.

I thought about it for a long moment.

"No, I don't believe I was. I liked her and maybe even loved her, but I wasn't *in* love with her."

"She told me something while you went to look for Spence," he said. "I am not sure I should even tell you, for it is not going to matter now. But I think it is the *right* thing I should say it."

I sat listening.

"She said she was sure she was pregnant with your child. I just thought you should know what she was thinking, what she was feeling."

I listened to the silence of the water, the quietness of sky. I wanted to tell Tom it wasn't possible for her to know such a thing with any certainty. But then a question pressed into my denial: *What if?* It was something I didn't want to consider. It felt like I'd swallowed a stone. *What happens to the dead? What happens to the person we were when the body dies? What happens to that thing inside us that causes us to love, to hope, to feel anguish that has nothing to do with the body?*

"We need to move on soon as possible," I said. "If you still want to go, that is."

"I've given it some thought," he said.

"Well," I said, standing and brushing off the seat of my jeans. "You don't owe me anything, Tom. If anybody owes anybody it's me that owes you."

"I guess nobody is indebted to anyone here, we've all paid our debts in full."

"I'm going to walk back up to the house."

I saw him stand and look off to where I'd dug Maize's grave, the large rock I'd found for a headstone.

"You picked a good place for her, Jim."

"I think so too."

He said, "I'll walk back up to the house with you."

And the late afternoon light threw our shadows long across the rock, shadows that seemed to follow us sadly.

23

We started early, Tom and me, the light without the sun in it shadowy and unkempt. Tom wore his arm in a homemade sling now and could close his hand about halfway. He still couldn't grip one of his two guns. We rode steady for most of the day, the loose caliche shifting under the horses' hooves. Riding toward the rising sun, a blaze of red lifted over the lip of the earth.

We arrived in Coffin Flats the second evening.

"I want to look in on Chalk Bronson," I said. "But we ought to find you a doctor to take a look at your arm."

"You go ahead and I'll go look for a physician," he said.

"We can meet up later at the Bison—that saloon yonder," I said, pointing out the Bison Club.

He nodded. "Might be a good place to ask where the doc is," he said.

"I'll meet you there in half an hour."

I rode on down to Chalk's place, dismounted and slapped the dirt out of my clothes best I could with my Stetson before knocking.

His wife answered the door and looked at me for a long moment, then said, "Oh, it's you. Come in."

Chalk was sitting at the table with a book open in the glow of a lamp. His hands were still bandaged, but the rest of him was looking normal again, the cuts on his face now like black marks someone had drawn there with a small paintbrush.

He looked at me as though he expected to see Antonia.

"What are you doing back here?" he said.

"I wonder if we might have a private talk."

He looked at his wife.

"Go ahead and say what you have to, Nora knows everything."

"Can I get you some coffee?" she said.

"Yes, that would be nice."

I sat down across from him, the book's pages falling back from where he had it opened.

"It's about all I can do these days, read," he said. "Forgot how much I used to enjoy it."

His wife set a cup of coffee down in front of me. "You take sugar with it?" she asked.

"No ma'am."

She took a seat next to Chalk. You could see how much she loved him.

"We got off the train in Refugio," I said. "The next morning the local law came and arrested us." I saw the worry come into his face.

"For what reason?"

"Because the lawman there happens to be a cousin or some such to Johnny Waco."

Chalk nodded. "He telegraphed ahead."

"Yeah."

"What about Antonia?"

"They took her. Escorted her back to Waco's. I think that's where she is now, with him."

"So it all went for nothing?"

"Yeah, pretty much."

"They just let you go?"

"In a manner of speaking," I said. "But not without a proper sendoff."

"Can you pour us something a little stronger than the coffee, love?" he said to her.

She rose from the table and went to a cupboard and got down a bottle of liquor and three glasses. He looked at her when she poured some in all three.

"Nora, when did you start drinking?" he said.

"I guess when you decided to go save your ex-wife and get yourself near killed for your trouble," she told him.

We all three drank down what she'd poured. I don't know it made any of us feel any better, but it probably didn't make us feel worse.

"Now what?" he said.

"I'm going to go get her."

"Let it go, Jim. You did what you could, it didn't work out. Next time he'll kill you."

"You know, Chalk, I would do that very thing, just let it go. Except I can't. It's just not in me to do so."

"I can't help you no more, Jim. I can't help Antonia no more. I've got Nora to think about. And these hands of mine ain't never going to heal right and I don't know if I'll ever be able to use them for anything. I already paid all the price I can afford."

He looked broken in more than just his hands.

"I'm not asking you to do anything more," I said. "I just came to see how you were making out."

She poured us another glass each of the liquor and we sat and drank like three old friends even though we didn't know very much about each other except we were all bonded by the same thing: injustice.

"All I ever wanted in life was just to be a footloose puncher," I said to neither of them in particular. "And I was fairly well content with my life till all this happened. I'd like for things to go back to what they were, and maybe they will eventually . . ."

"Some things happen that change us forever, Jim," he said, looking down at his hands.

"You're right, they do," I said, and stood. "Take care of yourself, Chalk."

"You as well, Jim."

His wife looked at me as though she was glad I was leaving. I didn't blame her.

The night air breathed a cool wind and I walked over to the Bison and went inside where men tended to their needs and commiserated with their own brand of misery, lives not all lived in the way they'd hoped, just as my own wasn't lived in a way I'd once dreamt of. They stood along the bar and gathered around the few tables. Bill was there at his usual spot behind the bar. I did not yet see Tom.

I walked to the bar and took up residence near the far end and Bill came down and said, "I never thought I'd see you 'round these parts again. I heard you ran off with Johnny Waco's woman, stole her after you delivered her up there from Pink's hog farm . . ."

"You just here to ask questions or do you still sell beer in this place?" I said, ignoring the comment.

He moved down and pulled a tap till he filled a beer glass then walked it back and set it in front of me. "Takes some balls to show back up around here." It was a caution not a threat. "They'll be looking for you they hear you're back in town."

"I'm supposed to meet a friend of mine here, fellow with his arm in a sling. You seen him?"

"He was in a little while ago looking for a doc. I sent him over to Doc Flax's place."

I drank my beer and watched four men at a table playing poker, listened to them grouse and tell jokes and lose money and win it. They were playing for low stakes, no more than a fifty cent limit. They weren't the sort of men who would play for big money, just cattlemen and punchers looking to lose themselves from wives who were waiting home, or to avoid empty cots in a bunkhouse somewhere.

I paid for my beer and told Bill that if my friend returned to tell him to wait for me and walked out again into the black night and looked to the far side of the tracks were a few lanterns were hung in the doorways and windows. A locomotive stood on the tracks, behind it a line of passenger cars, quiet and dark as a dead beast waiting the morning run.

I walked across the dead line and reached Pink's place. Inside I could hear a man's laughter, and then a woman's. I knocked on the door and Lorri answered.

"Well, my my," she said with a smile. I could

see she was a little drunk. A fancy dude was sitting there on the horsehair divan across from the pimp, Pink Huston. They were passing a crystal decanter of what looked like some expensive whiskey back and forth.

Pink looked toward the door and said, "Who is it?"

"An old friend of ours," Lorri said and stepped back to let me in.

"The pugilist," he said. It sounded more like a cuss word than a compliment. "You bring Antonia back to me?"

The other man had thin graying hair combed over from a part just above his left ear. His face was red. His shoes were soft and black and polished. He was heavy as a grass fed heifer.

"I'd come to see if she maybe had made her way back here to you," I said.

"Can I get you something, cowboy?" Lorri said. She was standing with her back to Pink and I could see the look in her eyes held the promise of more than just a drink if I wanted it and was willing to play a game of deception.

"I just came to see about Antonia," I said. It gave me a little satisfaction to say that to her, as though she and I were playing a game that only the two of us knew the rules to.

"Oh, is that all?"

"She ain't here, and the way I see it, you owe me for her services unrendered," Pink said. He started to stand, I guess to make himself look tough in front of his friend, maybe in front of Lorri too.

"You a slaver?" I said.

That stopped him short, that and the fact he'd

had too much to drink and was unsteady. He fell back down.

"Slaver?"

"The last I heard people were free to go where they wanted. Unless of course you're a slaver, which would make you something illegal."

The other man was eyeing me with mild curiosity, maybe waiting for something bad to happen between me and Pink, a bloodletting perhaps.

"T'fuck ya want here! Git him the hell out," Pink shouted at Lorri.

She took me by the elbow and guided me to the door, stepped outside with me, pulling her red silken robe tight to her against the cool night air.

"Why don't you come back later, after Pink's passed out. No sense in all of us having a lousy night," she said.

"You know, if it were a different time and I was in a different mood, I'd probably take you up on that offer," I said. She reached down and took my hand and placed it inside the robe.

"You sure about that?" she said.

She was warm and soft and round where my hand touched, like a dream you want to fall into on a cold night. I let it linger there for a second then withdrew it.

"Oh, that it were so simple," I said, and turned and walked away.

"Oh, but it is," I heard her say.

I walked back up to the Bison and Tom was there. Standing alone, looking out of place.

"How'd you make out at the doc's?" I said.

He looked down at his arm.

"He said I was on the mend and there wasn't

much more he could do for me than what had already been done. He gave me these pills . . ." He reached in his pocket and took out a small envelope. "For the pain. I took one and now I'm feeling sort of okay."

"Cocaine pills," I said.

"Really?"

"They'll do the trick."

"So I'm finding out. How about you, you see your friend?"

"Yeah."

I ordered us a beer then said, "You drink beer, don't you?"

"Sure, why not? I'm a two-gun killer and a doper now. What harm's a little glass of beer?"

We drank slowly.

"What's your plan?" he said. "You got one yet?"

"I'm working on it."

He flexed the fingers on his bad hand.

"They don't hurt so bad," he said. "Nothing does."

"That's why people like those pills," I said.

We sipped our beer.

I didn't notice the four punchers that came in until Bill eased down to our end of the bar and said, "Those boys that just came in—down the other end of the bar—those are some of Waco's boys."

They were hard-looking men in long coats and chaps with their hat brims set down low over their eyes, and they stood at the end of the bar without talking, just drinking their beer.

"They see you here they'll run back and tell Johnny and he'll come with even more of 'em and probably tie you to a horse and drag you till you're nothing but raw meat and rags."

"When'd you start to worry about guys like me?" I said.

"Ain't you I'm worried for, I just don't want my place tore up he finds you here."

I looked at Tom and he looked at me.

"They look like working boys to me," I said.

"Waco pays 'em regular if that's what you mean," Bill said. "But he pays 'em for whatever he wants done and not just running his cows and mending fence."

"Yeah, well, I guess we'll have to see," I said.

Tom slipped his revolver out with his good hand and held it just inside his duster and said, "Go ahead, I'm right behind you."

He followed me down to where they stood drinking and I said, "You're off Johnny Waco's outfit?"

They turned their heads to look at me and Tom.

"I'm not looking for a fight with you boys," I said. "I just wanted to know if he got his wife back all right."

The one, a knotty fellow you could see had some bulk to him, gave me a hard stare.

"What business would that be of yours?"

Before I could answer him another one, a tall hook-nosed, sandy-haired puncher said, "That's the old boy was with Chalk that day, you remember, Hank?"

The knotty one rubbed his chin.

A smile parted his rough beard.

"I'm a mother's son," he said. "You run off with ol' John's woman then bring your sorry ass back here. Mister, you must have a death wish."

"No," I said. "I just came back to see if she got home again safe and sound."

"Goddamn," another one said. "You believing this?"

They all four grew grins.

"Maybe we ought to truss him up and take him back with us as a early Christmas present. Ol' John would probably put something extra in our stockings."

They were laughing but you could feel the tension.

"It's just a simple question," I said. "Is she out there with him now?"

The knotty one shoved me away suddenly, nearly causing me to lose my balance, which only added to their perverse humor.

"Tell you what," he said. "Git on your goddamn nag and ride clear out of the territory and we'll forget we even seen you. And take that lame arm sissy standing there with you."

"Yeah, you're probably right," I said. "I should do that."

Then I hit him so hard I couldn't tell for a moment whether it was my hand that shattered or his skull. And when the other three started to make their play, Tom brought out his gun and said, "I got enough pills in this to give you two each. Sleeping pills, and death is a long sleep. My friend asked you a civil question and he'd like an answer."

They looked from the barrel of Tom's fancy pistol down to their friend who lay cold as stone at their feet. His head had struck a spittoon and turned it over onto himself so that along with the blood there was the stain of tobacco juice and old chewed plugs and wet cigar stubs.

"She's out there," the hook nose said. "I don't see where that's no business of your'n."

I stepped over the one I hit and said to the three, "You boys don't know how close you come to dying tonight. That one there," I nodded toward Tom, "is John Wesley Hardin, and most generally when he pulls his piece somebody ends up dusted." I don't know if they believed one damn word but at this point Tom and me had gotten the upper hand on them and the answer I'd wanted and that was enough.

We watched them pick up their smashed friend and carry him by the arms out the door, presumably on their way back to Johnny Waco's to tell their tale, which was exactly what I wanted. If I knew anything at all about Antonia, she was a woman who could read a plan even if it wasn't completely spelled out for her.

We walked out after the punchers rode off and stood there in the night air.

Tom said, "You're going to get me killed, aren't you?"

"I'm going to try my best not to. That's why this is where we part company, my friend."

"You're going to try and do this alone?"

"Look, two against all them or one against all them, it isn't going to matter. We're too few in number, me and you, Tom. Even if you *were* John Wesley Hardin it wouldn't matter. Waco will send as many men as he needs to. I can't outfight them all and I don't plan to. People don't live as long as we do because we're tough, we live as long as we do because we're just a tad smarter than the other guy. At least I'd like to believe that."

"Okay," he said.

"Let's get us some rooms and then you head out first thing tomorrow in case they come early."

He nodded. Somewhere a dog barked. Somebody laughed from inside the saloon. Lights from across the tracks beckoned the lonely. The town was heading toward sleep.

24

She held the bottle of mercury in her hands, the one she'd gotten Pedro to get her the last time he'd gone to town. For days she'd been struggling with the decision: life, or death?

Maria, had, if anything, become more cruel toward her, had chided her at every opportunity, and she'd had no will to fight back. The only one who showed her the least bit of kindness was the old man, Maria's henpecked husband, Pedro.

On the day she'd asked him to buy her the mercury, he'd been grooming one of Johnny Waco's favorite horses, a tall roan with a coat like polished mahogany.

She could tell that Pedro felt a kinship to the animals, for he spoke to them lovingly whenever he groomed them.

When she pressed the money into his hand and asked him to buy her the mercury, he tried to refuse.

"*Por favor, no pida el de mí,* missus."

"You're the only one I can ask such a favor of, Pedro."

He acted at first as if he hadn't heard her, ran

his brush down over the haunches of the big horse until she stopped him by touching his wrist.

"Please," she said.

He nodded finally and took the money and had brought the bottle under his serape when he returned from town and gave it to her with the saddest eyes.

"What will you do with it?" he asked her, though he was pretty sure he already knew, for he'd seen a prostitute in Nogales drink it when he was a young border outlaw, before he took a bullet to the hip and gave up his wild ways. In death her lips and flesh were as blue as winter ice.

"*Está de ninguna consecuencia,*" she said. It's of no consequence.

He crossed himself, though he was no longer sure if God paid any attention to him because of all the bad things he'd done in his youth. And he was sure that as part of his punishment, God had given him Maria, who, among her other distasteful actions, had lately taken to sneaking up to the *jefe's* house late at night. His Maria had turned him into something less than a man. It was only the *jefe's* wife, Antonia, who treated him with respect. But he knew he had to be careful and not show her too much attention or deference, or Señor Waco would do to him what he'd done to the gringo lawman.

Still, he liked her and was willing to take some risk, just as he had done when she'd asked him to get her a gun the last time she ran away. It was a pity to see her brought back by an armed man and handed over once more to Señor Waco; if anything, Antonia looked even more pitiful and sad than she had before she ran away.

Every night in their bed, when she had not snuck off to the big house, his wife complained to him about Antonia. "That woman!" she called her. "She's no good for Mr. Waco," she would say. "He needs a good woman, not some *puta* who will run off the minute he turns his back."

He told her to hush her harsh talk, which only incited her all the more. He had come to conclude there was no use arguing with his wife, that he had no more power over her than he had over anything else. His time had come and gone with the coming and going of his youth. Old age had left him a man simply waiting for the end to come and to take him to whatever heaven or hell awaited men like him. He had thought when he married such a younger woman it would somehow return to him at least a little of his youth, but instead it had done the opposite, made him feel even older and more useless.

It gave him a good feeling to help the woman, even if it *was* to kill herself, he thought when he'd handed over the bottle of mercury. At least he would help her escape whatever misery she was in. *Such beauty, such a waste. If only I were a young bandit again, I would steal her away for myself.*

She heard the commotion downstairs and went to the door and listened. Some of Johnny's hands had come in talking loud, telling him, "That fellow was with Chalk that day—the one who stole your wife, Mr. Waco—well, we by God run into him at the Bison Club. He was in there bold as brass."

Another of them said, "He hit Rolle straight in the mouth, knocked him cold as the bottom of a well. Show him where your tooth is missing, Rolle."

Her heart raced a little. *Was it even possible Jim had come back for her?*

"He had to know we'd come tell you, Mr. Waco. You know if we'd been armed we'd taken care o' him for you, don't you, Mr. Waco?"

"You get some of the boys, a dozen or so, and have them ready to leave here first light. Tell them I want them armed, pistols and rifles."

"Yes sir," they said. She heard them shuffle out and went to the window and saw their shadows crossing the ground toward the bunkhouse.

She heard him call her name.

"Antonia!"

She did not answer. She heard his heavy steps ascending the stairs.

"Antonia," he said again as he approached her closed door. She slipped the bottle of mercury under a satin-covered pillow there on her bed.

He opened the door and stood there.

"I guess you heard," he said.

She feigned ignorance.

"He's back and I aim to kill him. I'm tired of this goddamn business."

She looked at him without trying to hide her hatred.

"If I have to kill every man in the territory who would have you or who you'd go off with, then that is what I'll do. And if need be, I'll kill you as well."

She pulled at the bodice of her dress so that her flesh was exposed, the upper swell of her breasts.

"Shoot me right here—through my heart," she said. "Why not do it and end it and go and live with that Mexican wench and then you both can be as miserable as I've been."

He took one step into the room. She remained defiant.

"Do it, John."

He turned suddenly and left, closing the door behind him.

She quickly went to the window and saw the lights still on in the small adobe—Pedro and Maria's quarters just off the west corner of the house. She stood watching until the door opened and Maria emerged and then closed the door behind her, then watched as she went around back of the main house. Satisfied that Maria and Johnny would be occupied for some little while there at the back of the house in one of the spare rooms, she then slipped down the front stairs, pausing only long enough to take money from the safe and to write something on a piece of paper that she wrapped the money in, then went down to the adobe.

Pedro had a rope in his hand he'd been weaving.

"I need you to go and find the man named Jim Glass and tell him to meet me at the grove as soon as he can come."

"No, señora, I cannot go. Señor Waco will fire me, or worse . . ."

"*El consiste en allí coger a su esposa, Pedro*—your wife and Señor Waco, right this moment."

The old man dropped his eyes in shame.

"I know what they are doing, señora."

"Take a horse and this money and go home," she said. "After you've found Mr. Glass, go back to your home in Mexico."

He looked at it. She'd never seen such sorrow in a man's face.

"Take his best horse and the saddle," she said.

"This is a bill of sale for it. No one will question you as the owner."

He looked on the verge of tears.

"I will do it," he said, "if you do something for me."

"Anything."

"Let me kiss you."

She saw in his eyes that it wasn't so much desire as it was loneliness and drew his face to hers with both hands and gently kissed him on the mouth.

"It is enough," he said when she pulled back. "*Gracias* . . ."

"Hurry," she said.

"Maria will tell Mr. Waco that I've gone as soon as she returns and finds me missing."

"Write her a quick note telling her that your heart is broken because she is being unfaithful to you and that you can't take it anymore and that you are going home to Mexico. They will believe it."

He smiled. "You're very devious for someone so young," he said.

"I'm a woman," she said. "All women are devious." It was of course a veiled reference to his own wife and he knew it and smiled sadly.

"Sí, all women are so."

She hurried back to her room and stood by the window and watched until she saw him come out of the adobe again and head for the corral. Then she saw the shadow of him astride the horse, the glint of silver from the saddle in the moonlight, and smiled. In a short time, she told herself, she would be free—one way or the other—and set about making her plan of escape.

And as Pedro rode away to the town on his good horse and fancy saddle, his pocket full of more money than he'd seen since a bank he'd robbed near Paso Robles and his old revolver stuck down in his belt, he felt again vital—like in the old days—and once more felt the wind against his face and the blood of a bandit rushing through his veins.

25

I was already awake and dressed when the knock on my door came. The light outside was still struggling against the fading darkness—dawn against night. I opened it and found an old man standing there—Mexican under a big frayed sombrero, face as cracked and brown as old leather. His shirt was buttoned at the throat and his eyes held secrets I'd not want to know about. His ears stuck out like jug handles.

"Señor Glass?"

"Yes."

"She say to meet her in the grove soon as you can."

"Antonia?"

He nodded. "Sí."

"That's what she told you?"

He nodded. "You better hurry. Señor Waco is coming soon to get you."

"How many men?"

He shrugged. "Many," he said. "More than you."

I considered for a moment it was a setup. But looking into that ancient face, I didn't see anything dishonest, just a face that had seen its share of troubles and hardship.

"What's your name?" I said.

"Pedro Montero," he said proudly. "I used to be a pretty bad hombre in my day." Then he grinned a mouthful of butternut yellow teeth and I didn't have any reason not to believe him.

"You know they might kill you for telling me these things," I said.

"Shit," he said. "They'll have to catch me first . . ." Then he turned and walked stiffly down the hall then down the stairs. I went to the window and looked down onto the street and saw him mount a good-looking animal with a saddle that had silver ingots inlaid in the pommel and wondered how a broke-down old Mexican could afford such finery. But then, like he said, he used to be a pretty tough hombre in the old days, and maybe he still was.

I pulled on my coat and hat and went down and out the front door and down the street to the livery where I'd boarded my horse. I gave the man three dollars for its keep and asked him to saddle it for me. I knew if Waco and his boys were coming, he was already on his way. I'd have to find a different route out to the ranch in order to avoid passing them on the road. I walked up to Chalk's place and knocked on the door and this time it was Chalk himself who answered even with his damaged hands.

"I'm learning to do things I used to take for granted," he said, standing there. "Like opening the damn door."

I told him the situation.

"They might burn the town," he said.

"No, I don't think so. Some old Mexican brought

me a message from Antonia. I'm to meet her in the grove again."

"You sure he's not setting you up?"

"Could be, but the old man seemed honest enough."

"Pedro," he said. "He's worked for Waco long as I can remember."

"I think he was doing her bidding."

"I can't help you, Jim. You're smart, you'll ride away from this and not look back."

"Tell me if there is a different way I can reach the ranch other than the road."

"You could swing wide west, go up through Dead Horse Canyon then cross Bitch Creek and come into the ranch from the north."

He called his wife and told her to draw a map as he gave her instructions. She didn't seem very happy I had returned but set at the table and drew the map as he described it on the back of a piece of butcher's paper and gave it to me.

"Thanks," I said. "I might not ever see you again, Chalk. Either Antonia and I will get away or they'll kill us both."

"You take care," he said. "I wish there was more I could do."

I went back down the street to the livery and Tom was there with his horse saddled.

"You heading out too?" I said.

He nodded.

"Good luck to you, Tom." I held out my hand.

"I guess I'm not ready yet to quit," he said.

"Quit what?"

"Whatever it was we were doing before."

"We weren't doing anything before."

"Yes, we had set out to save the woman," he said. "That's what it was."

"You don't want to go no farther with me, Tom. This is getting into some serious business. Waco and his men are on their way here now."

"Then we better get going," he said.

"No."

"I can't believe you're going to argue with John Wesley Hardin," he said. "Why I've shot men for less."

I shook my head and mounted up and rode off in the direction Chalk had said but Tom wouldn't quit following me and after a time I just let it go. If he aimed to get himself killed, there wasn't anything I could do about it.

We reached the canyon about noon and rode down into it and the red rock walls rose on both sides of us a good hundred feet or so and the echoes of our horse's iron shoes rang off the loose rock in a way that sounded like there were more than just two of us.

"Beautiful, isn't it?" Tom said, looking up at the walls. "Reminds us of what small and sometimes insignificant creatures we humans are . . ."

I didn't say anything; for me, it wasn't an adventure or some sort of picnic we were on and the beauty of the land had to it an unforgiving nature and could be just as cruel as any human as far as I was concerned. I felt closed in and kept wondering if Waco and his men had for some reason decided to come into Coffin Flats this same route instead of the road. But then, why would they? I didn't know, but it was in my mind a possibility. And if we encountered them in the canyon, me and Tom wouldn't stand any more chance than a block of ice in hell.

We came out of the canyon just as the sun was setting low, and there ahead of us, twinkling with that last bit of sun, was what had to be Bitch Creek, the sun on it causing it to light like it was on fire.

We crossed it and as the water came up to our stirrups I told Tom to hold his feet high unless he wanted wet boots and he said, "I'm already there," and we rode on across like that, our feet high.

Once on the far side, we let the horses have a blow and chewed on some jerky.

"What's the plan when we find her?" Tom said.

"To get the hell out of the country as quick as we can and leave as few tracks as possible."

"Which direction?"

"Texas, I'm thinking. The Panhandle possibly. Big country, easy enough to get lost in it."

He nodded.

We tightened the cinches and got on board and rode on swinging slightly northeast this time, calculating we were already on the ranchland and just needed to locate the grove.

Dusk drew in around us like a curtain of purple. We found ourselves sitting atop a bluff looking down to some distant lights winking in a wide valley.

"That's it," I said. "That's Johnny Waco's place."

"So while we're here looking for his wife, he's in Coffin Flats looking for you?"

"From what the old man said, yes."

"Where exactly are we supposed to hook up with her, and how?"

"She'll meet us in a grove beyond those hills," I said.

"I think the Spanish word is *bosque*," he said.

"There anything you don't know?"

"Plenty, and I'm still learning."

"Well, let's go see if we can find that *bosque* in the dark then."

"Let's."

Once I got my bearings straight we eventually saw the shadows of the grove standing against the night sky. We drew reins and I gave a sharp whistle. We sat there listening. Finally we heard the footfall of a horse.

"Jim?"

"Over here," I called.

She came toward us slowly. Having a full moon helped matters. We heeled our mounts to meet her.

"Who's this?" she asked when we drew up together.

"His name is Tom, he's a friend."

"Tom Twist, ma'am."

"Johnny rode out with a dozen or so men this morning," she said. "He's looking for you in Coffin Flats."

"I know."

"I wasn't sure if Pedro would find you or just keep riding."

"He found me."

"Thank God."

"You set to go?" I said.

"Ready."

"I'm thinking we'll make a run for the border—

Texas. I still got some old contacts over there I can trust. It's a good place to get lost in."

It was then that a voice shouted.

"Don't move or we'll cut you down like grass."

We whirled our animals around and saw them there astride their horses in a moonlit meadow maybe a hundred yards away.

"Ride into those woods," I said, and slapped her horse, and me and Tom were right behind her. Gunfire erupted and you could hear the whine of bullets as they went past our heads, could hear them snapping limbs and busting against the trunks of the trees.

Tom's horse got shot from under him and I raced up fast and offered him my hand and he took it with his good hand and swung up behind me. I heard him groan as he did. We got just to the edge of the woods and my horse got shot and we both went tumbling.

Antonia's scream cut through the racket of gunfire. I pulled Tom to his feet and we found her just inside the woods trying to control her frightened animal. I told her to dismount and took the reins and forced the animal to the ground using a technique an old vaquero once taught me.

"He knew I'd come here," she said breathlessly.

"You hurt?" I asked.

"No. A bullet passed right through my blouse and I thought I'd been shot. But I'm not."

"Tom, what about you?" I said. The bullets came in through the woods like angry hornets.

"I think I broke my arm in the fall," he said through gritted teeth.

"Which one?"

"Guess."

"That arm is a curse," I said. "You might be better just cutting it off."

"I'm beginning to think so."

"How about we do some firing back," I said.

"I dropped my guns," Tom said, reaching around for them.

My own rifle was still in its scabbard.

"You two wait here," I said and began to crawl back out again, feeling along the ground as I went. I found one of Tom's pistols and grabbed it and stuck it in my belt then crawled on till I got to my own shot horse and jerked the Winchester free of the scabbard and began to lay down a field of fire at the muzzle flashes coming from Waco's men. They looked like large fireflies in the darkness. Knowing they'd quickly pick up where I was firing from, I crawled back into the woods.

"We can't stay here forever," I said.

"You two go," Antonia said. "He wants me. I'll go to him."

"No," I said.

"It's the only way you and your friend stand a chance."

"I think he's pissed off enough to kill us no matter what you do."

"Maybe, but he'll surely kill you if you don't run."

The gunfire stopped suddenly. We all took a deep breath.

"What's he planning?" Tom said.

"Who knows?"

"I'll give you about five minutes to come out—then I'll set those woods afire with you in them."

Antonia said it was Waco shouting the command.

Before I could stop her, she cried, "I'll come to you, Johnny, if you let them go!"

"Sure," he called back. "Why wouldn't I? What the hell I want with them?"

"Even I know a damn lie when I hear one," Tom said quietly.

"You glad you came now?" I said.

He didn't say anything.

"This is stupid," she said. "I won't let you die because of me."

"You two take out of here on your horse," I said to them. "I'll hold them off long as I can."

"No," she said.

"Tom don't deserve this," I said. "Neither do you. Get the hell out of here while the getting's to be had."

Tom said he wouldn't go either.

"Goddamn it, go!"

"What difference will it make?" she said. "He'll just find us and kill us anyway."

"He can't track you in the dark and by morning maybe you'll have found a place to hide. Take Tom and get in the wind."

Tom refused to go until I cocked the hammer of my pistol and put it against his head. "Either they'll kill you or I will," I said. "Get the fuck out of here, both of you!"

They got the horse to its feet and mounted double and I laid down more fire to hide the sound of their leaving and Waco's boys returned my fire with equal measure and I figured this was it—this was how I was going to die—just like those soldiers in the old battles when I was nothing more than a snotnose kid in a bad war—shot or burned to death, or both, in a wood without any name.

I emptied my guns then settled in and waited.
Something calm came over me.

I stopped fearing death altogether in those next few moments.

I could hear them coming.

— 26 —

They rode swiftly through the night of moonlit landscape. Tom could see the shape of things and it was like riding through a dream as he clung with his good arm around the woman's waist. She was a skilled rider. They rode wordlessly and there was just the sound of the horse's labored breathing, the ring of its shoes on rock and the thud of them in the soft soil, the creak of saddle leather, the whisper of wind.

They rode until the woman pulled reins and said they needed to give the horse a rest, then stood together in the moonlight looking back at the direction they'd come from. They stood quietly and listened, thinking they'd hear the rumble of other riders pursuing them. But there was just the great empty silence.

"We shouldn't have left him," Tom said softly.

"It's what he wanted," she said. "You must be good friends . . ."

"No," Tom said. "We hardly know each other."

The night air was cool against their skin and she buttoned her coat around her and he said, "Are you all right?"

"Yes, I think so."

"May I ask what it was between you that made him so determined to find you?" Tom said.

She shrugged. "Nothing," she said. "Money? I don't know what else it could be. Maybe he's just one of those damn fool men who once they take on a job want to see it through."

The horse cropped bunch grass. It was like they were two lovers out for a midnight ride.

The moon stood balanced on the jagged teeth of a mountain range.

"Hunter's moon," he said, looking at it.

They mounted again and this time she rode the horse at a trot rather than a gallop, trying to preserve its stamina.

"I know of a cave not far from here," she said. He could feel the strands of her hair against his face; they were like silk threads.

The cave was covered in brush at the foot of a smooth rock wall that had been carved and shaped by a million years of wind and rain, the same rock he'd seen earlier in the day in the canyon, beautiful if foreboding.

He helped her clear away the brush enough so they could enter and bring the horse in with them.

"We'll need a fire," she said, and together they gathered some of the brush that lay along the slope of the ground leading to the cave and dragged it inside then recovered the entrance once they'd got a fire started. The floor of the cave was sand with scattered small rocks and clay chips she said were from the days when the ancient people lived in this cave. "It's shards of their pots and dishes," she said.

"I know," he said.

"You've been in these caves before?"

"No. But I have read about these people."

She unsaddled the horse and it stood out of the fire's light, sleeping on its feet, weary from the weight of two riders, the pace.

The light danced along the cave's ceiling, which was several feet taller than Tom when he stood.

"I brought a little food," she said, reaching into the saddlebags she'd placed next to the saddle. She retrieved a large wedge of cheese and some crackers, a bottle of whiskey and one of wine. He took notice.

"How's your arm?" she said.

"I'd just as soon I didn't own it."

They ate measuredly, taking small bits of the cheese and crackers. She said, "Do you prefer wine or the harder stuff?"

"Wine," he said.

She handed the bottle to him and he watched as she took the cork from the whiskey and tipped it to her mouth. She did not drink indelicately, but he thought she was someone who wasn't tasting whiskey for the first time. He noticed too the way her hands shook.

"What causes that?" he said.

"Causes what?"

"Your hands to shake the way they are."

She looked at them then took another drink of the whiskey.

"I'm just cold," she said.

"Not some other reason, afraid maybe?"

"No," she said. "Just cold."

Later she lay with the saddle blanket over her, her head resting on the saddle, the bottle cradled in the crook of her arm; she'd drank nearly half. He knew then what caused her hands to shake.

He sat with his knees pulled up, feeding the fire when it needed it. Inside the cave it was pure silence except for the sound of water dripping somewhere deeper, a rhythmic steady sound. He did his best to ease the pain of his broken arm; he didn't think it was broken badly, a small bone somewhere in the forearm, he guessed it to be. Just added misery to the healing snakebite. He closed his eyes and tried not to think of the sharp little stabs of pain that came and went. His weariness overcame him.

He awoke to the darkness and saw needle points of light penetrating the brush covering the entryway. The woman was yet asleep and he took the half-empty bottle from her and replaced it in her saddlebags then shook her shoulder till she came awake.

"God," she moaned, cupping her head in her hands. "I always forget what whiskey does to me—not like opium at all . . ."

Then realizing what she'd said, she tried making a joke of it.

"It's okay," he said. "I understand."

She looked into his eyes and saw something she hadn't seen in a man's eyes since she saw it in those of Chalk Bronson's.

"We better get the hell out of here," she said, and rose and took the saddle blanket and saddle and swung it up on the horse's back and tightened the cinch while he went to the entrance and tried to see out through the brush pile.

"What's it look like?" she said over her shoulder as she made the final loop of the cinch strap.

"Looks clear," he said.

"How's your arm?"

He looked down at it, his fingers cold and stiff, but he could flex his hand at the wrist without too much pain.

"It's good," he said.

She came over and said, "Let me see." He held it to the light coming through the brush. Her fingers felt his.

"This hurt?"

"No."

"How about this?"

"Yes, a little."

They were standing inches apart and he could feel something tense between the two of them and he wasn't sure what it was—his imagination or something other.

Her fingers lingered a moment longer there along his wrist.

"I thought at one time I wanted to be a nurse," she said. "I don't know why I never did anything more with my life than I have . . ."

"You're still young enough yet to do things you want," he said.

Her gaze lowered from his.

"We should try and find you a doctor soon as possible," she said. He looked down at her lingering fingers; there was nothing unusual about them except for the way they felt against his pain.

She turned then and went and took the horse's reins while he pushed aside the brush enough so she could lead the animal out. The sun had not yet risen above the red rocks, and the sky was colorless at that hour. Somewhere in the chaparral they could hear quail dusting themselves and cooing. She swung up into the saddle and kicked a foot free from the stirrup so he could swing up behind her. She waited until he put his good arm around her waist. She felt somehow safe with it there.

For him, the feeling of holding to her was different somehow this morning than it had been last night. They were pressed together in a way that was comforting to each of them. It seemed to him like she waited a long time before heeling the horse into a lope, but it had only been a moment in their lives.

⇥ 27 ⇤

I'd heard rumors that the last of Custer's men shot each other to prevent their enemies from capturing them, knowing as they must the results if taken alive. Whether or not it was true, I could understand men in dire straits doing that very thing. I'd half considered saving my last bullet for me, knowing as I did what Waco would have done to me by his drovers.

But when it came right down to it, I'd rather have spent that last bullet in the hopes it would blow up one of their hearts than to take my own life with it. Something about shooting myself seemed cowardly, or maybe it was just the opposite—maybe it was too brave a thing.

I sat there like I was waiting for them when they found me. They leveled their guns and I figured it was execution time until Waco said, "Don't kill him, not yet anyway.

"Where are they?" he said.

"Gone," I said. "Fled. Left me here to die, the dirty bastards." I said it with a smile.

"Where'd they go, goddamn it!"

"Big country," I said. "Your guess is as good as mine."

"And you just what, stayed behind to be the hero?"

"I would have gone with them," I said, "but we flipped a coin and I lost."

"Get him on his feet, boys."

Two of them yanked me to a standing position and Waco backhanded me hard, but I'd been hit harder.

"You *will* tell me," he said.

I spat out a mouthful of blood.

"Probably not, since I don't know any more than you do where they're at. They say ignorance is bliss."

"Who's the other one who was with you?" he asked.

"John Wesley Hardin."

He backhanded me again and my ears rang.

"Can't get blood out of a turnip," I said.

"Yeah, you're right, but I sure as hell can get it out of you."

He hit me again, this time with his closed fist, and it would have dropped me to my knees except for the two holding me up.

"Take him back to the house and lock him in the smoke shed," Waco ordered. "We can't track them tonight but we'll head out first thing in the morning. Harker, go find the Indian and bring him."

I was tied at the wrists and a rope was dropped over me and cinched around my middle by some chap-wearing waddie who dallied the other end of his lariat round his saddle horn. He said, "You best keep up, or this is going to hurt."

Then he spurred his horse into a trot and of

course I ran for about twenty paces before I stumbled over a rock I couldn't see in that nightglow of moonlight and fell and that waddie was true to his word about it hurting, being dragged through the chaparral like that.

Time we reached the ranch I was feeling about half dead and almost wished I was because being bounced over that rough ground like that wasn't anything you'd want to do twice. He dismounted and let the rope go slack and a couple of others came up and lifted me and half carried me to the smokehouse and locked me in it. I by God didn't do much but try and not think how bad off I felt over every inch of my body. Hadn't been for that canvas coat of mine and those tough Levi's, I wouldn't have been fit to feed to the dogs.

I wondered why Waco didn't just have me killed instead of going to all this trouble. But it was late and I was too tired and hurting to care. At that point killing me would have been doing me a favor. I closed my eyes. I'd made my peace.

The door rattled open and morning light came in so sharp it hurt my eyes and two of Waco's men dragged me out by the arms and dropped me at the feet of a few dozen horses upon one of which sat Johnny Waco in a big sheepskin coat.

The morning was cool and bright as polished steel. Next to Waco sat a dark-skinned man I guessed to be the Indian. He sat staring balefully down at me the way you might look at horse apples.

"It's not over yet, if that's what you're thinking," Waco said. Then to the boys on either side of me: "Get him on a horse."

I didn't figure they were going to go through all

the trouble of riding me out a ways just to kill me, that there was some purpose to his madness. But I was damned if I knew what it was.

We rode to the grove again and the Indian began to cut sign and we rode on through the grove and out the other side and I looked but couldn't see how the Indian could cut sign when nothing seemed visible. But he did and we rode in a due westerly fashion, down the slope of a ridge and across what I guessed was still part of Bitch Creek and out the other side. We halted while the Indian rode up and down then waved us on. I counted nearly thirty riders and I didn't know why he needed so many other than to make sure there was nothing left to chance. Waco rode out in front of his crew but behind the lead of the Indian.

That Indian tracked over hard rock and how he did it was anybody's guess, but Waco seemed to have full faith in him and by mid-morning we reached a rock wall with lots of brush blown up at its base. The Indian pointed and Waco pulled his gun and ordered some of the drovers, "Go see what that fucking Indian is pointing at."

Several of them rode forward and dismounted and turned and one of them said, "We don't see nothing what he's pointing at, boss."

Waco looked at the Indian again and he heeled his horse forward and leaned and pulled away a chunk of brush and there was a hole in the wall.

It proved to be a cave but there wasn't anyone in it.

"Looks like they may have camped the night, or somebody did," one of the drovers said, coming out again and brushing gray ash from his hands.

Waco looked at the Indian, and he rode up and down cutting sign and it didn't take him long before he started off in one direction—this time east. I figured Antonia was doing as I suggested, heading for Texas.

We rode on at a steady pace till noon when we had to give the horses a blow, and I stood feeling weak and sore as hell and some of the drovers took out jerky from their saddlebags and chewed on it while we waited and others smoked. Waco was talking to one of his hands and looking over at me and I figured it could come at any moment—my execution. Then the two of them walked over and I could see now that he had his coat unbuttoned, Waco was heeled with a Colt revolver with staghorn grips riding his hip; he wore it butt forward in his holster.

"How'd you get involved in my business?" he said.

"Money," I said.

"You are going to live to regret your greed."

"I already do."

His gaze was unflinching. He removed his Stetson and slapped it against his leg and I saw he had a receding hairline and was probably younger than he looked.

"Why carry me along on this?" I said.

He nodded as though I'd just told him something important and he was in agreement with me.

"I want you to see what I'm going to do to them—Antonia and your friend. I want you to watch them suffer before I kill you. You see, that's the way it is with me; I want to know that the man who crosses me does have to pay a heavy price.

Shooting you in the head wouldn't give me any
satisfaction. Having my men kill you slow after
they've finished with her and him, that will give
me satisfaction. You ever think you'd live to see a
woman killed in a very bad way, Glass?"

I didn't doubt he'd do it and with his own hands.
Me and Tom he might let his men do, but with
Antonia he was going to extract his own personal
revenge.

I could tell he was looking at the cuts and
scratches on my face, examining them closely like
a doctor might.

"You shouldn't have come into this county and
gotten into my business," he said, then turned and
walked away.

We were on the march again in thirty minutes.
I couldn't help but wonder how Tom and Antonia
were going to outrun them riding double. I figured
at best they had a couple hours lead on Waco, if
that.

I figured by nightfall we'd all be dead.

28

The horse was starting to break down under their weight so they took turns walking, knowing it was going to slow them down.

At one point Tom said, "You go on."

"No," she said.

"They'll catch us at this rate. No point in both of us getting caught. Your husband doesn't know who I am. Even if they catch *me,* I can deny I even know you."

"You're the one with the broke arm," she said. "You best go on."

"I'm not the kind to leave a woman behind."

"Really? Don't tell me you're one of those do-gooders."

"How'd you know?"

She looked down at him and he was smiling.

They kept moving, neither one willing to give in. Late afternoon they reached a spring and knelt and drank using their hands to scoop up the cool clean water and filled the one canteen.

"You know where we're going?" he said.

"I think to Texas if we keep going this direction," she said.

"How far do you reckon it is to Texas?"

"It's a good ways yet."

Their horse drank. The sun was gaining strength. Things almost seemed normal.

"You think they're following us?" she said.

He shrugged. "You know him better than I do. I don't know him at all."

"I think they're following us."

"We better not sit here then."

"I think I recognize some of this country," she said.

He looked around.

"It all looks pretty much the same to me."

"I came up through here once with Johnny, back when things weren't so bad between us. He was going to a place called Gando to buy some horses. I don't think it's all that far from here."

"You think you can find it?"

"I think so."

They debated whose turn it was to ride; he finally convinced her it was hers.

By the time they topped a rock ridge and looked down on a set of shacks, the sun was a foot off the lip of the horizon.

"That's the place," she said. "That's Gando as I remember it."

He studied it.

"Looks deserted to me."

They each felt hope sink as they made their way down the loose rock slope.

He had been right, the place was deserted. The last of the day's light fell on ridged but rusty tin roofs that covered ill-constructed buildings of weathered gray planks, the broken glass of their windows glittering in the dying sun. A wind that cut down through a gorge whistled like a lonesome man as they stood there feeling defeated. The stock pens stood empty, as though they'd never been used. A couple of the buildings had been burnt to charred remnants.

They picked one of the buildings and tied off their horse and went inside knowing it wasn't much if any sort of refuge but knowing they couldn't go on either.

"I think this was the place where Johnny did business," she said, looking around. It was empty except for motes of dust swirling in the light. The floorboards creaked underfoot.

"What now?" she said.

"I was about to ask you the same thing."

"We can't go on, the horse is shot."

"I know it," he said.

"Wait here."

She left and returned carrying her saddlebags and set them on the floor between them then slid down and sat with her back against the wall, and he sat with his back against it too. She opened the bags and took out the two bottles—one of wine and the other of whiskey and something else too: a small silver derringer.

"Whiskey and guns don't mix," he said, "so I've heard. What do you intend to do with that?"

She uncorked the bottle with the whiskey and took a long drink and said, "I don't know. But I figure when the time is right I'll know what to do with it." She held out the bottle for him. He declined.

"You *are* a do-gooder," she said.

"Why, because I won't drink with you?"

She looked suddenly sad. "I'm sorry. I guess I just think everyone should feel as miserable as I do."

He watched her tilt the bottle to her mouth again. "Tell me your story," he said.

She arched an eyebrow.

"I'd like to know more about you," he said. "I mean we have some time, right?"

"You tell me yours," she said.

So he began to tell her about himself and his late wife and how she died and his lonesome wanderings ever since and meeting Jim—how he'd found him and how it seemed to him all so strange and yet predestined somehow.

"Even this, the two of us sitting here waiting for death to come," he said, "seems to me somehow predetermined and I'm okay with that."

And after he finished she told him about herself, the pain of losing the person you loved and being with someone you didn't, and somewhere in the middle of telling their stories, their hands met and held to each other and he even shared a little of the whiskey with her. And then they drank the wine. And by the time they'd done all this, the sun had set off in the west and the room had grown almost completely dark and he found an old bull's-eye lantern that still had some oil in it and lit it and sat back down next to her.

"When do you think they'll come?" she said.

"I don't know. It doesn't matter now, does it?"

"No, it doesn't."

"May I ask you something?"

She shrugged.

"I was wondering what it would be like to kiss you. Would you allow me to?"

She thought of Pedro, of his request to kiss her—how his voice and eyes spoke of the deep loneliness. His need wasn't born of desire. But Tom's was, and it raised her own desire as well.

"Funny," she said.

"What is?"

"I was just about to ask you the same thing, about kissing you."

"Because you're scared this may be the last time you ever kiss anyone?"

"No. I'm scared this may be the last time I ever get to feel something real again."

"That's what I was thinking too. But even if those men weren't coming to kill us, I think I'd still want to kiss you."

She closed her eyes and tilted her face to him. He kissed her and she kissed him.

"Would you like to turn out the light?" she said as they held each other.

"Yes," he said.

29

As luck would have it—or fate, which he knew was how Tom would put it—the pursuit got delayed when the Indian's horse came up lame. There was some debate about what to do, and the sun was dropping out of the sky, making our shadows long.

"Why don't we just shoot that son of a bitch, boss, and give the Indian his horse," the man who seemed closest to Waco said.

"No, I'm saving him for something special. Let the Indian keep afoot."

So we went with that plan for a time and I was pretty amazed how much stamina the Indian had, running about as fast as a horse could trot, but even he couldn't keep it up long and stood at some point bent at the waist with his hands resting on his knees.

It had been a mistake on Waco's part to slow the chase, and he realized it when the last light went out of the sky and we still hadn't caught up with Tom and Antonia. Waco cursed his decision and ordered his top hand to pick a man to give up his horse and stay behind come morning—that we'd make camp tonight. I was ordered away from the campfire and tied to the trunk of a small blackjack tree. I was also damn glad to be off a horse; every bounce rattled my already sore bones.

I sat there in the dark watching the others crowded around the campfire moving in and out of the light, filling their plates from a cook pot of beans and their cups with coffee. My belly crawled with hunger.

I tried closing my eyes and not thinking about what was going on or how hungry I was or how much I ached. It didn't do any good to think on it. Instead I thought about Maize and Fannie Watts and several of the other women I'd been with. Even if I hadn't loved them, they still provided me some nice memories—except for the bad parts—and I could lose myself thinking about them, about particular moments, and it helped ease my troubled self. About all a man has to rely on is his mind and what's in it and what all he's done in the past—the good and the bad. It's like looking through an album of photographs somebody took of your life and all the people you'd ever met.

I was roused from my reverie by the sound of approaching footsteps. A shadow stood over me when I looked up. He was holding something. I did not care.

"You remember me?" he said.

I shook my head.

"Bob," he said.

"Sorry, I don't."

He squatted down and I could see and then smell the plate of beans and the cup of coffee he was holding.

"You hungry?"

"This bound to be my last supper?" I said.

"No. I don't reckon it is," he said. "I think the boss wants to use you pretty good before he drops you down a hole." He leaned forward and untied me and then handed me the plate.

"Your boss know you're doing this?" I said.

He shrugged, said, "What do I give a shit?"

"Bob?" I said, trying to remember the name; nothing came to mind.

"Back at the line shack that day. Me and my pard came 'round and you jumped us and tied us up and I had to piss and you were decent enough not to make me piss in my drawers. You remember now?"

"Oh, yeah. I do."

"Go on and eat 'fore that gets cold."

I ate and he retied me to the tree.

"I figure this way we're even on things," he said.

"Much appreciated," I said.

He stood then. "Take care friend," he said.

"Wait."

He paused.

"We're not quite," I said.

"We're not quite what?"

"Even."

"How you figure? You done me a good turn and now I done you one."

"You remember the last thing I did that day?"

He stood silent.

"I left your ropes loose enough so you could work your way free."

"That make us even in your book, I was to do the same thing, knowing if Mr. Waco learned of it he'd probably break my hands then have the boys use me for target practice?"

"You seem like a man who don't let his debts go unpaid."

He looked back down to the campfire. A lot of the others were already wrapping up in their blankets for the night.

"Shit," he said, and bent and retied the ropes nice and loose.

I was already working my way out of them by the time I saw him dip into the camp's firelight. I stayed put until it looked like most everyone in the camp was asleep. The remuda was tied just on the other side of the campfire. I didn't have anything to lose.

I came up on the horses easy and untied the first one, a dark bay, and led him off away from the camp, rubbing his muzzle as we went. A gun or two would have been nice and so would a saddle, but all the guns and saddles were with those sleeping men and I couldn't risk charging into the camp.

Then something cold and hard pressed to the back of my skull and a low voice said, "Where do you think you're going?"

"Nowhere, I guess."

Then the pressure relieved itself and Bob stepped around in front of me and said, "You're probably going to need this," and handed me a Winchester.

"We're more than even now," I said.

"You goddamn straight we are."

I swung up on the back of the bay.

"Oh, by the way, that's Waco's horse. He's going to be real pissed you took it."

"What about you?" I said.

"Me? Shit, I'm in the wind as of this night. I guess I about used up any welcome I once had here."

I reached down a hand and he shook it and I heeled the horse to a walk moving away from the camp and didn't stop till I topped a ridge and looked back and it looked peaceful, the firelight flickering down there in the great darkness. I could see them rising in the morning, stretching and yawning and trying to work the kinks out of their stiff bones, because I'd done it a thousand times myself. I could see the man who came and told Waco his horse was stole and then hear the confusion about where old Bob had gone off to and how all I managed to get away.

The Indian would stand looking baleful as usual, not letting any of them read what was in his thoughts, and pretty quick they'd get it figured out and find Tom and Antonia and do their business.

I knew I had to reach them first.

⇥ 30 ⇤

He woke and wept alone—away from his wife, where she could not see or hear him. He held his broken hands up in the air and stared at them and it brought tears to his eyes each time he did. The bones had been more than broken, they had been smashed, and even though they were healing slowly, they would never heal right and he couldn't look into the future and imagine what it would be like to be a cripple after he had all his life made his living using his hands.

He worked his revolver out of its holster and tried to hold it and fumbled it and picked it up and tried again but it was a useless frustrating exercise. His fingers would not bend to the trigger, his thumb had no leveraging strength to cock the hammer. Even with two hands he had difficulty.

He had let everyone down—Antonia, his wife, and maybe the town, if Johnny Waco took it in his head to burn it down.

He hated having Nora see him this way. Hated having her wait on him, tie his shoes, button his shirt, while he held his broken hands like claws. He considered in those dark private moments of getting on a horse and just riding away. The towns people looked on him with pity, kids stared at his hands. His two deputies showed no respect for him any longer. Life went on. He felt left behind.

On just such a morning there came a knock at the door and using both hands he fumbled the latch open and saw a face he hadn't seen in years.

"Chalk," the man said.

"Dalton."

The man was well-dressed in a fine suit and overcoat and a sugarloaf hat; he wore kidskin gloves. He was a tall angular man, well groomed with neatly waxed moustaches that were more gray than dark.

"You mind if I come in?"

Chalk stepped aside and the man entered, ducking his head slightly as he did.

"When'd you arrive in town?"

"Late last night, on the flyer," he said.

"Why you're here is the more important question."

"What happened to your hands, Chalk?"

He looked again at his hands then into the slate gray eyes of the visitor.

"Long story I'd just as soon not go into."

The man nodded and took off his hat as he followed Chalk into the front parlor—a small room just to the right of the front door whose windows looked out onto the street and were draped with tatted curtains.

Chalk nodded toward a chair with padded arms, and the man sat, crossed one leg over the other and rested his hat on his knee.

"I came to see my daughter," the man said.

"She's not here," Chalk replied.

"Perhaps you could tell me where she is?"

Chalk shrugged, said, "I ain't sure, Dalton."

"I see. I'd gotten a letter from her recently that concerned me. In it she wrote some veiled references. Antonia always was a bit cryptic. I thought I'd come and find out what's going on for myself."

"She's in trouble."

"Do you mind if I smoke?"

"No."

Dalton Stone took a ready made from a silver case and struck a match with his thumbnail and fired the end of the cheroot, then snapped out the match and looked for a place to set it. Chalk walked over to a small table and took a pewter tray from it with both hands and brought it to his visitor.

"Thank you."

There was a long moment of silence where only the sound of a clock in another room could be heard.

"Tell me about the trouble my daughter is in, Chalk."

"How much do you know about her?"

"Not much. It's been several years since I've seen her. She rarely writes. I knew she had left you when she thought you were dead and married John Waco, that he's a rancher. She didn't invite me to the wedding. I asked then if I could come and see her and meet him and she told me not to. I respected her wishes. I figured then there was a reason behind her not wanting me to meet her new husband and I am guessing the reason still holds true. That's why I came to you first."

"Johnny Waco turned out not to be a blessing to her."

"He's mistreated her?"

"I'm not sure how much or in what ways."

"Tell me what you do know."

"I know she left him and ended up here in Coffin Flats working for a man named Pink Huston."

"Odd name."

"Fits his profession."

"What do you mean?"

"Jesus, Dalton, I hate to even have to talk about this with you."

The man drew deeply on his cigarette and exhaled the smoke in a long blue stream, his gaze fixed on Chalk Bronson.

"Whatever it is, I can take it," he said.

"Pink runs a hog farm."

"You mean a house of prostitution."

"Yes."

"And Antonia became one of his girls?"

Chalk shrugged. "Something along those lines."

He saw Dalton stiffen but only slightly, saw him touch the brim of his hat resting upon his knee as though to brush something from it.

"So she's working for this Huston?"

"No, not anymore."

"Let's not be mysterious, Chalk. Say what you know."

Chalk told him the story—all of it that he knew so far. Dalton listened intently, stubbing out his cheroot by the time the marshal had finished.

"So you think this Jim Glass has gone to rescue her?"

Chalk looked at his hands.

"That was his intent, yes sir."

"But you don't think he's capable?"

"No sir. I don't see how with it being just him against Johnny Waco and all his men."

He saw Dalton Stone lower his gaze then in a contemplative manner, heard him take a deep breath and let it out again.

"Then I must go and do what I can," he said.

"I don't know what that would be, Mr. Stone."

"Nor do I."

"I'm sorry I let her down," Chalk said.

"Your hands," the man said. "Have you seen a doctor, and what does he say?"

"Says I'll be lucky to tie my own shoes once they heal."

Chalk watched as Dalton Stone took out a card and wrote something on it and handed it to him.

"That is the name and address of a doctor—a surgeon I know in Denver. I want you to go there and have him examine your hands. I'm sure there is something he can do for you."

"I appreciate it, but I can't afford trips to Denver and special doctors. I can't even get a job sweeping out a store . . ."

Dalton Stone took out a black leather wallet and took from it two hundred dollars and set it on the table next to the ashtray.

"For tickets and a place to stay. Tell Dr. Jameson to send me his bill."

"I can't accept your charity."

"The hell you can't. Don't be a fool. You were always good to my daughter as far as I know and you tried to help her when she was in trouble and it's little enough I help you now."

Chalk felt contrite, slightly embarrassed, but grateful.

"I'd like to hire as many men as I can—men who aren't afraid to use a gun. Can you recommend any?"

"Not in this county, but the next county over maybe. I've got a contact or two there."

"Can you send a telegram on my behalf to your contact?"

"Yeah, I can."

"How long do you think before your man could get some people here?"

"Two days."

"No sooner?"

"Two days would probably be the soonest."

"Then if you would."

"Yes sir."

"I'll be at the hotel, just ask for me."

"Yes sir."

Dalton put a hand on Chalk's shoulder. "I'm sorry about your hands."

"I would have let him cut them off if it would have saved her."

"I believe that you would, Chalk."

He put the sugarloaf hat back on his head and went out, and when Chalk turned back from the door, his wife was standing there.

"Who was that?" she said. "And would you really have traded your hands for her?"

He didn't know how to tell her—how a man could love two women at the same time, how he could give his hands or even his very life for either one. There were just some things you couldn't explain.

☞ 31 ☜

I knew I'd never be able to locate Tom and Antonia in the dark, and even when it grew light I'd have a hell of a time finding them. So instead of riding away trying to stay ahead of Waco's men I went up to a ridge and waited. It was a long cold night of waiting and two or three times I started awake from a doze.

But finally the dawn came over a ridgeline or rocks to the east and I saw the small figures in the distant camp below me stirring awake. I saw too the small panic among them when they found out I was missing. It seemed to quicken their pace and in short order they were riding out, led by the Indian, except two left short of horses.

I kept my distance in following them. If the Indian was as good today as he had been yesterday he'd find my friends for me.

We rode till near noon and then I saw them stop atop a bluff of red sandstone. I wasn't quite able to see what they were looking at below. But it looked like Waco gave them orders and they descended the bluff slowly.

By the time I reached the spot where they had

been I saw what they'd been looking at: a collection of shacks, a ghost town, it seemed.

Waco's men were spreading out through it then they gathered around one building in particular that had a weary looking horse tied up in front.

I could hear them shouting something.

Then suddenly there were two shots spaced out about a second apart followed by utter and stunned silence. I had dismounted and lay flat on the sandstone with my rifle ready. I had it aimed at the fellow wearing the sheepskin coat.

Several of the men dismounted down below and cautiously approached the building, their pistols drawn. Johnny Waco sat his horse, content, I suppose, to let his boys do the dirty work.

Like rats, the men slipped in through the doors and windows.

I held my breath, keeping the front blade of the Winchester aimed at the center of Johnny Waco's back.

And when the men came out dragging the bodies of Tom and Antonia and laid them at the feet of Johnny's horse, I pulled the trigger and watched him topple from the saddle and fall beside them.

It set up panic among them of course, and I shot the Indian next just because he was the son of a bitch that led them to my friends. And then I shot another and another until I had shot at least half a dozen before they figured where the firing was coming from and had scattered like quail into the buildings.

But I was already riding back down the ridge, circling in a wide loop, maybe one or two shells left in my rifle, my mind full of anger. I figured if they were fool enough to come after me, I'd take them away from the ghost town and circle back and get more weapons and make my stand. And if it came to dying with my friends, then I figured it was a hell of a lot better than dying without them.

I reached a point far enough away to wait to see if they were coming. I waited listening for the sounds of pounding hooves.

Nobody came.

I waited some more.

Still, nobody came.

I completed my loop and came within sight of the ghost town from the northwest. The bodies were all still there, lying like rag dolls, but the drovers were gone. I saw a dust cloud the other side of the valley. I figured it was Waco's boys, fled, all the fight taken out of them now that the man paying their wages wouldn't be anymore. Besides, if they were any sort of drovers, it would have been damn demeaning taking orders from a dead son of a bitch. Drovers, if nothing else, are pretty goddamn independent even if someone's paying them regular wages.

I waited a bit longer to make sure some of those old boys didn't come back out of a sense of misguided loyalty, then rode on down.

Tom and Antonia lay side by side as if they'd simply fallen asleep. She was yet beautiful even in death, and Tom looked as peaceful as he had ever been. I noticed how their hands touched. Each had a small bloody wound to the side of the head but were otherwise unmarked.

Johnny lay facedown next to them, his face in the dirt turned away from the woman he'd wanted to possess more than he'd wanted to love.

My curiosity caused me to go inside the building I'd seen Waco's men drag them from. I found a small silver derringer with both shells spent and it confirmed my suspicions. Tom had done for her what she could not have done for herself. And knowing him, he probably told her he wouldn't let her go alone into that dark void, that he'd go with her just to keep her company.

I walked out again feeling sad and bitter because it shouldn't have turned out this way.

I scoured the ruined little town until I found the busted blade of a shovel with half a handle someone had left behind, as if whoever had left it knew it still had a purpose.

I dug a single grave and put Tom and Antonia in it, side by side. I suspected they would have wanted it that way—that she would have wanted him to hold her and that he would have wanted to hold her on their final journey.

My hands shook as I tossed the last shovel of dirt onto the mound and patted it down. I told myself that my tears were from anger and not from sorrow, but they were from both and I didn't really care.

Then I rode away again, as I had once come, a stranger to this place, these dead.

— EPILOGUE —

As they waited for the end they spoke of many things and told each other things about themselves they'd not told anyone until that time.

They slept and woke again and talked more and she told him of all the things she'd hoped she would have become if life had turned out differently, and all the places she would have liked to have traveled. And he told her of similar dreams he had, saying he had lost his way but understood there was reason to be found even in the confusion of being lost.

"One life is not enough," he said. "We should have three or four. One in which we learn, and another in which we live what we've learned, and one we spend in pleasure and one in which we spend in reflection."

"How do you know that we don't?" she said. "How do you know that when we die we don't go on to another life and do exactly that, and that maybe this is the life of reflection we are living now and all the other lives await us still?"

"I don't know," he said.

"Do you believe there are other lives after this one?"

"Yes, I do," he said.

"So do I."

"Then it won't be so bad, will it?"

"No. I don't think it will be very bad at all."

"It might be so beautiful we can't even begin to imagine it," he said.

"I'd like to believe that."

"Then we should."

"Yes."

And then they fell into silence, each feeling their separate thoughts as they held hands until she leaned against him and said, "Hold me, Tom."

And so he held her in his embrace knowing what was to come.

For they'd decided somewhere between that long night and when they heard the riders come that they would suffer no more at the hands of others.

She handed him the derringer.

"I want to go first," she said.

He nodded.

They heard the horses stop outside.

"It's time," she said. "Before they come in."

"Yes," he said. "Let me kiss you one last time."

She inclined her head to him and he kissed her.

Then they heard footsteps on the porch outside. She closed her eyes. He pulled the trigger once. Then he said, "Good-bye my sweet, sweet child," and pulled the trigger again.

Twenty men arrived from the adjoining county and Chalk was waiting for them.

"You boys go over to the Bison and get you

something to eat and something to drink and I'll go and get Mr. Stone and he'll tell you what he needs and what the pay is," he said, and they went quietly knowing that work was work and sometimes hard to come by unless you were willing to do whatever it was needed doing and were not afraid.

And just as he came out of the hotel with Mr. Stone walking at his side he saw the stranger riding down the street on a lathered horse.

The stranger stopped, and Chalk said to Mr. Stone, "This is Jim Glass. Jim, this is Mr. Dalton Stone, Antonia's father."

And the two men shook hands and then Jim told him about the daughter he had come to find and where he could find her.

"Would you be kind enough to show me?" Mr. Stone said.

"I would."

And together they rode back out to the ghost town and Jim showed the father where the daughter was buried and explained to him the story and circumstance of her death and about his friend Tom Twist and what sort of man he was.

"I know he did right by her," Jim said. "I don't doubt that by the end he had come to love her." And after Dalton Stone had knelt there by her grave for a time, he stood and looked around and said, "You killed these men?"

"I did."

"Which one is Johnny Waco?"

Jim showed him.

"And would you, sir, do such a thing again if the need called for it?"

"I would," said Jim.

"Then we need to talk, you and I."

And together they rode back to Coffin Flats, two men who were once strangers but now had found a common cause.

For Bob Faulkner,
writer, pal, muleskinner,
and a pretty good man
to go upriver with, I'm betting.

1

You couldn't hear it falling, but you could tell from the rattling wind and the cold creeping in under the door that it had snowed the night before. I rose and put on a pot of Arbuckle after hopping into my pants and boots.

Luz was still asleep in the bed. I was tempted to stay in there with her. She had a warmth that made me want to be lazy and playful.

I rubbed frost from inside the window and looked out at the horses that were strutting around in the corral blowing steam from their nostrils. The buckskin stud was boxed off from the mares, and he was nickering and daring them to kick down the rails.

I put on a wool shirt and threw some more chunks of wood into the stove's belly. I tried to be quiet about it, but Luz rose to one elbow and smiled.

"You hungry?" she said.

"When am I not?" I said.

She came out from town once a week to clean and keep me a little company. That's how it began. She was the widow of a man who broke his neck

from falling under a wagon he'd been loading with
bricks. The workhorses spooked just enough to
roll the wheel over him. From everything she'd told
me about him, he was a good man but full of bad
luck. She had two half-grown children her sister
watched on the nights she spent with me.

She started to get out of bed.

"Why don't you let me get you some coffee," I
said. "I'll make the breakfast too."

She liked to switch from English to Spanish
when we talked, and over time I'd learned quite a
bit of her language. Now she smiled and said in her
own language, "*Me siento como soy una esposa
otra vez.*"

"Yes, it feels like you're my wife too," I said.
"It's not so bad, is it, to feel like that?"

"But when you cook for me," she said in English this time, "it is like you are *my* wife." Then
she laughed and brushed away the hair that had
fallen over one side of her face and tucked it behind her ear.

"Why didn't you ever remarry?" I said, mixing
some flour and water and a little yeast for biscuits.

"I don't know," she said. "I guess the same reason you never did."

"I've never been married," I said.

"So you said. But the question is, why not?"

I shrugged.

"Just never got around to it, I guess."

She shrugged.

"Now you know why I didn't remarry, too busy,
too much work. And besides, all the hombres who
aren't married are either old or have buck teeth."
She laughed again.

She had straight black hair she normally kept parted down the center and twisted into braids or wrapped atop her head and held with large combs. But when her work around my place was finished and we'd sit down to have supper, she'd unpin or unbraid her hair and let it all fall free, and it made her look younger and more at ease, and I think she knew it and that's why she did it.

Over the weeks we'd flirt and eat. The flirting with each other began about the fourth or fifth time she'd come out to clean. She had a friendly way about her and was always singing softly while she worked. But when I talked to her I could tell she always kept something back—like a gambler with a pretty good hand, but not necessarily the *best* hand at the table.

She'd be in the house doing something and I'd be out on the porch mending a broken stirrup or just having a cup of coffee, and she'd come out and ask if she could get me anything and we'd just get to talking. Then she told me about her husband, how he'd died, and I could see that even after three years she was still affected by the loss—the way her bottom lip quivered sometimes when she talked about him. She would apologize as if she had something to be sorry for. I told her she didn't and she could talk to me about anything that she wanted to.

"He was a good husband and a father . . ." she said that first time. I remember how the light from the setting sun turned her brown skin golden, how it caused her eyes to shine like wet black stones. I kept on thinking about her long after she headed home and finally decided I didn't want the day with her to end so soon, and so worked up the cour-

age to ask her to stay and have supper with me. I
thought for sure she'd turn me down, make some
excuse as to why she had to get back to town to
take care of her kids. But she stayed, telling me that
her sister, Carmelita, watched her children when
she went off to clean houses.

We'd carry my small table outside and eat our
supper there because the weather was warm and
pleasant. I found some candles and set them atop
the table and we ate with just the light from them.
We started out sitting at opposite ends of the table
and ended up sitting next to each other, the third
or fourth time we ate together.

She asked me to tell her about myself and I probably talked way too much—more than I had with
anyone about my own past. I told her I'd once been
a Texas Ranger but I didn't tell her why I'd quit. I
told her about herding cattle up some of the trails
from Texas into Kansas and once into New Mexico, which is how I'd come to eventually settle here.
But I never told her about the ranch owner's wife in
Nebraska and why I finally left that job. I told her
lots of things but not everything.

"I did a lot of drifting," I said. "But I always
liked this country best and knew someday I'd come
back. And, well, here I am."

"I was wondering what brought you here," she
said.

"Now you know."

One other thing I never told her about me was
that I'd most recently killed a man named Johnny
Waco—now nearly a year ago in the history book
of my life. Everyone in Coffin Flats knew about it
at the time, and why I had done it. But she lived

out nearer to Wild Horse River than Coffin Flats, and if she did know about it, she never brought it up in our conversations, and I appreciated that about her.

Her laughter was something to behold. She was beautiful when she laughed. She was no young girl and her age and looks, by most men's standards, probably put her in the average category, I guess you'd say. And being a widow with children didn't exactly endear her to the few eligible bachelors worth a peck when there were so many younger, fairer Mexican women whose folks wanted to see them married off down in this part of the country. But what Luz was, was just about right for me at this time of my life. That first night we had supper together I rode with her back to her home. She had a little paint mare. She insisted she could make it home by herself just fine like she was accustomed to doing, but I now felt an obligation to make sure she got home safe and sound.

We both knew something had changed in our relationship that night—that if she continued coming out to the house and we continued along the same lines it was going to be more than just her cleaning my house and more than just us having supper together.

We got to her front door, the night having long descended, the inside of the casita dark, and we just sat there for a moment.

"What do you want from me, Señor Glass?" she finally said.

"Nothing, Luz."

She gave me long enough to explain it.

"I don't know," I said. "I liked tonight, having supper with you, talking, laughing, telling you about myself. I like the fact you smoke cigarettes even though I never have, but I'm thinking of taking up the habit. I like the way the evening sun looks in your eyes. I don't know what it all means. I just know I liked it and wouldn't mind if we made it a regular deal."

"I liked it too," she said. "But what might people say?"

"Hell, I don't care if you don't. We're both still vital people, me and you, Luz. You're widowed and I'm single; what can they say that's so terrible?"

She touched my hand for the first time and I leaned and kissed her soft cheek.

"Then I'll see you next week," I said.

"Yes, you'll see me next week."

So that's how it began, like that—two strangers who'd come to know each other a little more each time over the ensuing weeks and decided at some point we didn't want to stop with just supper.

When the coffee was ready I poured her a cup, remembering she liked two spoonfuls of sugar in hers, and brought it to her and said, "I'm going to go out and break ice off the water troughs for the horses, then gather some eggs if those chickens didn't all get et last night by the coyotes and we'll have some eggs and biscuits with honey for breakfast, how will that be?"

"In bed?"

"Sure. We'll pretend we're rich people."

She reached up and kissed me, letting the blanket drop away when she did, her warm brown breasts pressed against me as she hugged my neck. And it roused my desire all over again.

"Don't go anywhere," I said. "I'll be right back."

The horses pricked their ears at my approach and I took the hand ax and busted the plates of ice off their water and said, "There you are, ladies." The stud stood off watching me cautiously as I went to his pen. I shattered the ice on his water and said, "Just so you know, we're going to have us another go-round today, so you might just as well get used to the idea."

He tossed his head and pawed the cold earth just as if he knew what I was talking about. The thought of getting bucked off on such a cold morning was a little more than I wanted to think about. I'd wait till around midmorning, then give it a go—when it was a little warmer and the ground not so damn hard.

I went over to the chicken coop—one I'd constructed myself and surrounded with chicken wire but didn't seem to do much good when it came to crafty coyotes and zealous badgers. Even had a hawk once that flew down and took one. I strung more chicken wire for a barrier. Those chickens acted scared and I couldn't blame them. I unlatched the wire holding the small gate so I could enter and hopefully find a few eggs for breakfast. The rooster squawked like someone told him he was about to be murdered and the hens ran about with their clipped wings flapping and squawking too.

Then I saw something way out on the road that caused me to pause: a quarter-top leather buggy, black against the snow, pulled by a single trotter. I didn't know anybody in Coffin Flats who owned such a rig except the new doctor. I wondered what the hell the new doctor was headed to my place for.

I got my eggs, holding them in the fold of my shirt-tails, and hitched the gate shut again and started up to the house. Inside I set the eggs in a bowl on the sideboard next to the stove and said to Luz, "Some-one's coming. Looks like that new doctor. Maybe you ought to get dressed. You know I'm a jealous man."

She smiled boldly, said, "Oh, you are, huh."

"Maybe just a little."

"I like that you are," she said.

She tossed back the covers and stood fully naked before me, her arms out away from her sides.

"You're a sight and half, woman. And if you keep that up, I'm going to crawl back in the bed with you, and that new doctor will just have to wait outside till we're done in here."

She laughed and came and threw her arms around my neck and kissed my mouth.

"Okay," she said. "I'll get dressed, and I'll make breakfast too."

I stepped out on the porch, closing the door behind me.

But the man riding in the hack wasn't the new doctor. Instead it was a man I hadn't seen in almost two years and never thought I'd see again.

His name was Gus Rogers, Captain Gus Rogers, and I knew he hadn't traveled all the way from Texas just to pay a social visit.

He halted the hack, the morning sun glistening in the new snowfall, his horse blowing steam.

"Jim," he said in that South Texas drawl of his as he just sat there huddled inside a mackinaw with his hat pulled down tight to the top of his ears.

"Cap'n," I said. "You're quite a ways from home."

"Hell if I ain't, old son."

"You lost, or just out wandering the earth?"

He smiled like a man who didn't do it much.

"Neither," he said. "I come looking for you."

"Get on down," I said. "Was about to have some breakfast. You hungry?"

"No, not too much. Could use a taste of hot coffee though, maybe just a finger or two of something in it to ward off the chill."

I watched the way he stepped out of the hack; like a man who had something in him broken.

He stood for a moment straightening himself, hands pressed to his back, looking around.

"Nice little place you got here," he said.

"Ain't it though."

"Never thought I'd see the day Jim Glass had himself a house." He looked to the corral. "Nice horses too. Hell, old son, you've become like some sort of potentate."

"Hardly," I said. I was trying to kill enough time for Luz to slip on a dress but I figured by now she had. I almost smiled at the thought of the look on the Cap'n's face was he to see her innocent beauty in all its glory, a man like him, who was all Bible and by the book.

"Let's get in out of this morning cold. Coffee's already on," I said.

I waited for him to go first and saw the way he was listing and moving slow. I'd known the man for a goodly number of years, knew him to always be tough as a blackjack stump, figured even bullets couldn't kill him, which they hadn't yet after being shot at least three times I knew about.

His face was ashen, his features drawn, and he

looked like he had aged twenty years since I'd last seen him.

I introduced him to Luz and told him to take a seat at the table. He gave her an appraising eye and smiled like a coon eating melon.

"Ma'am," he said, touching the brim of his Stetson with a finger. Supporting most of his weight on the back of the chair and edge of the table, he eased himself down.

I went to the cupboard and took out the bottle of bourbon I kept there for special occasions, which were mostly for the nights after Luz and I had supper together and would sit out on the porch and watch the sun set and sip and talk till it got dark. She confessed she quite liked the taste of my whiskey.

I poured the Cap'n a cup of coffee, then poured in some of the whiskey till he waved a hand over the cup. "Good enough," he said.

Luz threw together our breakfast but he just let his plate sit in front of him, trying to be polite, but only picking at it, saying, "This is real good, ma'am."

I could tell by the look on Luz's face she had several questions but knew to wait to ask them. Finally she took up our plates and cleaned them, then put on her wrap and said, "I have to be going, Jim. I'll see you next week."

I walked her out to her little horse and helped her up after a long good-bye kiss.

"Who is that man?" she asked.

"Just somebody from my past," I said.

"He looks sick."

"I'll see you next week then?" I said.

She looked at me in a way that made me wonder if everything they said about a woman's intuition wasn't true.

"Whoever he is or whatever his problem, he feels like trouble," she said.

"Not far as I'm concerned," I said.

"I'll bring some silk flowers for the grave, next time I come," she said.

"That would be nice."

She clucked the little horse to a start, and I stood and watched her head back toward Coffin Flats.

I went back inside dreading whatever it was that had brought Cap'n Gus Rogers to my front door on a fresh winter day.

2

Nice lady, your friend," the Cap'n said when I stepped back inside.

"Yeah, you want a refill of that Arbuckle?"

He held out his cup and I filled it with coffee, then my own, and set the pot back atop the stove plate. He looked at the bottle of bourbon.

"Help yourself, Cap'n," I said.

He spilled in a nice portion and stirred it with his spoon and sipped it.

"So you want to tell me why you came all the way from Texas?"

He took his time sipping the coffee, blowing off the steam, and said, "Thank Jesus for the whiskey 'cause you still can't make coffee worth a holy damn, Jim."

"Kinda early to be drinking, isn't it?"

He arched his back as though it was aching, then relaxed. He had lost weight since I'd last seen him, though he never was a big man to begin with: maybe a hundred fifty, tops, but a solidly built man of good coloration and clear keen eyes that seemed to see everything at a glance. Now he was down to a lot less and looking gaunt, his gray eyes sunk back inside their sockets under a ridge of forehead. His cheeks were sunk in and his color an unhealthy pale.

"I came to ask you a favor and you know I don't ever ask them easy," he said.

"Yes sir, I know that."

He looked uncomfortable.

"You okay, Cap'n?"

"Depends which day it is. Today's worse than yesterday was."

"What's the favor?" I said.

He looked grim.

"Got me this real bad problem, Jim. First thing you should know is, I'm dying. Doctors tell me I got five, maybe six weeks left at the outside . . ."

"Sorry to hear that," I said, and I truly was. The Cap'n was one of the best men I'd ever met in my life. He waved a hand.

"Didn't come looking for pity, just need to tell you this so you'll know why I come this far and what I come for."

"Go on with it," I said.

"You remember I got two grandboys?"

"Seems to me I do."

"Billy Edward, he's the oldest, and Sam Houston is five years younger, nineteen and fourteen."

I faintly remembered him speaking of them when I rangered for him.

"They're my Laura Lee's kids, and as you know she's my only child. Never had no boys of my own, just Laura Lee. Had her, then JoAnn died right after and I never married again because there was no use to it. You love a woman as hard as I loved JoAnn, well, what's the use of trying to find something to compete with that. I raised Laura Lee best as I could and she turned out a good woman with poor judgment when it came to men.

"Went through two marriages herself before she met the right man. That's how come the difference in her boys' ages. Billy was fathered by her first husband, Wayne Brown, and Sam was fathered by her second, Orville Cutter. Anyway, neither of them was much count and took off soon as they found out she was pregnant. Then she met this Jardine Frost fellow. They were living together over in Tascosa, her and this Jardine raising the boys together, Jardine adopted them and gave them his last name. From what she'd written me, Jardine was a good, decent man, hard worker, and treated her boys like they were his own, she said. Then he got himself killed in a dispute over a horse."

Cap'n Rogers told it with his eyes cast down, remembering it all, and when he mentioned about this Jardine Frost getting killed, he just shook his head slowly.

"Well," he said, sipping from his cup, "like I said, Laura Lee never did have any luck with men, good or bad. Frost getting himself killed just about done it as far as those boys standing a chance of getting raised right. They just went wild after he passed. I'm sure she did her best to raise them right, but you know when boys don't have no father to discipline them, they can get off the track real fast.

"I didn't learn about a lot of this till later on— till after it was too late for me to do anything about it. Not that there was much I might could have done living three hundred miles away at the time. But maybe if she'd come lived with me and brought those boys with her, I could have been some sort of father to them and taught them the right thing to do . . ."

He looked pained and he drank down more of the whiskey-laced coffee, and I wasn't sure I wanted to hear more of this story because it just felt like it wasn't going to get any better the more of it he told.

He looked up at me with those gray eyes, and I didn't see in them what I once had: a man too tough to be whipped. What I saw now was a man who had five, six weeks at the outside to live and a peck of personal problems.

"The way it turned out was Billy and Sam drifted off and started getting themselves to doing bad stunts."

"What sort of bad stunts?" I said.

"Mostly minor stuff at first—gambling, drinking, fighting, petty thievery. But like most wild boys who start out slow, they did not stay that way. Pretty darn soon they progressed up the ranks to become true outlaws—stealing cattle and horses and even got accused of robbing a bank in Las Vegas, New Mexico, though they didn't get but pocket change according to the report I got. I heard all this secondhand from Laura Lee through letters had the ink stained with her tears. Broke my heart to hear about it. I went down there to visit with her and get the whole story just after I got word I was in a fix my own self. Cancer of the stomach," he said with a finality that was like letting his breath out.

"And that's where the real tough news came, when I got down that way."

I thought about Luz, my life here, how I'd pulled away from the violent life I'd once lived. I looked up at the gravesites of my friend Tom Twist, on the hill where I'd buried him, and the woman he'd loved and died over, both of them buried side by side now and forever together. I thought about the men I'd already killed and sometimes dreamed about—the dreams always bad, but what told me it was time to quit was when I stopped dreaming about them.

Then for a time I took to drinking hard and fell pretty low on the ladder of humanity.

I drifted for a year or so, mending fence and working for other men and getting into my own sorts of trouble with liquor and women. I got into fistfights because I was good with my fists and I liked how it felt to beat a man down who gave me trouble, like it wasn't so much beating *him* down as it was the trouble that dogged me.

Then I woke up one morning from a hard drunk, lying face up on the high desert with rain in my face and my horse and saddle stole along with my boots. And if whoever it was hadn't also stole my guns, I do believe I would have killed myself then and there because I was a man past forty without a future and I knew I either had to lie there and die or get up and walk.

I was cold and miserable and hung over, and out of nowhere a dog came up and started licking my face, and something made me hug it because it was love I was most in need of, and I guess that old dog was looking for the same thing.

I asked the dog if it was Jesus come to save me and it barked and I said, "Well if you ain't, you're close enough." And I got up and started walking and the dog followed me and stayed with me for a time, then went off on its own soon as I got to within sights of the next town.

I hated to see that dog go, but I knew we all had to choose our own way and it had to choose its own way as well. That's just the way life is.

I ended up getting hired on as a deputy town marshal and tending bar in some broke dick Texas town that has since burned to the ground and never rebuilt as far as I know of. Then one day a telegram showed up for me from Dalton Stone, the father of the woman buried up on the hill next to my friend Tom Twist.

It said in effect he'd been trying to find me ever since that day I showed him her grave and told him the story of how she and Tom had died at Tom's hands. He'd wanted to do something for me then but I'd refused, because I didn't take pay for doing what was the right thing to do. He went on to say in the telegram the offer of money or whatever I needed was still standing and he'd like to hear from me and know what I was up to, that he'd feel forever indebted to me and would I please wire him back.

Well, I thought about it for a few days and counted what I had in my savings account—forty-four dollars and seventy-five cents—a dollar for every year I'd lived and change. I remembered there was this little place I'd seen for sale on the Rio Penasco that used to belong to Charlie Bowdre, who'd run with Billy the Kid until Garrett put a bullet in them both.

Charlie's place was a little run down but it had

a good view of the river and the grass around it was sweet for grazing horses—a venture I thought I could do well at: catching and breaking wild horses and selling them. So I wired Mr. Stone back and thanked him and said if he wanted to do something, he might consider loaning me the money to buy the place and I'd pay him back as my horse venture grew.

That's how it came to pass that I'm in this place now, with horses in the corral and a woman who comes and cleans my house and has supper with me and stays the night once a week. I built a little porch on the front too. Now here was a sort of trouble I didn't need or want at my kitchen table.

"What is it you're asking of me, Cap'n?"

He leaned forward, setting his cup down, then stood and walked over to the window above the sink. He stared out for a long few moments, the sun on the glass now so that the frost was melted away.

Without turning to look at me, he said, "This is the part that's real bad, Jim. I have to kill one of them boys."

⇥ 3 ⇤

I sat listening as the Cap'n explained it. All the time I'd known the Cap'n, I'd never known him to fail at anything he set his mind to, and I never saw him flinch from danger or falter under fire. But now I noticed his body tremble as he spoke.

"What do you mean, Cap'n, say it plain."

He turned to face me then, his features drawn into a mask of sorrow.

"They made a big mistake, those grandsons of mine," he began. "They crossed the border into Old Mexico and something real bad happened—a woman got raped and killed, the daughter of a Ruales general. They caught Billy and Sam at the scene. Billy confessed it was his doing and none of Sam's. And the General would have probably let Sam ride but Billy broke out of jail, and he was the only one got away. Sam's still locked up down there in their calaboose. Billy made his way back across the border and wired his mother what happened, asking her to wire me and send a company of Rangers down there. I still got some contacts down there and found out who it was, this general. Just so happens I knew old Pancho Toro from back during my border days, back before he *was* a general or even a soldier.

"We worked the same cattle outfit together and used to drink and gamble together, both of us still green kids."

Cap'n shook his head, remembering.

"He was a hell of a vaquero is all I knew. We grew to be friends. He was even set to marry my sister Alice but she died of the influenza before they could tie the knot. After that we just sort of went our separate ways. Once I got word it was Pancho holding Sam I wired him direct and explained to him who Sam was to me. He wired me back saying he had a lot of sympathy for me but if I wanted to save Sam's skin, I would have to track Billy down and kill him since he and his Ruales couldn't cross the river north and do it themselves . . ."

Then a great weight seemed to settle on the Cap'n's shoulders, for he visibly sagged.

"He says to prove I killed Billy I had to cut off his head and bring it to him or else he was going to execute Sam in Billy's stead. Said somebody had to pay, and if not Billy, then Sam. I don't doubt for a minute he'll do it. You know anything about Mexican men, you know they got a lot of pride in their manhood and are real macho types. Says I've got two weeks to get Billy killed. Not much more time than what the doctors tell me I got to live. So you can see I'm in a bit of a tight spot here, Jim."

Cap'n came back over to the table and sat down and said, "Maybe you could pour me another bit of that forty rod." And I filled the bottom of his cup with whiskey.

"You want me to find Billy and kill him for you, is that it?" I said.

His face knotted in pain.

"No sir. Not quite."

"Then what?"

"I'd just like you to go along with me in case my own deal goes bad before I can see it done. You'd be my backup plan."

"You mean kill Billy in case you don't make it that long, then go get Sam from the General?"

"Yes sir. That's about the way of it. I can't save them both but if I can save one, it will be better than watching them both go down."

"And you think you can kill your own grandson, do it the way the General wants it done?" I said.

He looked at me level then, with a gaze I'd seen before.

"You know I've always been a man who does whatever needs doing," he said after taking another swallow of the whiskey. "Even if it is about to be the most terrible thing I've ever done."

"Can I ask you something?" I said.

"You've every right."

"How come you want me in on this and not one of your other men?"

"You were right on the way," he said.

"How come I don't believe that's the real reason?"

"You know that ain't it, but do I have to explain it?"

I shook my head. I knew what he meant: I was as bad as him when it came to killing men. How could I convince him I'd changed, that I'd met

Luz and just the pure gentleness of a woman can change a man's heart and make him want more than what he's been used to all his life? Luz's love took all the fighting out of me, all the bloodletting ways I used to have.

His gaze continued to hold mine steady. There was one other reason I think he was asking me, even though he didn't say a word about it: the fact he'd saved my life once. But the Cap'n wasn't the sort of man to come right out and say he was calling in his marker.

"What if we can't find Billy in the time the General's given you and goes ahead and executes Sam?" I said.

"Then I aim to go down there and kill him, and if I ain't able, then I'm asking you go down and kill him for me. But I don't think it will come to all that, because I know where Billy is and how to get him."

I heard the stud whicker out in the corral. Cap'n looked up, and for a brief moment I saw light in his eyes. He was a pure horseman.

"Well, think about it at least," he said, standing and turning stiffly toward the door. "I'll be waiting for the afternoon flyer to Tucson. Billy's locked up in jail down near there. All I got to do is go on down there and take him out and . . ."

He opened the door, and the cold touched my skin like a piece of flatiron.

I walked him out to the hack and watched him struggle to get up and in. He sat there a minute catching his breath, looking off toward the horses.

"That big buckskin stud looks like he'd rip you a new one," he said. "You tried to ride him yet?"

"Every day since I caught him. Keeps pitching me off and trying to stomp my brains out. Don't know why I just don't cut him loose and let him go on back to where he came from."

"Where'd he come from?"

I pointed.

"Way out yonder beyond those hills," I said. "I don't know why I wasted my time catching him in the first place. Should have known better."

"He'll make you a hell of a horse if you can get him rode."

"I don't know as he can be rode."

Cap'n looked at him for a long time, then said, "He can be rode, old son. Any horse can be rode, just like any cowboy can be throwed. It just takes the right man on the right horse to do it is all."

He snapped the reins and turned the hack back toward the road to Coffin Flats, and I stood watching him go and half wished he'd never come in the first place because I sure as hell hated to see a good man like him so busted down and sick and with such troubles to deal with in his last days.

There was snow on the mountains that would be there all winter no matter how warm it might get down here in the valley. I turned to walk back to the house when my gaze swept the ridge where Tom and Antonia are buried, their headstones with a cap of snow on them.

I walked on up there. It was a bit of a climb. The wind was blowing up from the south now, bringing some warmth.

"Got me a problem," I said when I reached the graves, kneeling in front of Tom's. Tom was always a good listener. "Cap'n wants me to go help him kill his grandson, just a kid, really, nineteen, but old enough, I reckon, to pay for his crimes. I don't want to do it. I like it right here just fine. Me and you and Luz and this old place and them horses is about all I ever wanted and all I'll ever need."

Way off down in the valley the other side of the river, I could see a lone coyote loping along, its rough, rusty fur catching the sun.

I brushed aside some of the snow on the ground and picked up a handful of pebbles.

"I don't want to do no more killing either," I said. "I go do this thing, I'm right back where I said I'd never go again."

A gust of wind brushed along the ground.

"And I still got that damn stud to ride so I can get him gentle enough to be bred up with those mares and maybe sell him to a rich man. I got lots of damn things to do right here without running off to Arizona or Old Mexico, or some such."

I watched the coyote come down to the river's edge, look back the direction from which it had come, then straddle and drink.

"What would you do were you me?" I said.

Tom had been a chaplain's assistant in the Union Army and later a preacher before his wife died and he began to drift in search of answers to questions he said pressed on him after her death. And by the time I'd met him, he said he hadn't found any answers yet. All I could hope was he found them in that last hour of his life, or he'd found them when he crossed over from this world to the next.

"You're not going to tell me, are you?" I said.

The coyote loped off upriver like something was chasing him but he wasn't scared.

I shook the pebbles in my hand like dice.

"Why the hell did you have to go and die on me?" I said. Another gust of wind caught in my shirt.

I stood and walked back down to the house, but instead of going inside, I went to the shed and got my saddle, then walked to the small corral I had the stud in.

I slung the saddle on the top rail.

The stud eyed me like he knew the jig was up for one of us.

"Today's the day," I said. "I'm feeling like a dance."

He whinnied and tossed his head.

"You're going to get rode or I'm going to get throwed, but this is the last day we do this thing if it ain't one or the other."

He was a block of muscle and fury, a cyclone of a horse the color of the desert, with a line running down his back, black as death. Just standing there looking at him reminded me I still had plenty of bruises from the last several times I'd tried to break him.

I crawled between the lower rails and took my rope and let out a loop. There was no place for him to run except along the back rails. I tossed my rope and let it fall over his head, then wrapped it twice around the snubbing post, and he kicked and screamed like a banker who was being robbed.

"You can raise all the damn hell you want," I said. I waited till he settled into a stiff-legged stand.

Sometimes you fail at something and you can't understand why you did. You figure you gave it all you had and it still didn't work out and you're ready to quit it all, figuring you got nothing left to give. Then something makes you try one last time. And this time you dig down deep into a place you never even knew was there, just an extra inch more, an extra ounce of strength. Your mind locks down tight on the thing you're determined to do— and suddenly it's just enough to get it done.

So I got my blanket and saddle on him and my bit in his teeth and swung aboard. The first few seconds forked on the stud was like riding a run-away freight train that had crashed off a gorge into a rocky canyon bottom. I thought he was going to snap my head off and pull both arms out of the sockets. But when he hadn't thrown me on the first several tries, I got into a rhythm with him, and it was like dancing with a crazy woman. Only I felt even crazier this time. Whatever move the stud made I anticipated. It was like I suddenly was part of him and he was part of me.

He kicked down the rails and busted down the gate. He snorted and stomped and kicked and bucked all over what you might call a yard, and then suddenly there went my chicken fence and coop— those hens and that rooster scattering like ten sorts of hell was after them, the coop busted to boards. The stud was just a damn cyclone but I stuck and finally rode him down.

And then he just stood there under me, blowing hard, his whole body quivering, and I waited for him to make another go at it but when he didn't, I touched my heels to his sides and walked him around with that Spanish bit in his mouth, and he learned fast what it was there for. I stroked his powerful sweaty neck and walked him over to the water and let him take a drink, then rode him all the way to the ridge and showed him off to Tom and Antonia. And for a time we just sat there with the wind in our faces. Then I rode him back down and the stud did everything I asked of him, though he still had a lot of strut to him, but that was okay—it was the way I wanted him.

I had myself a good horse.

And an old man who needed my help.

I went inside and packed a bedroll with a few extra clothes in it: shirts, socks, pair of jeans. Packed my saddlebags with razor, soap, comb, two boxes of shells for the Merwin Hulbert that was in my bottom dresser drawer, pocket knife, general things I'd need. I went and got my pistol and unwrapped it from the towel and slid it into the shoulder rig, then strapped it on before putting on my coat. I took the Henry rifle from the corner by the door and slipped it into a scabbard and walked outside again and rigged everything to the saddle. I looked around at my wrecked yard and thought I should probably try and round up those damn chickens and that rooster, but decided against it. You can always buy more chickens and a rooster.

I rode to Gin Walker's place halfway between my place and town and stopped and asked him if he'd look after my stock—that I'd be gone a few weeks, maybe longer. I knew he'd do it because that's what neighbors do for each other. He said no problem, and I could see him eyeing the brass butt of the Henry sticking out of the scabbard and probably wondering what I was up to, but he didn't say anything.

I thanked him and headed for town.

It was a pretty day.

I figured I'd better stop and tell Luz I'd be gone for a time. It seemed only fair.

I just hoped that, unlike the chickens, she'd be there when I returned.

4

He was sitting there in front of the station, in the shade of the eaves on a wood bench smoking a cigarette. He was leaned forward with his forearms resting on the thighs of his faded jeans, his mackinaw unbuttoned and hanging loose. The sun had come up and melted most of the snow that had fallen through the night, and now the streets and roads were just a reddish mud the horses and wagons slopped through as they passed up and down. Women held their skirts up above the tops of their shoes as they walked wherever there weren't boards to walk on, and dogs stood grizzled with muddied legs, looking forlorn.

I rode up and stopped in front of the station, and he looked up and I could see just the merest recognition on his face and a sign of relief that I'd come. He looked at the stud and said, "I see you got him broke."

"Not without some disagreement," I said.

"You going to haul him along?"

"That's the plan. What about you?" I said. "What you going to do for a horse once we get down to Tucson?"

He drew on his cigarette and exhaled a cloud of smoke, his fingers stained yellow from years of tobacco use.

"I'm going to rent a hack," he said. "Can't sit a horse no more. This burg they got Billy in is about fifty or so miles southwest of there, a place called Finger Bone. Train don't go there."

Stacked there beside him next to the bench was a small trunk and a Winchester rifle. He saw me glance at it.

"How'd you learn of him being in jail down there, Cap'n?"

Cap'n leaned his head forward and spit between his boots.

"Like I said, I got friends all over the Southwest."

I dismounted and went in and bought myself a ticket and stuck it in my shirt pocket, then came out and unsaddled the stud, and set the saddle along with my bedroll and kit there next to his things, and my rifle still in its scabbard next to his, and he looked at it and said, "I see you still favor the Henry rifle."

"It was good enough for me in Texas," I said. "I guess it's good enough for me here in New Mexico."

He drew on the smoke and shucked the nub into the muddy street, where it fizzled, and said, "I reckon so."

I glanced at my pocket watch, and there was still half an hour before the train was set to come in.

"I need to go do something," I said.

"Go ahead," he said. "I'll watch over your gear."

I went up the street toward Luz's place—a small adobe at the edge of town that had an ocotillo fence around it. She was there in the side yard hanging clothes from a wire line, white blouses and black and red skirts.

She turned when she heard me open the gate.

"Didn't think I'd see you again so soon," she said.

"I've come to tell you I'll be gone for a little while," I said.

The smile faded from her face as she brushed some loose strands of hair away from her forehead with the back of her wrist, a wet piece of clothing clutched in her hands.

"I thought you liked it here," she said. "Did you just say the other night how you didn't think you were ever going to leave here again?"

"Like it here more than anyplace else I've ever been."

"Then why go?"

"No choice."

She looked beyond me as if someone was standing behind me.

"We can choose to stay or we can choose to go," she said. "If you're going, it's because you choose to go, because you want to go, not because you have no choice."

I came up close to her. She was wearing a long-sleeved blouse and I could see the heaviness of her breasts loose inside, and I wanted to take them in my hands through the cloth and hold them and feel their firm softness once more. Something dark and troubling had been working at me ever since I first saw the Cap'n's buggy black against the snow.

"It's because of that man that came to your house, isn't it?" she said.

"Yes."

She crossed herself as if she'd just stepped into the little church at the other end of the street—the one by the plaza where bailes were held every Saturday night if the weather was decent—and had a bell in the tower that would ring in the believers. An old padre with one good eye preached there, and some claimed he could perform miracles.

"I knew it," she whispered.

"He needs my help," I said. "I owe him from the past."

"What do you owe him?"

"My life."

"And now he wants it back."

"No. Not if I can help it."

She shrugged in resignation, shook loose a wet skirt she'd been holding, and hung it on the line.

"It's none of my business what you do," she said. "When and where you go and come. I'm just the woman who cleans your house."

"And sleeps in my bed," I said.

"Yes, and sleeps in your bed."

"I just wanted you to know," I said. "I figured I owed it to you to tell you."

"And now you have told me."

"Yes."

I turned to leave. She called my name.

"Jim."

I turned back, and she came close to me and pressed the palms of her hands against my chest.

"I'm afraid for you," she said. "I'm afraid you will go away and I will never see you again."

"You don't have to worry; there's nothing to this. I'm just going to ride along with the Cap'n while he does some business. You were right about him looking sick. He is. He's dying and is worried he won't get his business done before he passes on."

"What sort of business needs you wearing this?" she said, patting the bulge under my left armpit.

"You know how it is out here in this country," I said.

"Yes, I know how it is."

"I best get on," I said.

"I'll wait for you until the spring," she said. "After that I'll stop waiting for you." I wanted to laugh at her foolishness.

"I shouldn't be more than a couple of weeks at the outside."

"Do you want me to go and feed and water your horses?"

"No, I've asked Gin to do it."

"What about the chickens, should I go collect the eggs?"

"They're scattered all over hell," I said. "I broke the stud earlier and he kicked down the coop and fence and everything. I reckon those chickens could be in Colorado by now."

She smiled. I kissed her, then walked back up the street to the station.

Cap'n looked up when I approached like he knew something.

"You let her know you're going off?"

"Yes."

"You think you might end up marrying her?"

"It's possible."

"She strikes me as a good woman besides being real easy on a man's eyes. Women like that are hard to come by way out here in this frontier. Even no-account ugly women are hard to come by, but especially the real good-looking ones."

"There's more women than you might imagine if you like the Mexican kind," I said.

"I got nothing at all against Mexican women," he said. "They work hard and laugh a lot from what I know of them. I imagine yours does too."

I reached inside my coat pocket and took out the pint bottle of forty rod and handed it to him because he looked like he could stand a drink, and I sure as hell knew I could.

He looked at it before taking hold of it and pulling the cork, then he put it to his mouth and swallowed. Then he looked at it again and handed it back to me, and I took a pull and plugged it and put it back inside my coat pocket.

"Sun's pretty on the snow on them mountains yonder," he said.

"It is, ain't it."

Way off in the distance we heard the train whistle blowing.

"She's coming," he said.

I pulled my watch and checked the time.

"Way early," I said.

"Lucky we're here then or we'd of missed it," he said.

"Ain't we though."

He stood slowly as though he had to fit everything into place, all his bones, before he could move properly.

"You don't owe me nothing," he said. "I don't want you to go on you thinking you owe me because of what happened that time in Caddo."

"I'm not thinking nothing like that."

He stared hard at me then.

"'Cause if that's the case, I don't want you helping me. I don't operate like that, figuring a man owes me anything because of the past."

"Look, maybe it is some of that, but so what? You saved my skin in Caddo and if it wasn't for you killing those two bandits, I'd have been planted and no chance to help nobody or eat a nice breakfast this morning or spend my nights with a good woman. So maybe it is a little of my thinking I owe you for something. But it's not just that."

"What is it then?"

The whistle grew louder, and you could see the black smoke of its engine chuffing into the air off in the distance like a small dark cloud.

"I guess you already know."

He nodded.

"I always just did my job, Jim, keeping you boys alive, you and the others. I didn't always, that's a natural fact, but I did the best I could because it was my job, that's all."

I couldn't say I thought of him like he was my own daddy, which he'd just about had been when I first joined the Rangers. I couldn't tell him that, nor would he have wanted me to. Men like him and me don't talk about such intimate things, but it didn't mean we didn't feel them.

"You did more than your job, Cap'n, a lot more."

He looked off again up the tracks.

"Here she comes," he said.

I held the reins to the stud. He was jumpy at the sight and noise his iron brother was making. I stroked his muzzle and spoke to him gentle. "Don't raise no fuss and make us have to go through what we did earlier all over again," I said. The stud tossed his head and whinnied.

"Maybe we ought to have another sip of old Mr. Fortifier," Cap'n said. "Before we get on that train. Maybe you ought to give that half-broke horse a swally too so he won't kick out the sides of his car when they put him aboard."

I took out the bottle and handed it to the Cap'n, and he bit off a piece and handed it back.

"I used to be a teetotaler when I was married up with JoAnn. She was a righteous woman and wouldn't let me keep none in the house, and so I just gave it up along with every other wickedness when I got with her. She got me to being baptized standing waist deep in the Canadian River by a tongue-speaking preacher. She cleaned me up pretty good from what I had been. But I never claimed not to miss a good glass of whiskey or a good smoke, and now I just look at it as the best medicine a man can get himself."

"You don't need to explain nothing to me," I said.

"I know I don't."

Then we stood there waiting for the train to shudder to a stop.

5

The Cap'n slept on and off as the train rolled through countryside that was mostly tan hills shaped like the crowns of sombreros, and laced with ocotillo that glittered in the sun like the white of an old man's hair. The red country turned to brown and the creek beds and washes we crossed were mostly dry, strewn with rocks and boulders— here and there thin streams of water laced down through the sandy draws.

Once I saw a herd of antelope way off in the distance grazing contently, their tails swishing the flies.

The Cap'n would wake every now and then and say, "Where are we, Jim?" And I would guess and he'd nod and then close his eyes again, and I thought, *You must be plum wore out, Gus, go ahead and sleep in peace while you can.*

His coat was parted open and I saw the familiar pearl grips of his Smith & Wesson Russian model—something he'd always carried ever since I've known him. It was a .44 caliber that had seen its fair share of work. I knew because I'd seen it in action up close and personal on more than one oc-

casion. The Cap'n was a dead shot even under fire.
I asked him about that, how he never missed.

He said, "You just can't think about it, you just
aim and shoot what you're aiming at. You start
thinking, you're probably going to hesitate, and
that can be a fatal mistake in a gunfight." He
proved his point that time in Caddo when we ran
this half-breed gang to ground. We'd been dogging
their trail for weeks over some robberies and killings they had committed in the Panhandle. Our
party of Rangers took them on in a last stand
they'd made there in that little town, and we killed
five of them and they two of us.

We thought we'd killed them all, and while the
Cap'n went to send a wire to our headquarters in
Fort Griffen that the Juarez Gang was no longer,
the rest of our party licked its wounds and set
about burying our dead. Then when that was complete, we allowed as to how we needed to rest our
horses a day or so before starting home. I took the
opportunity to go into the town and get myself a
haircut and shave.

It was while I was there in the barber's chair with
a hot towel on my face I felt something small and
hard suddenly pressed against my temple and the
stink of bad breath. I heard the hammer of a pistol being thumbed back, accompanied by a rough
Spanish voice saying, "*Señor, usted mata a algunos
de nosotros, nosotros mata a alga de usted, eh?*"

I'd learned enough Spanish to understand he
was telling me it was my turn to die, to more or
less even the score for the ones we'd killed of his.
I peeked up through the towel and saw it was
old Vaca Juarez—a half Apache, half Mexican—

himself standing there, short and heavyset like
a man who ate too much beans and fried bread.
With him was a rough-looking character of about
the same stumpy stature, holding a Walker Colt
the size of a small cannon. Cross-eyed little bastard with a wispy mustache and whiskers looked
like they were made out of black silk threads sewn
into his upper lip and chin.

I eased the towel from my face and saw the barber standing there holding his straight razor down
along his leg, looking about as fearful as I was beginning to feel. You always think you're ready to
die when the time comes. But the simple truth is,
you never are when it actually comes. You could
be eighty years old and bullet shot and still not
ready. I was still relatively young at forty-five and
in pretty good health, and sure as hell not ready to
cash in my hand.

I saw the bottles of shave lotion and talc sitting
on the shelf in front of the mirror, saw my reflection and that of the three men standing—the barber and the two bandits holding their pistols on me
had every right to be pissed off, because we'd flat
laid out their companions in the earlier fight like
planks, side by side, so the local newspaperman
could take photographs of them before we buried
them in a hasty common grave.

The sour smell of the bandits mixed with the
talcum powder and shave lotions on the barber's
shelf. I saw patches of hair that had been cut from
my head lying there on the floor, and thought that
dying in a barber's chair was about the last place
I'd have guessed I was going to fold my hand if
somebody had asked me. But it sure as hell looked

that way, and I just hoped old Vaca had a good aim and generous heart and finished me with one bullet and not two or three. Sometimes a man wanted to make you suffer before he finished you off; he shot you in the knees or through the hands, just to make you suffer awhile.

I waited for the bullet that would kill me, knowing I'd never even hear the shot. I closed my eyes because I didn't want to see it. But then I did hear a shot that caused me to flinch. And when I opened my eyes, the man holding the pistol to my head fell like a stone dropped down a well at the same instant his blood and brains splattered across my unshaven face. The Mexican with him yelled something I couldn't make out, a bastardized cussword. But before he could get the word all the way out of his mouth the Cap'n shot him too, dead center of his forehead. The bullet bucked him back and he crashed to the floor and lay there next to old Vaca, who had a ribbon of blood coming from underneath his head.

I swiped the bloody offal from my face as I saw the Cap'n standing there, his gun still held straight out, smoke curling from the muzzle before he slowly lowered it and slipped it into his holster.

"You okay?" he said that day.

"I'm not sure, but I don't hurt nowhere."

He took his bandana from round his neck and dipped it a pan of water the barber used to wash off his razor off, and handed it to me, saying, "Warsh your face, Jim. Get that stinking bandit's blood off you."

He never once mentioned how I should have been more careful, or lectured me about making the mistake of letting the bandits get the cold drop on me. He just shot those two like they were quail, then put his gun away, waiting for me to wash my face. I'd always wanted to talk to him about it, about what it felt like to be so near being murdered, because a thing like that sticks with you worse than your worst dreams. I wanted to just talk about it after I'd had time to get my wits about me, but I knew he wasn't the type to discuss such matters— that life was just what it was; you either lived or you died and that was the end of it. Didn't matter how close you might *have* come to dying. Life for him at least was like a game of horseshoes—*close didn't count*. And if it didn't count, then why talk about it?

But I figured I owed him my life even if he didn't.

I saw a sign the following day out the window that read: NOW ENTERING ARIZONA TERRITORY. And when the Cap'n woke up from napping, I told him we'd crossed the border and he nodded and said, "Well, it don't look no different, does it?"

"No sir, it don't." Then he closed his eyes again and I walked out to the platform of the caboose.

A black porter was standing there smoking. He started to strip away his shuck but I waved him not to.

"Don't need to put it out on my account," I said.

"Yas suh."

The clatter of the train's steel wheels against the track rose and fell with an easy steady rhythm. The porter said, "Nothing like train music."

"You like working on the railroad," I said.

"Beats lots of other things," he said. He was

middle-aged with very black skin, and wore a black jacket and wrinkled trousers that were a few inches too short and a pair of rough brown brogans.

He reached in his pocket and took out his makings and extended them to me, and I thanked him and rolled myself a shuck, then handed his makings back. He handed me a match, and I struck it off the side of the car and cupped the flame in my hands to light my smoke, then snapped out the match and flipped it away. I never smoked before I met Luz. She's the one got me into the habit, just watching her smoke there in the evenings out on the porch of my place after supper. I liked the smell of it and I had her roll me a shuck, and after the first few draws I got used to it. She's the only woman I ever knew who smoked cigarettes and looked good doing it.

The porter and me stood there smoking with the rocking of the car beneath our feet, not saying anything because we were of two different worlds, the porter and I, but maybe not so different than a lot of people might think. I'm sure, like me, the man had seen his share of troubles and heartache. And I'm sure, like me, all he mostly wanted was a decent life, a steady job, and to live in peace.

"You like horses?" I said.

He smiled broadly.

"I used to ride 'em in the army," he said. "I was a buffalo soldier with the Ninth. Fought the Comanche, the Apache and Kiowa too. All over Texas mostly." He had a wistfulness about it when he spoke of it. He took off his cap and rubbed his shaved head.

"The Indians gave us the name because they said our hair reminded them of the buffaloes. I always kept mine shaved because I figured if they ever killed me I didn't want them to hang my scalp from their belts." The corners of his eyes crinkled when he smiled.

"We got that in common," I said, thinking aloud about how in my early years as a Ranger we fought some of those same peoples at places like Adobe Walls and Palo Duro Canyon.

"Huh?" he said.

"Nothing," I said. "Just talking to myself."

"It ain't no problem," he said. "I best get back on inside."

I nodded and watched him take one last precious draw from his shuck, then grind it down under his shoe heel.

Light lay along the twin ribbons of steel tracks that ran like two thin rivers behind the train. The smell of hot cinder rose from the track bed as a black erratic cloud of engine smoke floated lazily overhead. I thought of the thousands of Chinese that laid these tracks in their cotton pajamas and coolie hats, their backs bent to the task, how they must have squatted in the shade of their own making for lunch and the few daily breaks from the onerous work and chatted in their own language about their faraway homeland, wondering no doubt if they'd made a mistake coming here to this wild and endless frontier. I guess in some ways they were like that black porter; designated to their lot in life by the color of their skin and nothing else. Just men trying to make it from one day to the next while waiting for something impossible to happen that would change their circumstances, like a man who waits for love or money or God.

I went back in and sat across from the Cap'n. A woman in a dark blue gingham dress sat across the aisle from us reading a small book with red leather covers, her feathered hat resting on the empty seat beside her. She glanced up when I came and took my seat, and our eyes met, and she smiled and I returned the smile, then she returned to reading.

We rode on through the day and into evening, into the darkening land that lay ahead of us and descended behind us. We rode on like two errant knights off to slay the dragon—only the dragon was a kid named Billy, son of the Cap'n's daughter who always made poor choices when it came to men.

6

We stepped off the train in Tucson at around noon the following day. It looked ramshackle, like a bandito hideout. Up the street a group of men were gathered watching a cockfight. Two oily red roosters with steel spurs were tearing into each other, and I don't know who was squawking more, those chickens or the men betting on them.

Cap'n shook his head and said, "What men won't bet on."

He spat in the dust.

"What's our next move?" I said.

"We go and rent me a hack and drive to Finger Bone."

"You know how to get there?"

"No, but I can ask."

I unloaded my stud and saddled him, and tied on my rifle in its scabbard and bedroll behind the cantle. Cap'n carried his Winchester in one hand and his valise in the other. The sun scorched the dusty street so that when we walked our footsteps raised little puffs of brown dust that settled over the toes of our boots, and we got as far as a saloon that simply had the word SALOON painted in black on the adobe facing over the wood door.

"Maybe we ought to stop and get us a cold beer and something to eat," he said. "I'll bet you're hungry." We hadn't eaten anything since yesterday. We went inside and found a table, and the waiter came over and we ordered a couple of ice beers, and the Cap'n said, "Can you read that menu?" It was a chalkboard above the bar and featured beef stew and sausages and cabbage. I read it aloud and he said he'd try his hand at the sausages and cabbage. I ordered the stew. The Cap'n only nibbled at his food.

"It ain't setting too well with me, Jim. Not much is these days." Then he motioned the waiter over and asked if he had any bread and milk, and the waiter said he thought he had but he'd have to check the ice house. Then soon enough he came back with a saucer of milk and a loaf of crusty bread, and this the Cap'n tore off in small chunks and dipped into the milk and ate fairly well for a man in his condition. I could only imagine what that was like—to have cancer in your stomach.

We mostly ate in silence. Finally the Cap'n had enough and ordered us each a glass of whiskey.

"Finger Bone's where you said they got Billy locked up?" I commented as I washed down the last of the food with what was left in my beer glass before tossing back the shot of rye.

"Yes sir." Then he proceeded to tell me about Ira Hayes, the local lawman in Finger Bone, how Ira used to be a cattle and horse rustler and real hard drinker till the Cap'n caught up with him in a whorehouse after dogging him for the better part of a month.

"Ira at that time was living with a three-hundred-pound whore and selling snakehead whiskey to the savages down in the Oklahoma panhandle. The marshals were after him as well, but I caught him first. I come up on him taking a siesta, his big feet sticking off the end of the bed. The son of a buck was well over six and a half feet tall. His big gal jumped on me like I was a pony at the fair and tried to bash my head in with her fists. I had to lay her out, Jim. I swear I'm not about hitting women, but this one was about to ride me under. Then I called for him to surrender. Which he did quite well. He asked me right off as I was putting the manacles on him if I was a God-fearing man, was I in the Good Book regular, and I said I was, and even if I hadn't been, just looking around that den of iniquity of a town, where the saloons maintained a noticeable predominance over every other sort of dwelling, I'd sure enough become a righteous man from thinking I'd just landed in hell itself . . . Then I asked him why he wanted to know and he said because he'd been having thoughts lately about turning his life around . . ."

The Cap'n again displayed a rare smile in the telling of how he first met Ira Hayes.

"He wore two guns, real rare," the Cap'n said. "But one had a busted hammer and the other had busted grips, and when I relieved him of them and made commentary on his poor firearms, he laughed and said, 'Hell, I ain't a killing man no-how. Onliest way I'd kill a feller with my guns was if one went off accidental, or I was to throw one at him and it somehow knocked his brains out.' I said, 'Well, you are under arrest for horse thieving and cattle rustling and that's that.' He asked me would I pray with him and help show him the way to the Lord. I said, 'Right here, you mean?' His whore was laid out like a Belgium carpet there on the floor where I knocked her, and it was such a bad place you could taste the sin in the air. 'Yes sir,' says he, 'right here and right now, for I am sick to death of my criminal ways and want the good Lord to take mercy on me like he did them sinners on the hill.' So we prayed and I felt a change in him and promised if he ever needed anything when he got out of the jailhouse to let me know. Didn't hear from him for several years, then one day I got a letter from him telling me he was doing all right for himself, going to church regular, and wanted to know if I'd write a letter of recommendation for this lawman's job in Finger Bone—said he had a wife and a new child on the way and could use regular work. I wrote the letter and sent it to him and he wired me back later and said he'd got the job. That was three years ago."

It was the most I'd ever heard the Cap'n say at one time. I wondered if he'd gotten windy knowing his time was short, and everything he needed to get said, he needed to get said before it got too late. He swallowed down the whiskey the Mexican brought to the table, and it allowed some color back in his sallow cheeks.

"So the second stroke of luck, if you can call it that, was it was Ira who arrested Billy for trying to steal a horse, and Billy ended up confessing to him the whole sad story about what happened down in Old Mexico and that he'd wired his ma to try and get me to come down with my Rangers, and that's how it come out about who Billy was to me. Ira right quick sent me a telegram. I wired him back and said, 'Hold him till I get there.'"

"You tell Ira what's going to happen once you get Billy?"

"No sir. That's between us."

I saw how the thought of it drew down the corners of Cap'n's eyes and mouth into something grim and weary. He swiped whiskey dew off his mustaches with a forefinger and stood and took a moment to straighten himself, leaning his weight on the back of his chair but acting like it was a natural act and not something born of his pain.

"We best go rent that hack," he said. On the way out he asked the waiter where there was a stable, and the man told him and we went up the street past the cockfight where the dead roosters lay in a pile of bloody feathers, their owners having twisted off their heads and fed them to several stray cats lurking about.

Cap'n said, "I guess a man takes his pleasure where he can find it," as we walked past the knot of shouting men. "I personally don't see no sport in killing chickens."

A caballero sitting under a big straw hat with some of the crown eat out probably by rats was dozing on a three-legged stool in front of the barn. You could smell the sweet scent of hay and horse-shit lingering in the heat.

The man's arms hung straight down from his sides like he'd been shot dead, only hadn't yet fallen over. Cap'n kicked him lightly on the sole of his huaraches, and he woke with a start, pushing back the flop brim of his sombrero.

"Sí!"

Cap'n told him in Spanish he'd come to rent a hack, and they haggled the price because it was a common thing to do, haggling. Most of these birds felt slighted if you didn't haggle with them. They came to terms in short order because the Cap'n was by nature an impatient man. The caballero went and hitched a horse to a hack, and the Cap'n paid him in silver. Then the Cap'n pointed and said, "That the road to Finger Bone?" The caballero nodded.

"Sí."

"You're a fellow of few words, ain't you?" Cap'n said.

The caballero shrugged, not understanding the joke.

I mounted my horse and rode alongside the hack at an easy pace.

"We should get there by nightfall," he said.

And I couldn't help but think that by morning, Billy would be dead and the old man would feel worse than he ever felt in his entire life, and I probably would as well, just having to witness it.

7

In the dying heat you could smell the greasewood. The horses stepped along, raising dust to their fetlocks, their tongues fighting the bit.

"You doing okay?" I said.

The Cap'n kept a steady eye on the road in front of him. Off to the north a distant ridge of gray mountains seemed to shimmer in the haze.

Suddenly his horse shied in its traces and he fought it down while I shot the rattler that had crawled out onto the road, the Cap'n saying, "Snakes and horses just don't mix and never will." He skirted his rig around the carcass because the horse wouldn't have none of it. The damn thing was long as a man's leg and thick through the body as your wrist.

"Everything bites, stings, or sticks you in this country," he said. "They even got what they call jumping cactus out here—cholla, they call it." Then he grimaced in pain from something obviously troubling him on the inside, and his face was bathed in sweat, his color ashen.

I spotted a lone cabin off the road to our right, up a trace that cut through the desert.

"Why don't we pull off and see can we water the horses at that house yonder," I said.

"Lead the way," he said without debating me on it.

The house set back about a quarter of a mile and the trace was rutted with deep wheel tracks that had cut through the earth when it was wet from the rainy season and baked hard again with the sun, and each time the Cap'n's wheels caught and jiggled the hack, his face took on the look of a man being punched in the gut.

We got within calling distance of the house—a combination of mud and wood with a tin roof run through with rust streaks, a small stone chimney at one end and a by-God gazebo in the yard. Off to the right was a couple of lean-tos, a wagon with the tongue laid on the ground. Farther on was a privy. Off to the left rear stood a pile of rusting cans.

I called the house.

Old man stepped out with a big bore in his hands down below his waist, not aiming but ready to use it if he had to.

"What you fellers want?" he said cautiously.

"Wanted to know if we could water our horses," I said.

He looked from me to the Cap'n.

"Don't figger you're trouble," he said. "Never known killers and troublemakers to go around in a hack. Water trough is out back."

"You mind I step down and stretch my legs and maybe use that privy of yours?" the Cap'n said.

The old man nodded.

"Hep yourself," he said.

I led the horses around back to the water trough and let them drink while the Cap'n trudged off to the outhouse, then pretty soon trudged back again. I heard him in there retching. Then I walked the horse back round to the front where the Cap'n now sat making palaver with the old man there in the shade of a partial roof of what could be considered the start of a porch, but I'd never bet it was going to get finished anytime soon, if ever.

"How you making it way out here?" Cap'n was asking the old man. Well, I say old, but truth be told, the old man was probably the same age as the Cap'n, just more gnarled, like a wind-twisted tree trunk.

"Making do as best I can," the old man replied. "I come out here in '50, back when it was still wild and overrun with Chirichua and Lipan Apaches. Met old Geronimo and Natchez and their bands right here, near my well yonder. We palavered some and I think they would have cut my head off and put it on a pike, except I was married to an Apache woman at the time and she spoke up for me, saying how I was a good man and friend to the Induns, and they said long as I was married to her I didn't have nothing to worry about from them. That son of a bitch Geronimo had eyes like candle flames."

"That so," the Cap'n said. The old man nodded.

"You want a drink? I got some peddler's whiskey in the house I could abuse you boys with."

"Yes sir, we sure could use a drink of something stronger than well water," the Cap'n said.

"You look as if you could. Wait here, I'll go in and get the jug."

Cap'n looked at me and nodded.

"You learn to talk to folks right, you can get along pretty well in this old life," he said.

I looked off to where the sun was edging down behind some low brown hills, the rays of its light glancing upward and outward like the earth was catching fire.

"I bet that old boy has seen some things in his times," the Cap'n said. "I heard Geronimo was a real bad actor. Heard they put him in a jail down in Florida, Natchez too and their whole band."

"I bet he knows he's a lucky man to still be living," I said.

The old man came out, said, "My name's Torvor, Waylon Torvor, 'case you was interested," and handed Cap'n a brown glazed crock jug. The Cap'n took it up by the handle and hitched its bulk over his shoulder and tipped the neck to his mouth for a good long pull, then swung it over to the old man, who held it out to me. I stepped forward, and he grinned a dark brown–toothed grin through the grizzle of his maw and said, "You ain't Mormons, are you?"

"No sir, we ain't. What makes you think we are?"

"Nothing," the old man said.

I took a pull and was surprised how top-notch the liquor was. I handed it back and he took a pull and said, "Goddamn," and did a hitch step.

"You want another?" he said to the Cap'n.

"No sir, we got several miles yet to go and I'd not want to fall out of that hack and break my neck along that there lonely road and have to be buried so far from my home."

"Where you hail from?"

"Texas," is all the Cap'n would say.

"Texas," the old man said, like he was tasting the word. "Now that's a goddamn place and a half, it sure is. I once got married in Texas to a six-foot-tall whore—this was before I married the Apache woman, of course—who outweighed me by thirty pounds. This was in my wild youth. They grow everything big in Texas including their women." He cackled and snapped the jug up to his mouth again, happy for a reason to drink and palaver. And when he finished, he wiped off his mouth with the frayed cuff of his shirt sleeve.

"I buy my liquor off a whiskey drummer comes through here in the spring and fall. Says he has it shipped in from Kentucky. It fortifies me against all illnesses and dark times."

"Yes sir," the Cap'n said, trying to be polite. He wasn't a man to carry on an overlengthy conversation, nor listen to one either. He edged away from under the overhang and stepped toward his hack, and I could see it took every ounce of his strength to make it that far.

The old man called, "You boys is welcome to stay the night. Can camp out there in that shed if you like. Don't make nothing to me if you do. Got water and feed for your hosses. Just charge you a dollar for the feed. Good straw in that shed to make you a bed."

Cap'n looked at me.

"What do you think?" he said. The sky overhead had turned the color of sheet iron now that the sun had nearly gone out of it.

"How far is it to Finger Bone?" I asked the old man.

"Oh, I'd say another twelve, fifteen miles, but you daren't get caught out on that road after dark—too many highwaymen. They catch you out on that road, just the two of you, they'll set on you like chickens on a june bug. Real bad fellers patrol that road at night."

"I'm about tuckered out, Jim," the Cap'n said.

"You want us to bed down here for the night, that's okay with me," I said.

He looked off toward the dimming sky.

"It'll be dark before we got another two miles," he said. "I don't guess it'd make no difference if we get there late tonight or first thing in the morning."

I couldn't tell if his reluctance to push on was due to his feeling poorly or just that he knew what lay ahead of him, what he had to do once he got there.

"Maybe we ought to give it a rest then," I said.

He nodded.

The old man said, "I got a pot of beans with some fatback cooking in the firebox. We can all sit down to eat whenever you're ready."

I walked over and paid him the money for the horses' feed and then turned both animals out into the small corral he had there with his bunch of nags. I grained them down, then went and washed my hands and face at the pump and wiped off with my bandana.

The Cap'n was seated on one of the chairs the old man carried out from inside and set in the front of the house. The last of the sun was just then winking out beyond the smoke gray mountains off to the west. A soft dying wind ruffled the Cap'n's striped shirt. I sat on the edge of the porch.

"You thinking about tomorrow, when we get to Finger Bone and get your grandson?" I said.

"I am, can't help but to think about it."

"I'll do it for you if you want," I said. "I'll take care of that business for you."

He looked at me with troubled eyes.

"I couldn't ask that of you."

"You don't have to ask it."

"Shit," he said. It was one of the few times I'd ever heard him swear.

"You think about it," I said. "It's no skin off my neck you want me to do it."

"You think you could, just shoot a man like that?" he said. "A kid who never did a thing to you and wasn't trying to kill you back?"

"Put a gun in his hand if it will make you feel better."

He grunted.

"Ain't me that would need feeling better if *you* was to do it."

"It wouldn't make me feel better either way."

"I keep wondering what would get into him so bad, make him do something like what he done to that woman."

I shrugged and took out my makings and rolled myself a shuck, and it made me think of being out in the evening after supper with Luz, the two of us smoking and sipping liquor and talking.

"I sure wish I had a cold pear," the Cap'n said suddenly, sipping another bit of the peddler whiskey. "I do admire cold pears. Ever since I got told what I had by the physician, I'll get a craving for something now and then. The sweet kind you get in a can with the syrup in it."

I knew he wanted to change the subject, and I did too. I'd kill the kid if he wanted me to. I'd do it to save him the grief, but I sure as hell wouldn't feel good about it and knew it was something I'd have to live with forever.

The old man came out with his kettle of beans and salt pork and set it on the ground and then went back in and came out with three tin plates and some spoons and another jug of whiskey.

"Dig in," he said. "Ain't nothing formal round here."

So we ate till our bellies felt like they were full of buckshot, except the Cap'n didn't eat but a spoonful or two.

"Ain't it to your liking?" the old man asked.

"It is, I'm just not feeling up to snuff is all," the Cap'n replied.

To be honest, I wanted to say it was about the worst meal I ever ate, but I held my tongue in order to be polite.

Afterward we smoked and the old man said, "What you all going to Finger Bone for?"

It wasn't common for one man to ask another his business, but there wasn't anything overly common about this old buzzard. I just supposed he was lonely for talk.

The Cap'n said, "Buy some horses."

"Horses, huh?"

The Cap'n nodded as if to say, *What part of that don't you understand, old-timer?*

The old man pushed the jug toward the Cap'n and he tipped it up, and I could see the liquor was beginning to take its effect on him from eating so little and drinking that hard whiskey.

"We best turn in," I suggested. It was nigh on full dark now, stars beginning to sprinkle the sky and a half moon rising over the rimrock.

"Go on, make yourselves to home," the old man said, standing away and stretching. Then he hooked a forefinger through the jug's ear and took it up and swallowed what little was yet still in it and said, "You boys sleep well." Then he trudged off inside his door and closed it.

"I'm about all in, Jim," Cap'n said.

"Let's go saw some wood then," I replied, and we stood up and walked to the shed and pitched down some saddle blankets hanging from a nail hook onto the thicket of straw there.

"Boy, it feels like I've swallowed a belly full of bent nails," Cap'n said as he lay down. "It's pretty bad how life treats you when you get old . . ."

In a few minutes I could hear him breathing like a man will when he's first asleep. I was myself tired but not so much, and I lay there in the darkness with only a little of the moon's light coming in over the partial shed wall above my head.

I kept thinking about Luz, and how it would feel to be lying with her tonight in a regular bed and when was I ever going to get too old or tired of sleeping on the ground or some old man's shed floor and finally settle down permanent? I vowed once I got back home again, that was it for me; it would take hell and high water to ever get me to do anything like this again. Jesus himself could ride up to my place and say he needed help with the Philistines and I wouldn't go with him.

I was thinking all this when I must have drifted off to sleep, for I suddenly started awake when I heard the crunch of boot just outside the shed.

⤛ 8 ⤜

The Boys

Billy said after the funeral of their stepdad, Jardine Frost, when he and Sam went off behind the saloon in town after asking the drunk, Thompson, to buy them a bottle and giving him a dollar to do it: "We ought to skin out of this town."

Sam, barely fourteen, was still weighing the loss of the only daddy he knew with an ounce of kindness in him. Jardine never beat them, never laid into them, real soft-spoken sort and good to their ma as well. Would come riding home some days after his job as a horse trader with bouquets of wildflowers he'd stop and pick and sometimes bags of rock candy for the boys. One time he came home with a baseball for them. It was a treat to wait for Jardine to come home from his work.

But then one day he didn't come home till some men brought him home in the back of a wagon wrapped in a tarp, saying how he'd gotten into an argument with a fellow over a horse the fellow claimed Jardine sold him that had the bloat and how Jardine refused to refund the fellow's money and how the fellow went up the street and got drunk and came back with a long barrel pistol and shot Jardine through his rib meat, the first round, and the second through the back of his "goddamn skull" to quote the fellow who shot him. The fellow was arrested and a quick trial was held and the fellow was found innocent of murder in the first degree and every other degree because nobody could prove one way or the other whether it was a justified shooting or not, seeing as how the horse in question actually had the bloat and in fact died only one hour before Jardine was himself shot.

So there he now lay in a cold dark grave with nothing but Billy and Sam's memory of him photographed in their minds, this mild-mannered fellow with eyes blue as ice water, closed forever against the stain of the world wherein men could shoot you over practically nothing at all and get away with it.

"Where would we go?" Sam asked when Billy suggested they leave Tascosa. "And what about Ma?"

"Ma can make out a lot easier she don't have our hungry mouths to feed. We'd be doing her a favor."

"How'd we make a living and feed our own hungry mouths?" Sam asked.

"Hell if I know, but we'll make out one way or the other."

Billy was nineteen, and growing up as he had,

with a mother who couldn't pick the right man till she picked Jardine, or rather, Jardine picked her, had made him grow up fast.

He passed the whiskey bottle to Sam, and Sam took a hit off it while Billy rolled them a shuck and smoked it first, then handed it to Sam when Sam handed him back the bottle.

"You know that son of a bitch Longly that killed Jardine and got away with it ought to pay something for his sin," Billy said.

"How you mean?"

"I mean he ought to pay something."

"Like what?"

"I don't know, but we ought to ride over there and make him pay something to Ma, and to us."

"How we gone do that? We ain't even got no horse to ride over there with."

"We got the keys to the padlock that holds the gate to those horses Jardine was trading for that man in Uvalde."

"You mean steal us some?"

"You think that fellow from Uvalde when he gets here is just gone give us two horses for showing up and asking him?"

"No, I don't reckon he would."

"We got Jardine's pistols," Billy said. "We'll need 'em."

Sam remembered the Remingtons Jardine kept in a red velvet–lined case made of mahogany he'd shown them once from his old days of being a town marshal in Dallas. The citizens there had given him the set for his faithful duty of keeping law and order. They were even inscribed on the backstraps with *J. R. Frost*.

"His prize pistols?" Sam said.

"You think he's gone need them anymore?"

"No, I reckon not."

"Time we went out on our own, became men,"
Billy said. "Pass me that shuck."

They drank half the whiskey before Sam puked
up his portion and slumped down green. Billy,
nearly fallen-down drunk, laughed at his little half
brother.

That night after they'd all gone to bed, Billy woke
Sam and told him to pack some things and off they
snuck out the back door with Jardine's prize pistols
stuck inside their belts and walked clear to town
where Jardine kept the man from Uvalde's horses
locked up in a corral with a big brass padlock.

Billy undid the lock with Jardine's key, and they
slipped inside among the horses, some of whom
slept standing, their heads down. Billy picked his
way through the small herd to where some saddles
and bridles were kept next to a big grain bin.

"Pick you out one," Billy whispered.

The each took a bridle and saddle and picked
them out a horse and slipped the headstall over
their horses' heads and the bit between their teeth
and saddled them up, then walked them out slow
through the gate, with Billy dismounting and locking the gate again before remounting, telling Sam
to take it slow, to walk up the back alley behind
the town's buildings till they hit the road leading
south.

It was half a moon that night, enough to see by
but not easily be seen unless somebody was looking for them.

When they reached the south road Billy said,

"Okay, let's ride these sons a bitches like they was horses we just stole."

"We *did* just steal them," Sam said.

"My goddamn point exactly," Billy said with a grin.

The found Longly's place easy enough. Just a lone little shack looked like a shadow in the half light of night, sitting just off the road three miles outside of town.

"What if he keeps a dog?" Sam said. "And it sets to barking loud."

"Then I feel sorry for that old dog," Billy said and pulled the Remington out of his waistband, and holding it like that, knowing what he might end up doing with it, gave him a whole other feeling than he'd ever had before.

"You best pull your piece too."

Sam followed suit and they rode up to the house slow, thinking any minute some hound would come out barking and snarling. And such would have been the case, but Longly's hound had been bitten a week earlier by a rattlesnake several times and died an anguished death. The man Longly had not yet replaced him, much to Billy and Sam's good fortune and not to Longly's.

They tied off their mounts out front, and Billy stepped up to the door with Sam across from him, both of them holding their pistols at the ready. Billy rapped hard at the door and kept rapping till a light came on inside.

"Who is it?" they could hear a man calling from within. "Who the hell is there and what do you want?"

Billy shouted, "It's the law, open this goddamn door!"

It opened slowly and Billy stuck the muzzle of his revolver in Longly's face and walked him back into the room with Sam following.

"You're the brats of that whore Frost was living with," he said, and Billy struck him across the ear with the barrel of Jardine's pistol, and Longly yelped like someone had scalded him.

Sam was feeling nervous.

"Give me all your money, you son of a bitch," Billy commanded. "What you owe my family for taking the life of a decent man."

Longly held his bleeding ear, the blood dripping through his fingers and down his hand to his wrist.

"I'll give you shit and call it money, is what I'll do, you mealymouth little peckerwood."

Billy struck him again, across the collarbone, and dropped the man to his knees. Billy thumbed back the hammer and put the muzzle to the man's head and said, "You think I won't, just go ahead and call me another name and find out."

Longly relented, and Billy let him get a tin box from under his bed and take out the money he had in it, then Billy ordered Sam to take a rope and tie Longly to the bed, and Sam did what Billy told him. And once he had Longly tied to the bed, Bill went into the small kitchen and broke off a table leg and come back in and set to whaling on the bound man till Longly stopped screaming, passed out from the blows.

"I reckon playing all that baseball come in handy, huh?" Billy said, standing there breathless.

"You killed him," Sam muttered.

"Nah, I didn't. I just busted him up good. Look, he's still breathing fine. Let's get."

So they left with Longly's money and the man from Uvalde's horses and Jardine's pistols and Longly's canned peaches and a slab of fatback bacon and coffee in a burlap poke tied to Sam's saddle horn, and Billy wanted to burn the place to the ground with Longly still in it, but Sam talked him out of it.

And they rode hard for a time but then Billy said, "We ain't safe nowhere this side of the border, we best go to Old Mexico, cross the river and get on down to where they don't care who we are or what we've done."

And along the way they sustained themselves by holding up small stores to get supplies, and once a saloon for whiskey and a box of cigars. They even robbed a bank in Brazos but hardly got more than pocket change because all the money was kept in a large steel vault the banker said couldn't be opened till the next morning.

They camped out in canyons so nobody looking could see their firelight. They drank the whiskey till they passed out from it and smoked the cigars till they got used to smoking them.

One night while thus camped, Sam said, "I miss Ma."

"I miss her too," Billy said. "And as soon as we get a little extra money, we'll send her some of it to help her along and let her know we're all right."

Sam sometimes wept in his sleep.

And once they got down near the border, Billy said, "Time you and me became full-fledged desperadoes."

"How do you mean?" Sam said. "I thought we already were with all the crimes we been committing."

"We stole things, yeah—whiskey, horses, and even a box of cigars, and robbed that bank in Brazos." They both laughed at the fiasco of it. Billy continued, "And we come close to killing a man—which is the truest mark of a true desperado," Billy said. "But we ain't blooded yet."

"How do we get blooded?"

They were sitting their horses atop a rocky ridge looking down on a small village below. And perhaps a mile or two beyond, if their judgment was worth a spit, lay the river that once you crossed you were in Old Mexico. The river shone like a wire in the fading light.

"Come on, I'll show you," Billy said and spurred his mount down the slope, and Sam followed him on down.

They rode into the village with their pistols plainly showing, and folks outside their haciendas stopped to look at them. It was just one dusty street leading up to small adobes on either side, ramadas with roofs made of ocotillo that threw down patches of striped shade. They came to a cantina halfway up the street, and Billy said, "Let's rein in here."

They tied off their horses and went in without trying to hide the fact they were wearing pistols, and strode to the plank bar. A small, thin man with a horseshoe of gray hair stood behind the bar.

"We'd like some whiskey and a woman."

The man looked from Billy to Sam.

"You boys got a red cent to pay for the booze and pussy?"

The man had a deep Southern drawl.

"I guess we wouldn't be standing here asking for

it if we couldn't pay for it," Billy said, and slapped five silver dollars on the table. "What'll that get us?"

The man smiled enough to show he had buck teeth.

"Zee!" he called to a woman seated at a table by herself on the other side of the room. Near where she sat, a man sat with his head lying down on his table, snoring.

She was a lot bigger than anyone else in the room, and she lifted that bulk from her chair and came over. She was wearing a loose, thin cotton shift that showed the outline of her breasts and the patch of dark hair between her legs when she waddled over.

"These boys say they want a piece of beaver," and he pointed at the money on the bar. "What do you think, Zee?"

She looked at each of them.

"You little peckers think you're up to handling Mama Zee?" she said.

"I reckon we're about up for anything," Billy said.

"Shit then, follow me."

"I'll wait here," Sam said.

"Hell you will," Billy said and tugged him by his collar to follow the woman out back to a small shack that was barely large enough for a bed and a basin, which was all there was in it.

"How you peckers want it, one at a time or both together?" she said.

"One at a time," Billy said.

"Strip off your duds then, or if you'd rather, leave 'em on, but let's get started because it's tight in here and I don't mean this," she said, lifting the shift above her fat thighs. "I'm not laying in this stifling room any longer than necessary."

Sam cut his gaze away as Billy dropped his pants and climbed on top of the woman. Sam wished he could shut his ears as well—the ache of bedsprings and the woman grunting like a shoat hog. Then Billy climbed off and said, "Your turn."

It was something awful and at the same time fixating, Sam thought as he tried not to think at all. And when it was finished he and Billy went back into the bar while the woman cleaned herself up standing over the washbasin and had themselves a shot of tequila each, then left and headed for the river.

And when they'd crossed the river and made camp for the night, Billy said, "How was that back there?"

"Plain ugly," Sam said.

"Yeah, but you liked it too, didn't you?"

"I guess it's second best to using your hand."

Billy laughed and said, "Well, we're both blooded now."

"I feel like I ought to jump in that river and warsh."

"Go ahead."

"Think I will."

"Hell, I'll join you."

And for a time, as the sun sank beyond the brown hills, they frolicked in the cool waters of the river like fishes until they were exhausted and climbed out and lay on the grass naked and wet, semi happy knowing they'd probably never cross north of the river again—that what had been home was home no more.

Billy lay on the grass thinking, *I guess what we have done can never be undone. I should have left Sam out of this, but too late, too late.*

The stars looked like God's own eyes staring down at him.

Sam said, "I hope we didn't catch the pox from that fat whore."

"What do you know about the pox?" Billy said.

"Nothing, except it's supposed to be something bad and something you get from whores. I heard it makes men go crazy and some blind. I heard old Wild Bill Hickok had it and he went near blind, and that's how come that fellow shot him in Deadwood City because Bill couldn't even see the fellow pull his pistol."

"I don't think we caught the pox, do you?" Billy said.

"I don't know."

They closed their eyes and fell silent, each wrapped in his own thoughts. A coyote yipped from somewhere off in the dark hills. Another yipped back.

9

Jim & the Cap'n

I eased my Merwin Hulbert from my holster and brought it out and ready waiting for the next footstep to crunch into the caliche. The Cap'n lay asleep, his snores light, rhythmic. I leaned and touched his shoulder, and he awoke instantly, sitting up, his hand full of pistol. I touched the back of his wrist to keep him from firing at me.

"Someone's outside," I whispered.

We didn't hear anything.

"Maybe nothing," I said.

Then we heard it again, something, someone moving around outside. I rolled away from the Cap'n so that I was pressed up against the wall of the shed nearest the sound. There was a slight crack between the weathered boards and I put my eye to it. The moon was bright enough to show a shadow of a man carrying an ax standing there several inches from the shed as though listening for us. I shifted back to the Cap'n and whispered, "Start snoring again," then rolled back to the wall as soon as he did.

As I watched through the crack, the figure outside simply stood there holding the ax down alongside his leg, and the hair on the back of my neck rose. But it rose even more when a second figure appeared and stood next to the first. He was also carrying something in his hands—a shotgun it looked like, judging by the short length of it. I heard them whispering.

"You know what to do," the one said to the other. It was the voice of the old man who a couple of hours earlier shared his grub and whiskey with us. I guess he was about to put an end to all that hospitality. They took a single step forward toward the shed and I shot the old man, the flash of light blinding my night vision for a moment.

I heard a yelp and the Cap'n crawled over quickly and said, "What's going on?"

But instead of answering him I kicked down the loose boards of the wall and fanned the hammer of my pistol into the body of the man with the ax who'd paused and bent to his fallen comrade. I was pretty sure I hit him four out of four because every shot coming in rapid fire as it did caused his body to jump and jerk. He dropped the ax with the second round, spun completely around with the third, and went down with the fourth. The old man was on the ground moaning. The Cap'n was right there, his gun held straight out in front of him, cocked and ready.

"Get a lantern if you would, Cap'n," I said. He crossed the yard to the house and took a bull's-eye that had been hanging next to the door on a nail and struck a match to the wick, then lowered the glass and brought it near the two shot men.

One, the one holding the ax, was a younger version of the old man. He was shot through the belly and writhing on the ground, groaning through clenched teeth.

"Bring your light over here to this other one," I said, and the Cap'n walked it over and lowered it to the old man's face. His eyes were crossed in death as though he'd been trying to look down his nose at where my bullet struck him—top button of his shirt. Cap'n flashed the light around the ground till it fell on the double barrel. He bent and picked it up and looked at it close. Then he looked at the one moaning and groaning and said, "You chickenshit son of a bitch. How many others you done this way?"

He gasped and said, "I need a doctor, oh . . . oh . . ."

"You're gut shot, among your other wounds," I said. "A doctor won't do you any good."

It was a mean goddamn thing to say to someone dying, but I owed him no sympathy for trying to waylay me and the Cap'n.

"Oh . . . help me . . ."

"You bought the ticket, now do the dance," I said and stood away.

Cap'n, still carrying the shotgun in his hand, his

pistol now tucked down in his holster, said, "The old man must have thought we had money we were going to use to buy horses," he said. "I wonder who this other'n is."

"Looks enough like the old man I'd say he was kin, son or something."

"I don't guess it really matters, does it?"

"No sir, I don't suppose at this point it really does."

"What do you want to do about him?" Cap'n said, pointing the barrels of the shotgun at the dying man, whose boot heels kept digging for purchase into the ground.

"Leave him," I said. "He'll not make it till daylight."

"Can't just leave him like that, Jim. Wouldn't hardly be Christian."

I looked at the Cap'n as he handed me the shotgun.

"No, I'm not going to kill him," I said.

"I know," the Cap'n said. "I know you ain't, Jim." Then the Cap'n stood over the wounded man and drew his pistol quickly and shot him through the skull, and reholstered his revolver.

"I didn't see no other way, did you?" the Cap'n said.

"None at all."

"What time you figure it is?"

"Two, three in the morning," I reckon.

"Still can catch a few hours of rest and head out first light," he said.

"All right, if you think you can after all this."

"Might just as well make use of that bed inside," he said. "Beats hell out of sleeping in the shed like a couple of dogs."

"Be my guest. I'll wait out here 'case there's any more of his boys comes home."

"There won't be," Cap'n said. "I think we done all the killing tonight we're meant to."

The Cap'n went inside and I took out my makings and rolled myself a shuck to ease off the things I was feeling. Then I took the dead men by their boots and dragged them both into the shed and laid them there, and went out again and sat down on one of the supper chairs that was still out front.

I never have found out all the reasons that possess men to set upon one another, money, hatred, just pure meanness. Whatever it is gets in a fellow's mind makes no sense if in the end the man you set upon puts a bullet through your brain.

I smoked my shuck down, and then I guess I dozed fitfully in the chair until first dawn. The sky was as gray as a ghost with just a seam of silver light between it and the horizon. I went inside to wake the Cap'n, but he was already awake, but just lying there. He sat up and said, "Was it a dream I had about last night, me shooting a fellow in the brains?"

"No sir, it was real enough," I said.

He rubbed his eyes, then pulled on his boots, and we went outside again. We went out to the pump and washed our hands and faces and strung water through our hair, and then went back inside, where I fixed us some breakfast of fatback and beans from a can. We ate there at the table without speaking anymore about last night till we finished and stood away from the table and went outside again, leaving the dishes just setting there.

I saddled my horse and then put the Cap'n's in the traces of the hack, and he climbed aboard and looked off toward the road and said, "What'd you do with the bodies, Jim?"

"I put them in the shed."

He nodded.

"The wolves and coyotes smell death, they'll be round soon enough."

"I'm not that far gone as a human being yet to let them have at dead men," I said. I went over to the shed and searched around till I found a can of coal oil, then shook out the contents all over the boards before striking a match and setting the whole place afire, the bodies still inside. The fire caught slowly at first, then built quickly enough, like a maw of flame swallowing everything.

We rode off toward Finger Bone, the hungry flames behind us just as if we were riding out of Sodom and Gomorrah.

"I wonder how many others them two has way-laid over the years?" the Cap'n said as we rode along.

I said I didn't know but I guessed we weren't the first, that they just didn't suddenly start with us, because of the way the old man had set it up.

"I'm surprised he didn't try and drug us with that whiskey first," Cap'n said.

"You and me both know, criminals was smart, wouldn't none of them get jailed or shot," I said.

"Well, their souls are with Jesus now," he said.

"I doubt Jesus will have any truck with them," I said.

"I doubt it too, Jim. I doubt it too."

We were leaving death to go and create more of it, and that was an unsettling thought if ever there was one.

It was like death was dogging us just so it could learn how to do it proper. Last night, when I shot that man, I realized then and there, I didn't flinch at the thought, my heart never quickened, my hand never wavered, and it made me realize that in whatever ways I thought I'd changed, I hadn't changed all that much.

The road lay long and straight ahead of us, the sun just now rising above the rimrock to our rear, and the world seemed no wiser or bereft because of what we'd left in our wake.

= 10 =

Billy & Sam

They wandered from place to place, striking up friendships with the locals because they were in a strange country and Billy had heard some tales from Jardine back when Jardine was still alive and talking about the things that went on in Old Mexico. Said he'd been there a time or two, back in his wild youth, Jardine called it. "It's easy country if you know how to get along with the natives," he'd said. "Hard country if you don't.

"Me and some of my pals went down there that first time to see could we steal some Mexican mustangs off a big ranch down there. Ah, hell, we were only half-baked boys without no mothers and fathers. Most of us jumped off the orphan trains rather than be put to work as slaves for some farmer or rancher. We had to grow up hard and do what we could to survive. But it ain't no sort of way to live, boys. That's why I want to be a pa to you—to show you there is a better way. And I love hell out of your ma, too."

Jardine always had good stories to tell, and Billy and Sam would listen raptly as Jardine told them. He always wore a workshirt buttoned to the top button winter and summer and was fastidious about having clean hands, would wash them ten, twelve times a day and clean under his fingernails.

"So we get on down there," Jardine said of that particular time, "and first thing we did was come into this little town where all the women were as pretty as young colts and batting their eyes at us, me and Clarence Harper and Gil Westmore, and not a one of us over the age of seventeen, eighteen years old, and still green peckerwoods as you'd ever find.

"We practically fell out of our saddles from looking at them and having them look at us. Then some big-bellied man standing out front of a cantina us over and we stopped to see what he wanted and the son of a gun, and I swear this is the God's honest truth, had nothing but gold teeth in his mouth." Billy remembered how Jardine would shake his head over something he found hard to believe even when he was the one saying it was true. Jardine showed them his own teeth for emphasis.

"This fellow owned the cantina and a cathouse as it proved out. You boys know what a cathouse is?"

Billy and Sam shook their heads, and Jardine grinned and looked round to make sure their ma wasn't anywhere within earshot.

"It's a place where a man can buy himself a whore," Jardine said and waited for the effect to take hold of them, and when they both grinned he continued, "Anyways he says to us, 'Hey, gringos, you want some tequila. Real cheap, ten cents a glass, and I got some nice women, real cheap too.' And he called some of them outside there on the veranda of his cantina and we liked to have fallen over because she wasn't nowhere near the beauty of the ones we'd been seeing till then. She was real skinny for one thing, and not very good-looking unless you squinted. She was wearing nothing but these little cotton shifts you could see the dark of her tits through. Had this straight chopped-off hair and stuttered when she talked."

Billy and Sam tried hard to see it in their minds: the ugly woman standing on the Mexican's veranda in a cotton gown so thin her dark tits showed through.

"Well, I won't go into any of the dirty details," Jardine said. "Let's just say me and Clarence and Gil had us one heck of a time for a couple of days there even if we had to stay drunk as sailors. We went in that place with about forty dollars in money in our pockets and come out picked clean as chickens, with hangovers the size of Montana. We ended up crossing back north of the river with nary a stolen horse or a centavo to our names. But we was burning up with desire to go back again soon as we could put a little stake together. But then Clarence got hitched to a gal he got in the family way, and Gil got drowned in the Canadian River trying to cross where the ice was thin that winter. He was trying to save a yearling that had fallen in."

"What about the other time you went to Old Mexico?" Billy asked that time.

Jardine simply shook his head and said, "Boys, you don't even want to know about that time. Let's just leave it at it wasn't nothing like the first time. And you'll learn soon enough, nothing ever is." Then he showed them a puckered scar just below his shoulder. "That's all that needs to be said about the second time I went into Old Mexico." They knew it was a bullet wound that had left the scar.

"Remember some of those stories Jardine told us about?" Billy said as they rode along a white dust road with the sun straight over their heads.

Sam smiled and said, "I sure do. Wouldn't it be something if we could find that Mexican with the gold teeth that ran that cathouse and give that same skinny gal a go like he did?"

"It sure enough would," Billy said. "We'd have to get drunk like he did, but we'd get her done, wouldn't we!"

They both laughed. But neither could remember where or if Jardine had said the name of the town, and all they could do was hope that each town they came to might be *that* town. Some of the smaller villages didn't even have a cantina.

Soon enough they ran low on their luck, their pockets nearly empty and sitting in the shade of a ramada, sharing some tamales they'd bought from a local woman.

Sam said, "What's our next play?"

Billy shrugged. A grungy hound had come sniffing around, its coat dirty and rough. Billy broke off a piece of the tamale and fed it to the dog.

"Now git," Billy said and the dog slunk off.

"I guess we need to rob something," Billy said.

Sam looked around at the small, dusty village. "Rob what?" Sam said. "There ain't nothing here."

"Not here, but maybe the next place we come to. A store or a bank. Might even rob a railroad train if we come up on one going slow enough."

"Railroad train," said Sam incredulously.

"Well, something. I don't know what yet till we get to it."

Their boots were dusty with the white dust and so were their jeans.

"It's pleasant country, ain't it?" Billy said.

"I reckon. You miss Ma?"

"Some," Billy said.

"I do."

Billy ate the last of his tamale and wiped his hands on his jeans. "Eat up," he said. "We still got some daylight to burn."

"How you think Jardine got shot that time he was down here?" Sam said, still chewing his tamale.

"Hell if I know. Probably did something with a married woman and her husband shot him over it." Billy grinned at the thought. "Knowing Jardine, how wild he said he used to be in his youth, it wouldn't surprise me now, would it you?"

Sam shook his head. "I miss him too," Sam said, swallowing the last little piece of his meal.

"Yeah, well, we pretty well took care of that son of a bitch who killed him, didn't we?"

Sam didn't say anything but instead stood up from the shade and went over and tightened the cinch on his horse.

The sun burned through his shirt, drying the sweat stains, and he told himself as he fixed the saddle that he sure didn't feel fourteen anymore, but felt more like a grown man, him and Billy running all over the country taking what they needed and living free like they were, probably wanted outlaws north of the river so's they could never go back. It left a bad taste in his mouth thinking about it, and in some ways he regretted ever having taken off with Billy in the first place.

Finally he put a foot in his stirrup, realizing he didn't have a say in things now, things had gone too far for either of them to have a say in it. They could quit and turn themselves in to the law back north of the river and get locked up in a jail, or they could just keep going and see what happened.

The other thing troubling him was it seemed to hurt when he pissed.

"I think I caught the pox from that fat whore," he said as they turned their horses out to the road again heading south. He mentioned how it hurt when he went.

"I'd say it's a sure sign," Billy said. "I think I got it too. Started out tickling a little and now it feels like I'm trying to piss razor blades. We'll look for a doctor the next town we come to."

"Can you die from it, the pox?"

Billy shrugged.

"I never heard of nobody dying from it. But I did hear it can drive a man insane, he carries it in his blood long enough."

"It's like our own sins are eating us up," Sam said.

Billy looked over at him.

"Shut up," he said.

"Hell," Sam said. "I don't guess I have to if I don't want to."

= 11 =

The wind-waggled sign read: CIUDAD DE TONTOS. A sagebrush tumbled wildly across the road.

"What's it mean?" Sam asked.

"I look Mescan to you?" Billy said.

"Hell, I figured when you were running with that Mescan gal back home you knew some of the lingo."

"I knew enough to say let me kiss your lips and feel your titties," Billy said with a grin.

They spurred their mounts forward. It was a good-size town set between twin mountains whose slopes were prickled with hundreds of saguaro cactus.

Most of the buildings were adobe, low slung and whitewashed so it hurt the eyes to look at them under the blazing sun. Judging by where it stood, it was sometime late afternoon, four or five o'clock.

"You think maybe there's a doctor here we can get ourselves checked out and fixed up?" Sam said.

"I reckon, if we had something to pay him with."

"I'd trade my pistol for some relief."

"You'd be a damn fool then. In this country."

"I can't hardly stand to sit my saddle."

They reined in at a merchant store.

"What we aim to do here?" Sam said. "We got no money."

"We'll figure it out," Billy said and dismounted.

Sam followed suit and followed Billy inside. It was quiet and cool inside the store, with the scent of dry wood and blankets, coffee and tea.

Nobody was in sight.

"We could just grab some things and go," Sam said.

"That's what I was thinking. See can you find a gunny and then put some of them canned goods on that shelf yonder in it."

"What you gone do?"

Billy was eyeing a big brass cash register.

"What you think I'm gone do?"

Billy went around the other side of the counter, keeping an eye peeled for whoever owned the place while Sam poked around for a gunny till he came up with one.

"Eureka!" he said.

"Keep quiet," Billy said as he punched the buttons on the cash register in an effort to get the drawer to pop open. Finally it did with a ring and the drawer popped out. But the money was Mexican money, paper and copper and silver pesos.

"Shit," muttered Billy, but scooped them out and stuffed what was there in his pockets while Sam hustled cans of peaches and pears, beans and potted meats into the gunny.

Billy saw a rack of rifles across the way and went over but the rifles were chained to the rack and held with a padlock and he wondered where the key was.

"I can't believe this, can you?" Sam was saying when they heard something from behind a door that stood to the rear of the store. They froze listening.

"What was that?"

"I don't know but we best get in the wind," Billy said.

Then they heard something else, a sharp cry of pain sounded like a woman crying out.

"Something's wrong," Sam said.

"Don't worry about it, let's get the hell out of here."

"No, somebody's hurt back yonder."

"It's not our problem unless we make it our problem," Billy said, tugging at the gunny Sam was holding, trying to pull him toward the door.

"No, it wouldn't be right to let a woman lay back there hurt." Sam started for the door, then they heard the sound of breaking glass and a loud crash and Sam pulled the pistol from his belt and cocked it and Billy said, "You're a crazy son of a bitch you go through that door."

But Sam went through it anyway and Billy yanked his piece and followed his kid brother, figuring he couldn't just leave Sam hanging like that.

What they saw on the floor stopped them dead in their tracks: a woman lying in a pool of blood, gasping, her dress torn away, everything exposed, and several bloody stab wounds in her chest.

"Jesus God!" Sam said.

Billy saw the torn dress lying to the side and grabbed it and knelt by the woman, pressing the folded cloth to the woman's torso to try and stanch the flow of blood. She looked at him wild-eyed and gasped, only the gasp was more a rattling gurgle than anything.

Sam stood frozen, gun in his hand as Billy struggled to stop the blood. The woman squirmed and Sam shouted, "She's dying, Billy!"

"Goddamn, help me with this. Do something."

But neither of them knew what to do, and Billy looked into the frightened eyes of the woman that stared at him with so much fear, it went straight into him. His hands were soaked in blood up to his wrists now, the dress soaked too so that you could wring the blood out of it, and Billy thought, *How much blood can a body have?*

Sam ran out into the store and grabbed a striped blanket from a shelf and came back and pressed it to the woman's nakedness even as she thrashed about in her agony.

"Please, lady," Billy was saying. "Please . . ." Then he looked at Sam and said, "Run get somebody, see can you find a doctor, anybody."

But when Sam turned there stood a man in a tan soldier's uniform with a tan cap, clearly a uniform, and the man was nearly as tall as the doorjamb. He had dark fierce eyes and long black mustaches and wore a pistol in a black holster with a flap over it he'd already unbuttoned and was pulling the pistol from.

He spoke to them harshly in Spanish and aimed his pistol at them, waving them away from the body. Then he came and knelt next to the woman and spoke her name, "Maria . . ." They saw her eyes roll toward the man as if she was trying to speak to him with her eyes.

More Mexican soldiers poured into the room, their guns drawn.

"Shit," Billy said.

Then the woman shuddered and the man cried out to some of the other soldiers in Spanish and they came and lifted her and carried her out of the room in a hurry.

"You killed my child," the man said to Billy and Sam in English while the remaining soldiers kept their guns leveled at the boys.

"No sir!" Billy said. "We didn't have nothing to do with this."

"You little shits!"

The tall man stood, stepped forward, and slapped Sam with an open hand hard enough across the face to stagger him. Then he cocked the pistol and put it against Billy's head.

"Maybe I blow out your brains, eh."

Billy closed his eyes expecting the bullet. But then the man finally growled something to the others, and before Billy or Sam knew what was happening, they were dragged from the store and up the street to a large adobe building with bars on some of the windows. Even then the streets had suddenly filled with people, the word having gone out that Señorita Toro, the General's youngest daughter, had been murdered, her throat slit, that she had been "*violado*," they whispered. The rumors were rampant. Of course they were wrong on some of the facts, but what were facts when such a thing happened?

The General had been at home eating a meal when his brother-in-law, his wife's brother, came rushing in breathlessly to tell him there had been trouble at the store.

"What sort of trouble?" the General said. He'd been eating a chicken.

"Very bad trouble," the brother-in-law said.

"Maria, is she all right?"

"I don't know," the brother-in-law said. "You know I just left for a little while to go get lunch and when I returned I saw two hombres there in the back room with her on the floor. They both had pistols, and, well . . . I came right away for you."

The General stood with such a burst of energy he knocked over the table and the platter of chicken and everything else and grabbed his cap, hurrying after his brother-in-law toward the store, telling him as they went to go and round up some of his men and have them hurry to the store.

What he saw broke his heart when he entered.

His lovely and beloved Maria, her bare legs sticking out from under a blanket, the pool of blood flowing outward across the wood planks of the floor. He bent and took the blanket away from her and saw the numerous stab wounds, the two boys with blood on their hands. He'd pulled his pistol and ordered them to stand away from her, then knelt next to his daughter.

"*Oh, dios querido!*"

Then he'd wanted to know why these gringos did this thing but they denied having anything to do with it, and he became instantly angry and slapped the one boy hard across the face and nearly shot them. But instead his logic took over and he ordered some of his men to take the girl to the infirmary and the others to place the boys in jail until he could learn the truth of what had happened.

He told himself that if his child died, he would

immediately execute the two boys without benefit of a trial. He would have them shot by firing
squad; he himself would take up a rifle and make
sure they paid for their crime.

He was at once angry and aggrieved, and the
two emotions struggled within him to find some
balance.

For now, he must go to the infirmary and await
the outcome.

At his advanced age, he had learned it is always
best to keep your anger at bay until all the facts
were known and then proceed with due speed to
bring about justice where wrongs were committed.

But it was hard not to want to kill those two
muchachos then and there.

Very damn hard.

12

Of course the General had them beaten to get them to confess to their crime, to say why they did it. The men who did the beating tied Billy and Sam to chairs and hit repeatedly with a leather strap that cut and stung until their heads rang. At one point the General himself did it.

"What I want to know is, why did you come here and do this thing?" he said to them in between the beatings, between the buckets of water poured into their bloody mouths until they choked and almost drowned.

"We didn't!" Billy sputtered. "We found her like that."

"Oh, is this why you had her blood all over your hands, eh?"

The General's English was quite good. He was by far the most threatening of the many men who stood in the room along the walls looking on with passive faces.

Billy tried to explain it, so did Sam. Tried explaining it over and over again. But whenever they tried explaining it, the General or one of his men would hit them with the razor strap.

"Why don't you just kill us then, you believe we did it?" Billy screamed against the pain at one point.

The General shook his head, wiped the sweat from his forehead with the sleeve of his shirt, and drank from a bottle of tequila.

"If my *hija* dies, you can count on it, amigo."

The boys continued to deny their involvement with the savagery.

"You just happened to be there by accident, is that it? You came in and found her like that, is that your story?"

More beating.

Finally Billy said something that gave the General real pause: "If we done it, where's the damn knife we done it with!"

The General stayed the hand of his man holding the strap now.

"Did you find the knife?" he asked his men. They looked at one another, shrugged, until an older man said, "No, General, but then we did not look or even think about it."

"Go and see if you can find the knife," the General ordered.

Several of them raced from the room and went to the store.

The strap stung like a razor being slashed across their skin. Sam couldn't help but cry. Billy bit the insides of his cheeks till they bled.

Then their mouths would be forced open and buckets of water would be poured down their throats until they thought they were drowning and would pass out, only to be awakened again, to be beaten again until they both thought they would go crazy.

"I did it!" Billy finally muttered. "I stabbed her for the money, but Sam didn't have nothing to do with it . . ." Billy couldn't take seeing Sam done that way; he knew if it kept up, Sam would probably die first. Sam didn't deserve any of what was happening to him, Billy told himself, and if he had to confess to try and save Sam's life, then that's what he would do. And did.

The General nodded his head slowly, looked round at his men with a sagging satisfaction that he had gotten the confession.

"Why did you do it?" the General asked. "Did you do it for the money or because she was just there and an easy target for you? I want to know why."

"Yes . . ." Billy said, his will completely broken. What difference would it make what he confessed to? The General was bound to kill him either way.

"What is your name and where do you come from?" the General said. "I want to put it on your death certificate and send it to your mother. I want her to feel what I am feeling."

Billy told him the only true name he knew of, his mother's maiden name, because he didn't really know who his father was or even who Sam's father was—both men had fled before they were born. And it wasn't right in his book to use Jardine's name, because Jardine was no kin at all; he was just a dead man lying in a grave with all those stories left untold.

"Billy Rogers," he said.

"And where do you come from Billy Rogers?"

"Tascosa, Texas."

"Tejas, eh?"

Billy nodded.

"Tell me your *madre*'s name and I will write and send her your death certificate and tell her how you have died from your sins here in Mexico. I'm a fair man."

"Don't have no living kin," Billy said. He could only imagine how hard his mother would take hearing that he and Sam had gotten themselves killed down in Mexico, accused of rape and murder. He didn't want her to have to bear that.

"So you come from the North and yet you have no family. Were you born of chickens? Hatched from eggs?"

The General motioned toward one of his men and said, "Kill that one," pointing at Sam. The soldier took out a black revolver and stepped forward.

"All right, damn it!" Billy said. "Her name's Laura Lee Rogers. And I'll tell you something else, you goddamn son of a bitch, you kill either of us, she send her daddy down here to wipe all you bastards out."

The General snorted his derision.

"This is what you think, that some old man will come down here for the sake of you two and himself be killed in the trying?"

"Gus Rogers is one mean son of a bitch," Billy declared. "And he'll bring every Ranger he knows down here and burn this town and hang you and all these others . . ."

Again, the General took pause. He knew a Gus Rogers from his youth who later joined the Texas Rangers and became well known on both sides of the border.

"So your *abuelo* is Gus Rogers, eh? You think he will come and save you two little shits? No, he won't save you. And if he tries I will have him buried in the same grave as you."

The General motioned for the Ruales to lower his weapon. Tears streamed down Sam's cheeks. It was so awful, the beating they'd given him, he'd just as soon be shot and put out of his misery.

"Put them in separate cells," the General ordered. Then he went out, and some of his men shadowed him because he was *the* General. He went first to the store where his men were searching for the knife.

"Have you found anything?"

"No, General."

"Keep looking."

"Yes, General."

"And wash that stain."

"Yes, General."

The General was full of sorrow for his young daughter, the issue of his third wife as it turned out. He'd been married before, and one wife had died in childbirth and the baby as well, and the other had gone off with a young vaquero and disappeared after giving birth to a daughter, Edwina, and left him to raise her alone, and she was nearly grown by the time he met his third wife, a young woman forty years his junior named Phillipina with whom he'd had, very late in his life, this child that now lay in the infirmary possibly dying.

He went home to tell his wife what had happened and she wept bitterly.

He said simply, "I'm sorry. I've caught those

who've done this thing and will see that they are punished severely." It seemed to the General too little consolation.

It was this wife's brother, the one who had informed him of the tragic events, who owned the store originally. Maria had gone to work there at first to learn to become a business woman. She proved very good at it due to her education at a girls' academy while an adolescent. It was at the General's wife's insistence that he bought the store outright from the brother-in-law, who'd gotten himself into gambling debt. The General gave the girl the deed and said, "It is yours," but again at his wife's insistence, the General let the brother-in-law stay on as an assistant to his daughter. And so it had been until this very day.

What of course the General could not have known was the effect that the lovely Maria would have on her uncle. How, having worked so closely with her day in and day out, Don Domingo had secretly observed the young woman's beauty, practically breathed it in and became intoxicated by it. How his passion for her was like a small flame that built into a raging fire. And how on that particular day the two young gringos had come into the store, he had already lured her into the storeroom and set upon her. And when she refused his advances, he put his knife to her breast and cut away the dress and threatened that she would give herself to him one way or the other, so impassioned was he. And that as he was finishing with her and they heard someone enter the front of the store, the ringing of small bell above the door, this man, this Don Domingo, panicked when she cried out and plunged his knife into her several times. And then crashed through the tall window and ran down the alley.

No, the General would have never thought such a thing of his brother-in-law, the affable Don Domingo, who was by nature a quiet and unassuming man.

Absorbed as he was in his misery, the General waited with his wife at the infirmary; waiting, waiting, until she drew her final breath. Then the women who themselves were widows and prayed every day in the church came and said they would care for her. His wife, distraught beyond consolation, threw herself over the girl's body screaming, "No! No! No!"

The General could stand it no longer and wandered out into the night, then into the cantina, and proceeded to drink tequila while some of the men who always accompanied him stood by and watched somberly.

"What will you do, General?"

But he only wanted to erase the memory of seeing his daughter as he had—naked and terribly wounded and now peacefully dead. How does one wash away such a memory?

He fought the impulse to go straight to the jail and kill them both. That would be too easy; they deserved greater punishment before he killed them. For what would they suffer in comparison to what Maria had suffered if he gave each a quick bullet to the head? No, let them think about it, the hour of their death, in a way that his child had no time to think of her hour of death. Let them think about it and wonder when that hour would come to them. His military training had taught him much about how to punish the enemy. He would wait until after Maria's funeral.

He drank for a time, then said, "I want to go see the fortune-teller." His head was abuzz as though full of bees, from the absinthe and the tequila.

And so his soldiers walked him up the street to the house where the fortune-teller lived. The windows were dark. He rapped hard until a light came on and the door opened and the woman recognized her visitor.

"Sí, General," she said, and he removed his cap and heeled back the hair that had been sweated to his forehead and told her why he'd come. She invited him in, and he told his men to return and be with his grieving wife.

He stepped into the little house, and she led him to a settee and then sat in a chair near him and said, "Give me your hands, General." He extended them to her, and she turned them over and looked at his palms.

After a moment or two she released his hands.

"What do you think?" he said.

The fortune-teller said with all authority, "You have suffered greatly, but you will suffer even more . . ."

"Tell me how I could possibly suffer more than I am at this moment?"

She shook her head and said, "I don't know. It is not clear to me. But the lines in your palms tell of more trouble."

He gave a sigh and paid her for the fortune, stood and said, "Pack your things and be gone from this place by the morning."

His anger and pain were redoubled by the old

woman's predictions. What did she know anyway? Everything around him seemed unpleasant; his life was ending in ruin.

And in those very hours while he was away from the jail, sitting at the infirmary and later in the saloon drinking, followed by his visit to the fortune-teller, the General could not have known that the old guard watching over the gringos was smitten with Billy. The old guard was of a secret nature, and his desire ran counter to most men. And when he first saw Billy, he began to speak to him in soft tones while Sam slept on the floor in the adjoining cell with his hands clamped between his knees.

This old guard said to Billy, "You are a very handsome boy." Billy had removed his shirt to inspect his welts and bruises. "Yes, very handsome. Would you like a cigarette?" At first Billy did not know what to make of this odd fellow who was old enough to be his grandfather, a man with small rat's eyes narrowly set into his thin face and greasy gray hair that lay plastered to his bulbous head when he removed his cap and combed it to one side with his dirty fingers. He had a sour smell to him.

But young Billy had good instincts for sin and so saw it as an opportunity even if he had to swallow down the bile created by his disgust of the old bastard's intentions.

And when the leering guard stood and went out into the outer office for something, Billy whispered to Sam, "I think I got a plan to get us out of here. You just be ready to go when it happens."

Sam started to ask a question but Billy silenced him with a finger to the lips.

"Just be ready to run when I make my play."

Sam nodded.

Then Billy kicked at the barred door till the old guard returned, his eyes bulging from his thick face.

Billy met his gaze as they stood separated by the bars.

"I need to use the privy," Billy said.

"I get you a bucket, amigo."

"No. I thought maybe we could go out back. You got a privy out back, don't you?" Then Billy glanced at Sam, who pretended to still be asleep.

"I don't want my brother to have to see anything," Billy whispered.

The guard nodded.

"Sí," he said. "We go out back, me and you."

The guard went and got a pair of manacles and put them through the bars and told Billy he must wear them.

Then he winked and said, "It's okay, you won't need your hands, hombre."

Sam watched through half-closed eyes the two of them going out the back door.

13

He waited till the old man had placed himself in a vulnerable position, then brought his manacled hands down hard, using the heavy cuffs to knock the guard senseless. The old man let out a hard groan after the first blow but did not make a sound when Billy struck him a second time, splitting open his head.

"You dirty son of a bitch!" Billy muttered, then took from around the man's neck the key that he'd used to unlock Billy's cell and rushed back inside. But the key would not fit or would not work the lock on Sam's cell. It was either the wrong key or the lock was jammed.

"Hurry up," Sam pleaded.

"I'm trying, goddamn it."

Sam was so frightened, his hands shook and his body trembled as Billy fumbled with the lock.

"It don't want to work," Billy said. "Goddamn it."

"Maybe there's another key somewhere."

Billy ran out into the jailer's room and searched through the drawers of the desk but could find no other keys. There was a shotgun sitting in the corner of the room and this he grabbed up, broke it open, saw that it was unloaded but held on to it anyway. He ran back into the cell area and tried the same key again, only in forcing it to try and open the lock he broke it off.

"Son of a bitch!" he yelped.

Sam looked at him through the bars with the saddest eyes Billy had ever seen on anyone.

They could hear approaching voices through a small open window there in the back.

"I'll have to come back for you," Billy said.

"No use to it," Sam said. "They'll kill me sure."

"No they won't. I won't let them." Billy touched Sam's hands that gripped the bars of his cage. "I'll come back."

Billy burned with guilt at having to leave Sam. He wanted to stay and fight but he had nothing to fight with. Two Ruales entered the jail through the front door. Both had been drinking heavily, and Billy could hear them talking loudly to each other. Billy fled out the back door, stepping over the prone body of the old guard, and ran down the darkened alley into the night.

Stealing a horse should be easy enough, he told himself as he ran away and came out at the far end, where he rounded a corner and stood in the shadows of the main street again. He could not tarry, he told himself. The Ruales would discover soon enough he'd escaped and sound the alarm. There were several saddle horses tied up on the street in front of a cantina. Billy was already formulating a plan in his head. The river was a good fifty miles north, but if he chose a good sound horse and rode like hell, he could make the river by daybreak, cross it, find the nearest town, and sent a wire to his granddaddy.

He chose a big roan mare and knocked his heels into its flanks and rode it fast out of town and all night northward, resting only long enough for the horse to catch a blow and drink a little and eat a little. He'd read dime novels about the Pony Express riders and thought if they could ride at such a pace, so could he. He didn't care if he rode the horse to death as long as he could reach the river and cross over.

By dawn the next day that's exactly what he did, splashed across the river and into the States. He passed the dugout that had a sign crudely hand-painted that read: WHISKEY & ICE BEER and kept on riding. He needed to find a town that had a tele-graph and remembered a town not many miles yet north of the river. And less than five miles more he came to a town with the funny name: Finger Bone. He learned from asking strangers where the tele-graph was. He used his last dollar, that he'd stuck down inside his right boot for safekeeping, to send a telegram to his mother. Its contents explained in brief that Sam was in a Mexican jail in a place called Ciudad de Tontos—and that she should wire her daddy, Cap'n Rogers, and have him come quick with a company of Texas Rangers.

The last line of the telegram stated: "*I took blame to save Sam*." The telegrapher looked at him when he read it and said, "This true?"

"Just send it," Billy said.

Exhausted, he found a place to lie down in an alley to try and sleep and woke with a mangy dog licking his face. A dog with worse than dog's breath, and he sat up swatting at the creature. It yelped and growled once, then trotted off looking back over its shoulder at him.

"Boy, I'm piss poor and run down at the heels," he muttered to himself. The light in the alleyway was dim, indicating the sun was close to setting, he figured. He had no watch to tell time by. His welts and bruises felt like fishhooks in his flesh every time he moved. He stood with great effort. He'd been wise enough to have tied the reins of the stolen horse around his wrist before lying down. The horse stood with its head drooping, and he knew he'd pretty well worn it out on the hard ride.

He took pity on it knowing it wouldn't carry him another five miles. He turned it loose and walked out of the alley carrying the shotgun over his shoulder, on the scout for another horse to steal. Whoever he pointed the scattergun at wouldn't know it wasn't loaded and would be a fool to take the chance it wasn't, the way he figured.

He wished he had a dime for a cold beer and a sandwich, but he'd spent his last dollar for the telegraph. Well, that was where he was smart, to carry that empty shotgun, he told himself. It was all about taking risks now; he told himself he had nothing left to lose.

But goddamn, he was weary of running, of being chased, of all the bad stuff and none of the good. And the pox he'd caught from the whore didn't help his disposition any either.

He cracked the scattergun open again, hoping somehow, magically, two shells would appear. But the chambers were still empty. He snapped it shut again and stood there on the sidewalk in front of a closed millinery shop, trying to decide his next play.

A bank stood across the street, but it was closed as well, the last of the dying sun reflected in its plate glass windows. ARIZONA BANK & TRUST was lettered in gold leaf. He thought of all that money that must be in that bank, and he thought of his empty pockets and nothing standing between him and riches except twelve inches of brick wall and probably that much of steel where the money was no doubt kept in a vault.

Well shit, he told himself.

He figured to rob someone since there was no store or bank open to rob. First man who came up the walk looked like he had a few bucks was who he'd rob. The problem was, it was the supper hour and most folks were either home eating supper with their families or in the saloons drinking their supper. He was glad he wouldn't have to kill anybody, and in that way the empty shotgun was a blessing.

It was a wild-assed idea, but he even thought if he could steal enough money, he could hire some gunslingers to ride with him back down across the border and break Sam out of jail and thus save face all around.

But shit, that was like asking for the moon.

He leaned against the wall of the millinery and waited as the shadows closed in around him. Now he held the shotgun down along the side of his leg so it wouldn't be so obvious. Somebody come up, he'd just raise it and point it and ask for their wallet. He had his eye on a little paint tied

up down the street in front of one of the saloons.
Mustang, it looked like. Nice little horse.

How long he stood there waiting he couldn't say,
but the lights began to come on in the saloons up
and down both sides of the street, and somewhere
far off he could hear the rumble of thunder. It was
almost as if he could taste the air, the way it tastes
when it has rain in it, or about to come.

A stiff wind blew along the street kicking up
dust, and some cowboys rode in off to the right of
where he was standing, four or five of them in a
bunch, and tied off up the street and went into that
particular saloon, laughing and talking loud.

He realized it was Friday. First time he'd thought
about the day because ever since him and Sam had
left home, time didn't mean nothing to them. They
didn't have to be anywhere at any particular time
and had no use for watches or calendars. Time
simply became lost to them.

But if he remembered correctly, it had to be Friday. Or maybe it was Saturday. He closed his eyes
and saw the General bringing down the strap, felt
the sting, the way it stung like when you got cut by
a knife.

The anger and hatred welled in him suddenly
and he didn't give a shit what he had to do, he was
going to rob somebody, and if they put up a fight,
well, too bad for them.

Then he heard the clomp of boots on the boardwalk coming from his left. A tall man wearing a
frock coat with his trouser legs tucked down inside
the tops of his boots, whistling softly to himself.
Billy gripped the shotgun tight, hoped his ruse
would work.

And when he stepped from the shadows, shotgun coming up in both hands, he faced the barrel of a pistol inches from his nose.

"I don't know what you're intending, son. But you look way too young to die like this," the man said. Then showed Billy his city marshal badge pinned to the backside of his lapel when he flipped it over.

"Now set that shotgun down easy or this could be the last thing you're going to see—the dark hole of my pistol barrel."

Billy swallowed hard and let the shotgun slip from his grip till it clattered to the boardwalk.

"Now put your hands where I can see them plain," the man said. "I'd not want to get caught by surprise at some little gun you might have hidden up your sleeve."

Billy raised his hands, and the lawman told him to turn and face the wall and not move because "I've got a slight case of the palsy, and this Colt has a hair trigger, and I'd sure hate to blow your brains out if I didn't have to."

Billy felt the lawman patting down his pockets and down the inside of his legs and into his boots looking for a gun or a knife. And when he was satisfied, the lawman said, "Now just march down the street ahead of me till I tell you to stop."

Billy did as directed, and soon enough he was sitting in another jail cell, this one only slightly better than the one in Mexico.

The lawman, once he'd turned the lock, stepped back and said, "You ain't a local, so what I need to know is where'd you come from and what are you doing here?"

Billy told him what had happened.

"So you killed this daughter of a Ruales general, is that what you're telling me?" the man said.

"No sir, we didn't, but I said I did so I could hopefully save my kid brother from getting shot, figuring if they thought it was just me who did it, they wouldn't hurt Sam. But we didn't do nothing but try and save her life, and that's what thanks we got for it."

And when Billy told him the rest, how he'd wired his ma to try and get his granddaddy to come down with a company of Texas Rangers and said who his granddaddy was, the man offered a crooked smile and said, "Jesus, boy, I know your old granddaddy. You are one lucky peckerwood to be landed in my jail, and luckier still I didn't leave your brain matter splattered all over Mrs. Thurgood's hat shop. She'd hated like hell to have to wash up such a mess and who can blame her. Where's old Gus living these days?"

"Eagle Pass, the last I heard."

"You hungry, kid?"

"Enough to eat a damn dog."

"Well, we got plenty running around here."

"I know it."

"I'll be back in a little while."

Billy watched the lawman go out. He was an old bastard for doing law-dog, Billy thought. Old but way out in front of trouble, it sure seemed like. He had pulled his pistol without Billy even seeing it, and in a heartbeat too.

Then the fellow returned in a little while with a plate of food and slid it in under the door of the cell, and went and got Billy's stolen shotgun and broke it open and saw it wasn't even loaded.

He came carrying it to the cell door and held it up and said, "Jesus, boy, you must have yourself a real death wish."

"I reckon I must," Billy said, eating hungrily.

— 14 —

Billy was lying there on the cot, his arm flung over his eyes, his body aching like a fever from the whipping he'd taken at the hands of the General. *What right did that son of a bitchin' Mescan have to whip us?* He lay there seething, which did not help his physical condition any. He thought about Sam, wondered if maybe they'd taken him out and shot him by now, figuring that they'd not risk letting another escape their puny jail. He fretted over Sam terribly. His own guilt was like a sharp rock in his belly. He slept that night with a head full of bad dreams, of seeing Sam hanging from a tree, of the stabbed girl laughing at them, of his flesh being chewed by dogs.

He awoke to a stream of morning light angling in through the barred window above his head. Then heard the door to the jail open and the clomp of boots. It was the old lawman bringing him another tray of food, covered with a cheesecloth to keep the flies off. Ira slid the tray under the door and stood back and watched Billy eat.

Goddamn but it tasted good, a thick slice of

fried ham, fried potatoes, two corn dodgers, and a scoop of applesauce.

"My missus fixed it," the lawman said, retrieving a chair from the outer room and bringing it back to sit outside Billy's cell. He took out his makings and rolled him a handmade, and struck a match head off his belt buckle and held it to the tip of his shuck, then snapped it out. The smoke smelled good and reminded Billy of better times, like when Jardine would smoke in the evening on the porch of his mama's house, and him and Sam would sit at Jardine's feet there on the steps and listen to Jardine tell stories about all what he did in his life.

"Thank your missus for me, would you?" Billy said when he finished the plate.

"I'll do it," the lawman said. "I wired your granddaddy, told him I had you in the jail down here. I reckon I'll get an answer back from him pretty quick if he's still alive. You know if he's still alive?"

Billy shrugged. In truth, he did not know if Gus was still alive. He could only hope that he was.

"From what I know about him, I'd say he's too tough to be dead. Hell's bells, I figure he cares anything about us he's already on his way with a passel of Rangers," Billy said bravely.

The lawman looked at him askance through a veil of his cigarette smoke.

"I know those Rangers is some bad sons a bitches," Ira said, "but even they wouldn't cross that river and go into Mexico. It'd start another damn war if they did."

Billy suddenly felt glum.

"You don't know him then," he said defiantly. "I mean he whipped the Comanches all up and down Texas every which away. He sure as hell can whip a few of them damn Mescans."

"Hell, I know old Gus Rogers is bad on miscreants and such," Ira said. "He arrested me once and put me in prison. Hadn't been for his hard ways, I'd probably be dead my own self right now. He prayed with me to turn my life around before they took me off to the jail and I'll never forget him for that."

It was something Billy didn't know about his granddaddy, that he was a praying man. But then there were a lot of things he didn't know about his granddaddy because his mama had moved them away every time she got up with some man or another, and only occasionally did the Cap'n drive to wherever it was they were living at the time and see them. One Christmas he brought presents, and another time he stayed a week and took Billy and Sam fishing and they caught a catfish the size of a man's leg out of a muddy river. But that was about all he knew about Cap'n Rogers directly; the rest of his granddaddy's history was learned from Billy's mother whenever she felt in the mood to talk about him. Now Billy wished he'd learned him better.

"He might just do that very thing," Billy said, trying hard to raise his own hope. "Come all the way down here and bust Sam out of the jail."

"Might grow wings and fly with the angels too, boy," the lawman said. "You play checkers?"

Billy thought of it more as an opportunity than simply passing time. Figured he might find a chance to distract the lawman and get hold of his gun or some such.

"Like a son of a bitch," Billy said.

"All right then, I'll go get the set."

Billy and Ira played nine games straight and Ira whipped him like a rented mule and said, "It's a good thing we're not playing for money or you'd be broke as old Aunt Hattie."

"I *am* broke as old Aunt Hattie," Billy said.

"They skinned you in every way a man could get skinned down there, didn't they?"

"Worse than you can know."

"I'll have the doctor come and look at you soon as he gets back from the Johnson place. Mrs. Johnson's about to have her eighth child and Doc's been out there all night waiting on it."

"I appreciate it if he was to come and give me something for these whip marks."

"You want to go again?"

Billy saw there was no opportunity to reach through the bars and grab the lawman's gun since Ira wasn't wearing one. He'd obviously left his pistol in the outer room.

"No, I guess not," Billy said. "You've already whipped me so bad, I don't see as how there'd ever be any pleasure in it for either one of us."

"It's the only game I know," Ira said. Then he stood and folded the checkerboard after putting the checkers in a wood box with a sliding lid. He carried them out and returned with a wool blanket and handed it to Billy through the bars.

"'Case you get cold during the night, otherwise you can fold it and use it for a pillow," he said and went out again, and Billy could hear him locking the front door after he went out. Then it was just silence.

He lay upon the cot and stared at nothing, trying hard to think how he was going to break jail again. It was break jail or face the consequences once old Gus Rogers showed up—if he showed up. He was sure if Gus thought he'd killed and raped that General's daughter, his granddaddy wouldn't take any mercy on him. From what little he recalled of Gus's nature, he was a stern man when it came to serving the law. *Well, maybe I could convince him the truth of it*, he thought, lying there in the growing heat.

He closed his eyes, and when he opened them again the lawman was standing there with another man wearing pince-nez glasses pinched on the bridge of his nose. A sleepy-looking little man with a bald head holding a black leather bag in one hand.

"This your victim?" the man said to the lawman.

"It is. Boy says they whipped him with a razor strap—some Ruales down in Old Mexico."

"Razor strap? That right, boy, they whip you with a razor strap?"

Billy nodded.

"Like I was a goddamn dog that ate off their plates," he said.

"Well let's have a look," the man said. "I'm Doctor Bunyon, and all you're about to find in this town that passes for a medico. I also cut hair and embalm if you ever find yourself in need of such services."

He nodded to the lawman, who unlocked the cell door and let him stroll in like he was visiting a sick aunt in an infirmary.

"Take off your shirt," the doctor said.

Billy did as ordered, feeling ashamed to have to let people know he'd been whipped like that. Told himself a real man wouldn't have allowed it.

The doctor touched the welts with delicate fingers, but it still hurt like the blazes while he was probing and prodding. He reached into his bag and took out a jar of something and unscrewed the lid.

"This is some healing ointment," he said. "Dab some on you every little while like this," and showed Billy how much to slather on. "Don't get it into your eyes," he said. The ointment had a distinct smell to it and even caused Billy's eyes to water a little bit.

The doctor looked at the lawman and said, "I don't find no broken ribs or nothing. He'll heal but he'll have some scars to show the ladies."

Then he stepped out of the cell, and Ira closed it again and locked it and thanked the doctor, saying how he'd walk with him up the street to the café where they could get some coffee. "'Cause what I cook ain't worth drinking," Ira said.

Billy put the ointment on his cuts and welts, and it cooled the places it touched. He was grateful for any little relief.

Later the lawman came back with yet another plate of food, announcing, "Lunch," and set it under the jail cell door where Billy could get it.

"I'll go over to the telegrapher's and check and see if your granddaddy sent a wire back yet," Ira said. "You drink coffee?"

"Yes sir, I do."

"I'll bring you back a cup."

"Thank you."

The lawman reminded Billy of Jardine a little

with his easy manner. *I'm sure going to hate it if I have to shoot him*, Billy thought as he sat on the side of the cot and ate his lunch, a liverwurst sandwich with a slice of onion. *But I got to do what I got to do.*

15

Jim & the Cap'n

We made Finger Bone midmorning. The dead men, the fire, the near to coming to being assassinated in the middle of the night was still playing in the back of my mind. How many others did those two murder and bury somewhere was the question the Cap'n asked and the one I asked myself as well. It was a question I came to conclude that would never find an answer. But I told the Cap'n we ought to mention the attack to his friend Ira Hayes, the lawman in Finger Bone, just in case he knew of anyone missing lately—it might give a clue as to what had happened to them.

"You're right, Jim. Could be all sorts of folks them two killed and buried somewhere."

His voice was near a rasp by now, and I could

tell his flame was burning out sure as anything. I pretty well figured too that once he killed his own grandson, that would just about finish him, that he'd never make the trip back to Texas, much less on down to Old Mexico to retrieve his other grandson from the General. I doubted that boy was even alive.

Finger Bone would prove to be a typical little desert town: dusty and not much to it, but the sort of place that attracted bad men on the dodge from the law from either side of the border that lay just south toward the river. It was a place where the saloons outnumbered the churches ten to one and where the indecent women ruled the roost, because not many decent women would so much as hit the town limits before turning round and heading back to wherever it was they'd come from. It was also a town of men, mostly, and a handful of whores who kept them from going completely crazy. I'd ridden into a dozen such towns before, back when I was a Ranger and otherwise. They were towns that often would spring up because of a silver or gold strike or a railroad spur. And for a while, the town would beat like a young heart for a few years until the gold or silver played out, or the railroad stopped coming.

Then such towns would die a slow hard death, like a man gut shot, and be forgotten except by those who'd once been there and raised a little hell.

It was the bottom of the barrel for a lawman, the last stop before the grave, or worse, clerking in a store. I'd never met Ira Hayes, but I felt as though I already knew him because of what all the Cap'n had told me about him. My gut started to tighten the minute we entered onto the main drag because I knew that probably within the hour, I'd have to witness a killing that, no matter how you sliced it, didn't have any good to it. Killing never does, but this was going to turn out awful.

We were just coming up the drag when we heard the blare of trumpets.

"Sounds like a welcoming committee," Cap'n said.

"No, Cap'n, that sounds like funeral music to me," I said.

Then we looked on ahead and saw a black hearse pulled by a pair of Percherons followed by a bunch of people walking or riding horses or in gigs: men in bowlers and a few women in black dresses carrying umbrellas to shield against the sun. Behind the mourners was a brass band, their instruments catching the sun's glare, and a fellow beating a big bass drum slow and steady.

"Somebody sure enough is dead and getting buried this fine day," Cap'n said. The sky was as blue as a painting I once saw of the Pacific Ocean hanging in a whorehouse in Northfield, Minnesota.

"There shouldn't never be no funeral without rain," Cap'n said. "God's tears is what rain is."

I couldn't disagree. We were at a slow walk ourselves with the funeral procession a hundred or so yards ahead of us. The Cap'n took off his hat and held it to his chest, and I could see him mumbling what I supposed was a prayer and wished I was somehow better at it myself, but just dropped my eyes away out of respect.

We reined in at the saloon next to the building marked JAIL. There was black bunting in many of the storefront windows, including both the saloon and the jail.

"Must have been somebody important," I said.

"Must have been," the Cap'n said and climbed down out of his buggy with a grimace. He stood for a second getting himself back in order and I pretended not to notice. I knew his blood must be ticking in his wrist like a cheap railroad watch winding down, close as we were now to taking charge of his grandson Billy.

He turned the handle on the jail door's office but it was locked. Cap'n offered me a troubled look.

"Let's go next door," he said, "and get us something to swallow down this road dust and find out where old Ira Hayes is."

We entered the saloon through the batwing doors, and the place was virtually empty, except for one man behind the bar reading a newspaper held up to the dim light falling through a window there at the back wall.

He looked up when we entered and folded his paper and set it atop the bar before coming down to wait on us.

"Gents," he said. He was a smallish man with handlebar mustaches and garters on the sleeves of his red shirt. "What'll it be?"

"Whiskey with a beer back," Cap'n said. "And could you kindly tell us where I might find city marshal Ira Hayes? I've come to see him on some important business."

The man paused in his reaching for a bottle on the shelf behind him, all three of us framed like a photograph in the back bar mirror.

"I'm afraid you're a little too late if you're here

to conduct business with Marshal Hayes," he said, turning slow and pouring the shot glasses he'd set on the bar full to the brim with whiskey, so full you'd have to lift it gentle not to spill any.

"How's so?" Cap'n said.

"Marshal's been kilt. They're hauling him up to the boneyard now. Surprised you didn't hear what passes for a town's band playing his dirge. They just went by here couple of minutes ago. Would have gone myself, but he was no friend of mine."

"Who *kilt* him," Cap'n said. His voice was low now, tired as I'd ever heard it. I knew what he was thinking and wishing against—that it wasn't Billy that killed Ira.

"Kid he had locked up in his jail is who kilt him," the barkeep said, pulling the porcelain tap handle to fill our beer glasses, then slicing off the heads with a wood paddle before setting them before us.

Cap'n took off his Stetson and set it on the bar and rubbed his scalp, then tossed back his whiskey before setting his hat back down on his head again.

"How and when did this happen?"

"Yesterday evening," the man said, pouring himself a shot of the forty rod and tossing it back. "It's kinda early for me to be drinking but what the hell."

"You didn't say how it happened and I'll ask you again," Cap'n said.

The barkeep looked from him to me, then back at him. There was an element of danger in the Cap'n's voice when he grew irritated with someone, and the way the barkeep was casually talking about the death of Ira Hayes, I'm sure was irritating him more than just a little.

"Shit, nobody knows," the barkeep said, shrugging his shoulders. "Somehow the kid got hold of a gun and shot him, right there inside the jail. Then he run out and stole the first horse he come to—Charlie Kilabrew's fine gray racer it was—and rode out of here like his heels was on fire."

"Which direction?"

"South," the man said.

The Cap'n stood there, tired eyes ablaze with disappointment and maybe a mixture of relief that he didn't have to kill his grandson this hour. I was still wondering how he was going to do it when the time came.

"What lays south?" the Cap'n said. "Between here and the border as far as towns go?"

The barman thought for a moment.

"Just some little crap heap don't have nothing there except for a dugout run by Terrible Donny Dixon, who sells whiskey he pisses in and un-branded horses that are to say the least suspect as to their prior ownership. He also rents cots to men equally suspect, bordermen and others whose faces adorn wanted posters; they take quite well to Terrible Donny's place. Plus he keeps a couple of fevered whores whenever he can get them. Heard you can buy you a piece of beaver for little as fifty cents, you get there on the right day."

"That's it?" Cap'n said, "the only thing between here and the river, this man's dugout?"

The man nodded. "Far as I know, unless some-one's come and built a metropolis since I was last there."

"What you want to do?" I said.

The Cap'n coughed and said, "What the hell do you think I want to do?"

He put a dollar on the bar for the refreshments, then said, "You got a telegraph in this burg?"

"Out the door and up the street, three doors down on your left."

We walked out into the sunlight again, the glare of it causing us to squint.

"I'm a son of a buck," Cap'n said, shaking his head. "That grandson of mine has turned feral . . ."

"I guess if he thought he was going to hang," I said, "it made him a desperate man, like it would any of us, you and me included."

"That boy would have had a father, or if I'd taken over that role, none of this would have ever happened."

"You can't blame yourself. You can't say one hundred percent certain either it wouldn't have happened. You remember that Forbes boy who killed his whole family? He was, what, all of fifteen? His daddy was a banker, his mama a school-teacher. They were as good a folks as you're likely to find, living in that nice house in Houston, money in the bank. Well, he had a daddy and a mama too and everything a kid could want, and he still murdered them in their beds. And you remember how when we caught him in Ulvalde, he wasn't sorry one bit for it. Went to his hanging with a smile on his face. Some are just born with bad blood in 'em, Cap'n. Maybe that's the way Billy is."

He turned to me then and said, "That's the longest damn speech I ever heard you give, Jim."

"I know it."

We found the telegrapher's and went in, and Cap'n had him send a telegraph to his daughter, reassuring her everything was going well.

"I hate having to lie to her," he said when we walked out again. "But I don't want her worrying herself sick over this business."

"What about afterward?" I said. "If you get Sam back. She'll have to learn about Billy then, what happened down here."

He leveled his gaze at me and said, "I don't think I'm ever going to make it back to Texas, leastways not alive, so I'll not concern myself about the consequences . . ."

"Why do you think he headed south and not north?" I said. "After what happened."

Cap'n shook his head.

"There's not a thing I know about that boy except that at one time he was sweet with blond hair and loved to fish." Then he added, "We best get going, see if we can catch up to him before something else bad happens. This whole thing is turning into a nightmare, Jim. Just a damn nightmare."

"You don't look fit to even ride," I said.

"I'm here to tell you, it's not the easiest thing I ever done and it's plumb wore me out to come this far, but unless I'm dead, I got to catch Billy and put him down and all the rest of what the General wants me to do to get Sam back."

I saw a sign across the street in a small plate glass window that read: DOC BUNYON, PHYSICIAN, UNDERTAKER, BARBER.

"Let's take a walk across the street if you're up to it," I said.

Cap'n saw what I was looking at.

"You think I'm that far gone, I need embalming?"

"No sir, but you could stand you something a

little more potent than that cheap whiskey you been guzzling."

We entered the door, and it set off a little tinkle bell. The place had a strange odor to it like nothing I ever smelled before, a combination of hair oil and camphor. A man came out from the back with his shirt sleeves rolled up. The room we stood in had a barber's chair with a fancy steel footrest, leather seat, and porcelain arms. There was a small shelf of bottles and a mirror behind it. There were three chairs along the opposite wall with some old issues of the *Police Gazette* and a couple of DeWitt's dime novels lying on one of the chairs. Sunlight streamed in through the plate glass and lay in a patch on the floor that had tufts of hair around the chair.

"You boys need a haircut or a burying?" the man said with an affable smile that reminded me of a man whose daughter I had once courted in Amarillo. His eyes settled on the Cap'n.

"You look ailing," he said.

"I am," the Cap'n said. "Damn fine observation, but then that's your job, ain't it—to tell the sick from the dead?"

"'Tis," the man said without any indication of affront from the Cap'n's reply. "And you are in need of something that will not cure you but make the unpleasantness go away slightly, am I correct?"

"You are."

"I'd need to know what ails you in order to prescribe?"

"Cancer, if you must know," the Cap'n said. "At least according to those Texas medicos I've seen. Got it of the stomach."

"Sorry to hear. What troubles you the most, the pain or nausea?"

"Both, but mostly the pain. I got no appetite and can't sleep but a little at a time. Just wore out is all."

The man nodded, and you couldn't tell whether he was contemplating the Cap'n's situation or measuring him for a coffin.

"Just a moment," he said and went into the backroom whence he'd come and returned again in a matter of moments with an amber bottle in his hand. He held it forth to the Cap'n.

"What is it?"

"Laudanum. The only thing I have to help you. It won't cure anything, but it will help with the nausea and the pain. And if you take enough of it, it will put you out like a candle flame in the wind. It will make everything seem less important."

The Cap'n hesitated taking it.

"I need to be in my right head. There's something important I've yet to do."

The physician seemed resigned and lowered the bottle.

"Well, your choice, sir."

"How much is it?" I said.

"Three dollars."

"I'll take it," I said.

"It will turn a healthy man into a dope fiend," he said by way of warning.

"I'll take my chances."

I dug out the money and handed it to him and put the bottle into my back pocket.

The Cap'n waited until we were outside before saying, "What the hell you going to do with that?"

"Take it along with us just in case."

"Just in case what?"

"You change your mind."

"I won't."

"Well, we'll have it along just in case."

He shook his head and we crossed the street again to where our animals were, and he climbed up into his hack with grit and took up the reins and snapped them. I put the bottle into my saddle pouch and climbed aboard the stud and followed along with him down the south road and the unknown, and all the while, I'm sure, even though neither of us talked about it, we were both thinking the same thing: how it was going to be once we caught Billy, and the Cap'n had to put a bullet in him.

⊰ 16 ⊱

Billy

The gun had gone off as they struggled for it. Billy said how he had to use the privy; it had worked before. Ira Hayes knew his own boy would have been about Billy's age had he lived from childbirth. But he hadn't. The doctor came out wiping his hands on a towel, his face hangdog, that blustery night so many years before with the wind slashing across the Kansas prairies like sharpened knives that wanted to cut everything in their path, a hard snow ahead of it that rattled the windows till they came near to breaking.

"I did what I could, Ira, but your baby boy came out of the womb lifeless. Tried to breathe air into its nostrils, but to no avail. Stillborn is the medical term, but tragedy is the human one."

Ira and his wife were always careful after that not to try and make another one. His wife was fragile as a wildflower.

"You think we should?" she said that first night months afterward, knowing he was lonely and she was too; the two of them lying there in the dark listening to the last of the winter winds crying as if the winter was trying to stop the land from being born again.

But already fresh grass stems were struggling from the rich earth. Nature, an unstoppable force.

He'd shrugged, full of doubt whether he was too old to make a child with her, whether she was too old. The doctor had said one more miscarriage could take her too. Ira didn't want to run the risk of losing the only woman he'd ever come to love. They had named their unborn William.

"I reckon we should wait," he said. And so they had waited all through the spring and into the middle of summer. Then one day they were out cutting sod together to repair that same west wall the winter had nearly battered down, and it came a sudden rainstorm. The sky darkened the color of ripe plums and the air seemed to shimmer with something uncertain and became very still for a time. Blackbirds hurried away from the storm's approach, winging their way across the sky. They could see lightning like twisted wire dancing in the distance. Ira remembered an abandoned bachelor's one-room soddy within a mile of where they were and rushed her into the wagon and whipped the team of horses with a fury. They arrived just as the first raindrops the size of liberty dollars began hammering down.

They huddled inside under a smidgen of roof rafters that still had some sod on them, and the storm quickly surrounded them with a roar and a fury that wasn't uncommon on the plains. At times the ground shook from the thunder and she clung to him, afraid, and he held her, unafraid, even though he'd seen what a storm like that could do to beasts and humans. He'd once been a drover on the long trails out of Texas when he was just a kid and had seen men and cattle killed dead by lightning. He had seen dry washes and gullies suddenly roaring with a wall of water that would and could drown a cowboy looking for strays. But he was unafraid, because he was a man who believed firmly in the fates—that if it was your time to go, you were going to go, and not heaven nor hell nor all the gods, Christian or otherwise, could prevent your going. He believed, and he told her this one time while they were courting, that a man's days are numbered in the book of life, and when your number comes up, that's it.

She'd said to him at that time, "Are you a Christian, Ira?"

"No ma'am, I don't reckon so," (this before he met Cap'n Rogers, who'd arrested him and prayed with him till he felt born again).

"That's too bad," she'd said. "I was raised to believe in Jesus and the Holy Bible."

"I hope it don't change things with us," he said.

"No, I don't suspect it will. You can't always help who it is you fall in love with, can you?"

"No ma'am."

So there they were now cleaved to one another with the rain coming in and her trembling in his arms and as sudden as a lightning bolt his desire for her flashed within him. The next they knew they were being intimate there on the ground of that old bachelor's hut, the rain falling in around them, the mighty sky dark and brooding, the ground trembling, and she kept saying, "We must be careful, Ira. We must."

"Yes, yes," he said. And he tried his best to be careful, but neither of them was sure afterward if he had been careful enough. Then the late fall arrived and trouble arose within her pert body. The baby she carried because he was not careful with her wanted to come early. He remembered blood and water on the floor. He remembered her cries of agony as they waited for a doctor who never arrived. He remembered burying her in the same ground they'd used for a garden when it was planting time. He remembered how alone he felt and all the rest till he went way wrong in life and became what he became—an outlaw of sorts. Then fate brought him Cap'n Rogers, and it all got better after he stepped out of the prison gates.

He was thinking about all these things that evening as he sat playing checkers with Billy, how he'd have liked a son with her, and mourning the loss of his wife and the two babies she nearly had, both boys as it turned out. Then Billy suddenly said, "I sure got to use that privy, Mr. Hayes."

Ira didn't see much caution in it. The boy was soft-spoken and respectful enough, and besides, he'd go and get his pistol and strap it on, and nobody but a crazy person who was unarmed would try a man wearing a gun.

Ira walked him out back and waited outside the

shithouse door studying the night sky laced with stars like the sequins on a gown of a songstress he'd seen one time at the Birdcage Saloon in Tucson. And as much as he reflected on the sorrows of his life, he was grateful for what he presently had, a good new wife and a baby on the way, a decent job, and a little money in the bank. He thought himself a lucky fellow.

He was leaning there looking up at the sky when Billy suddenly burst out and grabbed hold of him quick as anything Ira could have anticipated. His fatal mistake: forgetting how old he'd become and how slow his reflexes compared to those of a wild youth.

They struggled for the gun and Billy wrested it from his grip finally, and aimed it cocked at him and said, "Don't make this harder than it has to be, Mr. Hayes. I don't want to shoot you." Then Billy marched him back inside the jail.

"Just undo these manacles round my wrists and let me go and you'll be home this night safe in bed with your wife."

"There sure is nothing I'd like more, son."

Billy had the revolver aimed at Ira's chest as he used the key to unlock the manacles. And maybe Ira just didn't think Billy would shoot him. He knew if he let a prisoner escape, the city council would probably fire him, say he was too old for the job. Incompetent. If it hadn't been for the letter of recommendation from Cap'n Rogers, he might never have gotten the job in the first place. He sure didn't want to lose it, he told himself. He had Jane to worry about as well. Jobs were scarce as it was. He could wait and see what was to happen and let

fate take its course, as he'd always done. But maybe
this was one time where he had to take a hand in it.
And as he stared down the barrel of his own pistol,
he decided fate was dictating he take action.

He made his play, and Billy pulled the trigger,
and Ira dropped back like somebody had clubbed
him. He fell to the floor groaning.

Bill shucked off the remaining manacle and bent
over the fatally wounded man and looked him in
the eyes.

"Why'd you do it, Mr. Hayes? You could have
just gone on and let me leave out of here and
you'd be . . ."

"Jesus," Ira muttered and reached his hand forth
to Billy, who thought he was saying an epithet but
quickly realized he thought Billy was Jesus. Billy
backed away, just out of reach of Ira's trembling
fingers. "Jesus, where's Katherine?" Ira said in a
voice so low and soft, Billy barely could make out
the words. "Didn't she come with you?" Billy knew
from Ira's having spoken of her that Katherine was
Ira's first wife, the one who lost the babies and died
in childbirth.

Billy stood away, tucked the revolver into his
belt, and ran out the door. There were half a dozen
saddle horses tied up in front of Avery's Wild
West Billiard Emporium & Oyster Bar, and Billy
jumped the first one he came to and rode off into
the dark just as several men came out talking loud
and laughing. The men were cowboys off a nearby
cattle outfit, and when they saw one of their horses
had been stolen they gave chase but lost the vil-
lain in the darkness, and returned to learn that the
sheriff had been murdered by his boy prisoner. It

was what everyone talked about the rest of that
night in every saloon, the killing of old Ira Hayes.

Doc Bunyon came and got the body with the help
of his retarded assistant, Olaf, and laid Ira on a table
fashioned from an old wood door with the knobs
removed and set on a pair of sawhorses. Drained
him of his blood and fluids using an embalming
machine he bought off an army surgeon who'd used
it in the Civil War, a dandy little machine made of
copper and rubber tubes. He then sent the retard
to Ira's house to ask the widow Hayes to pick out a
suit of clothes. The town preacher had been notified
of the killing and had gone straight to Ira's house
and informed Jane Hayes of the tragic events and
sat with her for comfort's sake. It was the preacher
who answered the door when Olaf knocked and
stated his reason. Jane Hayes was too distraught,
and so the preacher told Olaf to go and pick from
the closet what he needed. The retard came back
with black coat and checkered trousers and a blue
shirt.

"What about the shoes?" Doc Bunyon wanted to
know, and the retard started back to get shoes but
Doc said, "Never mind, he don't need shoes where
he's going." Then he trimmed Ira's hair around his
ears and combed the rest down with rose water,
parting down the middle with a rubber comb. He
finished the task by waxing Ira's gunfighter mustaches, and powdered his cheeks.

"How's he look?" he asked the retard.

"Pretty," the retard said.

17

Jim & the Cap'n

We'd not gone a mile from Finger Bone when the Cap'n slumped over in the hack. I rode alongside and grabbed the reins and brought it to a halt.

"Cap'n!"

His eyes rolled my direction but I could see he was in a terrible way. A grove of cottonwoods stood just off the road and I led the hack over there, then lifted the Cap'n out and laid him under the shade. I got the laudanum out of my saddle pouch and told him to take a swallow. He tried waving it off, but I insisted, and he finally took a long swallow of it, then lay back and closed his eyes. I wondered if this was it, if the Cap'n's string had run out.

He lay there for a few moments, then opened his eyes again.

"I'm sorry, Jim . . ."

"Nothing to be sorry for," I said.

"Maybe this dope the doctor give me will take hold in a few minutes and I'll be able to go on."

"I'm going to take you back to Finger Bone," I said.

He shook his head.

"No, I need to go find Billy before it's too late." He cringed, then took a deep breath and let it out again. "Maybe I could stand another swallow of that." I put the bottle of laudanum to his mouth and he drank. And after a few minutes he said, "That's helping some."

I waited another half an hour, then said, "What do you think?"

He shook his head.

"I'm not sure I'm able to move just yet."

"I've got an idea," I said.

"I'm listening."

"I'll take you back to Finger Bone and let you rest up there, and I'll go on ahead and see if I can find Billy. I'll ride to that dugout on the river and see if he's there. How will that suit you?"

He slowly nodded his head.

"Maybe it's best," he said. "I sure hate to leave this on you, Jim."

"You're not leaving anything on me I didn't want put on me," I said. "That was the case, I wouldn't be here now." I helped him up into the hack, tied the stud on back, and rode him back to Finger Bone. I got him a room at the hotel and got him into it.

"I'll be back in a day one way or the other. If

not, you know something didn't go right. Otherwise, I'll see you back here tomorrow."

By late afternoon, along toward dusk, I came to the dugout the barkeep back in Finger Bone told us about. Just beyond it ran the river, glittering like broken glass with the last of the sun in it.

There were three saddle horses and a mule tied up out front. The dugout was long and low and had but two windows notched into the logs; one was covered in oilskin and the other had cheap glass. The doorjamb was without benefit of a door but had a heavy tarp rolled up and tied off above the frame I supposed was used instead of a door when the need arose.

One of the saddle horses was a gray, the same color the barkeep described as having been stolen.

I reined in and tied up next to the gray, then dismounted. I didn't know what the kid looked like but I'd figure it out.

I stepped in through the opening of the doorway. It was cool and dark inside, and it took time for my eyes to adjust to the poor light. Two men stood at the plank bar and one behind it. The rest of the room was in deep shadows.

I stepped to the bar and said, "Whiskey."

"Right-o," the man behind the bar said.

"You Terrible Donny Dixon?"

"Who'd be wanting to know?"

Terrible Donny Dixon had a blind eye—his left—that was the color of spoiled milk, and a long horsy face, a nose looked like it had been broken more than once, and a receding hairline with a widow's peak.

"I heard a man could buy some cheap beaver at your place," I said.

"A man could," he said.

"How much?"

"Twenty dollars, stranger. That cheap enough for you?"

I sipped the whiskey as my eyes adjusted to the dark interior of the place. There were two other men sitting at a table with a bottle between them watching me closely. They could have been on the dodge and thinking I was a lawman. Or they could have just been the curious type. My eyes scanned the room, and I saw someone sitting in the farthest corner alone, but it was too dark to tell if he was young or old. He was hatless, and I thought not many men of this country go around without a hat on.

"Too much," I said.

"How much you willing to pay?" Terrible Donny said.

"Hell, I don't know, where's the merchandise?"

He said, "Just a minute," and went around the end of the bar and over to the doorjamb and shouted, "Maize, get your goddamn ass in here!" In a few moments a thin, emaciated woman came in through the door and over to the bar, and the other men watched her like she was a prize steer they were getting ready to bid on for supper. "Fellow is looking for some beaver," Terrible Donny said. "Wanted to see the goods before he plunked down his money. Show him the goods, honey." She pulled down the top of her shift to reveal two small breasts the size of pears. Just looking at her eyes, the way they were sunk in, the dark circles under them, the sallow skin, the skinniness, you could tell she was a dope fiend and probably not more than eighteen or nineteen years old, but looked twice that if you knew anything about dope fiends.

"Think I'll pass," I said, still keeping an eye on the fellow in the corner. If he came up out of his chair I was set on shooting him and anyone else in that stinking place who might want to give me trouble. I was tired and longing for home again, and I wanted to get this business over with soon as possible.

"How about two dollars for her," Terrible Donny said. "She's worth a good two dollars."

"No," I said, "but you can tell me where your privy is."

"Out back," he said. "And that will be one dollar for the whiskey."

I paid it rather than argue and walked outside and waited around the side of the dugout to see who came out. I wanted to see who the man was sitting in the corner and if he climbed aboard the gray. I slipped my Merwin Hulbert from the shoulder holster and held it in my hand down along my leg.

One hour passed, then another, and the land started to take on the shadows of night, and I could hear the woman inside laughing at something, then heard something break, like glass. I heard Terrible Donny curse at something. His voice was distinct, nasal and high-pitched like you might think a man would talk who had had his nuts cut off. Then right after the sun set completely, throwing off the last of its light against a gunmetal sky, and buttery light fell through the two windows out into the darkness, a lone figure stepped out of the dugout and went straight for the gray.

I stepped out of the shadows and said, "Billy Rogers."

He paused, one hand on the saddle horn, staring over the back of the horse.

"You got me confused with someone, mister," he said.

"I'm here to arrest you," I said.

The horse was between us.

"No mister, you've got me confused with someone else. My name's not Billy Rogers."

"What is it then?"

He hesitated just a moment too long, enough to have to think up an alias, and I knew without a doubt it was him.

"Jardine," he said. "That's my name, Jardine Frost."

"Step away from that horse."

"No sir, I can't."

"You can go hard or you can go easy, son."

"Fuck, I don't guess I'll be going at all!"

He jerked the reins free of the hitching post and spooked the horse so that it twisted and reared, and when it did a blaze of light flashed and I felt the kid's slug go through the sleeve of my shirt between my left elbow and wrist, even as I brought up my own piece and fired back.

My first slug took his horse. It reared, then fell dead. My second slug knocked the kid down but he scrambled to his feet again and ducked into the dugout. I could hear him inside shouting at the others to back away or die. Then there was a burst of gunfire, something big—like a scattergun and two bangs from a pistol. Several men came rushing out with their hands in the air shouting, "Don't shoot! Don't shoot!"

I collared one and said, "What's happened inside?"

He stuttered that Terrible Donny had pulled his sawed-off from behind the bar aiming to kill the kid but that the kid shot him first and Terrible Donny's shotgun blast had taken off the top of the whore's head.

"Jeez Christ!" he said. "Jeez Christ! Poor Maize!"

I turned him loose, and he ran away like a frightened dog.

I ran over and jerked my Henry from its scabbard and unloaded all sixteen shots in through the windows in rapid order. I wanted the kid to know I wasn't fooling around.

"I'm here on behalf of your granddaddy, Gus Rogers," I called when the last shot's echo died. "You want to come out of there walking or feet first, it doesn't matter to me. But you ought to know Gus isn't going to save you. He's dying."

There was a long silence.

"Who you?" he said.

"Not that it matters, but my name is Jim Glass. I used to Ranger for your granddaddy."

"How I know you won't shoot me?"

"I just come to get you, kid, take you to him, is all. I've got no reason to shoot you unless you give me one."

"He come to help save Sam?"

"He did, but he's sick as hell in a town north of here a little ways."

"You said you come to arrest me, earlier."

"Arrest, get, what's the difference? You look

around and tell me if there's not been enough killing here today."

"They'll just hang me if I give up," he said.
"Might as well go out guns blazing."

"I don't know, kid. One way, you might stand
a chance with a jury, but with me, you'll stand no
chance at all. Your choice, but I'm not going to sit
out here all night. I'm going to come in there and
get you if I have to. I've done this sort of work before, and trust me, I'm good at it."

All the while I was reloading the Henry, not to
try and kill the boy, but show him some of the effect of no-holds-barred warfare. I slipped the last
round into the magazine and emptied it again into
the building as fast as I could lever and shoot.

Then I waited a moment till the silence surrounded us and said, "Well, you coming out or
not?"

⇥ 18 ⇤

Sam & the General

The Mexican general studied him till it got on his nerves. Just stood there and stared in on him.

"What you want?" Sam said, almost shyly, but with a hint of defiance too.

"You think he's coming, don't you, your famous grandfather, the Texas Ranger?"

"Yes, he's going to come and bust me out of this spit bucket."

The General sucked his teeth contemplatively.

"I think if he comes at all, he will have the head of your brother in a basket for me."

Sam felt the bite of the comment as if it had teeth.

"Tell me, was it your idea or your brother's to set upon my daughter?"

"I keep telling you we didn't do nothing but try and save her life, mister!"

"If you keep insisting you are innocent, then you leave me no choice to show you any mercy. How can I have mercy on someone so cold-blooded?"

"Did you all find a knife anywheres? Because me and Billy sure weren't carrying no knives on us. And I don't know how you could say we stabbed your girl if we didn't have no knives."

Thus far no knife had been found, and this troubled the General greatly. He was an observant man; his military training had caused him to be so. He was strategic as well.

"Tell me what you did with the knife," he said. "It might go easier on you."

Sam shook his head disconsolately.

"I don't know why you can't believe nothing," he uttered.

"You know how this is going to work?"

Sam shook his head.

"I have told your grandfather that if he will find and kill your brother, that I'll let you live."

Sam bowed his head, looked at the floor.

"I didn't do nothing. And Billy *didn't* do nothing either!"

"He confessed."

"Just to save me."

"Then he was a fool, it won't save you, his supposed lies. Nothing is going to save you, my young friend."

"Then why not just kill me if that's what you all are intent on doing? Why not just get it over with?"

"You must understand fully the gravity of what you've done and repent."

"Fuck, I don't even know what that means—repent."

"You are a crude young gringo."

"I reckon maybe I am, but I don't know how else to be," Sam said. "It ain't like I got much to lose at this point in the game by trying to show you my good side, now does it?"

"You think that is what this is, a game?"

"No sir."

The General thought the boy disarming in his manner: one moment talking tough like a man much older, the next shy as a schoolgirl. But he felt no compassion for him because of their crimes. Even a young snake can kill you with its poison.

"How does it feel?" the General said.

"How does what feel?"

"To suffer, to never know the hour of your death?"

Sam touched the lacerated places of his face and body where he'd been whipped.

"I guess I know a little of what old Jesus went through before they killed him," Sam said.

"You believe in Jesus?"

"I do, yes sir."

"You think he will be waiting for you in heaven?"

"Yes sir."

"You think he knows what you did to my daughter and that he will forgive you for it?"

Sam looked up, his eyes full of grief.

"He didn't see me do nothing like it. I may have done some bad things but I never did what you said."

The General slapped him across the face with an open hand so hard, the sound was like a pistol shot. It knocked Sam senseless for a moment.

"You will own to it before it is over," the General said.

"That what you want? Me to own to something I didn't do?"

The General slapped him again, just as hard, and Sam tasted the salt of his own blood as it leaked from his lips and his nose.

The General smelled of cloves, his eyes black as the beads on a woman's necklace. He just needed hooves and horns and he'd be the damn devil.

The General walked out of the cell and the Ruales guard with him locked the door.

Left alone finally, Sam felt himself shrinking inside. He tried hard not to think about what it would be like in those final minutes when they came and dragged him from the jail—for he would not go willingly—and stood him in front of a wall (wasn't that the way they did it?) and tied his hands behind his back. He tried not to think what it would be like looking down the barrels of their aimed guns and waiting for that instant when they pulled their triggers and how the bullets would feel punching into him, and if when you died did you float off this earth into heaven or was it more like just a forever blackness where you didn't think or feel anything.

Forever blackness. It broke his heart to think there might be a forever blackness.

He thought of Rebecca, their neighbor girl back home who lived in the house next to Jardine's place where his mama had moved him and Billy to be with Jardine. Rebecca had strawberry-colored hair and budding bosoms and a sweet way about her.

She was a year older, and seemed several years wiser. And when she kissed him that one evening underneath the tree with the sound of cicadas buzzing all around, he thought he had never felt anything as good or would again, until she reached for his hand and put it inside the top of her dress and he felt the small, firm, rounded bosoms and the rapid beating of her heart.

Something happened to him that evening. Something in him broke like a wall pushed by too much water behind it, and he felt a warmness issuing from him and wondered if he'd wet his pants. But it was worse than that. Much worse. And it scared and embarrassed him even as the pleasurable sensation washed over him.

"Oh my," she said when she noticed as he twisted away. Then giggled into her hand saying, "No, Sam. I'm not laughing at you."

He ran off leaving her there under the tree, too embarrassed to speak, and for a week or more hid out, Billy and his ma saying, "You sick or something?"

The last time he saw her, she wanted to talk to him about it, but he begged her not to and they kissed and sat sweetly holding hands, Sam pining away for her, to touch her again like he did when he had his accident, but afraid he'd have another.

Then Jardine suddenly got himself killed and it was a mournful time till Billy said they ought to leave off out of there and strike out on their own.

Now as he sat caged and bleeding, his whole face hurting like the blazes, he pined for her, for home, for his ma, even for Jardine. And it all got worse when he thought that maybe Billy was even dead, his body lying out there somewhere, the buzzards and wolves eating it.

I come into this world with nothing, he finally told himself. *And I guess I'll go out of it with nothing.*

He could not see them because there were no windows in the jail to see them with. But he thought the stars might be falling.

⇥ 19 ⇤

Jim & Billy

It went on like that for a while, me waiting outside the dugout for Billy to make his play—to go out in a blaze of glory as he said it, or to throw down his weapon and come out peaceful. The air buzzed with flies.

"You liking it in there with those dead people," I called at one point. "You're going to join them, you don't get your ass out here."

"I need your assurance you won't shoot me if I come out," he said.

"I already told you, kid, I'm not here to kill you. I just come to get you to your granddaddy."

Another thirty minutes ticked off, then he said, "I'm coming out!"

"Toss your piece out first," I said.

His pistol came out through the busted window and landed in the dirt. Then he appeared in the open door frame holding his shoulder, his fingers painted with blood.

"You busted my damn shoulder with one of your shots," he said, grimacing.

I told him to sit on the ground while I went inside to check on the scene. And it was as one of the patrons who'd run out earlier said it was— two dead, one a woman. I mean both god-awful dead with the flies eating their blood. There wasn't any time to bury them. I figured somebody would surely find them quick enough and do the job for me, or burn the place down around them. There just wasn't any time to waste.

I helped the kid struggle into the saddle of his horse that had run off a little ways but then stood cropping the local vegetation of grass there by the river's edge where I caught it up easy enough.

We rode north again with the rising sun off to our right painting the desert red, then golden. You could feel the heat already rising from the desert floor. A Harris hawk sat perched atop a saguaro and watched us with an alert eye as we passed down the road.

Then it suddenly took flight, went into a low glide, and snatched a packrat with its talons and lifted high into the air again, working its wings mightily, breakfast caught.

"I feel like that packrat," Billy said. "Just like it." He rode slumped to his offside where his shoulder was broke from my bullet.

"Don't die on me, kid," I said.

"Hell, why not?"

I didn't have an answer for him. And to tell the truth, maybe it wouldn't have been so bad if he had died. It would save the Cap'n the trouble of doing the deed. But still, something in me didn't want the kid to die.

We had to ride slow because of the kid's busted shoulder. But before we ever reached Finger Bone, I saw the Cap'n's hack sitting off to one side of the road, the horse still in its traces its head down, the Cap'n slumped over in the seat.

I figured the Cap'n was dead. That he'd got up his grit to follow us and just died, and the harnessed horse finally just stopped pulling without anyone to guide it.

I reined the stud in thinking the whole journey had been a failure, remembering what I'd promised the Cap'n if he died—that I'd go down and try and save the other boy and kill the General if I had to. I sure did not want to.

The Cap'n lay on his side across the seat with his eyes closed, his hat fallen off his head.

"That him?" Billy said.

"It is."

I dismounted and told the kid to get down and he nearly fell getting off the horse because of his bad shoulder.

"Sit on that rock yonder," I said, and he went over and sat on it because he looked like he was close to fainting.

I went over and shook the Cap'n, and at first he didn't move. I shook him again and he roused, but slowly, never even reaching for his pistol, which told me he was in bad shape. I've never seen him come awake without reaching for his pistol.

"Huh . . . what is it?" he muttered.

"You okay?" I said.

He looked around till he saw Billy sitting there on the rock. His eyes narrowed. I saw the lines around his mouth tighten. The boy looked up.

"You my granddad?" he said.

Cap'n nodded.

"Come here, boy," he said.

"I can't."

Cap'n looked at me.

"What's wrong with him," he said. Then he saw the blood on the side of my shirt, dried now to a reddish brown.

"We had a problem," I said. "He didn't want to come along. His shoulder's broke from a bullet."

The Cap'n looked aggrieved.

"You been taking your medicine?" I said.

"Too much of it, it seems. I thought I had it in me to catch up with you. Didn't want to lay this whole thing on your back, Jim. Last I knew I was just driving along, and gawd almighty, I wake up and you're standing here. My head feels like it's stuffed full of cotton."

"You don't look too well."

"I don't feel too well, to be truthful with you. Had some real bad dreams."

"What do you want to do here?" I said.

"You know what I've got to do," he said.

The kid sat listening. You could tell he suspected something bad was about to happen, like a dog you're about to put down, or a horse when you approach it with your gun behind your back—they just know. The kid just knew.

"Listen," I said. "I'm going to walk off up that

road just a little and leave you to your business. Then I'll come back. That okay with you?"

He nodded.

I glanced at the kid one last time, then led my horse up the road where there was a bend in it that would take me out of sight of the Cap'n and his grandson. I didn't want to see it. I knew it would be a scene that would live with me all the rest of my days if I saw it.

I walked with an ache behind my eyes and wished I had a whole bottle of whiskey to drink myself into a stupor. Maybe it would help, maybe it wouldn't. I got around the bend and stood there in the road waiting for the pistol shot that would kill the kid. I wish I didn't have ears to hear with, either.

Time seemed to stand still like the whole world was frozen in a moment. Then: BANG! A single shot. The sound quickly got swallowed by the vast desert as though it never happened. I turned around and walked back, expecting to see the last thing I wanted to see.

Only what I saw wasn't at all what I expected.

The Cap'n lay dead on the ground, his gun still in his hand, one side of his head blown out, his boots pointed skyward, the dust soaking up his blood. Billy sat there on the rock staring at him.

"What the hell happened?" I said.

Billy shook his head.

"He shot himself," he said.

"Goddamn, I can see that, boy!"

"I thought he was going to shoot me," Billy said, his whole body trembling now. "He said he was bound to kill me in order to save Sam. He said, 'I

hate to do this worse than anything, son . . .' Then
he cocked his gun and I said, 'Yes sir, I understand.
You got to do what you got to do. Go on and do it.'
He told me to look away, that he didn't want me to
look at him. I told him I wasn't going to look away.
Told him that I wasn't afraid of dying as much as
I was to keep living. Told him that I'd messed up
my life pretty good, but if he by God was going to
kill me, I wanted him to look me in the eyes when
he done it.

"He said, 'Yes sir, you surely have ruined your
life. I just don't know why it was you went so bad
so young. I guess if I'd been there for you, you
would have turned out different than you have.'
I told him it wouldn't have made no difference—
that I'd probably have gone bad either way, that I
thought I just had bad blood in me. He said, 'Is
that why you killed that woman and my friend Ira
Hayes?' I told him I killed that lawman because
he was going to kill me for trying to escape—that
it wasn't something I wanted to do, that it was an
accident.

"He said, 'What about that woman, that just an
accident too?' I said, 'No sir. I never did kill no
woman,' and explained it all to him. You know
what he said when I told him that?"

I shook my head.

"He said, 'I believe you, boy. I been around liars
and cheaters and badmen all my born life and I
know one when I see one. You might be a lot of
things, but I don't think you're a liar.' I said, 'Well,
that's it then, go ahead and pull your trigger and
get this over with.'"

I waited as the kid hesitated, blinking back whatever was in his eyes.

"Then he just said, 'I'm all in, boy. I'm finished as finished can be, and I'll be damned if I'm going out with such sin on my head. So long, boy,' and turned the gun on himself before I could try and stop him . . .'"

Tears began to stain the kid's dirty cheeks, his resolve to be hard-bitten was broken at last, broken in a way no bullet or threat of death could break him.

"Thing is," I said, kneeling by the Cap'n and taking the gun out of his hand, then gently closing his half-open eyelids. "He wouldn't have lasted another week. He was eat up with cancer. I guess he just couldn't do what he'd always done in the past."

The kid rubbed the tears from his eyes with the heel of his hand.

"What's that?" he said.

"His job," I said.

"Where does it stand now," he said, "between you and me?"

"If your granddaddy didn't kill you and bring your head in a basket to him, the General was going to shoot Sam, that was the deal," I said.

"Then you best go on and do it. Sam's a good boy and never done nothing truly wrong other than what I talked him into doing. He don't know much better—he's just a kid. Hell, what difference does it make to me if I'm alive or if I'm dead." He looked at his bum shoulder. "I'll never be able to use this no more and I'd as soon be dead as be a cripple anyways."

I stood away from the Cap'n's body. My old friend. I looked at the kid. I told myself I should just ride away from this, that maybe the younger boy was already dead, and even if I killed this boy and did what the General wanted, I'd just be wasting my time doing a dirty business I wouldn't ever be able to wash from my hands.

There was already too much good blood spilled as it was.

20

I bent and picked up the Cap'n's body and got it into the hack.

"You think you can drive this with one arm?" I said to Billy.

He nodded.

"Then get in and take the reins."

"Where we going?"

"To Old Mexico," I said.

For the first time I saw something akin to fear in his eyes.

"They'll kill us both we go down there with no army of guns to back us," he said.

"I'm going to see if I can trade you for that kid brother of yours. That's the plan, kid."

He stiffened.

"I wish you'd just do it instead," he said. "Pull the trigger on me rather than let those dirty Mescans have at me."

"You don't always get what you want in this life," I said.

"I don't want that dirty Mescan killing me!"

"What difference does it make who does it?"

"Makes a lot to me. He whipped me like I was a damn dog. Whipped Sam too. He had no right."

"He thought you killed his daughter; you're lucky he didn't shoot you on the spot."

"I wished to hell he had."

"Wishing don't make it so, kid."

I told him to lead out and he took up the reins in his good hand and snapped them over the rump of the horse, and we splashed across the river, and I thought, *There is no turning back*. By midday we made the village of Arroyo according to the sign on a side of a livery; a sleepy little burg that stood baking under the noon sun. A collection of clapboards and adobes without a single thing I could see to recommend the place. But I was hoping we could find a doctor, though, to look at the kid's shoulder. It was one thing to take him down to Old Mexico to be murdered, another thing to let him suffer on the way. I am not by nature a cruel man, or at least I'd like to believe that I am not. And I needed to find an undertaker for the Cap'n. I wanted him to have a decent burial.

I stopped the first person I saw, a woman sweeping the front of her adobe stoop. She was fat and brown with raven black hair twisted into a cone atop her head. She wore a red blouse and dark blue skirt and sandals on her feet that were dusty. She paused when I rode up and spoke to her and asked her if the village had a doctor.

"*Qué?*"

"Medico," I said. She looked from me to the boy, then to the tilted form of the Cap'n, and crossed herself and pointed up the street. We rode on. I saw a man, a white man, washing the windows of a cantina and asked him where the doctor was, and he turned to look at me and the kid and the body of the Cap'n.

"Across the street upstairs over the jeweler's," he said. He was wearing a big Walker Colt on his hip. I thought it must be a pretty bad town if a man had to wear a sidearm just to wash his store window.

"Who does the burying in your town?" I asked.

"The German, Hass. Digs the graves, no undertaker; he just puts them in quick, if you know what I mean, it being hot as hell down this way." Then he paused and chuckled and said, "I guess it's hot as hell in hell too, if that's where you're headed."

"Where might I find this Hass?"

"Keeps a place out at the cemetery, lives there, can't miss it. Just go on up this road to about half a mile out of town. You'll see it on your right."

I thanked him and we went across the street and I tied up the horses and helped the kid out of the wagon.

"What about him?" he said, looking at his granddaddy.

"He's not going anywhere."

I guess he saw the wisdom in that and climbed the stairs ahead of me, and we knocked on the door and it was soon opened by a thin man with dark skin and a widow's peak of silver-streaked hair and spectacles.

"Got a patient for you," I said in Spanish. "You speak gringo?" He nodded, said, "Sí. *Poquito*, a little."

"This boy's got a bullet-busted shoulder, do what you can for him, I've got money."

He had the kid remove his shirt, then examined

his busted shoulder, shaking his head. "How did this happen?" the medico asked.

"That sum bitch standing yonder," Billy said, pointing at me with his nose.

I ignored the remark and rolled myself a shuck and smoked it while the doctor cleaned out the wound and wrapped it and set a sling for the boy's arm.

"I can't do much for you," he said. "I've not too much to work with here in this place. Do you use this hand or the other one?"

"This," Billy said, looking down at the hand of his wounded shoulder.

"Then you will need to learn to use the other one," the doctor said.

"How much for the services?" I said as the doctor shook some pills from a bottle into a small envelope and handed them to Billy, telling him to take them as he needed them for the pain. "Take one or two now, if you wish?" Then he said to me, "Five American dollars."

I dug around in my wallet for five dollars in paper money and handed it to him.

"We've got to go, kid," I said.

Billy stood unsteadily and we went down the stairs again, and we drove out to the cemetery, where we saw two men digging a fresh grave. We rolled up to the iron fence and I dismounted. They stopped digging as I approached.

"I got a man needs burying," I said. "A friend."

One was a large man with a barrel chest wearing a thin, sweat-soaked shirt with the sleeves rolled up past his elbows, and a beard that looked like a hawk's nest. The other man was short and dark-skinned, wiry as a terrier. His work clothes were dirty, ragged at the knees. His straw hat was busted out in the crown.

"Yah, I bury yer friend," the big man said with a German accent. "Where you have him, eh?"

"Over in that rig," I said, pointing to the hack.

"We get him for you, then," the German said, and both men laid their shovels aside and went and carried Cap'n out of the hack and laid him there on the ground near the grave they were digging.

"Head shot, eh?" the German said, looking at the Cap'n's bloody head wound.

"Yes," I said.

"Pretty bad deal for him."

"You going to bury him in that grave you're digging now?"

"Yah. Why not?"

I shrugged and nodded with approval. There was no reason not to bury the Cap'n as quickly as possible. No need for a funeral and no mourners except Billy and me to attend it.

"You think you can get a priest to come and say a prayer for him?" I said. The German nodded and looked at his smaller companion, who hurried off toward town.

"We dig all the time, eh. Always somebody needs buried, yah. We finish this, we start and dig two more right away. Always the same, three graves a day, more if we need to. That way we stay ahead of the work, yah."

"How much for the burial?"

"Ten dollars if you don't want no coffin, fifteen if you do."

I took out the last of my money, then realized I probably should empty the Cap'n's pockets of his possessions. I knelt and took out his effects: a wallet with close to a hundred dollars still in it, a tintype of a young woman holding an infant with a towheaded boy clinging to her skirts—Sam, I figured, was the baby and Billy the boy—a heavy pocket watch, the contents of his valise, and his fancy Russian model Smith & Wesson pistol. I stood and said, "Okay, make sure he gets the coffin and the priest prays over him."

"Yah, sure, sure. I make sure, for his soul."

Then I started to walk away. Billy was still sitting in the hack looking stunned, and I saw he had the Cap'n's bottle of laudanum with the cap screwed off in his hand.

"Hey," the German yelled. I turned around.

"What about the ring on his finger, your friend?"

He pointed. It was the Cap'n's wedding ring. I never saw him without it.

"You leave it on him," I said.

"Yah, yah, okay then."

I tied my horse on back of the hack and climbed in and took the reins from the kid and turned the hack back toward the town because we needed to eat something. My belly was rubbing my backbone and I was tired from not having slept all night. We needed to eat and rest a little while, then hit it hard on down to the border and across.

"We turning back?" Billy said.

"Just going to town and get some grub and a day's rest. We can't go on like this, neither of us, and our horses need rest as well."

We found a livery and I paid the liveryman

there to feed and water our horses while Billy and I walked up to a restaurant and bought a meal: bowls of chili with chunks of beef that made your eyes water. Coffee for me. Billy asked if they had any cold buttermilk. The waiter said no. He had big black handlebar mustaches and acted as though this was the worst work in the world for a man to be doing. Maybe it was. Billy said, "I'll have a glass of beer then if you don't mind."

When we finished we walked up the street to the one and only hotel according to the waiter. It stood on the corner across from a bank. On the opposite corners were also a hardware store and a saddle maker shop.

The clerk behind the desk at the hotel had long sideburns that came down to his jawbone and shifty eyes.

"Two rooms next to each other with locks," I said.

He asked me in Spanish how long we'd need the rooms.

"*Una noche*," I said. Just one night.

The room charge was ten dollars.

We climbed the stairs to the upper level and walked down the hall till we found room numbers nine and ten. I unlocked nine and we went in. It was just a room with a single bed, no chair, a small table with a lamp on it. Bare floor, window that looked down into the alley that ran behind it.

I opened the window to let in some air. The room was hot and dry, the wallpaper that had once been a pattern of roses and stripes was faded and here and there peeling.

"Why it's just like the queen's palace," Billy said, looking around.

"What would you know about the queen's palace?" I said.

"Shit if I know anything about it."

"You stayed in school long enough to learn to read and write?" I said.

"Some. I read about her once—Queen Victoria. Said she lived in a palace and had servants for her wolfhounds. You believe that?"

"I wouldn't know. You go ahead and get some rest," I said and went out locking the door from the outside with the key, then opening the door to my own room, which was nothing different from the kid's.

I took off my shoulder gun rig and laid it on the table, but put the pistol under my pillow, then I sat down on the edge and removed my boots and lay back. The weight of exhaustion pressed down on me like a slab of granite. The room was hot and still, but I didn't even care.

I closed my eyes, and when I did I fell into a sweet dream about Luz.

We were swimming naked in a pool of cool water and she was laughing and we wrapped our arms and legs around each other and became like one person and made love that way, standing in the water, wrapped round each other.

I awoke sometime later in the darkness, got out of bed, and looked in on the kid, half expecting him not to be there. But he was. Sleeping in the bed just like he was a normal boy. And I wondered what he was dreaming about.

It sure couldn't be anything as pleasant as making love to a woman in water.

21

Sam & the General

Sam heard the mournful music outside his cell, from beyond the adobe walls. Strained and halting, it seemed like at first. Then it became less strident and uneven and more like the sad weeping of women, and he realized that it was the funeral cortege for the General's daughter. He could hear the ringing of church bells, dull and heavy with a reverberation that he could almost feel against his skin.

A Ruale stood guard outside the cell—ever since Billy had escaped. He was armed with a rifle and he did not smile or speak, for he'd been ordered not to.

"They burying the General's daughter, ain't they?" Sam said.

The Ruale's eyes flicked his way.

"Boy, that's sure enough a sad thing to hear— that dirge. She was a pretty woman," Sam said. The Ruale looked away.

The day before, they had come and taken Sam from his cell, and he thought it was to shoot him. They marched him down the street to a vacant lot that had an adobe wall and three wood posts set into the ground. A crowd of people had gathered and there was a line of Ruales standing there in the hot sun with their rifles. And then the old guard that had allowed Billy to escape had been brought in a wagon. He was sitting atop a coffin of white pine, it looked like. The wagon stopped and the prisoner was dragged down, his wrists and ankles in shackles. His head was cut from the beating Billy had given him, and he stood trembling as the coffin was lifted out of the wagon and carried over to the middle post. Then he was marched over to the wall where the posts were and a rope was tied around his chest to secure him to the middle post.

The General came then, riding a large black horse whose tail nearly brushed the ground. The General sat there among the gathered crowd as though allowing everyone a chance to take notice of him before dismounting. Then he went and stood among his soldiers who were lined up twenty or so paces from the prisoner. Another officer who walked along with the General handed him a cigarette already made and lighted it for him with a match.

The General smoked casually while all around him everyone stood silent, waiting. The prisoner wept openly, his whole obese body trembling. He blubbered in Spanish. Sam reckoned he was pleading for his life. Sam felt sorry for him.

Then the General motioned for the Ruales holding Sam under the arms to bring him forth and Sam thought, *Well, this is it then*. It pleased him that he had no fear of what was about to happen to him. He'd been working it through his mind for days now. Sure it was going to hurt a little, but the pain would be so quick and done with he'd only have to stand it for a mere moment. It took him longer to work through the after-dying part. He wasn't raised under the Holy Book like some. He knew a little about it, knew there was such things as heaven and hell according to the preachers. But then he thought, *I didn't know nothing before I was born so why should I know anything after I'm dead?* And he'd prayed to himself consistently ever since the Ruales had grabbed them up. But no answers or no relief came as answers to his prayers. He finally just figured either God wasn't there, or he wasn't listening if he was there.

Once he got himself settled on that point, his fear subsided.

The Ruales stood him before the General, who looked down at him with the same dead eyes he'd seen in the fish he and Billy had caught out of the river.

"You shall see now your fate," the General said. "Look at him. Like a woman he has become. Weeping and begging me for his life. You see, this is what the fear of death does to a man. It reduces him to being a baby, but only if he has enough time to think about it."

"I ain't afraid," Sam said.

The General drew deeply on his cigarette, then exhaled.

"Oh, but you will be when it comes your turn. I've seen men much braver than that one break down and weep like babies when their time has come. You don't think so now, but you'll see. To stare down the barrel of a rifle and know there is no escaping. Well, that's quite different than to just think about it. You will be like him, like a woman."

Sam figured they were going to drag him to one of those other posts and tie him up but instead they turned him around to face the prisoner, whose pleas now were more like screams.

The General nodded to his man, who gave a sharp command to the Ruales, and they brought their rifles up to their shoulders—Sam counted twelve of them. The prisoner wiggled and fought to free himself as if he were a hooked fish.

The General's man barked a second order, and the guns clattered, and Sam could see the bullets striking the prisoner, punching holes in him from which blood leaked as he sank to his knees, his head slumped, and like that he was dead.

Some of the Ruales came forward and untied the rope and then lifted him into the coffin, then another hammered shut the lid before the coffin was carried to the wagon again and carted off. Sam could see the dark stains in the dirt; they were the only evidence the guard had ever lived. Then Sam was dragged back to his cell. The whole while he repeated to himself, *I'm not afraid. I'm not afraid.*

And so now in his cell he heard the dirge of funeral music, the blare of horns, the ringing of the heavy church bells and thought, *So much death for a place so middling.*

"That's her being taken to the cemetery, ain't it?" he said to the guard.

Sam could not know that on this same day his own grandfather was being buried by a fat German less than fifty miles north.

"We didn't kill her," Sam said suddenly, more as if to convince himself than the guard. As if hearing himself say it was important to him.

The guard said nothing.

"I just want you to know that, we didn't kill her. And if you kill me, you'll be killing somebody innocent."

The guard simply blinked.

Sam sat on the side of his cot, his face in his hands.

"I ain't afraid," he muttered.

The funeral dirge went on a long time, fading slowly until there was a longing silence again.

Later that day, the General came in still in his funeral finery; a young woman in mourning dress stood next to him. The General said, "This is one of them," to the woman, who pulled the veil away from her face. Sam could see she was much younger than the General and very beautiful as well.

She looked at him intently for a moment.

"Yes, you see how young these gringos are who come down here and commit murder on our children," the General said to her.

She came close to the bars where Sam stood and spat in his face, then turned and stalked out.

The General came very close then, his breath

454   BILL BROOKS

smelling of liquor, and Sam could tell, because he'd
seen it on Jardine's face lots of times, that the General was drunk.

"You see, you have made her a mother without
a child," he said. "You have just two days to live.
How does it feel now? Are you still unafraid?"

"You see me crying like that fat friend of yours?"

The General offered him a sullen smirk.

"He's in heaven with his Jesus," he said. "You'll
join him soon. Your grandfather, Gus, he's a man
of his word. He told me he will find your brother
and kill him and bring his head to me. I think he
will do this. And when he does, I will kill you.
Then there will be justice."

"He won't kill Billy."

"To save you? I think so that he will."

"If anybody, it will be you he'll kill."

The General reached into his fancy black coat
and took out a silver flask and drank from it.

"No," he said, wiping his mouth with the edge
of his hand. "He will not kill me. I will kill him if
he tries. I will wipe out his bloodline. Bang, bang,
bang. And bury you all three in unmarked graves."

The General used his finger as if it were the barrel of a pistol.

Sam could see that the black dye the General used
on his hair and mustaches had sweated down his
neck and his chin. He was an old man trying to look
young, no doubt for his young wife. Sam wiped the
spittle from his face. Old men and young women.
Sam couldn't understand it; why a man would make
such a fool of himself for a woman, why a young
woman would marry an old man.

"That stuff you put in your hair," Sam said. "It's leaked all over your shirt collar."

The General motioned for the guard to unlock the cell door, then struck Sam with a winging backhand that made Sam's world go suddenly dark.

Sam's dark dreams were of fish and murder.

22

Jim & Billy

Get up," I said, tapping the soles of Billy's boots. Billy stirred and sat up painfully, guarding his busted shoulder.

It was just turning daylight outside. A slow, steady rain pecked at the window, fell in through the bottom where it was open, and wet the flooring.

"I can't feel my hand," Billy said, flexing his fingers.

"Let's go," I said. I wanted to have sympathy for the boy, but it was damn hard considering.

"I don't think I can stand the jolt of that hack," he said.

"You'll stand it or else."

"Else what?"

He was damn defiant, and it took everything in

me to keep from busting him one. I took him by the good arm and helped him stand.

We went down the stairs and out the front door. Puddles of rainwater stood in the muddy street dimpled with the falling rain. The sky hung low and gray, the clouds bunched together, and there was nobody out on the streets.

"Let's grab some coffee and breakfast," I said, and we walked over to the restaurant and took a window seat.

"I ain't hungry," Billy said.

"'Cause of that?" I said, pointing at his slung arm.

"I had to get up in the middle of the night and puke."

He seemed to me like a beat dog, and I felt for him the way I would a beat dog. But I'd promised the Cap'n I'd do what I could to save the life of his younger grandson even if it meant letting this one slide into the darkest hell. So I held off letting my emotions speak reason to me.

Rain slid down the window glass, and Billy watched it like it was a thing to behold. I wondered if he was trying to take in all he could knowing he would soon be dead—that he was aware that his last hours were the most precious ones of his young life.

We ate, or at least I did, and drank coffee, something he seemed to tolerate as long as there was enough milk and sugar in it, and the rain continued falling steady on.

"You know something," he finally said. "I'd shoot you dead if I got the chance."

"I reckon you would," I said and paid the bill,

and we stood and walked out into the rain and down the street to the livery.

I paid the man for boarding our horses.

"How far to Ciudad de Tontos?" I said.

"Twenty or so miles yet," he said. "The road is very bad when it rains. It will make it slow going for you. Gets very muddy."

"Thanks," I said. "Can I board the buggy here till I get back?"

"Sí, sure."

I helped the kid get aboard the horse, then got aboard my own.

"One more thing," I said to the liveryman. "There someplace I can buy a gun?"

He shrugged, said, "Sí, the trading post has guns," and pointed up the street. We walked our horses up the street to the trading post and tied them off out front.

I had my Henry rifle and mine and the Cap'n's pistols. Somehow it didn't seem enough for the job at hand.

Inside smelled like wool blankets and beef jerky, dried chilies and coffee. A young, dark-skinned woman stood behind the counter.

"Sí?" she said.

"I'll need to buy a gun," I said.

She showed me a tray of pistols.

"Something bigger—*muy grande*."

She kept her eyes on Billy the whole while. They were compassionate eyes, but also the eyes of a woman in the market for a man. She was maybe thirty and had no wedding band on her finger.

She led us to another counter and pointed to a

rack of guns and right off I spotted something I wanted. A double-barrel ten-gauge L. C. Smith.

"How much?" I said, pointing.

She took it down.

"Fifteen dollars," she said.

"I'll take it."

I paid her from the Cap'n's wallet since I was down to broke. I figured he wouldn't mind the expenditure knowing what it was for.

"You got shells for this?"

She nodded and took a box of shells off the counter behind her.

"Not these," I said. "These are for a twelve-gauge. Those." I pointed to another box and she got them for me.

I looked at Billy, who was now trading looks with the woman.

"Anything you need, kid?"

It took him a moment.

"Just to go kill that damn Mescan," he said. I saw the way she flinched. The kid lacked any social graces whatsoever.

I asked the woman if she had slickers to sell. She didn't understand my meaning. I tried to explain it but didn't know the right word. I looked around and didn't see any, but did see some serapes.

"I'll take two of those," I said, pointing. She got some down, held them up to Billy and me to gauge the right size, then I paid for them too, and we slipped them over our heads.

I thanked the woman and we went back out again, and I waited till Billy got in his saddle and handed him up the shotgun.

"Carry this," I said. "Don't worry, I wasn't stupid enough to load it."

"Then what's the point?"

"To keep you from shooting me in the back, how's that for a point."

"It ain't as if I ain't got enough to do just carrying my own damn self without having to haul this piece of iron."

"Shut your carping for once."

"Ah hell," he said.

I mounted the stud and turned him back to the south road.

The liveryman had been right about the road. The horses sank down into the mud past their fetlocks and after just a few miles they were laboring.

"We're going to have to push hard to make it to Ciudad de Tontos in two days," I said.

"This shoulder of mine is hurting like a son of a bitch," he said. "I can't ride hard even if this damn mud wasn't slowing us down."

"You stay up or I'll tie you belly down, but either way, we're going to make these next twenty or so miles by deadline."

You couldn't tell you were in Old Mexico. It didn't look or feel any different. It was just a place where somebody had long ago decided one side of the river was the United States of America and the other the Republic of Mexico.

How the hell that got to be determined was way beyond me, and it didn't matter a spit's worth because whether I killed a man this side of the river or the other, or he killed me, dying was still dying.

"This is the worst fucking country I ever been in," Billy griped. The rain soaked through our serapes and eventually through our clothes and ran down our necks. The serapes became little more than an extra load wet like they were, but still of some unknown comfort.

"Shoulder feels like it's been cleaved with an ax," Billy said a little farther on. I kept thinking, *In a little while, kid, nothing's going to hurt you anymore.*

⊰ 23 ⊱

We rode on like that slow, the rain falling harder like nails spilled from a carpenter's barrel. The sky grew dark as night and lightning shook through it like fence wire, its flash lighting up the landscape and each other in quick bursts. I could see in those grim moments how much Billy was hurting. We slogged on still, then I heard a *whomp!* in the mud. I reined in my horse and waited till the next flash of lightning and saw Billy lying there in the road, his horse running past me, spooked by the crash of thunder. I charged off after it and finally caught it up by the reins and led it back.

I dismounted and lifted Billy from the mire.

"I'm finished," he said. "You want to tie me belly down, you're going to have to 'cause I can't ride another mile."

Then I saw with the next lightning flash his eyes had rolled white. I went and untied my soogins and wrapped it round him after I dragged him off the road into the scrub. He lay there without moving and I hunkered there on my heels, miserable and soaked to the skin. The rain hissed and boiled and took no mercy on us, and I kept thinking how much nicer it would have been to be home in my own bed with Luz's warm body wrapped against mine. I told myself that maybe I ought to make an honest woman out of her and ask her to marry me when I got back—if I got back. The idea appealed to me more than I thought it ever would. I had my share of women and ladies but none that ever made me want to marry one of them.

But a man reaches a point where he knows that whatever he's been doing all his life he can't go on forever doing. Something happens to you when you hit forty years old, it seems. And I'd hit forty sometime back.

The rain dripped down the back of my neck.

The lightning danced all around like it was looking for us to kill us. Anybody who's ever trailed cattle could tell you the danger of lightning. But still, there was nothing to be done about it.

Billy was almost dead and I wasn't feeling too spry myself.

It was a long, long damn wait sitting out there in that rainstorm, and by the time it quit, the first gray light of a new dawn cut through sky and you could have wrung our clothes out like washrags.

It took me several moments to waken the kid. But finally his eyes fluttered open like a busted shade in some cheap hotel room.

"Kid," I said. "We got to get a move on. It's Thursday. By Friday, that little brother of yours is going to be dead if we don't make it down there."

He shook his head.

"Can't . . . go . . . on . . ." he muttered.

I lifted him onto my shoulders and heaved him into the saddle.

"You die, he dies," I said. "Is that what you want?"

He waggled his head.

"Then take hold of that saddle horn."

I mounted my horse and took up the reins to Billy's and led him out. I didn't know where we were or how far we'd come or how far we had to go. I had to carry the shotgun across the pommel of my saddle since I couldn't trust the kid to hold on to it. He was barely able to hold on himself.

We crossed a swollen creek that had come over the road, and a short way farther on we came upon a sheep camp that lay just off to our right and you could smell the cook pot and coffee.

"Let's ride over and see can we get a little something for our bellies and some of that coffee," I said. Even my bones were cold and soaked from the all-night rain.

The sheep—and there must have been nearly a hundred of them—were cropping grass contentedly as their herder squatted by the fire. He had three black and white dogs patrolling the flock.

He looked up at our approach.

I greeted him in Spanish and with a touch of my hat brim.

"Don't suppose I could buy a meal and some of that coffee from you?" I said.

He blinked, looked me over, then looked over Billy.

"Come, sit," he said.

I dismounted and helped Billy out of the saddle.

"What's wrong with your friend?"

"He's feeling poorly," I said, helping Billy to ease to the ground by the fire. He looked worse than an orphan.

The man stood and went to his wagon and came back with two extra tin plates and cups and handed them to me and nodded to the cook pot. I spooned us out each a plate and then poured us each a cup of the coffee.

"You from around here?" I said, chewing the mutton stew.

He pointed to a line of mountains.

"Over there," he said. "Chipata."

I nodded. The coffee began to warm my blood and I was grateful for it and poured myself a second cup. It was strong and black as a crowbar.

"How's that suit you, kid?" I said. He was at least eating and sipping his coffee. He glanced my way and then across the fire at the shepherd.

"I ain't proud to be eating a Mescan's food," he said.

"You best be grateful he gave you anything to eat at all," I said. Then to the shepherd, "You'll have to forgive my young companion's manners. He ain't got any."

The shepherd laughed.

"The wild ways of the young," he said. As though he understood that boys Billy's age were tempestuous and often ignorant in their ways.

I asked if he knew how far it was yet to Ciudad de Tontos. He held up the fingers of one hand.

Smoke from the fire rose in gray wisps.

"They had some trouble down there not long ago," he said.

"What sort of trouble?" I said, believing I already knew but wanting to confirm it.

"There is a garrison of Ruales there and the General's daughter was killed, murdered by some gringos. So you better be careful when you go there. They might think you're the ones who did it."

"We're no sort of killers," I said.

"I did not think you were. A man who is so kind to a wounded boy, even a surly one, could not be a bad hombre."

The man kept his eyes on Billy when he said that. Billy did not return the man's gaze.

I reached into my pocket and took out two dollars for our meal and handed it to the shepherd. He looked at it and said, "No. This won't do me any good," and handed it back. "I would have just thrown out the extra coffee anyway and the stew, whatever is left over, I give to my dogs."

The sheep bleated whenever the dogs would nip at their legs if they strayed from the flock.

"Those look like some good dogs," I said.

"They keep me company and do a good job with the sheep."

I stood then and said, "Thank you for your hospitality. My name is Jim Glass and this is Billy Rogers."

"And I am Hernando," he said and we shook hands.

"And thanks for the warning about Ciudad de Tontos," I said.

He scratched under his sombrero.

"I think there is a doctor there who could look at the boy's arm," he said. "I think maybe he pulls teeth too if you have one that is bothering you."

"Let's mount up," I said to Billy and watched as he unscrewed himself from the ground. Got him mounted on his horse, and we headed the last five miles to the town where his death awaited him.

I felt gruesome, like a man taking a sheep to slaughter.

From what I knew of Mexican manhood, it might not be as simple as exchanging one boy for the other.

I was glad I had the ten-gauge.

⇥ 24 ⇤

Billy visibly stiffened when we saw the town rising up before us. At this distance, it seemed innocent enough. But then lots of things, women and towns and men included, seem innocent enough if you're standing a long way away from them.

"Hold your water, kid. This might not seem as bad as what you imagine it to be." I needed to do my level best to keep him calm, to keep the situation contained. Because if it got out of hand, it wasn't only the kid that might end up dead, and I sure didn't want to become a corpse in a place called City of Fools.

"How'd you know how bad it's not going to be," he groused. "Anybody ever kill you before? Especially some goddamn Mescan Ruale."

"You got a point, kid. I wouldn't know. But I made your grandfather a promise, and I aim to see it through."

"Least give me a gun, give me a fighting chance."

"You think having a gun would give you a fighting chance against a company of Ruales?"

"It'd be something."

"Something is all it *would* be."

"How you know they're not going to kill us all, you included?"

"I don't. But if what your grandfather said about him and the General being pals back in the old days is true, maybe he'll cut some slack for your brother."

"Yeah, and maybe that sum bitch won't either."

"Chance we'll have to take," I said, feeling about as uneasy as I've ever felt riding into an uncertain situation with the only promise being that there'd be some bloodletting.

I saw a man packing a burro and paused and said, "*Dónde está la oficina de los Ruales?*"

He was tying a diamond hitch on a load that looked like all the burro could stand.

He pointed up the street and said in Spanish that the Ruales were located mid-block center of town. I thanked him and spurred my mount ahead, still leading Billy's by the reins. He seemed resigned to his fate when I last looked back at him.

There were Ruales standing out front of the General's office in tan uniforms when we rode up. Billy said, "The jail's in back."

The Ruales were smoking, talking about something, but stopped when we reined in. One of them seemed to recognize Billy and quick ran inside and returned in a moment with a rifle in his hands and the General on his heels. His hair was uncommonly black for a man his age. His mustaches guarded the corners of his mouth and down past his chin.

"What's this?" he said with feigned surprise as he stared at Billy.

"I've come on behalf of Gus Rogers," I said. "You remember Gus Rogers, don't you, General?"

He looked at me with a baleful stare, then signaled to his men, who stepped forward to take Billy off his horse.

"Not yet," I said, raising the shotgun from where it had been resting across my pommel to let the stock rest atop my right thigh. "Tell your men to hold off."

He raised a hand.

"He is my prisoner," he said. "He escaped from my jail after murdering my child."

"He will be in your jail once again after we make the exchange for the one you're holding—young Sam Rogers."

The General got a look on his face as if someone had just whispered something pleasant in his ear.

"Where is my old friend Gus?" he said.

"Dead and buried north of here, not far if you want to pay him a visit—little town called Gonzales. Ask for the German, he'll show you the grave."

The smile dropped away.

"Did you kill him?"

"No, he killed himself."

The smile that had gone away turned into a frown.

"This I find hard to believe, a man like him," he said.

"Believe what you will. He asked me to fulfill his mission if he couldn't. That's why I'm here instead of back home in a warm bed with a full belly of beef."

"What is your name?"

"Not that it makes any difference," I said. "But

it's Jim Glass. I'm not here for a social visit. Let's get this done if we're going to do it."

"First you give me him, then I will give you the other one," he said.

"No, that's not how this is going to work."

He snorted his derision.

"Who are you to dictate the terms? I have enough men here to kill you and take him. You're just one man."

I leveled the L. C. ten-gauge so that the thick black barrels were aimed directly at the General's chest. And when I thumbed back the hammers, it gave you the same feeling you get when you're walking through the brush and hear the buzz of a rattlesnake real close and you're not sure where it's at, whether you've taken one step too many.

"That's true," I said. "I am only one man, but I'm man enough to take you and some of these Ruales out with me if that's what you want. You can go get that boy or go to fighting."

The Ruales around him shuffled their feet nervously till he waved them to stand still.

He showed me both his palms.

"I done what you asked the Cap'n to do," I said. "I brought you this boy in exchange for the other one. Now let's trade or let's do whatever it is you've got in mind, but I'm not sitting here all day in this fucking hot sun."

He looked at those empty black holes of the L. C. and I guess it made him rethink his plans just as it surely would mine if he was holding that bad gun instead of me. Finally he assented with the dip of his head toward one of his men.

"Go and get the boy," he said.

"One more thing," I said.

He held his chin at a stately angle, raised so that now he was looking down his nose at me.

"That boy needs some medical attention. I expect you to do whatever it is you're planning to do with some sense of decency."

"All matters will be done with proper attention," he said. He might as well have said Queen Victoria ruled England, for all the difference it would make.

The kid they brought out was smallish, baby-faced, and in a stupor till he looked up and saw Billy astraddle the horse.

"Billy . . ." he uttered.

"Sam. They're swapping me for you. This fellow will take you home. You're safe now."

"No," Sam said. "I'm not going to leave you."

Billy got down off his horse gritting his teeth and said, "Go on now, get away from here and this dirty business. Do it before something upsets the applecart."

Sam began to sob.

"Be a man," Billy said sternly. "I taught you anything, it was to be a man. Now git."

The General and his Ruales stood watching, listening, waiting for a mistake to be made. You been doing what I've done most of my life, you can tell if a man is full of bad intentions. It wouldn't take much to start a shooting scrap that would leave the sidewalks bloody and several of us dead. But I had no choice, I was already in it too deep to do anything other than stand my ground.

"Get on the horse, Sam," I said.

"No."

"Get on the goddamn horse, boy."

"Go on," Billy said again, pushing Sam toward the horse. "Go and tell Ma what happened here. Take care of her, Sam. I'm sorry I got you into all this."

Sam did a slow shuffle to the horse.

"Hurry it along there, kid," I said. The air was so thick with men wanting to let blood, you could cut it with a knife.

The Ruales took Billy in hand.

"There, you see," General Toro said. "We are both men who keep our promises, eh."

I gave Billy one last glance. He stared at me without a hint of worry in his gaze. I said to Sam without taking my eyes or the double barrels off the General, "Ride up the street that way, and don't dawdle. Ride fast and I'll catch up with you. Don't stop and don't turn around. And if something bad happens, keep riding till you cross the river and don't even stop then."

"Yes sir," he uttered and kicked his horse into a trot, then a gallop.

It left me, the General, and five of his Ruales— what you call a Mexican showdown, only I wasn't wanting to turn this into something bloody.

"Then our business is finished," the General said.

"It's finished," I said and backed my horse up far enough, then reined it round quick and spurred it into a full-out gallop.

Nobody took a shot at me. I was a little surprised they hadn't.

I caught up quickly enough with the little brother, whose horse was a lot less horse than the stud.

"Hold up!" I shouted, and he sawed back on the reins.

"I thought you told me to keep riding?"

"I did. But now I want you to stop a second."

He looked at me with the confusion of a boy who'd just escaped death and couldn't understand why.

"What'd they do to you back there in that jail?" I said.

"Beat me like blue blazes . . ."

"What else?"

"Said they were going to shoot me, made me watch them execute the man who let Billy escape. The brought in the General's wife and she spit in my face. Kept telling me how my day was coming, how I'd bawl like a woman when it was my turn."

"That's if they didn't get Billy back, right?"

He shook his head.

"Said they'd get Billy and kill us both, and Granddaddy too if he put up a fuss. They wasn't ever planning on letting me live."

"You certain that's what they said?"

"I swear to God, mister."

"One more question, boy. Did you or your brother have anything to do whatsoever with the death of the General's girl?"

"No sir. We found her stabbed and Billy and me did the best we could to save her. We had her blood all over us, but it wasn't because we were trying to hurt her none."

It was the same story Billy had told. They could have gotten together and made it up, but I doubted it; neither of them seemed that clever.

"You think you can reach the river on your own? You just have to stay on this road and keep going."

He nodded.

"What about you?" he said.

"I got something I need to do." I took out Gus's watch, wallet, and badge and handed them to him along with Gus's fancy pistol.

"These belonged to your granddaddy," I said.

"Where's my granddaddy at?"

"North of here, buried in the ground. He did what he could for you, he just ran out of time."

"I hardly remember him," he said.

"You have your mama tell you about him when you get home again. First town you hit that has a train station, you sell that horse and use the money and some of what's in that wallet and buy you a ticket home. You understand?"

"Yes sir."

"And don't ever come back across that river again—leastways till you're a man and can make up your own mind."

"Yes sir."

I slapped the rump of his horse, shouting, "Git," and sat until I saw he wasn't going to stop again. Then I turned the stud back around.

Shit, I was almost forty-six years old and not getting any younger and there was this kid in a jail they were going to shoot over nothing at all.

I just couldn't ride away from that. Even though I should, I couldn't.

25

As if it were some sort of Greek tragedy, the kind I'd seen performed in Dodge City when I was a young buckaroo, the sky grew ominously dark again, and raindrops the size of silver dollars splatted down, a few at first, then more, smaller but more intense as I rode back toward the town of Ciudad de Tontos.

But I thought the only fool in this whole business was me.

I rode at a walk, steady, determined, the stock of the shotgun resting against my thigh, both hammers cocked, ready to do some mean business if required, and it surely would be this day before the sun set again beyond those stormy clouds.

The storm had chased everyone indoors, and as I rode past the business establishments I could see faces looking out—clerks, bankers, hardware salesmen, men in the cantina standing in the open doorway under the shelter of a roof, leaning there with their bottles and glasses in their hands. Men in tall sombreros stood under the eaves with the rain dripping off, some of them held glasses of beer like it was a show.

I rode down past the first block of buildings, a stable with a corral with no horses in it; a black-smith's whose forge showered sparks as he fired the steel; a gunsmith's with a CERRADO sign in the window. The old man who been packing his burro stood in the rain, his serape heavy and wet about his shoulders, looked directly into my eyes as if he knew what was about to happen. He turned, un-tied his burro from the hitching post, and walked the other direction.

I crossed the only intersection in town, Segunda Calle—Second Street—and kept my attention fixed ahead. I saw a kid standing under the eaves in front of a barbershop. He stared at me like I was the devil incarnate, or Jesus Christ himself. He was a kid that would someday, if he was lucky, grow to be a man, maybe even an old man. I reined in and told him to get off the street. He was hesitant to go. I gave him two bits. He ran like hell.

I tied off the stud. The Ruale office was just across the street two doors down. I could see lights on inside. I didn't want to think what they were doing to Billy.

I had the shotgun and I had a pistol and either I'd get the job done or I wouldn't.

Rain fell out of the black heavens.

I crossed the street.

I didn't bother to knock. I just turned the knob and went in fast.

The General and two of his Ruales were sitting there drinking from a bottle of tequila. I leveled the ten-gauge.

They all looked surprised.

"I come to get the kid," I said.

The General looked at me with a great amount of empathy.

"You already have him," he said evenly.

"The other one—Billy," I said.

"Oh, but that is not possible," he said. I had to admit, the son of a bitch was a cool customer, showed no fear whatsoever. The other two weren't quite so calm. I could see the fear in their eyes and they had every right to be afraid.

"Yes, it is possible," I said. "Nobody has to get killed here. That boy didn't have anything to do with your daughter's death."

"So you say, Señor. But you see, my men here, they caught him with her blood on them. And he has confessed to as much. There is no injustice here, no reason for you to act like this. Gus, he would have understood it—what a man must do to remove the stain of dishonor from his family name."

"I'm saying he's innocent. Now let's go and get him out of your goddamn jail."

Still, the General did not make any move to do as ordered. I looked at one of the two with him—the one who showed the most fear—and said. "You want to live, you son of a bitch?"

I could tell he didn't understand so I said it again in Spanish so he would understand: "*Usted desea vivir usted hijo de una perra?*"

"Sí, sí."

So I told him to get the keys and go get the kid.

He started to but the General ordered him to halt. Told him who did he think his boss was, the General or me? The Ruale looked caught between a rock and a hard place, which is exactly where he was.

I moved a step and put the barrels of the L. C. right against his neck.

"Do it!" I said.

"You think even if we give you the boy we're going to just let you ride across the river to del Norte?" the General said. "We will hunt you down like rabbits."

"I'll take my chances."

He motioned for one of the Ruales to get the keys and he opened a desk drawer, and I told him to come out easy, and he did with a large key on a metal ring. I marched all three to the back of the place where Billy lay on his side on the cot.

"Get up," I said.

For some reason he didn't seem surprised to see me. He eased himself up holding his busted shoulder.

"I didn't think no kind of man who was a friend of my granddaddy would just ride off and let these Mescan sons of bitches murder me," he said with a whoop as if he'd just won first prize in a pie-eating contest.

I told the Ruale to open the door, intending to put the three of them inside while the kid and me got a jump start on them, but just then three more Ruales came busting through the door with pistols cocked and ready and I didn't have any choice but to pull the triggers of that L. C., knocking them down like tenpins. The L. C. roared like thunder in that small room, so loud it made your ears ring. But just that quick the General and his two boys were all over me before I could pull my pistol and I knew if they got me to the ground, it was all over.

I slammed an elbow into one face and threw a

crushing right-hand fist into the face of the other. But the General had a hard grip on me, his forearm from behind around my throat, trying to choke me out. He was a strong son of a bitch, I'll give him that, and we fought out into the other room, mostly him choking and me trying to break his grip.

I heard Billy yell something and a struggle still going on inside the cell area, but I had my hands too full to help him. He was on his own now.

My wind cut off, I was starting to lose my strength, which only encouraged the General to choke down that much harder. I had maybe thirty seconds before I'd go under.

I took him out through the plate-glass window with one mighty push, hoping to break his grip.

We crash landed on the wet walk outside and rolled into the muddy street and it momentarily loosened his chokehold on me enough so I could gasp some air. I reached for my pistol, but it wasn't in the scabbard. I'd lost it somewhere in the struggle.

I heard three sharp reports from inside the office—gunfire!

It was then I looked up and was staring down the barrel of the General's own pistol—a nickel-plated Smith & Wesson Russian model, like the one the Captain carried, and I wondered stupidly if theirs had been a matched set and where and when and how they'd come by them.

Funny what a man who's an instant away from death will think. I always heard your life flashed before your eyes and sometimes you saw the presence of loved ones who'd passed before.

But all I saw was a tall man in a muddy uniform standing there with his gun aimed at my face, saw him thumb back the hammer and thought, *Jim, you're going to die here in this muddy goddamn street and not in a nice bed like you'd planned.*

Then an explosion caused the General to jerk like someone had snipped all his wires, and he fell face-first into the mud dead as a stone.

Standing there a dozen paces behind where the General lay was the little brother, Sam, holding his granddaddy's pistol, the one that matched the General's in every detail.

He did not move or falter.

And when Billy came straggling out of the jail holding one of the *federale*'s pistols in his good hand, smoke curling from the barrel, I knew then old Gus's blood had passed on down to those boys in spite of everything else.

We rode north, the three of us, Billy, Sam, and myself.

We did not dally, for to be north of the river was to be safe again.

At least for a little while.

26

She was there at the house, my house, waiting for me as if she knew I'd come. She was stroking the muzzle of one of the mares, and it pricked its ears at our approach, and the stud whinnied smelling the mare, his muscles rippled, as glad to be home again as I was.

Luz turned and did not move but stood watching, and my heart quickened at the sight of her.

I rode up casual as if I'd been gone on a Sunday ride, but she could see my overall condition was pretty poor, my clothes dusty and mud-caked, my shirt sweat-stained and my boots all run down.

I reined in and stepped down out of the saddle.

She did not speak and I did not speak. I unsaddled the stud and turned him out with the mares.

"You earned it," I said. Then I turned to Luz and said, "How you been getting on?"

"Fine," she said. "And yourself."

"Been better," I said. "Am better now that I'm home again."

I saw my chicken coop was rebuilt and the fencing put up and some of the chickens put back inside, and that old red rooster that would wake me up every morning about the time it got light.

"You do that?" I said, pointing toward the chicken coop.

"Who else do you think would trouble themselves to round up your chickens and fence them in again?"

"Nobody I know but you."

"That's right, mister, and don't you forget it."

I took her in my arms then and gave her a hug and kissed her on the mouth like it was the first time—tenderly and gratefully.

"I've got some coffee on," she said.

"I'd rather just sit out here and have a whiskey with you, and a smoke."

"That can be arranged," she said and went into the house and came out with the bottle and two glasses, and we sat in chairs facing off to the west where the sun was setting a passionate red in the sky, throwing off its light up against fingers of clouds. I rolled her a shuck and rolled myself one, and we sat there smoking and sipping our whiskey.

"You want to talk about it?" she said at last.

"No, I don't reckon," I said.

"I half thought you'd show up with your friend," she said.

"I left him down there in that country," I said.

She didn't ask which country I meant and I didn't volunteer it. It was enough to know the Cap'n was at rest now, that his two grandsons were home with their mother, and that what he set out to do got done. It didn't really matter which of us had done what. A mama had her boys back—that's what mattered.

"You hungry?" she said. "I can fix you something to eat."

"I am," I said.

She started to stand to go into the house.

"But not for food," I said.

She turned and smiled and sat down on my lap.

"Oh," she said. "Am I to guess what you're hungry for?"

"This," I said.

The sun dropped out of the sky, the heat went with it. The land grew cool and pleasant all around us.

I said, "You know that little lake over yonder the river flows out of?"

"Yes, what about it?"

I don't think she ever looked as beautiful to me as she did in that moment.

"Let's go over there and take our clothes off and jump in," I said.

"Really?" she said, arching her eyebrow.

"Yes, I had this dream while I was gone, about you and me making love in the water, and I'd like to see if it would be as good in reality as it was in that dream I had, because that was about the best old dream I ever had."

She stood and took me by the hand.

And I followed willingly.